Relapse

THE ORDER OF RAVENS AND WOLVES
T.L. HODEL

This book is dedicated to anyone who's ever felt broken or defeated. You are valid. You are seen. And you are loved. Don't be afraid to spread your wings and fly.

Author warning: This book is a dark romance and contains violence, profanity, references to emotional, physical and sexual child abuse, nonconsensual and dubious consensual sexual scenes, addiction, degradation and humiliation, and bullying.

Book Four in The Order Of Ravens And Wolves Accident-Prone

The Order Of Ravens And Wolves Titles

KINGS:
- Louis Kessler (King go Kings)
- Dean Whitley
- Sebastian Creswell
- Dr. Martin Creswell
- Ryker Hudson

KNIGHTS:
- Micha Kessler (Future king of kings)
- Mason Kessler
- Logan Hudson
- Parker Whitley
- Preston Whitley
- Silas Creswell
- Finn Creswell

Name
Pronunciation

- Micha: Mike - ah
- Ryker: Rye - cur
- Silas: Sye - lass
- Riley: Rye - lee
- Paisley: Pase - lee
- Derek: Dare - ick
- Marnie: Mar - knee
- Trina: Tree - nah
- Logan: Low - gan
- Mason: Mase - on
- Preston: Press - ton
- Parker: Park - er
- Finn: Finn
- Junior: June - your
- Shelby: Shell - bee
- Naomi: Nay - oh - me (bitch)
- Chase: Chase
- Tanner: Tan - er
- Amy: A - me
- Ava: A - va
- Whitley: Witt - lee
- Kessler: Kess - ler
- Creswell: Cress - well
- Mathers: Ma - th - ers
- Grier: Gr - ear
- Harper: Har - per
- Louis: Lou - is
- Lana: La - na
- Sean: Sha - awn

Playlist

'Somebody that I used to know' by Gotye
'Let You Down' by NF
'Drink You Away' by Justin Timberlake
'Heavy' by Linkin Park (feat Kiiara)
'I Hate You, I Love You' by Gnash
'Just Give Me A Reason' by Pink
'In The Stars' by Benson Boone
'Eastside' by Benny Blanco
'Say Something' by A Great Big World
'Love The Way You Lie' by Eminiem and Rhianna
'Rehab' by Rihanna
'2002' by Anne-Marie
'Easy On Me' by Adelle
'Someone You Loved' by Lewis Capaldi
'Roses' by Benny Blanco
'Empty Space' by James Arthur
'The Tragic Truth' by Five Finger Death Punch
'24K Magic' by Bruno Mars
'Scars' by Boy Epic
'You Are The Reason' by Callum Scott

Prologue

Mason

11 YEARS AGO:

There she was. The most beautiful girl in the whole world was building a sandcastle. I couldn't stop watching her smack more sand in her pink bucket. She was so much prettier than the picture I saw, even with her tongue sticking out to the side.

How come Micha got to pick through that book first? What made him so special? Just cause he was older didn't mean he should get to do everything first. Just the other day Silas and I hunted down a ghost in my basement. Micha never did anything like that. He didn't even believe in ghosts.

My brother was so dumb. Instead of picking a girl from the book, he picked some stupid one because he said she needed to be

1

taught a lesson. Pfft. Why would he want to marry her just to give her a time out? Didn't make sense to me.

Standing up on my tiptoes, I shielded my eyes from the sun so I could see the girl in the sandbox better. I was glad Micha didn't pick her. She was so pretty, with big brown eyes like Bambi and freckles on her nose. I couldn't see her freckles from here, but I saw them in the picture.

They reminded me of the connect the dots games in my coloring book. What kind of picture would her dots make? Maybe a crown. The sun did make her hair shine like waves of rubies. That's what Mom called her red jewelry.

Huh? Could gems make waves?

That would be really cool if they could. It probably wouldn't feel very good to dive into a river of diamonds – they were hard. I knew because Micha cut me with one of our mom's bracelets. He got in trouble for that. Our dad took away his bike. Then he took away mine when he found out I threw a paperweight at Micha first.

That was a funny word. Paperweight. Why did anyone need to weigh down paper anyways? Yeah it fluttered in the wind, but how were you supposed to draw anything with a big rock in the way?

Rocks were dumb. They got in the way and hurt my feet when I tried to walk in the water at the hot springs. I bet diamonds wouldn't do that. Besides, no one would go swimming in water made from diamonds. What kind of sound would that make?

The docks had a soft lapping sound, but the water at the bottom of the bluffs smacked hard off the rocks. *Dumb rocks.* Then there were the geysers. They boomed out great big streams of red water. Micha tried to tell me it was blood 'cause there was a whale trapped underneath, but Silas and I looked and we didn't see no whale.

Anyways, I really liked her hair.

"Hey." Someone poked me in the back. "Are you gonna go, or what? You're holding up the line."

I turned around and eyed the girl's long black hair. Micha had been following her around since we got to the park. I wasn't sure why? I didn't really care. I was just happy he was annoying someone else.

"Hello," she sang and clapped her hands in front of my face, making me jar back a bit. "Go already."

No girl was going to tell me what to do.

"This is my slide," I spat and crossed my arms. "Go find another one."

"You can't own a slide," she argued.

"Can so," I argued back.

My dad said our family owned this whole town *which meant* this slide was mine.

The little girl grumbled and rolled her eyes before trying to slip past me. But I stepped in her way. She didn't like that. Her lips twisted in a frown while she glared up at me.

"You better move."

I smiled back at her. "Make me."

Her eyes got really small and her lips tightened, making them kind of pale, like when Mom put that skin colored cream all over her face. Girls did weird things. What was the point in putting stuff on if your face was already that color?

The girl puffed up her chest and crossed her arms. "Maybe I'll just push you down the slide?"

That made me laugh. I was way bigger than her, and Micha was bigger than me and I couldn't push him.

Speaking of Micha...

His head appeared at the top of the slide as he climbed up the ladder.

"Careful Mase, she's a dog killer."

That's where I knew her from. She was here the other day

3

looking for her dog. Micha said he was dead, but I didn't find a body.

The little girl's mouth fell open with a loud gasp.

"I am not!" she propped her hands on her hips and waggled her head at my brother. "We found Charlie."

"Or," Micha charged up to her with his chest puffed out, "you took someone else's dog."

I was too mesmerized by her pigtails swaying to hear what she said. They moved back and forth like slithering black snakes. My hand shot out, yanking on a bundle of hair. I'd make a good snake catcher.

"Ouch!" She spun around and shoved on my chest.

I tried to catch myself, but my feet slipped out from under me. Next thing I knew, I was barrelling down the slide, head first, on my back. I launched off the end and landed hard on the ground.

I was still trying to catch my breath when I heard Micha growl, "No one pushes my brother."

Followed by a little girl's screech.

There was enough time for me to blink my eyes open before she sailed through the air and slammed down on top of me.

"Ugh," I grunted.

Little girls were heavy. Stupid Micha.

But it wasn't over yet. There was a boy with brown hair standing behind Micha with a scowl on his face.

"You shouldn't push girls," he said, and shoved my brother down.

My brother was big. When he crashed down on the top of the pile, all the air left my body. I thought for sure I was flat like those cartoon characters that got pianos dropped on them. But my fingers were still normal, so I guessed I wasn't completely flat. That was disappointing.

It would've made getting out of this kid pretzel a lot easier. The little girl's arm was flung back, wrapped around my face, and

Micha's legs were trapping mine. I could barely move. Thank god there was no one else to be pushed down.

At least that's what I thought, until I saw Parker climbing the ladder.

I wriggled my head out from under the other two and looked at the boy who'd pushed Micha. He was grinning and rubbing his hands together.

Oh no. I'll definitely be flat if he comes down here.

As soon as Parker's head came into view, the other boy stopped smiling and shifted his gaze to the swings. Preston was leaning back against one of the bars with his eyes narrowed and focused on the slide. The boy just smiled at Parker as he walked by and slid down.

Probably a good choice. I overheard my dad saying Preston wasn't normal. I'm not sure what that meant. Maybe he was a superhero or something?

Once he was at the bottom Parker stood up, smiled down at us, said, "Hey guys," and skipped off to the see-saw.

"Smug prick," Micha grumbled.

I heard a muffled, "Get off me," followed by my brother grunting as he rolled off us clutching his balls.

Guess the little girl got him good and hard. Good. Micha deserved it.

A second later she jumped off me and kicked some dirt in my brother's face before running off. I kind of liked that girl. Her mom was not as impressed as I was though. At least that's who I assumed the woman with black hair was.

She ran after her, yelling, "Riley Marie Adams, did you just hit that boy?"

I was glad she wasn't my mom. She did not look happy and was really fast. When she called out, "Get back here right now," I almost wanted to tell the little girl she should listen. But I had my own mom to worry about.

She came rushing over with her eyes all big.

Uh oh, I was in trouble.

I was about to tell her that I didn't do anything and it was all Micha's fault, but she spoke before I could.

"Oh my God, my sweet boys. Are you two okay?"

Maybe I wasn't in trouble?

"I'm okay," I grunted and pushed myself up.

Why did girls always worry about stuff? We just fell down. It wasn't a big deal. And now she was probably gonna rub spit in my face again. Or worse, kiss my cheeks over and over.

But I wasn't the one she focused her attention on. When Micha sat up and a drop of blood trickled down from a cut on his cheek, I couldn't help but smile.

"Micha," Mom fell down to the ground and cupped his face. "You're bleeding!"

He slapped at her hands and muttered, "I'm fine. Go away."

"I don't know, he fell really hard." I tsked, "He might have a cusion."

I'm not sure what a 'cusion' was, but I heard Silas's dad talking about it and knew it happened when someone hit their head.

Mom immediately began fussing over my brother, twisting his head to the side to check him for more injuries. He clenched his jaw and rolled his dark glare my way. I just smiled back. Micha was not impressed.

I was definitely going to pay for that later. That was okay. Dad still had that paperweight. Besides, I had better things to do.

I looked over at the sandbox and narrowed my gaze on the boy kicking over my wife's castle. No one picked on my wife. If he was going to make her cry, then I was going to make him cry. I jumped up, ran across the playground, and shoved him on the ground.

"Leave her alone!"

For a second when he blinked up at me, I thought he was going to argue, or hit me back. Then he looked over at Micha, who was trying to stop Mom from kissing his face. If Micha was mean to me, then he was really mean to people that picked on me. He said it was part of being a big brother. I thought it was annoying.

When the boy just stood up and walked away, I kind of wanted to push him down again. I didn't need Micha to stick up for me. I could take care of myself.

"You didn't have to do that."

Oh, right, my wife!

"Yes I did."

I turned around and smiled down at her. She was a lot prettier close up. Her eyes glittered as the sun shone down on us, making it look like her skin was glowing. I didn't even mind that she was crying. I just liked looking at her.

She brushed a tear off her cheek and sniffed back a sob. "No you didn't."

"Yes I did." I puffed out my chest so she could see how strong I was. "All husbands should protect their wives."

It was part of the job. Just like wives had babies, husbands made sure they were safe and had food.

Maybe I should get her a snack?

"But you're not my husband."

"I will be. Cause I picked you and my dad says so," I insisted.

She sat back and looked at me for a second. "Do husbands help build sandcastles?"

I smiled and sat down beside her.

"Husbands build the bestest sandcastles."

Chapter 1
Mason

*A*ddict.

I'd heard that a lot lately. From my brother, my friends, Lou, and the doctors at the clinic he'd locked me up in. They dubbed me with this term and talked about my addiction as if it was a bad thing. They said I was hurting myself. But was I?

Had they ever been so suffocated by their own thoughts that they wanted to crawl out of their own skin? That's how I felt without the drugs and alcohol in my system.

Micha blamed one person and one person alone. While he wasn't entirely wrong, he should take a look in the mirror. I didn't question anything my brother told me growing up because he was my hero. Now, Micha was just another guy that hid shit from me. Someone else who thought I was too weak to handle the truth.

The day I opened those paternity papers was the same day I lost my brother.

Never keep a secret from your friend that your enemy already knows.

As far as my brother was concerned, betrayal was the greatest sin. Someone could lie to Micha, cheat on him, hell, they could shoot the fucker in the dick, but if they betrayed him... That was it. If he didn't kill them, he'd make sure they damn well wished they were dead.

Did that make my brother a dick? Probably. But he was born an ass so I kind of expected shit like this. What I didn't expect was finding out that my brother–the person I used to look up to and admire– was the world's biggest hypocrite.

Micha didn't just betray me, he hid the very foundations of my DNA. Secrets he kept under the guise of protection, and that was so much worse. Someone could come back from a betrayal, but secrets...

Those didn't just topple nations, they tore apart relationships, and left scars so deep they stained your soul.

The truth shall set you free. What a load of crap. Know what the truth did? It changed the way you looked at people. Once upon a time, Micha was my hero. Now all I could think when I saw him was 'what else isn't he telling me'?

That's exactly what I was thinking right now, as I eyed up Micha–who was sitting on the couch next to his girl.

It'd been close to a month since they got back from Canada. He told me all about the drive-by at Chase's clubhouse, and his time in the great white north.

Hell, I was even there when shit went down at the docks, but none of that quieted the uncertainty picking at the back of my brain. Now a shot, on the other hand, would definitely help quiet my thoughts. Too bad our local coffee shop didn't serve whiskey.

"Mase?"

"Huh?"

Silas sat forward, making the big plush chair he was on creak, and rested his forearms on his thighs. "You okay?"

There was a loaded question if I'd ever heard one, and one I'd heard a lot since my real father came back.

Was I okay? No. None of us were. My brother and friends could pretend everything was peachy keen all they wanted, but I knew the truth.

Ryker Hudson might be gone, but he'd won.

"I'm fine," I lied.

If Silas knew the truth, he'd try to save me. A wasted effort, in my opinion. Can't save someone who's already damned. I was the son of the boogeyman after all. Turns out I *was* the monster Harper Callaghan made me out to be. How's that for irony?

"You sure?" Silas asked while dropping his gaze down to the cup in my hand, and he wasn't the only one.

Micha and Logan were staring at me too, but it was Riley that made me snort. Her big sapphire eyes were glittering with suspicion.

The only high I was gonna get would be from caffeine. I was tempted to fuck with them and slur a couple words. Instead, I rolled my eyes and lifted the mug to my lips.

"Calm down, it's coffee."

I wouldn't argue a good strong drink right now. Maybe a pill or two. Anything, really. Not only was I in a room with Riley – a walking reminder of how fucked up I truly was – but Silas's girl was staring at me.

Star was alright, I guess. A tiny little thing with platinum hair and dark eyes that could give both Naomi Prescott and Logan's girl, Shelby, a run for her money. If my best friend hadn't shown an interest in her, I'd have fucked her.

It was probably a good thing I didn't. It'd been a long time since I'd seen Silas smile like that. I thought for sure the fucker would shit out a diamond one day. That, I'd always be thankful to Star for. Who knew some prissy little chick from England would be the one to finally pull the stick out of my best friend's ass?

It was her choice in friends I didn't like. Moreso the fact that she decided to get in the way of me and said friend. When I said Star could give Naomi Prescot a run for her money, I didn't just mean in the looks department. She could be vicious for a little thing, but so could I.

My eyes wandered over to the stairs. Harper disappeared up them six minutes and thirty-two seconds ago. Not that I was counting or anything. Besides, she was the one that came here. Walked in like she belonged. Rule number one of handling an addict, never dangle what he wants in front of him.

I'd already be up those stairs prying some sweet ass tears from Harper's eyes if it wasn't for Star. The other girls weren't much of an issue. Riley and Shelby were easily distracted by their boyfriends.

Hell, I'd been handling Lana's shit for years. Star was different, though. Constantly getting in my face and intervening in my shit. The stupid bro code of 'don't fuck with my girl' was getting really annoying.

Harper was mine to fuck with. My perfect little doll that deserved every goddamn tear I pulled down her pretty face. Did I hate her? Fuck yeah, I hated her. At least that's what I told myself every time I saw those big brown eyes. The same eyes I tried to forget at the end of a needle.

The hardest secret to keep was the one you told yourself.

Logan leaned back and flashed a sly smile my way. "You have fun with that girl?"

"Which one? The blonde, or the brunette?"

Shelby groaned while Riley muttered, "Manwhore."

If only they knew.

Since I got out of rehab, I'd been with exactly two girls. One of which I barely remembered. Pretty sure she'd remember me though. When we were done, the bitch couldn't get away from me fast enough. To say my desires had taken a dark turn would be an understatement.

Part of the reason why I hated being in this fucking room. I didn't avoid my brother's girlfriend because of what happened–I did what I had to do–I avoided her because the fear in her eyes got me off.

"A blonde and brunette, hey?" Logan sang with a mischievous smirk on his face. "All you need to complete that trifecta is a redhead."

"Yeah," I snorted. "Too bad there wasn't one there."

Sly motherfucker skipped his green eyes over to the stairs. "That's a shame."

If anyone else noticed Logan's implication, they didn't say anything. Then again, Logan had a way of redirecting people.

I was a perfect example of that. One little suggestive comment and my eyes were once again focused on the second floor. My brother thought he knew me, and maybe once upon a time, he did. But the little boy he grew up with died a long time ago. Years before any of this shit happened. My brother wasn't the only one with secrets.

Tearing my gaze off the stairs, I turned my attention back to my friends.

Silas kept checking his watch. He had a branding ceremony to attend today and didn't like being late. And by late, I meant less than fifteen minutes early. Star, however, was a hot mess.

I don't think that girl had ever shown up on time. It was a match that I thoroughly enjoyed watching. They once argued for an hour on the proper organization of socks. Fucking socks!

I did understand the frustration on my friend's face this time. I went through the same ceremony. Branded Harper when we were kids. I didn't lie to Riley about that. I did brand someone I loved, and now she was dead.

T.L. HODEL

Sometimes I thought about carving that mark off Harper's neck. Other times, I wanted to display it and parade her around like a fucking pet.

"Hey," Logan said, tipping his head at Micha, "you think we can get one of those chicken places down here?"

"For the love of..." Riley sighed and dropped her face in her palm.

Shelby shrugged. "At least he stopped complaining about the cold."

"There was one good thing about the cold. You remember when we..." Logan nuzzled into Shelby's neck and whispered something that turned her cheeks a bright red.

"Logan!" she chastised him with a light slap on the chest.

It was all for show, of course. Shelby was just as addicted to her boyfriend as he was to her. It was annoyingly sweet. Not because their disgusting public displays bothered me, but because I knew what it felt like when that sweetness turned sour.

"What?" he called out in an innocent tone.

Riley grumbled from her corner of the couch. "She's your girl-friend. Not your sex doll."

"Wrong on both counts, little sis." Logan threw his arm over Shelby's shoulders and pulled her in to kiss her cheek. "She's not my sex doll, or my girlfriend. She's my wife."

We all stopped and cocked a brow. Unlike the rest, mine wasn't out of shock. Neither was Micha's. Logan couldn't keep that shit quiet. He called us that night to brag about getting hitched.

I thought it was fucking hilarious, especially considering the dumbfounded look on Shelby's face in the picture he sent us. Smooth motherfucker probably slipped that ring on her finger before she knew what was happening.

Micha did the exact same thing I did. He slowly turned his gaze on his girl. Now, that arched brow *was* one of shock.

14

"I'm sorry." Riley sat forward and braced her elbows on her knees. "Did you say wife?"

I could literally hear everyone hold their breath as we all turned our attention to Shelby, who was white as a sheet. Her mouth opened as if she was going to say something, and then she looked up at the roof and sucked her words back.

Meanwhile, Riley's eyes were getting darker by the second.

"Um... well," Shelby paused and once again looked up with her brows knit. "The thing is..."

"You got married," Riley finished for her.

"Kinda?"

"And you didn't tell me?"

"Uh... Well..."

This shit was amusing as fuck. Never thought I'd see the day that that girl wouldn't have anything to say. Logan apparently agreed, because he threw his arms on the top of the couch and sat back with a shit eating grin. Then again, his smugness could stem from the fact that he'd sealed the deal before Micha. Either way, things were about to get interesting.

I thought for sure Shelby would try and come up with some excuse. Instead, she snapped her suddenly angry glare on Logan. "This is all your fault!"

"What did I do?" Logan whined back at her. "You said the vows."

"Don't turn this around on her," Riley piped in while waving her finger through the air. "What'd you do? Get her drunk?"

Logan's green eyes widened. "I didn't do anything."

"Don't act all innocent. I know you did something."

"You should hear what he just said to me." Shelby sat back, crossed her arms, and gave Logan a dirty look. "He has no control."

I couldn't help but snicker when Logan glanced from one to the other with his mouth hung open. Never come between two chicks. They'll always find a way to turn that shit on you.

I was so caught up in the amusement of watching Logan dodge their wrath that I almost didn't hear my phone ding. The second I read the text, I wished I'd ignored it.

London: Leave Harper alone!

When the fuck did Star leave the room?

Whatever, I blamed this shit on Silas. He couldn't have dated some bitchy cheerleader that minded her own business. No, he had to go for the girl with a savior complex.

Me: Blow me London, I haven't touched your friend.

London: Bullshite! I saw the bruises Mason.

Bruises? What the fuck was she talking about?

Me: What bruises?

London: You know damn well what bruises. Leave her alone! Or so help me...

Why would she think I hit her? Yeah, I was an asshole to Harper, but I never physically hit her. Fuck sakes, one slap from me could kill someone her size.

The soft clink of handcuffs rang through my head and suddenly I was ten-years-old again.

'I'm sorry Louis, but Mason is going to have to come with us.'

My fingers tightened around the phone. Did Harper say something? Of course she fucking did. Lying bitch. This shit was not happening again. People in town already gave me enough sideways glances. Seven years later and they still thought I was a monster.

My eyes rolled over to the redhead trying to sneak out the

front door. If she wanted a monster, I'd give her a fucking monster.

"Where the fuck do you think you're going, Freckles?"

Harper froze with her hand on the door. "I... um... my dad needs me to get home."

Interesting how she wouldn't look at me.

She turned the knob and moved to open the door.

Don't think so.

"If you take one fucking step outside, you'll be sorry." I marched forward, keeping my glare locked directly on her. "What'd you tell your friend, huh?"

Harper shied away when I slammed my hand on the door above her head. "I–I didn't say anything."

Bullshit.

"So you've got bruises, do you?" I dropped my gaze down her trembling form.

There were no injuries on her neck or forearms, meaning whatever the fuck Star was talking about must be hidden under Harper's green shirt and jeans.

"Well, come on." I waved my hand impatiently. "Let's see 'em."

I thought about stripping her – my dick sure liked that idea – but where would be the fun in that? Innocent little Harper Callaghan didn't like showing skin and I liked watching that humiliated flush crawl across her cheeks. How deep would she blush if she knew what I did with the panties I stole from her at prom?

Harper ducked her head and hid behind her hair. "I don't know what you're talking about."

Sure she didn't.

I don't know what pissed me off more– the lie that slipped through her lips, or the possibility that someone hit her. I might not like her – in fact, I fucking loathed her – but Harper was mine, and no one touched my shit.

17

"Leave her alone, Mason!"

I rolled my eyes over my shoulder at Riley, then tipped my head down to Harper's fingers. She was clutching awfully tightly to the bottom of her shirt.

"Whatcha trying to hide, Freckles? You got something under that shirt you don't want me to see?"

She pulled harder on the fabric and shook her head. "N-n-nothing."

Bingo.

"If there's nothing under there, then why don't you show us?"

Her eyes went wide as she snapped her head up and shook her head. I didn't need to see her arms shake to know she was scared. Harper's fear was my new addiction. I could smell that shit from a mile away.

"Do it," I bent over and growled in her ear, "or I will."

Riley, of course, wasn't having any of that shit. "Back off, Mason."

"Fuck off, Riley. This doesn't concern you."

"You're messing with my friend, so yes, it does."

"Oh yeah?" I stood up and looked directly in Harper's eyes. "Well, apparently someone was beating on your friend."

It wasn't just my attention on Harper now.

The corner of Riley's mouth turned down. "Is that true, Harper?"

Let's see you get out of this one, Freckles.

She ducked back down and shook her head. I couldn't help but notice how her fingers had tightened on the bottom of her shirt.

Enough with this shit.

I reached down, snatched both her wrists in one of my hands and used the other to grab her shirt. She struggled, which was about as useful as paper slapping on a rock. I had the fabric lifted before she could suck back her gasp.

The purple and yellow marking her skin blended into one

color. Red. Hot, deep, and full of rage. It bled into my vision then burned down my veins until it was all I could see. Someone didn't just hit her, they beat the fucking shit out of her.

Blood boiled through my ears muffling the gasps coming from behind us. I didn't give a shit what anyone else thought. There was only one thing on my mind. The name of the asshole I was about to fucking kill.

"Who the fuck did this to you!"

Harper tore her hands out of my grasp and yanked her shirt back down. "I fell."

"Bullshit!" I barked down at her. "You don't think I know the difference between an accident and a fucking punch?"

Half my free time was spent in a ring pounding on pricks. I knew what a beating looked like.

"I fell," she insisted again.

Suppose I shouldn't be surprised. She was a liar, after all.

"Tell me who did this to you." I slammed my fist on the door, making Harper jump. "Right fucking now!"

Riley stepped forward and placed her hand on my back. "Mason, you're scaring her."

Good. She should be scared.

"Did I ask for your fucking opinion?"

She didn't like that. Riley went from gently trying to lure me away, to yanking on the back of my shirt.

"When you start picking on my friend, it is my business."

Tension poured through my veins, clenching my jaw as I spun around and glared at my brother's girlfriend.

"Why don't you ask your *friend* what happened last time someone beat the crap out of her?"

Riley puffed her little chest out and met my glare with one of her own. "I'm not going to let you push her around."

"You're going to stop me, are you?"

I was tired of this shit. No one stepped up to defend me. They said they believed me, but I could see it in their eyes. The doubt and wonder if I was indeed the horrible person she accused me of being. I was the weak link, after all. The only member of The Order that couldn't be trusted with the truth.

Well, fuck them. And fuck Riley too.

"You're damn right I'm going to stop you," Riley growled.

I stepped in on her, pushing her back with my chest. "Try it and find out what happens."

The rest of the group had joined us in the entryway. Shelby's eyes widened as Logan pushed her back, while Silas stared at me with a sympathetic frown on his face. But it was my brother that got my wrath.

Micha reached out and grabbed my shoulder, pulling me away from his girl. "Back off..."

My fist sailed through the air before he could finish speaking. By the time I thought about what I was doing, it was too late. My knuckles were already clacking off Micha's jaw.

Time seemed to slow down. Micha's head twisted to the side while he staggered back. The only thing I could think as I watched a drop of blood trickle from the corner of his mouth was, *I just sucker punched my brother.*

"Micha–" I was cut off when my brother's dark glare snapped to mine.

"You wanna play this game, Mase?" He stepped forward and gave me a shove. "Come on, then. Hit me again, asshole!"

When I didn't respond, he shoved me again, which was not helping me calm my mood any.

"Stop it, Micha." He needed to back the fuck off before this shit got out of hand.

"Fuck you, Mase."

Another shove.

"You started this shit."

Another shove.

I balled my fists and gritted my teeth. "I mean it, Micha. Fuck off."

But my big brother didn't stop.

"What's wrong? Can't pick on someone your own size?" He reached out and slapped the side of my face.

That's when I lost it.

My fist swung as I lunged to vent my anger on my brother. Our size difference didn't mean shit to Micha. We'd been fighting each other for years. He took every hit I landed and returned it with one of his own.

I don't know who knocked who on the ground first, but the first time someone tried to pull us apart, I was on top. Throwing my fists down in a fury of wrath. The second time, it was Micha who had me down. By the time we were pulled apart, both Micha and I had swollen jaws and blood running down our skin.

"Fuck you, Micha." I threw my elbow back at Silas–who was trying to hold me back–and snarled, "This is none of your business."

Micha wasn't ready to give up either. He lunged at me, but Logan pulled him back.

"Eat shit, Mase. You made it my business when you threatened my girl."

He needed to chill out. That was barely even a threat.

"Micha, calm down," Logan tugged back on his shirt collar. "You know how worked up he gets about this shit."

I had every right to get worked up. Micha knew that better than anyone.

"Yeah, Micha," I shot him a smirk while struggling against Silas's hold. "Listen to your friend."

That got to him.

Micha's eyes darkened as he stilled and glared back at me.

"You know what, Mase, fuck you." He roughly yanked out of

Logan's grasp. "You want to destroy yourself, go right ahead. I'm tired of cleaning up your messes."

Logan stepped up and put his hand on Micha's shoulder. "Micha..."

"Oh, shut the fuck up Logan." Micha glanced over his shoulder and shrugged away. "Stop fucking coddling him."

I'd seen my brother pissed. Hell, half my childhood was spent fucking with him. But the way he was looking at me right now... That was the darkest I'd ever seen him look.

"Here's an idea, Mase," Micha charged forward with his chest puffed up. "Why don't you grow the fuck up and take some goddamn responsibility for once in your life."

What exactly did he want me to take responsibility for? The lies everyone told me growing up, or being betrayed by someone I thought loved me as much as I loved her? This was the exact same bullshit speech I got from Lou.

"You sound like your old man."

When were they going to take responsibility?

"News flash, asshole," Micha dug his finger into my chest, "he's your old man too. Just because you didn't spawn from his nut sack doesn't mean he's not your dad. He was there when you were growing up, dealing with all your shit."

"Yeah, sure." I rolled my eyes. "Next you'll be telling me to talk to Freckles."

"You know what, that's a good fucking idea."

Fuck that shit.

"She betrayed me!"

"Yeah, she did," Micha narrowed his eyes and leaned in. "You ever ask yourself why?"

I tried asking her, so many times. She blew me off. So no, I didn't ask myself why. I didn't fucking care. Harper said I was a monster, so that's what I became. The why didn't matter.

But doesn't it?

"You want the truth so bad, Mase, then go and fucking find it." Micha shook his head and stormed out of the room, grumbling. "Stop playing the goddamn victim."

I stood there staring after my brother. Maybe he had a point? I spent so much time focused on revenge that I forgot about the one thing I really wanted.

The truth.

If Harper was still here, I might beat it out of her right now, but she wasn't. Must've slipped out during the fight. I balled my fists and glared at the door. Yeah, I wanted the truth, but I also wanted revenge. There was no reason I couldn't have both.

Silas dropped his hand on my shoulder. "Mase…"

"Don't." I shrugged away and stormed outside.

Micha wanted me to stop playing victim, fine. I'd take on the role of executioner.

Judgement day has come, Freckles. I hope you're ready.

Chapter 2
Harper

*E*verybody had scars. Whether they be visible or internal, every person out there had their own story of pain and misery etched into their soul. Some carried nothing more than a paragraph of information, while others had already started writing over their first draft. Trauma is what psychiatrists called this distressing story.

But what if those marks weren't carved in by evil?

The worst scars weren't born out of hate and malice. They were self-inflicted. Lana argued that I didn't deserve Mason Kessler's wrath, but this was so much bigger than she thought.

Would you hurt someone you cared about if it saved them from something worse? How much pain would you endure to protect them?

That's why those scars were impossible to get rid of. They were born out of love. And love, no matter how small or fleeting of a moment, always left its imprint behind.

So yes, the pain and suffering was there, but deep down underneath was the smile of a green-eyed little boy. And that memory was the most heart-wrenching of them all.

Trauma didn't have anything on love.

My heart thundered as I ducked behind a bush and snuck along the treeline. I'd managed to slip out when Micha and Mason started arguing, but it wouldn't be long before someone noticed I was gone. Star had already texted me twice, and Riley...

I glanced at my ringing phone before tucking it back in my pocket.

This was her third call. I tried texting Shelby and telling her I was okay–she was the only person I knew that could calm Riley down–but obviously that didn't work. I didn't want Riley to show up asking questions. Or worse, her dad.

The last time I was questioned by the sheriff, I almost messed everything up. I still wasn't sure if he believed my story, but he'd left me alone. The last thing I wanted was for him to start poking around again. Look how that turned out for Tico.

How stupid could I be? I knew better than to expose myself like that around other people. I could've waited until I got home to check my injuries. Why did I have to look at them there? It didn't hurt that bad anymore. At least I could breathe now. There wasn't much I could do about it now.

All I had to do was convince them that it was an accident, meaning I needed a better excuse than 'I fell.' I needed something that they would buy.

A pair of angry green eyes flashed in front of my face.

I rubbed my hands up my arms, trying to warm the tremble trickling up my spine, but I couldn't chase away the look on Mason's face. My life was spent drowning in the cloud of his well-deserved wrath, but today... I'd never seen him like that.

He's not going to let this go.

If I didn't calm down before I got home, then my father would know something was wrong. Blowing out a breath, I put Mason out of my head and stared up at the sky.

This was my favorite time of day, when the sun was starting to drop behind the horizon. I soaked in every second the sky was lit up with that breathtaking pink and orange hue, because soon enough the moon would come out and darkness would take over.

My mother used to call this 'warrior's hour.' She said these few minutes were meant to remind us that even though darkness dampened so much of our lives, there was always a time to shine. We just had to find it.

I liked her analogy. It reminded me of how sweet she was. But her story was nothing more than a beautiful lie.

The sun didn't come back every day because it wanted to. It didn't shine down on the world to brighten our lives. It did it because it had to. The sun sat high in the sky releasing its energy on everything below, because if it didn't, the world would die. It didn't have a choice.

Just like me.

I pushed through the magnolias lining our property. The sweet champagne-like fragrance that was wafting off the pretty little pink flowers decorating the foliage hanging overhead quickly faded when a large black roof came into view. My stomach flipped as that colorful hue in the sky lowered behind the black of my house.

More like a prison.

Other people looked at the building I called home and saw a breathtaking scene full of lush greenery and flowers surrounding a Georgian style house. When I was a little girl, I used to think the same thing. My family's estate was a place of beauty and wonderment for someone so young.

The large white pillars surrounding our wrap-around porch used to be one of Lana's favorite hiding spots, and Mason and Silas were convinced something was haunting the woods out back.

27

Every time they came here they'd have a more intricate plan on how to chase the ghost away. We even had the same spiral staircase that Lana and I imagined princesses would descend to enter a grand ball.

That time of innocence was the thing I missed the most. When the only things we had to worry about were the beings created by our imagination. But there was no ghost waiting to be vanquished, or fairy living in the garden, because the sun didn't shine here anymore.

Not since Mom...

I closed my eyes and shook the memory from my head. I didn't want to think about that. Or the patch of Black Eyed Susans on the left side of the house.

The only parts of her that were left were buried under those flowers. Daddy made me help him put her there. Alone in the cold, hard earth, forgotten by everyone but me.

No eight-year-old should know how long it takes to burn a body to ash.

When my phone went off again I was tempted to ignore it, but something pulled at me to look. I wished I hadn't. That one text caused my stomach to swirl with dread.

> Mason: I told you you'd be sorry if you stepped out that door.

I swallowed back the lump in my throat and turned my phone off. Guess I shouldn't be surprised. I did bring this on myself. I knew not to argue with Daddy, yet I did anyway. Now my secret was at risk of getting out. And to the worst person.

Mason Kessler couldn't find out, ever.

Once upon a time, he was my everything. The white knight sent to protect me from the horrors of the world. Now he was the monster I'd turned him into. I twisted everything pure and happy in those bright green eyes with three little words.

28

'Mason did it.'

Now he was judging me. Everyone was. Even the eyes of the bronze wolf knocker stared back at me, silently picking apart every decision I'd ever made.

I saw that skeptical look everywhere I went. The way Micha curled his lip when I walked past, or how Logan glared at me. They were all watching me. Even Preston tipped a brow when I was around. I could feel the question in their subtle glances and wavering tones.

What kind of person betrays someone they love? To them I was the monster, and maybe they were right. Lana was the only one who didn't judge me. Maybe she should. After all, I'd lied to her too. She just hadn't figured it out yet, but one day she would.

Then I'd lose her just like I did that little boy.

I missed him. Every day I looked for some hint that he was still there in the eyes of my tormentor. There was nothing. No spark or fleeting glance that told me the Mason I knew was still there. Just the dark and hate-filled stare that assaulted me in the halls.

That's all my life was now. A constant shuffle between two monsters.

One I created, and the other...

I slipped inside and quickly darted across the marble floor to skitter into my room.

The other monster I lived with.

Not wanting to alert anyone to my presence, I carefully made my way around the various plants seated in front of the windows, past the blue velvet armchair Mom used to sit in to watch the sunrise, and ducked down the hall. So far so good. Mrs. Benson hadn't popped out of the shadows to welcome me home.

She'd been in this house taking care of Sean and I for as long as I could remember. If she saw me, then she would know something was wrong. It wouldn't be the first time I came home distressed, but I couldn't pass this off as bullying at school.

29

Besides, I felt horrible hiding things from her. She was the closest thing I had to a mother, and not even she knew what was happening under this roof.

Mason was right about one thing.

I was a good liar.

I had to be.

The light shining out from under my father's office door caused me to freeze at the end of the hall. Was he in there? And if so, what kind of mood was he in? When I left he'd seemed to be happy, but that didn't mean anything.

My father wasn't a bad man. He did all the things a loving parent would. Took care of me when I was sick, tucked me in at night, and kissed away my boo-boos. He was a good dad, until something set him off and he became a different person. Someone mean and cruel.

Sometimes that switch would flip over the slightest thing. A look, or whispered comment. The last time the devil came out, it was because I got home five minutes late. The bruises from that incident were still healing. No way I was going to let him know that I wasn't at Star's house.

It'd be better just to avoid him completely.

I carefully tiptoed down the hall, pulse picking up speed the closer I got to his door. It beat at a furious rate that had me convinced he'd hear it and catch me sneaking past his office.

Holding my breath didn't help. I kept glancing over my shoulder, watching the shadows move through the light cascading across the floor, as my father's footsteps echoed in my ears like the thundering of a drum.

Every step I took caused my body to tense more and more. By the time I reached my door and slipped inside, my chest ached from holding my breath. Once safely tucked inside, I fell back and gasped in a deep breath.

Fear was something I was accustomed to. That sticky cloud of anxiety was my home. It followed me through the halls of Ashworth where torment lurked around every corner.

Honestly, I didn't know what I'd do if I didn't have a sense of dread to cling onto. What would it be like to close my eyes and not worry about what might be hiding in the corners? Would I still hate what I saw when I looked in the mirror?

I sighed and ran my hand over my bookshelf, filled with treasured stories. These written words were my only escape. No one in these tales destroyed the people they loved. Peter Pan didn't drop Wendy. He held her tightly all the way to Neverland. The heroes in my stories didn't create monsters.

They slayed them.

I flipped through a book lying on the top of the wooden shelf.

Alice In Wonderland was a children's book, but it was still my favorite. When I was little and my father was in a bad mood, I hid in the corner and looked for a white rabbit that would lead me away. The only thing I ever found were the twisted shadows waiting to swallow me up.

They say a girl's first love is her father. Perhaps they were right. Why else would I have done what I did? At the time I told myself it was to protect Mason, but he wasn't a little boy unable to defend himself anymore. He was just as cruel as the thing possessing my father.

So which one was I trying to save now? The little boy with the green eyes? Or the man who tucked me in at night? Who would I choose when that dreaded day came? Because it would. Two monsters couldn't occupy the same space without eventually trying to eat each other.

Maybe I was just trying to save myself?

Huffing out a sigh, I started digging through my dresser for my favorite pair of pajamas. I suppose it didn't matter. Sooner or later, one of them would come for me, and I didn't have a white rabbit to lead me away.

My eyes skimmed over the bunnies decorating a pair of blue flannel shorts. All I had were the lifeless eyes of fake animals.

Mason was right. I was pathetic. Standing here like a little girl putting all her hopes and dreams in imaginary beings. How sad was that?

Riley and Shelby didn't have that problem. Then again, neither of them looked at their monster and thought how pretty he was. That was the really pathetic part. No matter what Mason Kessler did to me, or how much he made me cry, I couldn't stop my stomach from fluttering when he walked in a room.

I clicked on the bathroom light and winced as I pulled my shirt off. My finger skimmed over the purple and yellow bruises marking my abdomen.

They were still tender, but not as painful as they were a few days ago. When my shirt brushed against my skin, I didn't want to cry anymore. That was something, right?

That wide-eyed look Star gave me was stuck in my head. The way she stood there with shock and pity on her face broke my heart. She was worried about me. She was always worried about me. But I couldn't have her asking questions.

No one knew that Tico came to visit. He showed up here and tried to convince me to tell someone about my father. I had no idea how he knew—not even Sean did—but Tico knew.

I never told Star about it because I really didn't know what happened. Tico stayed for about twenty minutes and left. That was the last time I saw him.

I gazed into the guilty brown eyes of my reflection and clicked off the light.

Sometimes it was better to hide in an illusion.

Someone knocked on my door as I was climbing into bed. A second later, my father walked into the room. I slid up against my headboard and carefully eyed him, trying to gauge his mood.

Was he the man right now, or the beast? He looked like the man in his black suit with his dark hair bushed neatly back. Then again, the beast wore the same look.

"Going to bed already, Honey Bug?"

My entire body sighed with the use of my nickname. He only used it when he was in a good mood, which wasn't often lately.

"I'm not feeling great," I explained, and settled back in my bed.

"What do you mean you're not feeling great?" I flinched when he walked over and placed a hand on my forehead. "You don't have a temperature."

"I'm just tired," I said, and pulled the blanket over my legs.

Honestly, I just wanted this day to be over. Maybe I'd wake up tomorrow and everyone would magically forget what they'd seen.

He tipped his head and eyed me, which was when I forced a smile on my lips. I'd learned a long time ago not to let him know anything was wrong.

"Well," he pulled the blankets up and gently tucked me in. "You get some sleep then. I just wanted to let you know that I'll be out of town for a couple of weeks."

Mom used to tuck us in like this. She'd make sure we were all snug, and then read a story. Sean still had hope that she would come back, but she was never coming back.

"You can invite Lana over if you like."

My chest ached at the mention of my best friend's name. Lana and I used to do everything together. Lately she hadn't been around much. I got it. She had a family now, and the cutest babies to take care of. But I missed her terribly.

"Can Star come over?"

Daddy sighed and frowned down at me. He didn't like Star. I wasn't sure why. She'd never been anything but polite to him.

"I suppose," he muttered and added, "but no overnight stays."

I nodded and watched him run his finger over my bedside table. His hand stopped next to a picture of a little boy. I looked into the sparkling green eyes and resisted the urge to reach out and stroke his cheek.

Every night I whispered my secrets to that image, hoping that he'd reach out and hold me like he used to. But that little boy was dead. All I had now were memories, and a picture.

"Has Mason Kessler said anything to you?"

My wide eyes snapped back on my father. *Oh God, does he know?* If he did and I lied…

I forced the lump down my throat and prayed he wouldn't hear the thumping echoing in my ears. "N-no. Why would he?"

My father's brown eyes narrowed for just a second before a smile washed over his face.

"It doesn't matter." He waved his hand, then walked into the bathroom. "Things will play out as they should."

What things?

I heard the sink turn on as he called out, "I talked to your brother today."

Sean?

My brother was the one beacon of light I had. Things had been even more depressing around here since he'd left for college.

I sat up and peeked in the bathroom. "Is he coming home?"

Sean called or texted me every day, but I hadn't seen him since Christmas and that seemed like forever ago.

"He has classes, Honey Bug." My father appeared back in the room with a glass in his hand. "He can't drop everything to come home."

Right.

I hung my head and chewed at the frown tugging on my lips. Of course Sean couldn't come home. He was busy living his life. I should be happy for him. He'd gotten away from here.

My father sighed and swept the hair off my forehead. "I know you miss your brother, but you'll see him soon enough. And you still have me."

Which version of him was he referring to?

"Here," he held out the glass, "drink this. It'll make you feel better."

I smiled at the warmth glittering in his eyes and swallowed back the cool water. This man, the one looking at me right now, *he* was my father.

"That's a good girl." He set the empty glass on my bedside table and sat down on the bed. "Maybe when I get back we could take a trip to that ice cream shop you like?"

That made me smile. We used to have weekly trips to the little stand outside of town, but we hadn't been there in ages.

"Okay."

I stretched my arms over my head and yawned. My limbs suddenly felt really heavy.

"You lay down and get some rest."

Sleep sounded like a fantastic idea. I blinked my heavy lids up at my father and smiled before nestling back into my soft pillow. The stress of the day must've finally caught up with me because I was really tired.

When I felt my father's lips press against my forehead, I was already drifting off.

"Sweet dreams, my little Trojan horse."

Chapter 3
Mason

I ducked back into the shadows as the front door swung open and Harper's old man strode out. The bushes I'd chosen to hide in weren't the best – someone else might have snuck in through the magnolias where there was more cover and height – but where was the fun in that?

Besides, the last place anyone would expect to find a man my size was in these shrubs. Especially someone like Ned Callaghan.

That motherfucker walked around town in his stuffy three-piece suit with his shoulders rolled back. The only thing better than fucking with some uptight prick was when they didn't know it was you fucking with them.

I lost count of how many times I listened to Lou rant about some issue, all while smiling behind his back because I was the cause of said issue. If Silas had a stick shoved up his ass, then Lou had the whole damn tree.

Asshole practically strip-searched me every time I left the

house. Acting like he was all worried that I was back on the sauce. I was – took my first drink three days out of rehab. It wasn't like I drank everyday or anything, but I know what Lou and my brother would say.

They'd sit me down and give me some lecture about all that wasted effort. 'You spent all that time getting clean, Mase. Why would you wreck that?'

Personally, I thought rehab was a fucking joke. Every time we were forced to sit around and listen to some asshole talk about his bullshit problems, I wanted to slit my damn throat. Unfortunately for the doctors at Cedarbrea Addiction Clinic, I grew up with two world class manipulators.

Three months was all it took for me to play those pricks, and they weren't the only ones. My supposed father and brother had no clue about my extracurricular activities.

Looks like I was better than Lou's little golden boy at something after all. I did kick the drugs though, so I suppose it wasn't a complete waste.

Not that Micha would see it that way. No, he was too busy telling me what to do.

'You want the truth so bad Mase, then go fucking find it.'

I snorted. "Prick."

Ned stopped mid-stride with his foot suspended in the air and turned his eyes in my direction.

Fuck.

Just keep walking, asshole. You didn't hear shit.

For a split second I could've sworn he saw me. The intensity of his gaze seemed to penetrate the shadows I was hiding in, but then he straightened up and walked around to the back of his black town car. *That was close.* Was it wrong that I was a bit disappointed? Nah, that shit would've been fun.

My head tipped to the side when Ned dropped two suitcases in the trunk. Apparently Harper's old man was going out of town. Worked for me.

The only person who could give Louis Kessler a run for the stubborn asshole title, was Ned Callaghan. Harper and I used to make fun of them. Saying shit like, 'the world would end if they were best friends.'

Thankfully, they weren't. How fucking difficult would that make my life? They were barely acquaintances, because Lou didn't trust him. And neither did I. The only pricks that pranced around that self-righteous were the ones that had a shit load of skeletons in their closet.

That's one thing I could thank my supposed father for. Because of him, I knew how to deal with assholes like this. I'd like to see Ned try to stop me from ripping the truth out of his deceitful little girl.

Bitch dubbed me as an unhinged monster. Well, she was about to find out just how unhinged I was. And there was fuck-all her old man could do about it.

Of course, there was always her brother. Sean and I had gotten into more than one fight over the treatment of his baby sister. Too bad for her, he was away at college.

Tsk, tsk Sean. You left the fawn all alone in the bear's den.

Personally, if my sister was getting ragged on like that, I would've waited a year for her to graduate. Then again, I never thought my brother would betray me, so who was I to judge? Plus, now I was free to pry whatever information I wanted from Harper's pretty little lips.

See, I did some thinking before I came here. Drove around for a couple of hours going over shit. And no matter how many scenarios I went through, the one thing I couldn't shake from my head was the terror shining in Harper's big brown eyes.

She wasn't horrified that I'd seen the bruises. She was horrified that I'd find out who gave them to her. Why? After all the shit I'd done to that girl, why would she be more scared of that than she was of me?

The only thing that made sense in that scenario was if she cared about whoever did it. Meaning I had three suspects.

Her brother.

Sean always did have a short fuse. I'd seen him lose his shit more than once.

Mrs. Benson, a stuck up old bitch that would make a better drill sergeant than nanny.

And her old man.

I couldn't see it being him though. I'd met some abusive parents, and Ned Callaghan didn't fit the bill. The way he doted on his daughter was fucking nauseating.

I waited until the town car disappeared down the driveway before stepping out into the moonlight.

My money was on Sean. Lana was my biggest hint on that one. Something was up with the way she looked at him. He did something, I just didn't know what. Whatever it was, it was enough to drive a wedge between her and Harper.

At school they seemed chummy for the most part. But every once in a while, I'd catch Lana turning away from Harper. Almost as if it hurt to look at her.

I thought about asking Parker about it, but then I'd have him sticking his nose in shit, and the Callaghans were my business. Well, Harper was. If anyone was going to deal with her or her family, it would be me.

My brow cocked down at a patch of black-eyed Susans.

Those were new. The tree a few feet away however...

I stepped up to the base and gritted my teeth at the heart etched in the bark. Time had worn down the two letters carved in the center, but I could still see them. That M and H were as clear to me as the day I put them there, which also happened to be the last time I climbed this tree.

My nostrils flared as I looked up to the window on the second floor. The same blue curtains were still hanging on the other side. Despite being a little faded from the sunlight, I could still see the tiny white flowers decorating the trim.

I bought those for her so she would know that even if I couldn't physically be there, I was still there.

When I was a kid, I'd get a strange feeling that something was wrong. I couldn't explain it, I just knew that Harper needed me. So I'd come over here and hold her until she fell asleep.

For years I told myself it was my imagination, but now as I stood there staring at those blue panes of cloth, I couldn't help but wonder if I *was* picking up on something?

Did I see something that I wasn't old enough to understand? I spent the last two hours asking myself that question. Would the answer make a difference? She still betrayed me. I took two years of torment to keep her safe, and when it was her turn to be tested, she threw me under the bus.

So no, it wouldn't make a difference. But it might give me some peace. Let me go to sleep at night without seeing the sick twisted smile of the green-eyed bastard that spawned me.

Ryker Hudson was the boogeyman to everyone. To me… he was the living nightmare I had to endure to protect the girl I loved.

'Do you think she'd show you the same loyalty?'

That was one of the last things that sick fuck said to me. Turned out he was right. I faced a monster for Harper, and she turned me into one. How's that for irony?

I jumped up, grabbing onto the branch above my head, and grunted as I pulled myself up.

What was I going to do when I took Harper? I had no fucking clue, but I did have a few ideas. Time didn't heal a broken heart, it made it black. I didn't just want to see her cry, I wanted her to suffer.

Every time she ducked away from me or whimpered in despair,

I felt a little more satisfied. If I hurt her enough, then maybe I could chase away the image haunting the back of my mind.

When I banged some random chick, it wasn't their annoying face I saw moaning. It was hers. Harper's face was in every magazine I picked up and every porn I watched. It was her chest I saw heaving while her lips parted in ecstasy. I'd been jerking off to that girl since the day my balls dropped.

That was the truly fucked up part. I despised everything about Harper, yet no matter how many chicks I bent over, I couldn't rid myself of those fantasies. Maybe Logan was right. Maybe it was time for some good old-fashioned hate fucking.

No, hate wasn't the right word. Rage was much closer to what I wanted. I wanted to feel her pulse flutter while I choked the life out of her and used her cunt as my personal jerk-off toy. Maybe throw in some tears and a couple pleas for me to stop and I'd be good.

Yeah, that's what I wanted. To break the bitch that broke me. Harper could consider it payback. Then, when I was done, I'd toss her away. Nothing more than another notch on my bedpost. At least that's what I told myself.

I twisted my body and took the next step up the tree. Kicking off a flimsy twig to the bigger branch above. I barely made it before the twig snapped off and fell to the ground.

This shit was easier when I was a kid. Then again, I didn't weigh anywhere close to what I did now. At least I had strength on my side. Benefits of my many nights spent in the ring.

My phone went off when I was halfway up the tree.

"Fuck," I growled as the ringtone echoed in the night.

My first instinct was to hang up. In order to do that, though, I'd have to let go of what I was holding and grab my phone. Since I didn't want the entire household to know I was here–Mrs. Benson would come out here with a broom and beat me to death–I had no choice but to answer.

Tapping the headset in my ear, I barked out, "What?" and continued up the tree.

"Where are you?"

Fucking Lou.

"Banging your secretary." I stepped onto a branch and paused when it creaked. "What do you want?"

"I need to talk to you about something."

Of course he did. Lou always needed to talk about something. My grades, behavior at school, or the fact that he wasn't my real fucking father.

"Can it wait?" I looked down at the ground as the branch creaked again–this time with a significant pop–and carefully tiptoed my way to a thicker piece of wood. "I'm kind of in the middle of something."

"In the middle of what?"

I rolled my eyes at the worry in his tone. "Relax Lou, I don't have a needle shoved in my arm."

"Are you drinking?"

"No." *I'm trying not to die in this old ass tree.* "Don't you have other things to worry about. Like Grandpa's next task."

Lou grumbled out something inaudible.

He was not happy about his father's miraculous return, and neither was Micha. I found that shit was funny as fuck. Grandpa and Grandma Kessler could stay as long as they liked. Plus, Lou hated them, which automatically made me like them.

I could do without Grandma's slaps though. The back of my head never hurt this much. I got smacked this morning for not washing my hands before breakfast. Grandma didn't mess around.

Logan had it worse. I thought Ryker's old man would be some psycho, but he was actually kind of normal. And his wife was so sweet she made Paisley look like the boogeyman.

The fact that she'd survived as long as she had in a house with

Riley was nothing short of a miracle. I thought she'd have a fork in her eye by now for sure.

"I need to talk to you about your contract."

"What contract?" There was only one contract he could be talking about, but I liked fucking with him.

"You know damn well what contract."

Who pissed in his cornflakes? Oh, right, Gramps did. I loved that old fucker.

I stepped around the trunk, hoisted myself up and grunted out, "What about it?"

"Mason, what are you doing?"

"Climbing a tree."

There was a long pause in which Lou was probably trying to decide if I was hallucinating said tree, actually climbing one, or doing something dumb because I was drunk.

"Did you say you're climbing a tree?"

Was he deaf now? "Yes."

Another long pause that I used to swing around the trunk.

"Why are you climbing a tree?"

"I thought about going for a five mile run, but I saw this tree and thought fuck it. Let's climb that shit and see if I can fly."

"Mason," Lou sighed.

I sighed right back at him. "Lou."

"I suppose it doesn't matter, as long as you're doing something productive."

Really? This was what he considered productive?

"Now, back to the contract," he said, making me roll my eyes. "Harper's sixteen now. Do you plan on enacting it?"

Why was he in such a hurry? I wasn't fucking Micha. She only turned sixteen a couple months ago. It wasn't like the clock was ticking down.

"Why do you care?" I grumbled and shimmied my way higher up.

A few more branches left and I'd be perched outside her window.

"Ned called me last week inquiring about it."

That made me stop and arch a brow. "Harper's dad called you."

"Yes."

"About the contract I have on his daughter?"

"Correct," Lou confirmed.

Well, that was weird.

Did he *want* me to take his daughter? If someone in this house was hurting her, then I guess it made sense that he'd want to get her out. Especially if said culprit was his son. I never did like Sean.

"Ned is a businessman," Lou explained. "He understands the bonds of a contract."

Uh huh? Sounded like a bullshit excuse to me. What kind of guy hands over his daughter? A better question was, why the fuck was I still climbing this tree if I could walk through the front door?

I glanced down at the dark ground, then up to the last branch held tightly in my grip.

Ah, fuck it. I was almost there.

"Well?" Lou said when I finally reached Harper's window.

It was dark inside, but the moon lit up the room enough that I could make out someone curled up on the bed. My eyes roamed over the small blanketed form as I slowly slid the window open.

The scent of cinnamon and peaches smacked me in the face like a freight train. That smell was a part of me for so long, it still followed me around. Filling my nostrils with a temptation I both wanted to devour, and destroy.

"Mason!"

Harper sighed and rolled over. Did she know I was here? Could she feel me watching her? My dick twitched at the thought of those big doe eyes blinking up at me in fear.

"What?" I whispered in a growl.

"The contract?"

Harper kicked out, throwing the blankets off enough to expose her thigh. I watched the moonlight dance across her creamy skin and thought about digging my teeth into that flesh. Pierce her so deeply that the taint of her blood lingered on my tongue.

"If I enact the contract, that means I can do whatever I want with her, right?"

I could practically see Lou nodding in confirmation. "That's right."

"Enact it," I said, and tore the headset out of my ear.

Lou's voice echoed up as the earpiece fell to the ground. I didn't give a shit what he was saying, and sure as hell didn't want him mingling with the voices already in my head. Like Micha.

I was still pissed at him, but he was right about one thing. It was time to stop playing the victim. Victimizer was much more fun.

I ducked down and crawled through the window—which was definitely harder to do than when I was a kid. I had to twist around to get my shoulders through, but I made it. And with elegance. Micha was constantly giving me shit about my need to fight. I'd like to see him slip through a girl's window without making a sound.

My brother thought I had anger issues. He was partly right. My earlier fight with him was proof of that. If I wasn't so pissed, he wouldn't have landed half as many hits as he did. But fighting wasn't about venting my anger.

It was the other aspects I craved. The entire thing was a game. One that I was good at playing. I liked watching my opponent try to figure out my next move. Was I gonna go left, hit low or high? The mind-fuckery of it all was the best part.

My eyes landed on the sleeping girl across the room. Now I got to play another version of that game. The only difference was, this one didn't involve fists. At least, not mine. I doubted Harper would fight me, she was too timid to try some shit like that, but how hot would it be if she did?

Her tiny little fists beating against my chest in useless struggle. I'd let her fight for a bit, maybe even let her think she might win. All so I could crush her hopes like a bug. The trick to beating someone in the ring was knowing your opponent, and I knew everything there was to know about Harper Callaghan.

Not much had changed since we were kids. She still had the same white desk and pink canopy bed with fairy lights hung above. A sixteen year old girl with little twinkling blue and purple lights. What the fuck? If that didn't scream defile me, I don't know what did. My gaze trickled over to little navy shorts on her exposed thigh.

I stand corrected. That shit screams defile me.

Who'd have thought little white bunnies would be so fucking hot. I actually had to take a second to adjust my dick before strolling across the room.

I took my time, running my hand along her dresser piled high with stuffed animals. One in particular caught my eye. A white rabbit with a big red bow.

I gave that one to her for her seventh birthday. The rabbit next to it I gave her the year after, and so on. She still had them all. Four bunnies lined up in a neat little row from earliest to latest.

My jaw clenched. Was this shit trophies to her? Something to remind Harper that she got one over on me? Well, fuck that. I swung my hand out, knocking the pile on the floor. She always did have a thing for rabbits. Maybe I'd make her eat one.

Stopping at the side of her bed, I stared down as her eyes moved behind closed lids, causing her long lashes to flutter. She was fast asleep and completely vulnerable. I could do anything I wanted to her.

My dick twitched as I slowly pulled the blanket off her body. She was so fucking tiny. Her foot would fit in the palm of my hand. Like a doll. I watched her chest rise and fall, pressing those perfect handful sized mounds against the blue fabric of her shirt.

When I was a kid, I liked playing with dolls. Ripping their heads and arms off while little girls cried. Now I wanted to play a different game with a more realistic doll. She'd still cry though.

Big fat tears that I could lick off her face.

Couldn't taste those tears if she was asleep though. So I reached over and flicked on the fairy lights, waiting for her to wake up.

She didn't. All Harper did when the tiny purple and blue lights danced around the room was whimper and roll over.

My eyes automatically went to the tiny specks dotting her face. There were thirty-seven freckles across her button nose. I knew this because I counted them every time I saw her.

I knew everything about those dots. How far each one was from her big doe eyes, or plump pink lips. Which one was the darkest, which one was the lightest. I even remembered the ones that faded with time.

Twelve missing freckles that died with my love. Did I still want her? Yeah. That much I'd admit. I wanted to use Harper in every possible way a man could use a woman.

And why shouldn't I? I fought my desire long enough. Why shouldn't I take what I wanted? She did. She tore my heart in half without so much as a second thought.

It was my turn.

"What do you think, Freckles," I walked my fingers down her side to the dip in her waist, where I tightened my fingers around her small hip, "should I just fuck you and get it over with?"

My eyes narrowed when I rolled her onto her back.

What the fuck?

Harper's shirt was pulled up, exposing her stomach. The same stomach I'd seen bruises on less than three hours ago. Yet there weren't any now. Make-up rubbed off onto my skin as I swiped my hand over her stomach. I stared at my fingertips, then glanced back down at the purple marks seeping through.

What was she trying to do? Hide the evidence?

"Tricky, tricky, Freckles." I tsked. "You didn't think I'd forget about this shit, did you?"

The only response I got was a quick shuddered breath.

"Of course you did." *Conniving bitch.* "You thought you could pull another one over on old Mason. But I've got news for you..." I crawled on the bed and ran my hands up her legs. "I'm on to your games."

She still didn't respond. Not when her bed creaked under my weight, or when goosebumps trickled across her skin. How fucking deep did she sleep? I stared down at the bare skin of her leg and licked my lips.

Let's find out.

I bent over and grazed my tongue up her calf, groaning when her sweet flavor exploded in my mouth. Fuck, she tasted good. Too good. I could devour her right now. Too bad I fucking loathed her. Otherwise I'd lick every inch of that body until she was begging for more.

Harper muttered something and tried to roll over, but I tightened my grip and held her where she was.

Just because I didn't want to fuck her didn't mean I couldn't do other things. The sweet spot between her legs called to the beast inside me. Only one thought ran through my mind– does she smell as good as she tastes?

Like the addict I was, I dove in. Burying my nose in the fabric of her shorts to inhale that tempting scent deep in my soul.

"Fuuuck," I groaned.

If my dick wasn't begging for release before, then it sure as fuck was now. The fucker was so hard it thought it could punch through my jeans.

I sat up and palmed my aching cock while considering how far

49

I wanted this to go. I was going to fuck her, there was no doubt about that. But why rush things? When I took her pussy, I didn't want her scared. I wanted her fucking terrified.

My hand shot out, wrapping around her neck and squeezing until she gasped and her eyes snapped open. When those wide brown orbs met mine, I couldn't help but smirk at the shock glittering inside them.

"Rise and shine, Freckles."

Payback's a bitch.

Chapter 4
Harper

One minute I was lost in Wonderland, having tea with Alice. Then the next, I couldn't breath. A giant black snake had wrapped around my throat. I didn't know where it came from, or how it got there, but there it was. Making me struggle and lash out. My lungs burned as I desperately tried to gasp in oxygen and fought against the constriction getting tighter and tighter.

Breathe Harper, breathe.

When my eyes fluttered open I realized it wasn't a snake. It was something else so much worse than any nightmare monster I could imagine. A pair of sparkling green eyes punched me in the gut.

"Rise and shine, Freckles."

My heart stopped dead in my chest as dread set in, rolling through my body in a wave that froze my muscles. All I could do was blink and struggle for breath. This couldn't be real. I had to still be dreaming. Mason Kessler was not in my room.

Those green eyes narrowed as Mason's fingers tightened around my wildly flickering pulse, but it was his voice that smacked me in the face.

"There you are."

Oh my God, Mason Kessler was in my room!

Shock had rendered me useless. I couldn't even move when he pulled his hand off my neck and sat back. I just laid there coughing much needed oxygen back into my lungs.

What was he doing here? The answer to that question terrified me even more than the devious smirk on his lips.

Mason didn't say a thing. He didn't apologize for almost strangling me to death, or ask if I was okay. He simply sat there watching me choke on air.

"Stop being so dramatic." An annoyed look washed over his face. "I didn't choke you that hard."

I don't know what came over me, or why I said anything at all. But the instant the words, "You almost killed me," left my mouth, I regretted them.

Darkness flooded into Mason's glare, making me scuttle back against my headboard and hug my knees. "I'm sorry."

I knew better than to talk back. Nothing good ever came out of being the brave one. It was the timid mouse hiding in the corner that survived the cat. Though right now, Mason looked more like a lion ready to pounce. A mouse had no chance against a lion.

Awkward silence filled the room as I stayed still, afraid to provoke the boy on my bed. No, not boy. My eyes rolled over his broad shoulders and bulging muscles. Mason wasn't a boy anymore. He was a man.

A man with arms bigger than my thighs. I couldn't stop staring at him. Watching the way the twinkling blue and purple lights danced across his olive skin, or how the moonlight highlighted his chocolate hair.

Other girls would be delighted to find a guy like him in their room. Not me. I knew the pain and humiliation that came with that charming smile. I'd felt the wrath of his sharp tongue. The only thing Mason Kessler wanted to do with me was destroy me. I suppose I deserved it.

My eyes drifted to the picture of the smiling little boy on my bedside table.

I destroyed him first. That didn't mean I wasn't scared. I was terrified, because he was in my room. He never came here. Not anymore.

Anxiety had me wound up so tight that when Mason did finally speak, I jumped.

"Nice job trying to hide the evidence by the way," he nodded at my stomach. "But you don't think I'm that dumb, do you?"

My brows knit when I glanced down. I didn't have to pull my shirt up to know what he was talking about, because my legs were tucked up against me. I couldn't see the bruise on my left thigh.

It should be right there, just below the hemline of my shorts. But all I could see was unmarked skin. I could still feel it every time my muscle twitched, which confused me even more.

Where did it go?

I was tempted to inspect the rest of my injuries, and I might've, if Mason wasn't watching me like a hawk. I couldn't risk raising his suspicions. Then he might think I was hiding more than the bruises he'd seen and my lame excuse of falling wouldn't have a chance of working.

"Why are you here?"

His eyes snapped up to mine. "Why the fuck do you think I'm here?"

To ruin everything I sacrificed so much for.

"I fell," was the only thing I could think of to say.

When he released a disgruntled snort, I braced myself for the verbal lashing I was sure to get. But that wasn't what I got. My mind went on full alert when Mason pressed his palms into my mattress and crawled closer.

I never wanted to be able to disappear more than I did at that moment. He was slithering over me like a snake ready to strike and all I wanted to do was meld into the wood at my back.

He stopped an inch away from my face. "I'm done with your shit."

Each word he spoke lingered on my lips with the minty taste of his hot breath.

I whimpered and once again tried to push back into the headboard, but there was nowhere to go. Mason had me completely caged in. He loomed over me, blocking out everything behind his large frame.

Could I squeeze past?

I glanced to either side, feeling the heavy sense of doom close in on me as the hard muscles in his arm flexed.

"Thinking about running, Freckles?" He leaned in to growl in my ear. "Try it. I dare you."

Something in the back of my head told me to go for it and sprint across the room for safety. I didn't, because that would only spur him on, and I wasn't brave enough for that.

Riley or Star might've fought back, but not me. I knew what happened when you antagonized the monster under your bed. So I did the only thing I could.

I tucked my head into my knees and hid behind my hair. Sometimes it was easier when I didn't see it coming. Like I could trick my brain into thinking everything was okay, when it really wasn't.

Mason moved in a little closer and smoothed his palm down my head. Stroking me like I was a pet. The sound of his chuckle rang through my ears, making me shiver and hug my legs tighter.

It wasn't sweet and lighthearted like a laugh should be. It was an alarm that I knew well. There was only one thing that quick, huffed out chuckle promised.

Misery and darkness.

"I'm only going to ask you this once, and you better tell me the fucking truth."

My scalp burned when he speared his hand in my hair and yanked my head back. I cried out and twisted my neck to escape the rage tugging at his features. That was a mistake. Mason's fingers tightened their grip, turning that burn into a searing ache that crawled across my skull.

I couldn't stop my hands from reaching out to clutch onto his arm. "Please stop."

"You want me to stop? Sure Freckles, I'll stop," he growled, and pulled my head back more. "As soon as you tell me who the fuck hit you."

Tears leaked from the corners of my eyes as I cried out, "I fell."

"The fuck you did!" He moved in, pressing his hard body against my curled up legs. "Last chance. Who. The fuck. Hit you?"

Desperation seeped into my bones. Every time I lied to Mason my soul died a little more. But I couldn't tell him the truth. He could never find out. If he did…

Licking my lips, I pushed back the pain in my neck and forced out the words, "I fell."

That's when my need to retreat intensified. Mason's eyes darkened as a smirk curled the corner of his mouth.

"Wrong answer."

That was the only warning I got before my legs were yanked out from my arms and pinned under Mason's heavy weight. I flailed about, kicking my legs and slapping his arm. Maybe it was reckless, but I needed to get away from the judgement on his face.

I needed to retreat back into the safety of my huddled form. My fight was useless. Less than useless, because, like Mason had told me so many times, I was pathetic.

He slammed my head back against the headboard. "I'd beat the truth out of you if I thought it would work, but…"

He didn't have to finish speaking for me to understand what he was thinking. The way his eyes dropped down to my abdomen was enough for that.

I swallowed down the truth and whispered, "I fell."

If I said it enough, maybe he'd believe me.

"So you keep saying."

"It's the truth," I insisted.

I could feel the fury burning in those emerald depths. It raged around in a storm of resentment that shredded my heart. The boy in the picture on my bedside table would never look at me like that. He would hold me and tell me everything would be okay, and in that moment it would be, because I was with him. I missed that little boy.

Mason grabbed my chin, making me wince as his fingers dug into my cheeks. For a second I thought he might snap my neck. Instead he let me go – yanking his hand away like I disgusted him – and got off the bed.

The instant he was off me, I resumed my protective position and tucked my legs tightly into my torso.

A tear slid down my face as I shook my head. "You used to love me."

I'm not sure why I said that. Maybe I was trying to reach a part of him that I prayed was still there. Then I'd have a little bit of hope. I should've known better.

"And you used to not be a lying cunt, so I guess we're even." I felt something drop down on the mattress, followed by Mason's deep command. "Get up."

I peeked over my arms at the black bag sitting on the foot of the bed. What was that for?

"Now, Freckles!"

A shiver ran up my spine when he impatiently folded his arms across his broad chest.

My body twitched, itching to obey him, but my limbs were

frozen, weighed down by the terror coursing through my veins. He wanted to take me somewhere. Why couldn't he just torment and humiliate me? I could handle that.

At this point, pain and humiliation were my comfort zone. This was different than all the other times Mason Kessler confronted me. There was a determination on his face that had me horrified to find out what he had planned.

Still I asked, "Why?"

Four words caused my eyes to go wide.

"You're coming with me."

What? No, no, no.

"B-but I-I can't."

"The fuck you can't." A shiver ran down my spine when his eyes narrowed in on me. "If you don't want to tell me who beat the shit out of you, then I guess I'll just have to keep you by my side. Let's see how long you can keep the truth locked up behind those lying lips."

My heavy swallow echoed around the room like the beat of a drum.

"Mason, I can't…"

"Tell me you can't one more time, Freckles." He leaned over and braced his hands on the bed next to the foreboding black bag. "I dare you."

I SMACKED my fists off Mason's solid back. "Put me down."

Why was I being carted through my house like a sack of potatoes? Because, according to Mason, I took too long. I didn't argue. I never argued. My only infraction was staying hidden under my arms while I tried to wrap my head around things.

There was barely enough time for me to comprehend what he

was saying before I was hefted off the bed and thrown over his shoulder.

"Please, Mason," I winced and tried to shuffle to a more comfortable position. His shoulder was incredibly hard, which my bruises were not agreeing with. "Just let me go."

I couldn't go with him. Not to mention, I didn't *want* to go with him. If my dad came home and I wasn't there...

"My dad won't–"

"He knows the deal," Mason grumbled. "He signed the contract."

That made me gasp. I didn't even think about the contract. And why would I? That thing was signed when I was like six. Yeah, he was constantly claiming dominion over me, but I thought that was just part of the make me miserable motto.

"Y-you still have the contract?"

"Of course I still have the contract." His hand landed on my ass, making me squeal. "You didn't think I'd let you off that easy, did you?"

He rounded the corner and skipped down the stairs. At that point, the only thing I was concerned about was not falling. I closed my eyes and clung onto Mason's shirt like my life depended on it.

He was tall, and it was a long way down. A marble floor never seemed so daunting. I'd end up with a lot more than bruises if I landed head first on the ground.

When we reached the front door, Mason paused and looked back at me. "Any more arguments, Freckles?"

I opened my mouth but quickly clamped it shut. There wasn't anything to argue. I knew who Mason was, and what his family was capable of. I knew who they all were. The Order Of Ravens And Wolves wasn't a rumor like I tried to convince Lana.

They were very real, and had more power than anyone could

imagine. The problem was, so did my father, and he was more methodical than anyone knew.

Sean grew up in the same house and he had no idea what was going on. He'd never seen a single mark on me. Did that mean I was a good liar? Maybe? Maybe it just made me unlucky.

Unlike my brother, I knew what our father had planned. I'd seen what he was capable of, and I knew what would happen if I let Mason take me.

Mason stepped outside and carried me across the driveway. I listened to the gravel crunch under his feet. Each step echoing louder and louder through my ears. I couldn't let this happen. If my father's secrets got out…

I have to get home before he does.

I beat my fists against Mason's back and kicked my feet out, while screaming as loud as my lungs would allow. My throat hurt and my body ached but I continued to fight. I had to. I might get lucky and attract Mrs. Benson's attention.

My tantrum halted when Mason's palm landed on my ass with a resounding slap that blazed a path of fire across my hips and up my thighs.

"Quiet down or I'll fuck you right here."

The insinuation of that caused mortification to burn a trail across my cheeks and down my neck. But Mason would never touch me. He'd made that quite clear numerous times. He wouldn't do anything like that, would he? My mind flashed back to the way Mason looked at me at prom.

"But you said I-I disgust you?"

"You think that makes you safe?" His shoulder shook with a deep snicker. "Wanna know what I did with your panties?"

Oh God.

I shook my head and tucked my face into his back. My cheeks were on fire now, which wasn't helped at all by the way he smelled. Mason used to smell like dirt and grass. Not anymore.

Now he had a fresh citrus scent with earthy undertones. So masculine and tempting that it was hard to stop myself from snuggling into the firm muscles flexing in his back. Luckily I didn't have much time to soak up his scent, because next thing I knew, I was deposited in the passenger seat of his Corvette.

I looked up to the man looming over me and the stern finger he was pointing. "Don't fucking move."

The trees lining my house were just over his shoulder. The leafy branches beckoned to me, tempting me to risk it and run back to my house and hide in my room.

"Clearly you're not hearing me. If you so much as flinch your ass off that seat…" he bent over and leaned in, bringing his face a breath away from mine, "…the last thing you'll have to worry about is how many bruises I find on your body."

Alarm caused the hairs on the back of my neck to stand up. What did he mean, how many bruises he found? Was he going to inspect me?

I swallowed back a gulp. "T-there aren't any more."

"We'll see about that." His eyes narrowed for a second before he stood up and warned me again, "Don't fucking move."

The bang of the door closing wasn't anywhere near as loud as the lock clicking into place. That soft sound rang through my ears like the chimes of a doomsday clock. I shrank back in the seat and watched Mason stalk around the hood of the car.

I'd never seen him look so determined. Every time he questioned me when we were kids, I managed to blow him off. The pit growing in my stomach told me that wasn't going to happen this time. Mason wouldn't stop until he got what he wanted.

I could feel the walls closing in as he opened the door, tossed the bag he packed for me in the back, and climbed in the car.

"Buckle up, Freckles." He shot me a smirk and started the ignition. "It's going to be a wild ride."

I hugged my knees into my chest and watched the trees behind us get smaller. There was only one person in this town that scared me more than Mason Kessler. When he found out who I was with, he'd come and finish the job he threatened to do...

"THE COPS WILL BE HERE any minute, Honey Bug." My father swept my hair back and pressed his lips to my forehead. "You know what to tell them."

I turned away from his stern glare and watched the machine I was hooked up to beep away my pulse. "Yes Daddy."

"Good girl," he said, and stood up to walk across the room. "Remember what happens if you don't do what I say."

The pain wracking through my broken body was enough to remind me of that. And if it wasn't, what I'd seen him do to Momma last night sure was. He told me not to go in his office.

I should've listened. Now, I'd never get that empty look in Momma's eyes out of my head. She told me to run, but there was so much blood, I couldn't move.

Daddy hit me when I threatened to tell Mason.

After we put Momma under her flowers, he hit me again, and again, and again. I begged him to stop. Told him I loved him and asked him not to hurt me. But he didn't stop. He said I needed to learn to listen to him.

"Hello Harper." The deputy sheriff walked in and smiled at me. "How are you feeling?"

"Okay," I whispered and continued to watch the machine pulse.

I couldn't look away from the bright green lines bumping up and down. Every time they reappeared, they'd sparkle just a little. Like his eyes sparkled in the sun.

Deputy Adams sat down in the chair beside my bed and sighed. "You're a very strong little girl."

His words brought tears to my eyes. I wasn't strong. Strong people didn't listen to the monster in their closet. But I had to, or those beautiful green eyes would never sparkle again.

"Can you tell me who did this to you?"

A tear slid down my cheek as I whispered, "Mason did it."

Goodbye my beautiful green eyed boy. I'll always love you...

I SWEPT the tear off my cheek and stared out the window. Seven years ago I made a choice, and now I'd have to make another. Did I try to escape before my father came home? Or did I let Mason break me?

Back then it was an easy choice, but now...

I glanced over at Mason, searching for something I hadn't seen in years. Was there any of that green eyed little boy left to save?

Chapter 5
Mason

*H*arper's body trembled so violently that the vibrations of her quaking slithered across the center console and up my seat into my balls. Was I proud of myself? Fuck yeah I was proud of myself.

I'd never seen Harper look so scared, which was saying a lot considering my day didn't start off right until I pulled at least one tear down her face.

Sometimes I sent her a good morning text, just in case I didn't run into her in the morning. Couldn't have her showing up to school all smiles and giggles, after all. That shit would fuck my good mood right up.

Was it wrong that I got off on her fear? Probably. Too bad for her I didn't give a shit. In fact, I preferred wrong. It was so much more fun to play in the dark.

Lou and Micha were constantly preaching about the benefits of a diplomatic approach. Kind of condescending, considering how my brother got his girl. I'd like to see him explain where the diplomacy was in that shit show. But that was Micha, the hypocritical prick. Telling me to stop playing victim.

Who's playing victim now, asshole.

My fingers tightened around the steering wheel, pulling at the scrapes on my knuckles and reminding me of our fight. I shouldn't be surprised. My brother was a chip off the old block and Lou had his nose shoved so far up my ass he could smell what I had for breakfast.

Wasn't the first time Micha pissed me off, but it was the first time I sucker punched him over it. Or should I say, over *her.*

My gaze slid over to Harper, who was staring at me with wide eyes. What the fuck was she looking at? This was all her fault. I guess it didn't matter. It was over with now. Besides, I had better things to concentrate on.

Like why the fuck she's looking at me.

Moonlight glittered off those big brown orbs, taunting me to give her a firsthand experience of a deer caught in headlights. How wide would her eyes go if I kicked her ass out and revved the engine? That was one way to find out how fast she could run.

I blew out a breath while stretching the tension out of my neck. There was no reason to get all worked up. Things were finally going my way. I had the lying bitch in my clutches, and this time she didn't have any cops to hide behind...

"Stupid Dad," I grumbled while snatching my sweater off my dresser.

Didn't he realize there were more important things to worry about than being warm? Someone hurt Harper. I needed to get to her. Micha said we'd find who did it and make them pay, but all I wanted to do right now was make sure she was okay.

Everyone kept telling me that Harper was fine, but they didn't get it. She was mine. It was my job to protect her. If I hadn't left her house last night then she'd be fine, instead of in the hospital. This was all my fault.

I swept the tears off my cheek and tore down the stairs. Harper didn't need to see me upset. I had to be strong so she'd know that I could keep her safe.

But could I?

My wife was laying in a hospital bed because I didn't do my job. What if I failed again? Would she survive, or would I lose her forever?

No!

That wouldn't happen. If I had to glue myself to her side, I'd make sure she was always protected. She'd never be left alone again. That's when monsters attacked. When you were alone in the dark, they jumped out of the shadows and snatched you up.

That's when my monster came. When no one could hear me scream. But that was okay, because as long as he was coming for me, he left her alone.

Maybe he did get her?

I knew Ryker was dead. We had a funeral for him and everything, but I overheard Micha and Logan whispering about how no one could find out what happened. Maybe Ryker wasn't dead? Maybe he was just stronger? That thought alone was enough to send a shiver down my spine.

I had to get to Harper!

Tugging the sleeves of my sweater on my arms, I ran into my dad's study and announced, "I'm ready."

My dad wasn't alone.

Three uniformed men turned and looked at me. One of whom was the deputy sheriff. My heart lurched out of my chest. Were they here because of Harper? Was she hurt worse than I thought? Was she dead?

The monster did get her.

The deputy sheriff tipped his head and frowned. "Hello Mason."

He wasn't the only one whose lips were turned down. My dad wasn't saying anything. He was just standing there with sadness in his eyes. The last time he looked that sullen was when Mom died.

I woke up in the hospital and there he was, staring at me just like that. He told me we had an accident, but I knew that was a lie. Micha was way too mad for it to be just an accident.

Was that why my dad was looking at me like that? Was Harper dead too? I couldn't breathe. She had to be okay. She just had to. I couldn't live without her.

"Mason..."

I stepped forward, cutting the deputy sheriff off, "Is Harper alright?"

I needed to know.

My heart dropped right along with Deputy Adams as he crouched down to my height. "Harper's fine."

Thank God.

And suddenly my lungs could work again. I sucked in a big breath of air and let my shoulders relax.

"But you're going to have to come with us..."

A TINY SCARED squeak pulled me out of the past and to the bend curving around Cherry Lake that was approaching way too fast. For half a second I thought about slamming my foot down on the gas just so I could hear Harper scream when we flew around the turn. But I eased up instead. I'd already escaped one sinking car and wasn't in a hurry to do it again. Even if it would be fun to watch her face light up in terror.

How ironic would that be though? Micha and Lou still tried to paint this picture of a perfect mom for me, but I knew what she did. I also knew that it was Micha who pulled me out of that car. I didn't remember much about that night, but I got enough flashes that I could piece it together.

The car careening off the dock, water soaking my legs, and the desperation on my brother's face when he was banging that trophy against the window. I still had that thing. I looked at it sitting on my dresser every morning before I got ready for school.

It used to be a symbol of hope. Now it just reminded me of yet another thing my so-called family kept from me. Every time Lou told me another story about how I used to bake cookies with my mom, I internally shook my head.

The man was a shrink, he should've known my memories would come back one day. So much for being one of the top men in his profession.

I glanced over at Harper's tiny hand gripping tightly to the door handle and rolled my eyes. "Relax, I'm not gonna kill us."

I might hurt her a bit, but I wouldn't kill her. Not physically, anyway. Her soul was another story. I'd happily tear that shit apart. Maybe the broken pieces would mend mine? Not that it would matter. I gave up on any sense of peace a long time ago.

Harper didn't so much as peep in response. She just sat there staring. It was fucking annoying. I could feel her gaze pouring over my face. Almost like she was searching for something.

Maybe she thought she'd find some remnants of that little boy she used to know? But he was dead. I fed him to the beast of wrath she created.

My jaw twitched as I twisted my grip on the steering wheel. Fuck it, let her stare. I hoped she looked at me for so long that her hope built up, so I could stomp it back down. I wanted to crush that spark in her eyes under my boot, until there was nothing left but a hollow shell of misery and pain.

Why the fuck is she still staring at me?

Clearing my throat, I shook off her eyes and curved around the sign saying Oakleigh Manor. This road was another lie. More specifically, the oak trees lining it. Another one was planted every time a new Kessler male was born. The one at the end was mine.

Except I wasn't a Kessler. I was the unwanted son of the

boogeyman. How sad was that? Even a monster couldn't be bothered with me.

Harper's gaze never left me. Not when she shifted in her seat, or when we pulled up to the house at the end of the road. That innocent look on her face was pissing me off. I tried to ignore it and focus on driving, but she was still fucking there. Sitting right beside me, staring like some poor pathetic trapped animal.

"Stop fucking looking at me!" I snarled and clicked on the remote clipped to my visor.

That seemed to work. Harper quickly snapped her head in the other direction.

About fucking time.

I didn't get out after I pulled my car into the garage. I just sat there in the cemented room, listening to the door softly drop down and eyed Micha's Jeep. When I went to Harper's house, I had all this planned out. Go in and demand the truth–which I knew I wouldn't get–then take the lying bitch. What the hell was I supposed to do now?

What the fuck did I want to do?

Harper shifted beside me, and I could sense she wanted to say something. But she didn't. She sat where she was and kept quiet, which was fine with me. The temptation of her sweet scent was bad enough. I didn't need the fearful quake in her voice to add to that.

I had more important things to think about. Like how I was going to explain this to the two nosey pricks inside. Given the whole contract conversation, Lou might not say much. Micha, however...

A part of me felt sick at the fact that I punched my brother. Then again, the smug prick did ask for it. Getting in my face like he knew everything. He didn't know shit. He had no idea what I sacrificed for her.

Well, fuck him, and fuck her too.

"Are we going inside?"

Rage twisted my neck, snapping my glare back on the redhead beside me. "Why the fuck are you talking to me?"

She instantly ducked her head. That in itself was a taunt. I fucking hated the way she hid behind the soft, shimmering ruby curtain of her hair. I wanted to see her face and watch the misery trickle down her cheek in a fat salty drop.

Instead I got her quiet, quaky voice. "P-p-please take me home."

Was she still on this?

"You are home."

She lifted her head, bringing those big brown eyes to mine. That's better. Now I could see the alarm tugging on her features. My dick hardened at the pout in her full pink lips.

"You can't do this."

That made me laugh.

"Oh yeah?" I arched a brow at her. "Who's gonna stop me?"

Her mouth opened but no words came out. I tipped my head, waiting for her to say something, like 'my brother will stop you.' Fucking prick. I'd like to see him try. Maybe I'd get Harper to give him a call, then shove my dick up her ass? The arch in my brow deepened as I rolled my gaze down the curve of her hip.

That's not a bad idea.

How hot would it be to listen to Sean cuss me out while I fucked the shit out of his baby sister? I could practically hear his voice screaming at me through the phone. Would Harper moan?

Cause that would be awesome if she called out my name when I made her come, so her brother knew *exactly* what I was doing to her. I bet she'd come hard, too. There was a screamer somewhere in that timid little body.

"Tell me something, Freckles." I crawled across the console to her side of the car, making her squeak and jar back against the door. "When you have your fingers in your pussy at night," I braced my palms on either side of her and leaned in to whisper, "do you call my name?"

Her heavy swallow echoed through the air, making my dick twitch. "We should go inside."

Oh, she wanted to go inside, did she?

"You think you're any safer in there?" I pushed myself up and cocked a brow down at her trembling form. "Maybe I'll get my brother to hold you down for me?"

"Mason." A shiver ran down my body when her palms flattened on my chest. "You need to let me go home. This isn't right."

Really? That's where she wanted to go?

The only right thing in this situation would be to slap the shit out of her and expose her for the liar that she was. But I didn't beat little girls. Maybe I should? After all, she respected whoever gave her those bruises enough to keep her mouth shut.

"Let's get one thing straight, Freckles, the only place you're going is where I want you to. If that means you spend the night in the fucking car, then you will. Your only job here is to shut the fuck up and do what I say." I narrowed my eyes to emphasize my point. "Got it?"

She whimpered and jerked back, banging her head on the door.

I liked that. I enjoyed the way she twitched, all timid and scared in her bunny pajamas. I should rip that shit off her and take her now. It'd only be fair. She took my innocence, so why shouldn't I take hers?

Instead, I sighed and opened her door, letting her spill out. Did I care about the wince that came out when she landed on the cement floor? Not in the least. If Harper wanted to protect whoever gave her those bruises, then she better embrace the pain.

"Get your shit," I growled, while stepping over her prone form. "We're going in."

Like the little pet she was, Harper jumped up and followed. Gotta say, watching her struggle to haul that big ass bag I packed behind her was entertaining. Every grunt and groan that left her lips improved my mood a little more. Especially when I barked at her to hurry the fuck up.

Unfortunately, my entertainment didn't last long. We'd barely made it across the wingspan of the raven in the entranceway when Lou stepped out. The look on his face had me grumbling out a sigh. There was only one thing that expression meant. A lecture. Probably for hanging up on him.

"Mason Miles Kessler."

Oh, he was middle naming me, was he? I was definitely getting a lecture.

"You do not..." Lou stopped and slowly leaned over to cock a brow at the small redhead behind me. "Hello Harper."

Look at that, she was useful for something after all.

Harper whispered out a meek, "Hello."

Lou turned a judgemental brow on me. "Care to explain?"

"No." Why should I explain anything to him?

"We should've talked about this, son."

I'm not your son.

"Why?" I argued. "You said I could do what I wanted."

I couldn't help but smirk a bit when he straightened his suit jacket and let out a frustrated huff. The great Louis Kessler couldn't argue his own words.

"I had other plans," he explained. "Which you would've known if you hadn't hung up on me."

I knew he was pissed I hung up on him.

Wait... did he say other plans?

My eyes narrowed in on him. I may not like him much, but Lou was a sneaky bastard. The shit I'd seen him convince people to do was astounding. I kind of admired him for that.

If there was a secret out there, then Louis Kessler would find it eventually. A good skill to have in this situation. Not that I couldn't get the information, but it couldn't hurt to hear what he had to say.

"What kind of plans?"

"Your brother told me what happened today."

I rolled my eyes.

Of course he did.

"Guess I shouldn't be surprised. After all, who better to keep an eye on the screw up than your golden boy."

He huffed out a frustrated sigh. "No one is spying on you."

I couldn't hold back the snort to that claim. Part of me wanted to bring up the guy who rode his bike past Ashworth every morning at 8:17, then again at 3:23, or the three gangbangers who obviously weren't in a gang that mysteriously appeared outside of every fight I went to.

But why bother? Besides, I liked knowing who my watchers were. How else would I be able to fuck with them, and in return, Lou.

"Whatever you say." I waved my hand through the air and moved to step around him, but he stopped me.

"We need to talk."

"Why?" I scoffed. "Seems to me like your real son has done enough talking for the both of us."

I couldn't help but notice the spark of pain in Lou's eyes, or the way Harper's head tipped. Forgot she didn't know about that.

Welcome to the family secret, Freckles.

"I know you're not particularly happy with me right now."

There's the understatement of the year.

"But this is important. I've put some things in place..." He paused to once again glance over at Harper. "Perhaps we should talk while Harper gets settled?"

He didn't want to talk in front of Harper. I was officially intrigued. So I didn't argue when he called Marco over to escort

Harper. Nor did I say anything other than, "Make sure she's close to me," when they walked away.

It wasn't that I thought Marco wouldn't take her to the east side of the manor – which was my wing – I just didn't want him to put her in some random room that I'd have to walk down three flights of stairs to get to. It'd be kind of hard to keep my eye on her if she was that far away. I needed to keep her close if I wanted to catch her in a lie.

"Come on, son." Lou placed his hand on my back and steered me towards his office. "We have some things to discuss."

Chapter 6
Harper

When the sun hit my face, warming my skin, I wondered why Mrs. Benson hadn't come in yet. It was her voice that woke me up every morning. She'd come in, pull open my curtains and say, *'Time to get up, child'*.

My world didn't have many comforting people in it. My brother, Lana, and now Star. My governess was a stern woman – Sean often referred to her as Drill Sergeant – but she was one of the few that didn't hurt me.

It was strange not hearing her scuttle about my room. Once, when I was about ten, she came down with a really bad flu. For a week I didn't see her. That's when I learned not to pester Daddy.

He got annoyed with my constant questions about how she was doing. I spent the last three days of that week in bed, recovering from the repercussions. Maybe she was sick again?

That's when I remembered, Mrs. Benson wasn't here.

She wasn't waking me up because I wasn't in my room. There

was no safe place where I could tuck myself away in this house. I was in the lion's den.

The ravenous beasts were everywhere, tucked in the corners and halls, waiting for me to come out of the shadow I was hiding in, and I was the prey desperately searching for a means of escape. But I wouldn't find one.

That was proven by the guard standing outside my door. I tried to leave last night and was met with Marco's intense glare. That man terrified me when we were kids, lurking around with hulking muscles and an evil stare.

He reminded me of the villains in the cartoons I watched. That feeling didn't get any better as I aged. So when I opened the door and saw him standing there, I quickly shut it again.

Over the years I'd become good at seeking out safe places. Cupboards and forgotten rooms I could hide in. So I knew deep in my bones that it was safer alone in this room than it was out there with them.

I pushed myself up and trickled my gaze around my gilded cage. When I first stepped in here, I panicked. The black marble flooring and the light oaken furniture made me think this was Mason's room. It'd been awhile since I'd been in this house.

Back then, his bedroom was full of toys, a car bed and other little boy things. It was also next to his parent's room. But everyone at Ashworth knew the day Mason was given his own wing of Oakleigh Manor. It was kind of hard to miss the party announcements plastered all over the halls.

That was the day my entire world shifted. For the first time in years, I didn't know what his room looked like. I didn't even know where it was. Sometimes, when I saw him walking down the halls at school, I tried to imagine what it would look like.

How had his tastes changed or matured over the years. But all I could see was the red car bed we used to play Hungry, Hungry Hippos on.

Even if I could envision where Mason Kessler the man slept, it wouldn't be in a place like this. This was bare and vacant of any hint of personality. There wasn't so much as a picture on the dresser, armoire, or desk. It was so opposite from the boy I knew.

I got that teenage boys were different from girls, but even Sean had personal touches. Posters hanging on his wall, movies in his bookshelf, and a quilt our mother made him. Aside from the large stone fireplace on the other side of the room, there was nothing in here to warm the atmosphere. Had I broken Mason that bad? This place was so cold and unloved.

Like me.

All I wanted to do was curl up and go back to sleep. Maybe I'd wake up and miraculously be free of the nightmare I was trapped in. I needed Alice's white rabbit to lead me away, but I wasn't in a fairy tale. I was in reality.

The only tea parties here would be the ones that served my tears and misery. Some would call it vengeance, I preferred penance. After all, Karma always got what was coming to her.

That didn't make it any easier to control my nerves when a knock echoed through my room from the hall. I sat there holding my breath while the door slowly swung open. As much as I would love to stay hidden in my hole, I knew Mason wouldn't leave me alone. He never did. But it wasn't his green eyes I was met with.

My entire body froze the second a familiar dark glare locked on me. I held my breath as someone so much worse strode in. If Mason was a monster, then his older brother was the devil. Micha's eyes pinned me in place as he walked in. I couldn't do anything but sit there and feel each long determined step of his jean clad legs vibrate through my chest.

Why was he here?

For the most part he ignored me – which I was more than fine with. There was a saying at Ashworth, don't mess with the little Kessler or the head would bite back. The head, in this case, was

Micha. How Riley handled him I had no idea. Then again, she scared me too.

"Hello Harper." He stopped in the middle of the room and crossed his arms. "I hope you slept well."

No he didn't. I could tell that much by the scowl on his face. In fact, I was pretty sure he'd be happy to find me sleeping on a bed of broken glass, suspended over an active volcano.

"I did, thank you," I nodded.

Why was I being polite? Well, when one was faced with the devil, rudeness probably wasn't the best way to go.

I waited for Micha to say something. Maybe explain while he was here? He didn't. Not a single peep escaped his mouth as he stood there staring me down. The air grew dense with silence. So thick that I could feel it seeping into my bones, tightening my muscles. The only thing I did get was a slight jaw tick when I pulled the blankets up to my chin.

As much as Micha did hate me, we did have one thing in common. I loved Mason once. I'd have sacrificed anything for that green-eyed little boy, including my integrity. Then again, maybe I never had any to begin with.

What kind of person does that to someone they love? It wasn't even that hard to do. A simple action that would forever change both of our lives was no harder than taking a breath.

It was the guilt that followed that crushed my soul.

I couldn't pull my eyes away from Micha. The way he was standing there and glaring at me reminded me of the little girl that died. She was gone, and I was left behind. A hollow shell that to Micha was nothing more than the source of his brother's torment. And he was the giant fist grinding into my ribs with the weight of my choices.

It was an overwhelming sense that eventually made me crack.

"Why are you here?"

"Why are you?" he asked back.

How was I supposed to answer that? I didn't come willingly. He had to know that.

"Mason brought me."

The only response I got was silence.

Micha Kessler was one of the most intimidating people I knew – including my father. I'd take a taunt over this, or a yell. Hell, it'd almost be better if he marched over here and slapped me across the face.

"Where's Mason?"

Don't get me wrong, I wasn't under any misguided delusions that Mason would come and save me, but I couldn't take being under Micha's scrutiny anymore.

"Why?" he snarled. "Don't you think you've tortured him enough?"

My mistake. Scrutiny was better.

I ducked my head and chewed on my lip, attempting to hide the guilt welling up in my gut. But Micha Kessler was nothing if not observant.

He scoffed out a snicker and shook his head. "Play that game all you want Harper, we both know you're not innocent. In fact, your hands are probably dirtier than mine."

Tico's smile flew through my head as I blinked back the tears brimming in my eyes. Micha had no idea how true that statement was.

"I didn't want to hurt him."

Was it Mason, or Tico, I was talking about? So many people had been hurt by my silence that I didn't know who I was trying to protect anymore. The monster I called father, the friend who tried to help me, or the little boy with the green eyes?

Maybe I was just protecting myself? Hoping that one day the shattered pieces of my soul would magically mend themselves. Then again, how many people would pay the price if I did reveal my secrets?

That wasn't a risk I was willing to take. My torment was worth their safety.

"Sure." Micha rolled his eyes. "Look, I only came here to tell you one thing."

Intrigue drew my gaze to his.

"This is your last chance, Harper."

I had an idea about what he meant, but that didn't stop me from asking, "Last chance for what?"

"I've watched my brother destroy himself for years, all because of you."

Those last few words sunk into my gut. He wasn't the only one to witness Mason's destruction. I was there too. It broke my heart every time he looked at me. But that was better than the alternative.

"The only reason you're not dead yet is because Mase hasn't had his fun." He marched over, dropped his palms on the bed, and leaned in, bringing his face a breath away from mine. "And he will have his fun, won't he, Harper?"

I wanted to point out that that's what I'd thought he'd been doing for the past seven years, but I kept my mouth shut. Silence was something I was good at.

"I'd tread lightly if I were you." Micha leaned in to growl in my ear, "I've been itching to take out the trash."

That statement was very clear. So much so that I could already feel the cold touch of the reaper closing in.

"Get your ass down to breakfast." Micha spun around and walked out, pausing briefly to add, "Wouldn't want my brother forgetting about his new toy."

What did I do after Micha left? I got my ass downstairs for breakfast. Well, I tried to. It took me a bit to find my way around. I hadn't been in this part of Mason's house before. Marco followed me, of course. Would've been nice if he pointed me in the right direction. When I hit my third dead end I even asked him. He just stared at me.

By the time I found my way to the main part of the manor, my nerves had me trembling. While Riley and I didn't grow up in the same neighborhood, I grew up with Micha. I'd seen first hand what he was capable of, and the last thing I wanted was to end up on his radar.

Given the fact that he just threatened my life, that was probably out of the realm of possibilities. But there was no need to antagonize him.

Though I did wish I'd at least taken the time to change before I left. Especially when I heard a deep voice waft out of the kitchen.

"You have any idea how hard it is to find a unicorn car?"

Logan.

A chill rolled through my veins as I froze dead in my tracks. All of them hated me, but Logan took that feeling to a whole new level. I legitimately feared for my life when he was around. A completely justified feeling, considering he held me over the bluffs once and laughed while I screamed. I was twelve.

The voice that followed his didn't help my situation any.

"You got Shelby a unicorn car?" Mason asked.

"Damn right I did."

I glanced down at the black marble floor and tried to force my feet to move. They refused. My gut churned with dread.

"Can I be there when you tell her?"

The chuckle Mason suppressed should've made me feel better. That meant he was in a good mood, right? The only problem with that was good moods didn't mean good things.

Not for me, anyways. And especially not when you put those two together. Mason I could handle. Even Logan I could sometimes. But both of them...

"Come on," Marco growled and gave me a shove. "Get in there. I don't have all day."

I took a second to consider what option would be safer. The man with the gun, or the two men in the kitchen? Then I sighed and slowly tiptoed forward. One way or another I'd end up in that room. At least this way the armed man might stay out here.

That was a decision I regretted the second I walked through the large arched doorway.

A bad day was being met with one set of twinkling green eyes. A terrible, horrible, no good, very bad day was being met with two. I never understood that book as much as I did in that moment. Mason's eyes darkened in a glare while Logan's brow arched.

"Holy fucking shit." The corner of Logan's mouth tip up in a smirk. "Nice PJs."

"I should go change," I whispered, while dropping my gaze down to my wringing hands and trying not to focus on the child-like rabbits decorating the fabric I was wearing.

Mason rolled his eyes as if I was nothing more than a nuisance and turned his attention back to his breakfast. "Sit the fuck down and eat."

I opened my mouth to argue, but Logan interrupted before I could say anything.

"You heard the man." A screech filled the room as Logan kicked out one of the chairs between them. "Sit the fuck down."

Those four wooden legs taunted me. I could feel the weight of them pressing in as I stood there. The table they were seated at was small. I did not want to be that close to either of them, let alone trapped between them.

My gaze shifted over to the marble island across the room, and the leather bound stools.

"Aw, what's wrong Harper?" The frown on Logan's face did not match the twinkle of amusement in his eyes. "This chair not good enough for you?"

Mason didn't say anything. Not that I expected him to. Logan, however…

"Maybe we're not good enough for you?" He dropped his fore-arms on the table and leaned forward. "What do you think, Mase, is the little princess too good to sit with us?"

"I think she should eat on the floor like the dog she is," Mason muttered in response.

I swallowed back a bundle of nerves when Logan stood up. The squeak of his chair sliding across the floor sped up the thundering in my chest.

"That's a good idea." His piercing gaze locked on mine. "Sit the fuck down, Harper."

I slowly slunk down, because what else could I do? Mason's voice was the only thing that stopped me.

"Get the fuck over here and sit down."

For a second I was stunned. Did Mason Kessler actually save me from humiliation? Should've known that would never happen.

"Aw man, I was just starting to have fun." Logan crossed his arms and dropped back down in his seat as I tiptoed my way over there.

Mason cocked a brow at him. "You want to explain to Shelby why we have her friend eating off the floor?"

"That's a fair point," Logan nodded in agreement, then pointed a finger at me. "Alright Freckles, you're saved for now. You know what will happen if you say anything to my girl, right?"

I slid the chair up to the table and nodded. While I may not know exactly what he'd do, I did know it wouldn't be good.

Most girls would kill to be where I was. Logan, with his blond hair, bright eyes, and natural charm was the kind of guy every girl wanted to sleep with and every guy wanted to be. Then there was Mason...

I pulled my eyes over his broad shoulder, up to the dark stubble on his chin. This man made my life hell and even I had to admit he was handsome. No, he was more than handsome. He was hot, as Lana would say.

He instilled fear in me so bad that I jumped at my own shadow, and he still haunted my dreams. Making me think things that I shouldn't. Like how soft would his lips be? What would it feel like to have his hands on me? To see his green eyes looking at me like they did the girls he made out with in the halls?

Wait...

My head tipped as I glanced from Mason to Logan. Last night Mason referred to Micha as his father's real son. Did that mean *he* wasn't? He looked so much like his brother, and Micha was the spitting image of Louis.

Then again, their mother had the same features. Dark hair, eyes, and olive complexion. There was one thing neither of them had. Green eyes. In fact, the only person in town besides Logan that had that color of eyes was...

"Ryker."

I hadn't realised I said the name out loud until both Logan and Mason looked up at me.

"What the fuck did you say?" Logan growled.

I quickly dropped my head. "Nothing."

Though I couldn't see them, I could feel their anger. Ryker was a bad man. Everyone knew that. He was the boogeyman people refused to talk about, and I just said his name. Naturally it was Logan whose wrath I received. He was the spawn of a monster, I could just imagine what he went through.

"Saying that man's name is a good way to get your throat slit."

I shook my head and breathed out, "I didn't mean to."

"Uh huh." His hot breath smacked against my hair, warming the ear hidden behind with the threat in his tone. "When he fucks you, and he will fuck you, I hope he breaks you in half."

I didn't move. Didn't even dare to breathe. It was dangerous to poke the beast.

The next second he was back to charming, happy Logan, as he jumped up and sang, "Hey baby."

That right there was why Logan Hudson was so dangerous. You never knew which version of him you were going to get.

"Oh my God, Logan, it's only been one night."

I didn't have to see them to know that Logan had his hands all over Shelby. It was as common as the giggle that came from her mouth when he pawed at her. I had to give her props though. He gave new meaning to the term player.

The things I'd seen him get girls to do would astound the devil himself. No one thought he was capable of being faithful, let alone settling for one girl. Then came Shelby Grace, who not only locked him down, but caused the guy to look like a love struck puppy.

It was kind of adorable. Part of me was jealous. I had that once. I knew what it felt like to be someone's whole world. I also knew what it felt like to be the reason that person's world collapsed. Yet sometimes I still longed for that look Mason used to give me. How pathetic was that?

If I was someone braver, I might have chosen a different path. But bravery had never been my strong suit, and it was far too late to change my mind now. So I'd settle for sitting here with my head hung, listening to Shelby's heels click on the floor. That would be the only sense of security I'd get in this place.

Not because she would protect me – though I was sure she'd try – it was because I knew Logan would play nice while she was around. Riley, Star, and all the girls thought of me as an innocent victim, but they were wrong. An innocent person didn't think of the girl who'd always been nice to them as a shield for their boyfriend.

"Harper?" Shelby's sweet voice caused me to jar a little.

Was it wrong that I hoped she wouldn't see me here?

I slowly lifted my head and forced myself to give her a smile. "Hi."

"What are you doing here?" She propped her hands on her hips while narrowing her cinnamon eyes on Mason. "Mason?"

"Shelby," he sang back at her.

"What is Harper doing here?"

"Eating breakfast." He shot me a look that caused me to squeak and reach out to snatch a banana. "What are you doing here?"

"I live here, remember."

Mason took a drink of what I assumed was coffee and grumbled, "How could I forget."

Shelby returned his comment with an exaggerated eye roll, then turned her attention to her boyfriend.

"Do you care to explain this?"

Logan shrugged. "I just got here an hour ago."

"Mm hum. So you're innocent in all of this?"

Logan's jaw dropped as his palm flattened over his heart. "Would I lie to you?"

He should get an award for that acting job. If I didn't know him, I'd have fallen for it. Apparently Shelby was smarter than I thought she was.

"Don't play that game with me. Look at her." Her hand flung through the air, pointing at me. "She's clearly terrified."

"She's always terrified."

I mean... he wasn't wrong.

Shelby waved a scolding finger in Logan's face and I could feel the clock of dread ticking down.

"If I find out that either of you..."

"Oh calm down," Mason cut her off. "Her old man's out of town so she's staying with us."

That was a good excuse. I was kind of disappointed that I hadn't thought of it.

"That's right," I nodded in confirmation when Shelby's suspicious stare landed on me.

When that didn't work, I added a smile. That seemed to do the trick.

Shelby sang "Okay," shrugged her shoulders, and flopped down in the chair beside me – that was formerly her boyfriend's seat. Logan followed suit and took the seat closest to her. Though he did mutter something about that being his food.

I couldn't help but smile a touch at Logan's obvious annoyance when she snatched a piece of bacon off the plate and popped it in her mouth. She really did have him wrapped around her finger.

The only warning I got for the oncoming verbal onslaught was the deep breath Shelby sucked in.

"Oh my God, this is going to be so much fun, you have no idea how frustrating it is to be in a house surrounded by boys. I mean, I have my sister, but Mags is only like ten and I can't really do much with her. Besides, the last time I put make-up on her this one lost his mind, going all big brother, saying crap like wash that off, she's too young for that shit, what are you going to do when she gets boobs and starts dating. You can't lock her up forever, oh but I'm sure you'll try. All you men gotta act all macho and puff your chest out. Am I right, Harper?"

My mouth opened but I wasn't sure how to respond. I only caught about a tenth of what she said. Something about someone named Mags, boobs, and macho guys with their chests puffed out.

Luckily I didn't have to think about it for too long because Mason's cynical chuckle startled me out of trying to decipher the verbal vomit that had just been spewed my way. At least, I thought it was aimed at me. She could've been talking to the table for all I knew.

"See, I think it's funny that you think Maggie will be allowed to date at all."

"Ugh," Shelby rolled her eyes. "Typical man. Of course she'll date, and you know what else? One day she'll fuck someone too."

Mason's face dropped. "Not if I kill him first."

"Who says it'll be a guy?"

I kind of admired the way Shelby's brow rose, though I was

starting to wonder who this Maggie, or Mags was. Shelby's little sister, maybe? I'd never met her, but I'd heard about her.

Was Mason getting this riled up about a little girl that wasn't technically his sister? That was disturbingly sweet and a bit hypo-critical considering how he talked to his father last night. But who was I to judge?

Mason sat back and eyed her. "It doesn't matter who it is. If anyone touches her before she's thirty-five, I'll cut their fingers off."

It was scary how simple and easy he made that statement sound.

"Yeah," Logan snickered while stuffing his face, "good luck with that."

Shelby turned her arched brow on him. "The same goes for Tristan, you know."

"What!" My heart jumped as Logan slammed his fists down on the table. "Who the fuck touched my sister!"

"Oh, calm down. She's like one. You've got some time." Shelby rolled her eyes my way. "You see what I have to put up with?"

I was suddenly really uncomfortable. More so than I normally was. The fact that both Logan and Mason were now staring at me wasn't helping any.

"Um, I'm going to go shower," I said and jumped up, getting the hell out of there before I could be dragged into whatever messed up argument they were having.

Chapter 7
Mason

*J*stomped up the stairs, grumbling, "Should've made her eat on the floor like a damn dog."

Freckles was damn lucky Shelby lived here. Not that I particularly cared – fuck what she thought. It was Logan I respected. I may be an asshole, but I wasn't about to cause shit between him and his woman. If it wasn't for that, Harper would've been on the damn floor.

Out of all the people who liked to get up in my shit, I never thought it would be Logan's girl who fucked my day up. Riley and Star I could see, but not Shelby and her perky, sunshine smile. Though I was sure I'd face the wrath of the other two at school tomorrow. That should be fun.

I scrubbed a hand down my face and blew out a breath. Why the fuck did I bring her here? This shit seemed like more trouble than it was worth. Everything with Harper did.

Just when I thought I could ignore her and move on with my

life, I'd hear her voice, or see her smile and be sucked right back in. Why the hell should she smile?

I ran my hand down the tan wall, tipping the edge of various pictures as I went. The swoosh sound of them swinging back and forth was oddly calming. Until I got to the one hanging across from my bedroom door. The smile on my mother's perfectly painted lips was so fake, even I could see it.

Micha hated her and I got that, but I remembered how sad she was. All those times I walked in on her drying her tears were permanently ingrained in the back of my mind. Lou should've done something.

Then again, some people just can't be helped. For all I knew, he did try. He was still helping me, after all. Wonder how long he'd keep that useless fight up?

Speaking of losing battles...

My brow cocked at the sound of running water trickling out from the other side of the door at the end of the hall. Was Harper in the shower? I thought that shit was just another excuse.

So she was capable of honesty after all. Would you look at that. Now if I could only get her to tell me the truth about everything else. 'I fell'—still couldn't believe she was trying to spin that tale.

Guess I shouldn't be surprised, she had seven years to perfect her lying skills. She should be disappointed in herself. Fuck, I was disappointed. Thought she'd have come up with something better than that lame ass story.

I bet she was getting a kick out of this shit. Stupid little Mason Kessler will fall for anything.

My eyes narrowed on the door. Why the fuck was she in *my* bathroom? Who told her she could use *my* water? Well fuck that. If she wanted to wash away her lies, let her use someone else's shit. I paused and cocked a brow.

Wash away her lies. Huh?

Right now, Harper was on the other side of that door cleaning all that make-up off her skin. Meaning she wouldn't have anything hiding the marks on her body.

Exactly how many bruises did she have? I could go in there, drag her ass out of the shower and find out, but that seemed too easy and not at all fun. Besides, I had a much better idea.

The girl's locker room in Ashworth was a place I was very familiar with. I knew my way around those white tiled walls better than I did my own balls. It took some serious skills to sneak around in a room full of girls unnoticed, and this was *my* bathroom so...

I made my way over there, pulled a key out of my pocket, and unlocked the door. I didn't so much as glance the shower's way as I strutted around the room, snatching towels off hangers. After that, I stopped and eyed a bundle of clothing on the floor. Shorts, a shirt, and a pair of pink panties.

I still had her thong from prom but that shit – motherfucking cotton panties. Fuck me. I snatched those up in point two seconds, then stopped to cock an eye down at her pajamas.

Yeah, fuck it.

I took those too. Like I said, nothing screamed defile me like fucking white bunnies.

On my way out, I couldn't help but glance over at the steam filled shower. I could barely see her silhouette moving around behind the frosted glass. Nothing much more than a few curves and limbs, but it was enough to make me crack a smile before I slipped out into the hall.

"Let's see you hide now, Freckles."

There was no doubt in my mind that she'd try. She'd probably dart out and rush into the bedroom like a fucking fly after a lump of sugar. Oh, but I'd be waiting for her.

Every room in this wing was mine. I knew each and every one of them like the back of my hand. There wasn't a single corner or crevasse I didn't know about. Absolutely nowhere for her to hide.

I threw open the door to the room Harper slept in and marched inside. This place was a perfect example of how fucked she was. It wasn't just a guestroom that happened to me next to mine. It was connected.

I looked over at the gold swirls decorating the brown wall next to the fireplace. I did a good job with that wallpaper, couldn't even see the seam of the door cutting through it. Most of the time I used it to fuck with Silas. He'd pass out then I'd sneak through and paint his nails or some shit. Now that door was so much more than an easy source of entertainment.

It was my window to the truth.

Harper held onto her secrets for seven years. That took dedication. Unfortunately for her, I was just as dedicated and a lot more inventive. But first things first, I needed to find out exactly what she'd been hiding under all that make-up. Once I was satisfied that I'd found every mark on her body, then I *might* let her get dressed. If she asked nice.

A squeak caused my mouth to curl as I tossed the towels in a wicker hamper and sauntered across the room. Guess Harper figured out there wasn't anything to cover up with. Aw, poor little Freckles has to expose herself.

I snorted and fell back on the tan bedspread. Well she better get fucking used to it. This was just a taste of the shit coming her way.

My fists balled as hurried footsteps echoed down the hall, but I didn't move. Even when the door opened, then slammed shut, I stayed where I was staring up at the stars on the ceiling. Two five pointed shapes that were made with innocent hands.

One with a green H and the other a black M.

I'm not sure why they were here. They should've been left in my old room with all the other memories. Then again, I spent a lot of time fucked up, so there was a good chance I brought them here. Probably thought they were magical and Tinkerbelle would show up or some shit?

A high pitched shriek rolled through the air, burning my ears.

"Do you mind?" I grumbled. "I'm trying to reminisce about good times here."

Like when I could forget about all this shit and shove a needle in my arm.

"What are you doing in here?" Harper's voice was barely above a whisper, but I heard every word. I always did. The chick was literally impossible for me to ignore, and trust me, I tried.

"Clearly, I'm laying down," I scoffed.

"Don't you have your own bed for that?"

That made me cock a brow.

"This is my bed." Every piece of furniture in the west wing was mine.

"T-this is y-your room?"

I wanted to see the fear I heard in her tone. I wanted to revel in the way her small body trembled, but I couldn't pry my eyes away from those damn stars. They stood up there mocking me with what could've been. This wasn't how I used to imagine this moment going.

The first time I saw the girl I loved naked should've been tender and sweet. Where I could take my time and worship every part of her body. But Harper wasn't the girl I loved. She was the person that killed her. A part of me knew that the second I looked over there, the last tiny spark of that innocent little boy would die.

Harper shuffled across the room to pull open a drawer, and I still couldn't make myself look at her. That didn't mean I was going to let her cover herself.

"Don't even think about it."

She whimpered and I could picture her shuffling back into the corner. "B-but, I'm..."

"Naked?" I finished for her.

Did I say anything when she didn't respond? No. Why should I make this shit easy for her? It sure as hell wasn't for me. So I stayed exactly where I was, letting silence fill the room. Until I heard the rustle of fabric.

"What the fuck do you think you're doing?"

"Getting dressed," Harper bit back.

Who the fuck did she think she was?

"Did I say you could get dressed?"

"I don't care."

Did she just fucking talk back to me? Oh hell no.

I shot up and froze.

Harper was across the room next to the dresser, bent over as she slipped her leg into a pair of white panties.

Fuck me, that's a nice ass.

I couldn't stop staring at the firm little globes pointed in my direction. My dick jumped as my gaze raked up, over the curve of her hip, then back down to her now panty-clad ass and slender legs.

Then she stood up, causing her long ruby hair to sweep across the middle of her back, and suddenly all I could think about was biting into that tender flesh. That flawless complexion was begging to be marked.

How red would her ass get if I put her over my knee?

That thought fled my mind the second Harper reached out and grabbed a shirt out of the open drawer. I was up and across the room with my fingers curling around the back of her neck before she could pull the fabric over her head.

"What the fuck did I just tell you?" I snarled while ripping the shirt out of her hand.

The whimper that escaped her lips was one of the most erotic sounds I'd ever heard. The sweet sad sound shot down my chest and into my cock. But this wasn't about that. So, for now, I'd settle for the way her pulse fluttered under my fingers when I tightened my grip and slammed her face first into the wall.

"Mason..."

"Shut up," I hissed through gritted teeth.

I needed a minute to regain control and her voice wasn't helping any. Then again, neither was the sweet scent filling my nostrils. Why the fuck did she have to smell so good?

"Mason," Harper lifted her chin and peeked over her shoulder. "Please don't do this."

She picked a fine time to grow a backbone.

I tipped my head and looked deep in those big doe eyes. That glint of terror was still there, but this time it was different. If I didn't know any better, I'd say she was more afraid of what I'd find out than she was of me – which pissed me off. I should be the only monster in her life.

"What don't you want me to see, Freckles?"

My question caused her eyes to go wide.

Bingo.

The corner of my mouth tipped up. "Let's find out, shall we."

She fought when I spun her around – which was hot as fuck, but utterly useless. I had her wrists in my hand and back pressed up against the wall in under thirty seconds. That's when rage really rolled through my veins. Her abdomen wasn't the only thing marked up.

There was a bruise on her thigh, shoulder, upper right arm, and left breast. That one really pissed me off. Buried deep in the purple and yellow injury were distinct knuckle impressions.

"Who the fuck did this to you!?"

Harper's bottom lip trembled as unshed tears glimmered in her eyes. "I fell."

My jaw ticked.

Don't know why I bothered to ask. Of course she would say shit, because for some fucked up reason she felt the need to protect whoever beat the shit out of her.

Let's see just how much she wants to protect this fucker.

"Alright, keep your secret if you want, Freckles. But just know, the longer you keep your mouth shut, the more time I have to think about what I'm going to do to this motherfucker." I bent over to growl in her ear, "And I know a lot of ways to make someone scream."

She didn't say a thing as I felt her stiffen under my hold. I took a second to memorize each and every mark on her body before letting her go. Harper crumpled down on the floor and tucked her knees into her chest.

"You make me sick." I shook my head and walked out. "Get dressed."

I stormed out with the intention of going into my room to pound the shit out of the punching bag I had hung next to my bed. That thing had saved me more times than I could remember.

When I'd wake up in the middle of the night covered in a coat of sweat, I'd take my anger and frustration out on the bag. My nightmares had gotten worse over the past year. I'd replaced the bag three times and the one I had currently hung up was on its last breath.

That idea went out the window when I heard my name echo down the hall.

"Mason Kessler, you arsehole!"

I groaned and rolled my eyes. Fucking Star, just what I needed. Sighing, I spun around and crossed my arms. Silas was behind his girl, who was wagging her finger in the air while storming my way.

"Where the bloody hell is she?"

Silas shrugged when I eyed him. "Sorry man."

Yeah, sure. Pussy whipped prick. I'd get him back for this.

"Well?" Star snapped her fingers in my face. "Where is she?"

I cocked a brow down at the tiny platinum blonde. "Where's who?"

I knew full well who she was talking about. In fact, the person Little Miss Savior was trying to protect was right through the door next to her. Was I about to tell her that? Fuck no.

"You know bloody well who I'm talking about." She placed her hand on her cocked hip. "I talked to Shelby."

Of course she did.

"I don't have time for this." I waved her off and turned to leave, but Star reached out and grabbed the back of my shirt.

"If you don't tell me where she is…"

"You'll what!" I snapped and spun around to face her. "What the fuck are you gonna do?"

Something in the back of my head told me to back off when Star puffed her chest up and glared back at me, but the powder keg was open, and I had no idea how to close it.

"Huh Star? Tell me, cause I'd like to know how the fuck you think you can protect her from me when you had no idea someone was beating the shit out of her?"

It was pure speculation that Star didn't know, but that assumption was confirmed by the way her mouth tipped down.

"You didn't know either," she shot back, making me chuckle.

"That's because I don't give a shit."

"Is that right?" Star sang.

"That's right."

This time it was her that cocked a brow at me. "Then why's she here?"

That was the stupidest question ever. She was obviously here so I could get the truth. I snickered and glanced over at Silas, who tipped his head as if he was also curious to hear the answer.

Really?

Had everyone lost their minds? Did they all forget what happened seven years ago? Because I didn't, and I wasn't about to let that shit happen again.

I pinched the bridge of my nose. "Get the fuck out."

Silas tried coaxing his girlfriend away. "Come on, Crumpet."

"No," Star snarled, refusing to leave.

Why was she being so difficult about this? She barely knew Harper. "I'd listen to your boyfriend if I were you."

"I don't leave my friends behind."

I looked her dead in the eyes and said, "Did you tell Tico that?"

Okay, that might've been a low blow, and I may have deserved the slap that followed, but ask me if I cared. I could give two shits about what she thought or how she felt. That was Silas's job. Mine was to drive the nail in more.

"Look at it this way, London, at least you didn't make this one kill himself."

That's when Silas intervened, stepping in between his girl and I.

"Nope, you are not doing this." He waved his finger at me, "Not to her."

"Oh, fuck you Silas. When did you become such a pussy?"

My best friend wasn't known for losing control, but I knew what buttons to push. Just like I knew that tick in his jaw meant it was working.

"Look, you're clearly upset so I'm gonna let that one go, but you need to walk away now and calm the fuck down."

And there he was, Silas Creswell, the ever logical one of our duo. He should know better. When did that shit ever work on me?

"Or? Your girlfriend and I can have a chat on how to mentally destroy someone." I leaned to the side to look over Silas's shoulder at Star. "You're good at that, aren't you, London?"

"Alright, that's it." Silas's fist swung through the air, clacking off my jaw.

My head snapped to the side, twisting my neck as a dull ache spread across the left side of my face. The coppery tint filling my mouth helped calm the tide of rage burning through my veins. A few more of those and I should be good.

I spat some blood on the floor then looked back at the scowl on my best friend's face. "That all you got?"

I expected him to hit me again. Hell, I wanted him to hit me, but that wasn't what I got.

Silas wrapped his hand around the back of my neck and pressed my forehead to his. "I love you Mase, but I'm not going to help you hurt yourself."

What the fuck was that supposed to mean? Before I could ask, he grabbed Star's hand and walked away.

"Good," I yelled after them, "Go. I don't want you here anyway."

Star looked back and pointed a threatening finger at me. "This isn't over."

"Ooo, I'm so scared," I sang while pretending to shake in my boots.

Pfft, what the fuck was she gonna do? Seriously? The girl was ninety pounds soaking wet, if that.

Bring it on, London.

"I mean it Mason."

Whatever.

I rolled my eyes and walked the other way. They could both kiss my ass.

Chapter 8

Harper

*E*very weekday for the past four years had been the same. Sean drove me to school, or when he couldn't, Daddy did, then I'd walk in, collect my books and go to class.

Aside from Lana, no one paid any attention to me or stopped me in the halls for a brief chat. No one so much as even looked my way. I was the forgotten student, roaming around Ashworth like a ghost.

They say misery loves company, when in fact the opposite was true. Invisibility was the only place I could be comfortable. If I wasn't seen, then I couldn't be hurt, humiliated, or spoken to.

That's what I really wanted to avoid. I hated it when people talked to me because eventually they'd ask something I couldn't answer.

With Riley it was why didn't I ever stick up for myself? Shelby wanted to know why she'd never been to my house, and Star... Well, she had a lot of questions. Solitude was a safer option.

Unfortunately, some people wouldn't even let me have that.

I tucked myself back in the leather seat and peeked over at Mason.

He was staring out the windshield, seemingly focused on steering his car through the busy parking lot. But I saw the way his forearms tensed. I noticed his muscles flexing underneath that tanned skin. He was just as uncomfortable as I was.

I tried telling him this morning that he didn't have to drive me. Shelby was there, I could go with her. That didn't go over well. Now I was sitting in his car, fiddling with the hem of my skirt and trying not to blush when the sting from the handprint on my butt radiated up my back.

It was a different kind of pain than I was used to. Almost warm and tingly instead of sharp and hot. I didn't like it.

"You're trying my patience, Freckles."

Confusion knit my brows. I knew how to avoid angering Daddy, but Mason was a mystery. Sometimes I just walked by him and he'd get mad. Not that I could blame him, but given my current circumstances, it'd be nice to know what not to do.

"I didn't do anything."

Based on the way his jaw ticked when he pulled to a stop, that was the wrong thing to say.

"I'm sorry," I whispered and hung my head. "I'm not trying to argue…"

"Stop fucking around with your skirt," he barked back at me.

My hands snapped away from the comforting cloth and pressed up against my chest. Why would that bother him? I didn't get it.

Curiosity drove me to tip my head and peek around my hair. It wasn't the way Mason's gaze was locked on my bare knees that sent a shiver up my spine. It was the intensity darkening those bright green orbs that made me shift away.

For half a second I thought he was going to say something. I held my breath, waiting for him to speak. But when his stare finally rolled up to mine, the lines in his brow shifted from contemplative to anger.

"Get the fuck out," was all I got before he was gone.

I did what he said and stepped out into the parking lot. That's when my stomach dropped.

Everyone was staring at me, and I meant *everyone.* The cheerleaders, jocks, and others walking around out front swung their eyes my way. Even the couple making out next to the door stopped to glance over.

Mason didn't seem to notice, or care. He simply swaggered across the parking lot as if this was just another day. I guess to him it was? Mason Kessler was the new King of Ashworth. People watched him all the time. I know I did.

The way he carried himself with his shoulders rolled back in confidence was hard not to admire. Add in his sparkling smile, chiselled physique, tousled dark hair, and it was impossible not to stare.

When Logan Hudson was roaming these halls and girls were vying for his attention, it was Mason I watched. He shone above everyone else. A true God among men.

I stayed where I was, enjoying the morning sun warming my skin, until Mason glanced over his shoulder and curled his lip at me. A sigh escaped my lips as I slowly made my way across the cement to the front of the school.

It was hard to ignore the glances and whispers being thrown my way. I tried hiding behind my hair, but I could still feel them. Staring at me with their judgmental eyes.

At first I thought it was because of who I'd arrived with. Mason was popular. Everyone loved him. I didn't even have a circle to step into.

There was Star, Shelby and Riley, I suppose. They said they were my friends, but were they? Could you be someone's friend if you didn't really know them? All I had was Lana, and even she didn't know what my life was really like.

I was alone.

So it wasn't that surprising that people were staring. At least that's what I thought, until I walked inside and was greeted by Mrs. Grier.

"Ah, there you are Miss Callaghan."

Was she waiting for me?

"Could you come with me."

My gaze shifted from the receptionist's outstretched hand, signalling me to follow, then over to Riley. She was down the hall, leaning against the wall while shooting me a guilty frown. If that wasn't enough to make the pit in my stomach swirl, then the sympathetic look Star gave me was.

"Why?" I whispered. "I didn't do anything."

Mrs. Grier's cold eyes locked on mine. "The sheriff would like to speak with you."

If it was possible for the world to fall out from under me, it just did. I could literally feel myself free falling as I once again glanced Riley's way. That explained the frown. I'd hoped they all would've let what happened the other day go, but luck had never been on my side. Why would it show up now?

"Miss Callaghan?" Mrs. Grier coaxed.

There were a few people at Ashworth one could argue with. The receptionist was not one of them. Lana tried once during freshman year. Now she refused to go into the office unless absolutely necessary.

Mrs. Grier let out an annoyed sigh. "Come on now, child. I don't have all day."

Without another option, I hung my head and followed.

My mind was in overdrive. I knew why the sheriff was here. That much was obvious, but what kind of questions was he going to ask? Would the sheriff believe my 'I fell' excuse? Would he want to see the bruises his daughter said I had? And if so, could he?

I might be a minor, but I still had rights. Could he demand I lift my shirt without parental consent, or mine? Could he take me to the doctor? Could I be examined without permission? Suddenly I wished I'd taken that pre-law course when it was offered last year.

When we stepped inside the office I lifted my chin and stopped. "Do I have to talk to him? I'm only sixteen..."

Mrs. Grier waved her hand, cutting me off. "Your legal guardian is here."

What?

"My father's here?" I thought he was out of town?

"No," I jarred back when her eyes rolled my way. Riley wasn't kidding when she called Ashworth's receptionist a soul sucker. Her irritation was literally tugging at my insides. "Mr. Kessler is."

"Mr. Kessler isn't –"

I froze.

The contract.

I'd completely forgotten. Of course Mrs. Grier would think he was my guardian. He had all the legal paperwork to back it up and there was no way for me to argue it. Who would believe me? Arranged marriages and relationships didn't happen in the land of the free.

Besides, Daddy would be mad if I said anything. He'd have to cut his business trip short to come back home and deal with it. And deal with me. If I thought my latest injuries were bad, wait until he found out the sheriff was asking me questions. The fact that the sheriff got called at all would be enough to set Daddy off.

My gaze shifted over at the principal's door, where Mrs. Grier was pointing. It would be better if I dealt with this. Maybe then Daddy wouldn't have to know. Lying didn't cause me pain. Not physically, anyway.

Sighing, I told myself I could do this and slowly made my way over there. That confidence fled the instant I slipped through the door.

Three sets of eyes shifted my way.

Mr. Sampson, Sheriff Adams, and Louis Kessler.

And just like that, I knew what it was like to be a gazelle in the middle of a pride of lions.

The sheriff was the first to speak.

"Hello Harper." Warmth shone from his blue eyes as he tipped his head. "Do you know why I'm here?"

To screw up all my hard work and put everyone I care about at risk.

"No," I lied.

"Harper," he let out a breath. "I'm going to tell you a story."

I stayed where I was, comforted by the possible exit at my back, as he shifted around in his chair to rest his forearms on his knees.

"Last week I had the unfortunate task of notifying a woman that her husband had passed in a car accident. When she opened the door she got this look, like she knew something was wrong. You see, that's the response I normally get. Do you know why?"

I shook my head.

"Because when the sheriff comes calling, it's not with good news. But you don't have that doomed look in your eyes. Now why is that?"

I shrugged. "I don't know?"

"It's because you know everyone you care about is safe. Just like you know exactly why I'm here."

My eyes weren't the only ones that widened. Mr. Kessler also cocked his brow. If I didn't know any better, I'd say he looked impressed.

"So why don't you just tell me who gave you the bruises? Who hit you, Harper?"

I looked from the sheriff to Mr. Kessler, then over at Mr. Sampson. All of whom wore concern on their faces, except for Mason's dad. He stood there in his suit with the same cold look that Micha donned every day. That was more intimidating than anything the sheriff could ask. All I could hear was Micha's voice.

'I've been itching to take out the trash.'

I sidestepped away and whispered, "Lot's of people have bruises."

"Not like the ones my daughter described."

Summoning all my strength, I turned my attention back to the sheriff and said, "I don't know what she thinks she saw Sir, but I can't help it if I had a clumsy day."

He took a deep breath then huffed a frustrated sigh out through his nose.

I watched his nostrils flare and added. "Do you question all of her friends who might've tripped or fallen?"

"Is that what you're saying happened?" The sheriff's brow arched in disbelief.

"I'm not saying anything happened." I tipped my shoulder to my head. "I don't know what she saw."

Did I feel bad for lying to Riley's dad? Yes, but she was the one that involved him. She might not know how dangerous that could be, but I did. I'd seen the repercussions of involving someone in my father's personal affairs. I knew what the outcome would be.

He made me help him dispose of two people in the past year. One was a woman he brought home for the night and caught poking around his office, the other some guy I'd never met before. He came around asking about someone named Niles. Daddy lost it.

So yes, I would lie. I would cheat and bring my friend's character into question if it kept her off my father's radar. Riley may have thought she was protecting me, but it was the other way around.

She should've never sat down with me in the cafeteria that day. She should've walked right on by and picked a different table.

"Perhaps we should bring Riley in here?" the sheriff suggested.

Louis intervened before I could say anything. "I don't think that's necessary."

If looks could kill, then Louis Kessler would've dropped dead right then and there. I thought I'd seen hate before. Nothing came close to the look Riley's dad was currently giving Mr. Kessler.

"Well, I think it is," he ground out through gritted teeth.

"The girl said nothing happened." If Mason's dad was bothered at all by the sheriff's glare, he didn't show it. "Perhaps your daughter is overreacting?"

"Are you calling my daughter a liar?"

"Yes," Louis stated flatly.

The sheriff's face flooded with insult. "Maybe we should see these bruises. Then we'll see who's lying."

A pang of hurt swam through my chest at his words. What would it be like to have a father willing to stand up for you? How good would it feel to know that just once, he wouldn't come down on you for putting him in that situation? To have a father that actually cared.

I used to have that. Once upon a time I had two parents that cared, but that was so long ago it seemed like a dream.

Maybe it was that jealousy that drove me to bark out, "I don't have to show you anything."

"I'm the sheriff, Harper," he argued.

"That doesn't give you the right to examine her." Louis cocked a brow at me. "Go back to class, Harper. You're done here."

That was all I needed to hear. Before the argument could start, I was out the door, hoping that none of them noticed the angry tears in my eyes. I wasn't mad that Riley tried to help me.

I was mad that she'd risked something so precious for someone she barely knew. I hated her for that. Just like I hated others who took that special bond for granted.

That festering seed of darkness had been brewing for years. It pushed me further into solitude every time I watched Lana dance around the kitchen with her Nan, or when I saw Shelby arguing with her mom.

Misery was easy. I lived there for so long I embraced the sadness and pain. My day wouldn't be normal without it. But these tears burned down my face like acid, because in that moment I knew exactly how Mason Kessler felt. And I was the one that pushed him there.

Swiping the streaks off my face, I stormed down the hall towards my first class.

My anger didn't get any better after I stepped into the room. Everyone stopped and looked my way, but it was the smile underneath a pair of sparkling green eyes that made me ball my fists.

Mason didn't need to say anything to taunt me. The arrogance coming off him was so thick I could taste it as I walked past to take my seat.

"What's wrong, Freckles? You look a little mad." His gaze dropped down to my fists. "Did you forget to put your big girl panties on?"

I paused for a second to rear back the ugly voice in my head telling me to lash out. It might be relieving to vent my anger, but nothing good would come from it. I wasn't strong, or brave, or free to speak my mind. I was surviving.

"Oh, that's right." The smirk that spread across his lips caused my stomach to drop. "Virgins don't wear big girl panties."

"That's quite enough, Mr. Kessler," the teacher barked out.

I tried to ignore the heat flooding my cheeks and slid into the empty desk as snickers rolled around the room.

"Oh come on, Mr. March, it's not my fault no one wants to fuck her." Mason twisted his neck to glance back at me. "I don't think anyone's that desperate."

Our teacher was not impressed. "Alright that's it. You can meet me back here after school for detention."

The rest of the class, however, broke out in a fit of laughter that Mr. March had to calm down.

I dropped my head and chewed on my lip. Not because of what Mason said, but because the person who said it was the only man who'd seen me naked. Well, mostly naked. I had panties on. The memory of the disgust on his face was enough to bring tears back into my eyes.

You make me sick.

It was a fair thing to say. I couldn't even look in the mirror anymore without feeling a wave of nausea roll through me.

"Psst."

Relief washed over me when I was met with a pair of bright hazel eyes. Lana. My refuge and peace. The only person I could trust in this place.

"Why did the sheriff want to talk to you?"

My face dropped. "It was nothing."

"Uh huh?"

It was clear that she didn't believe me. Anyone could've seen that. Lana wasn't the best at hiding her emotions, or gossip, or anything, really.

"Seriously, it was nothing." I shot her a look, hoping she'd drop it, then focused on my work.

It was quiet for a while. Should've known that wouldn't last. I could feel Lana watching me. So I wasn't caught off guard when I heard her voice again. What she said, however...

"I talked to Riley."

The floor fell away again, dropping me down into a deep dark hole.

"Oh?" I sang feigning shock. "What did she have to say?"

"Harper," Lana sighed. "I know."

I was free falling now. Thrown from a plane without a parachute, and Lana was the ground quickly approaching.

Forcing my shoulders to relax, I scribbled down the equation the teacher was pointing at. "You know what?"

"I knoooow," Lana repeated, dragging out the word.

"Okay?" This was killing me.

Lying to Shelby and Riley was easy. I could even force myself to lie to Mason, but Lana... She was my heart, and I could feel it breaking. Each word that slipped through my lips ripped that tear apart more and more.

Lana leaned over, placed her hand on my arm and looked deep in my eyes. "You need to tell someone."

My heart stopped. Did she know? She was staring at me like she did. But how could she? Daddy was always nice to Lana. In fact, he treated her better than he treated Sean sometimes, and Sean was his pride and joy.

"I don't know what you're talking about," I insisted.

"Is that the same bullshit you told the sheriff?"

She was getting mad. I could tell by the way her attempt at whispering failed.

The teacher's gaze snapped our way. "Are we interrupting you, Miss Crawford?"

"Sorry Mr. March," Lana sang, and sat back.

"Unless you plan on failing another test, I suggest you pay attention."

Lana grumbled under her breath and rolled her eyes.

Since she'd had the babies, a lot of teachers were letting her slack – which she had taken full advantage of. Mr. March was not one of them. Not that that was a bad thing. I'd have done the same if I was in her shoes.

Unfortunately, my father wouldn't accept anything less than perfect, and I was far from perfect. Something I was reminded about daily.

Thinking the subject was dropped, I settled into class.

Five minutes before the bell rang, Lana leaned back over. "Are you still going to play daddy's princess, after what he did?"

Time froze as my eyes snapped up to hers. "After what who did?"

She knew!

My pulse thrummed wildly when her gaze shifted down to my stomach. Alarm bells rang through my mind and all I could think was, *not her. Please God, not her.*

"You know exactly what I'm talking about, Harper."

Doing my best to stop my stare from narrowing, I sat back and eyed my best friend. Searching the lines of concern on her face for any hint of confusion or unsureness.

She didn't know.

"Have you been listening to gossip again?"

"Fine, don't tell me." Lana rolled her shoulders back and slammed her text book shut. "I just have one question. Were you lying seven years ago, too?"

My mouth opened, but nothing came out. Technically, I didn't lie to Lana. She didn't ask me what happened when she came to visit me in the hospital, and I didn't tell her. I didn't correct her either. I let her believe what everyone else said. Why I never confided in my best friend, I couldn't say.

I thought about it. Sometimes we'd be sitting in her room alone and the words would be right there, ready to come out. Then I'd remember the last time I saw my mother and I'd swallow them back down. A part of me was terrified Lana would hate me if she knew how pathetic I was.

Lana was waiting for an answer, but I couldn't think of anything to say. I couldn't accuse him. Not again. I couldn't tell her the truth, either.

"Go on, Freckles." Mason spun around and narrowed his eyes on me. "Your friend asked you a question, and I gotta say, I'd love to hear the answer."

Not sure what else to do, I hung my head and hid behind my hair. "I don't want to talk about it."

"Of course you don't," he snorted.

I'd never been more happy to hear the bell ring out as I was then.

Mason didn't say anything else. Thankfully he just grabbed his books and got up. He wasn't the one I should've been afraid of.

"Alright Harper, if you don't want to help yourself," Lana tipped her head my way, "Then I'll do it for you."

Panic seized my muscles as she pranced past Mason and grumbled, "I'd look into her father if I were you."

Chapter 9
Mason

I spent a lot of time thinking about ways to fuck with people. Silas, my brother, and Lou in particular. Some might say I got a kick out of pissing people off, and I kind of did. But that wasn't why I had Silas's room made over in princess theme, or sent a male strip-o-gram to Lou at work. Anything was better than being stuck in my own head, trying to make sense out of the chaos storm waging a war in my brain.

Why did she do this? Why did he say that? And all the other crap I'd never get answers for. It was exhausting and unending. The only time I got a little peace was when I was high or drunk.

Alcohol and drugs helped numb the pain, but they didn't take it away. Nothing did. But numb was better than the alternative. Sucking back a nice cold beer sounded like a fantastic idea right now, and all because of one person.

Ned Callaghan.

All day I'd been going over every single thing I knew about the asshole – which wasn't much. Other than a few childhood encounters, I didn't really give a shit about the guy. I knew more about Silas's balls than I did about him. Seemed weird, considering how much time I used to spend with his daughter. I didn't even know the prick's birthday.

Why?

Was I not paying attention, or did he not want me to pay attention? How many skeletons did he have in his closet? What was he hiding? Because everyone hid something. And if I did figure it out, where would his secrets lead me?

Down a useless road of sketchy business deals, or to somewhere else? It was driving me crazy. I grew up with Ned. Fuck sakes, I spent more time at his house than I did my own. I should know something about him, right?

Fucking Lana Crawford. This crap was all her fault. She wasn't exactly what I'd call an ally. In fact, I was pretty sure if I was doused in gasoline, she'd be the first to toss a match my way. The girl fucking hated me.

Normally I ignored her snide little comments – seriously, what the fuck was she going to do? Come at me with all her one hundred pounds of fury? I bench pressed twice that for fun.

Telling me to look into Harper's old man wasn't the same as cursing my dick to fall off. Though I'd argue that the latter was worse. Messing with a man's twig and berries was just plain cold.

Don't see me walking around cursing bitches' pussies to fall off. And trust me, there were plenty of chicks wandering these halls that should have a permanent block slapped over their hole.

Edith's granddaughter was a perfect example of that. I had no problem with women exploring their sexuality – they had every right to get theirs. But Trina Dupire had been in Ashworth for a little over half a year and had banged more guys than I knew. Then again, I might be a little biased.

Waking up with a knife to your balls while being told to stay away from some chick kinda turned a guy off. Trina may not be said girl Preston was referring to, she was an exact replica though. That was enough to make me stay the fuck away.

"Hey," Silas nudged me with his elbow. "You okay?"

I gave him a look.

That was the dumbest question I'd ever heard. My brother was a dick, my old man wasn't my old man, and the bane of my existence was sleeping in the room next to mine. Don't think you could get much further from okay than that. I really needed a drink.

He rolled his eyes in response. "You know what I mean."

Yeah, I did. It was the same reason everyone asked if I was okay, when what they were really thinking was *'Did Mase fall off the wagon?'*

"Don't worry Captain Sobriety, I haven't had a drink." I slid my gaze his way. "Yet."

The grumpy fucker looked me dead in the eyes. "That's not funny."

"Who says I'm joking?"

There was a bottle of Jack tucked away in the corner of my room calling my name. I could already taste the sweet spice warming my tongue. My entire body was itching for it, tensing my muscles with need. I wouldn't drink it all. Just a few mouthfuls. Enough to forget about all this shit.

And forget about her.

Silas folded his arms and leaned back against his locker. "Do you want to go back to rehab?"

"I've been worse places." I shrugged and slammed my locker shut. "Remember Naomi's graduation party?"

"You mean the one you showed up to in dirty sweats and a t-shirt?"

Yeah, that was pretty good. Black tie event my ass. "I thought she was gonna kill me."

"No, motherfucker, I was gonna kill you." Silas raised a hand to wave a finger at me. "You know how many times I had to hide the bottles you were sucking back from your brother?"

"Fuck Micha," I grumbled, then sauntered down the hall.

"You know what, Mase," Silas skipped up behind me. "I'm not pulling your ass out of the fire this time."

"Whatever helps you sleep at night."

Silas could say that shit all he wanted, but I knew if I really needed him he'd be there, no questions asked. Hell, half the time he was there when I didn't need him, poking his nose in my shit. Not that I minded. I kind of loved the ornery prick. This however, was something he couldn't help with.

Then again, maybe he could?

"Hey, what do you know about Ned Callaghan?"

Silas's brow rose. "Harper's dad?"

I nodded.

Lou had his King's Ledger, a book he didn't think I knew about. Just like he didn't think I knew about his little collection, but I did. Thanks to Silas. He noticed shit other people didn't.

There was something to say about being the quiet one. I guess one could equate that with my brother as well. It pissed me off how often Micha was right.

All these years he'd been telling the guys that I'd eventually snap and sack up. Then my little Harper situation would come down to two simple things. Her and me. And now I had the lying bitch in my house because I was done with her shit. If that wasn't worth a snort of irony, I didn't know what was.

"Why the sudden interest in Ned?" Silas asked.

Really?

I was wrong, that was the dumbest fucking question ever asked.

"Why the sudden interest in Ned?" I tapped my chin and rolled my eyes up to the ceiling. "I don't know, maybe I just want to get to know the guy. Or, and hear me out," I pointed my tapping finger Silas's way, "It could have something to do with the fact that someone beat the shit out of his daughter."

Silas opened his mouth, then shut it as he swallowed down whatever dumb shit he was about to say.

"Okay, that's a fair point."

You think? "I mean, I thought it was."

"You don't have to be a dick."

I shrugged. "You're the one that asked a stupid question."

A sigh escaped his lips. "Don't make me shove my foot up your ass."

"Why would you go and ruin a perfectly good pair of boots like that?" I scoffed and dropped my gaze to his feet. "At least take them off first."

Silas's face dropped. "I hate you."

"Aww," I sang. "I love it when you talk sweet to me."

No one in this world knew me better than he did. Proof of that came when he raised his hand to stop my lips from landing on his cheek.

"I swear to god, if you kiss me I'm not going to tell you shit about Ned."

My brow rose. "But will you tell me how you plan on getting your boot up my ass?"

He lifted his chin to look up, and I could hear him praying for strength. This wasn't something new. Silas spent half our friendship asking the god of grumpy assholes for peace. They never answered of course, because as far as I was concerned *he* was the god of grumpy assholes. But hey, who was I to rain on his parade?

"You want to continue whispering praise to your deity, or are you gonna help me out?"

Silas's blue eyes rolled back down to me. "I hope a lightning bolt comes down from the sky and shoots up your ass."

"Do you have a fetish I don't know about?" My lip curled. "What is it with you and my ass? Don't get me wrong, however you decide to swing that thing is fine with me. But if I wanted something the size of a bat shoved up there, I'd go and piss off the baseball team."

There was no coming back from that.

"You done?" Silas grumbled.

Technically, I could carry this on for hours, but he'd run out of patience. That was evident by the way his fingers smoothed away the furrow on his forehead. The action was kind of useless. He'd need something a lot stronger than his fingers to get rid of that scowl. I was pretty sure he was born with it.

Silas blew out a breath. "Alright, so. Ned."

Oh great, we were back on topic. Finally.

"I don't really know much." He dropped his hand and continued down the hall. "The Callaghans moved here a couple of years before Sean was born. They had Harper, and his wife took off a few years after that. I think he works in mergers and acquisitions or something. He seems like a normal guy."

"Normal?" I cocked a brow at him. "No one with that kind of money is normal."

There were six families at the top of the food chain in Ashen Springs. The Kesslers, Creswells, Whitleys, Hudsons, Torres', and Callaghans. And the Callaghans weren't at the bottom of the list.

Silas waved his hand through the air. "I just mean I've never heard anyone say anything about him."

"No one?" Come on, that had to strike him as a little strange.

"Star called him a slimy twat once." He gave a quick shrug. "But she calls everyone a twat. Unless it's my old man. She prefers cunt when it comes to him."

Can't say I disagree with her there.

"Why? You think he's the one that fucked up Harper?"

"Maybe?" It would make sense, I suppose. It had to be someone close to Harper. Someone that she'd lie for. "Could be Sean?"

"I don't know." He shook his head. "Sean's a dick, but he was always on your ass for picking on her. Way too protective, if you ask me."

"Yeah, but her old man is *'super daddy'*. Always beaming and doting on his little princess."

I wonder what he'd do if I fucked her in front of him?

Silas pointed at me. "That's true."

We both stopped and tipped our heads as Harper rounded the corner. My eyes immediately zeroed in on her, rolling over the white blouse and skirt bouncing off her legs, before she ducked into the bathroom.

Ignoring the girl had become an impossibility. It didn't matter if she was in the near vicinity, or sitting right next to me. In point two seconds I'd memorized everything about her.

The accessories she wore, what color her nails were painted, and how her hair flowed down her back. Last Thursday at 2:43 she smelled like the cinnamon buns she'd baked in home economics. And the Tuesday before that she had a blue bow holding back the right side of her hair. Know what I didn't know? Who gave her the fucking bruises.

"Looks like someone's upset," Silas said, while nodding at the bathroom door.

Yeah, I saw the tears in her eyes. *Aw, was Freckles having a bad day?*

She had no idea what a bad day was. Not yet, anyways.

"Here's a question." He folded his arms and leaned against the wall. "Say one of them did do it?"

"Okay."

"What else have they done to her?"

That made me eye him. "What do you mean?"

"I mean, if someone's willing to beat on her, what's stopping them from..."

He didn't need to finish talking for me to get where he was going.

"You don't think…"

His shoulder lifted to his head in a quick shrug. "Why not?"

Suddenly all I could see was red. Beating on her alone warranted a slow and painful death, but if anyone went near her pussy… that was my shit to taint.

"She better damn well still be a virgin!"

"What if she's not?" Silas asked.

The look I gave him said it all. Preston Whitley himself wouldn't be able to pull off the sadistic shit I was ready to do. My hands were balled so tight my nails were piercing my palms.

Adrenaline rushed through my veins as images of hands grabbing flesh filled my mind. Hands that had no business touching her smooth skin. Did she like being caressed? Did she ask for more? Did she cry?

"Fuck this," I grumbled and marched down the hall.

"Where are you going?"

"To find out if she's still a virgin," I snarled back at Silas.

Some guy in the hall cocked his brow at me.

I responded with a loud, "You got a fucking problem?"

He shook his head and took off the other way. Good choice. If he'd have stuck around I might've beat the hell out of him for fun. Harper better pray she still had a goddamn hymen, cause if she didn't, all bets were off. I wouldn't just kill the motherfucker, I'd skin him alive. And make her watch.

Fueled by my boiling blood, I lifted my foot and kicked the door open. It flew forward, slapping off the door and sending a resounding clang around the room. Two girls standing in front of the mirrors shrieked and sprang back. Harper wasn't with them. I did hear a squeak come from the back stall, however.

A light clink drew my attention to a tube of lipstick rolling across the floor. It trickled over the white tiles and tapped against the red toe of a heeled shoe. What the fuck were these two bitches still doing here? Did they think this was show time?

"Get the fuck out!" I snarled at their wide eyes.

Did I give a shit about the dirty looks they gave me? No. They could fuck right off and deal with their precious female needs somewhere else. I didn't even bother to give them a side glance.

One of them muttered, "Asshole," as they scuttled past.

"Blow me," I grumbled back, before closing and locking the door.

Wouldn't want anyone coming in here to interrupt us. I rolled my glare back to the closed stall in the back corner. Harper hadn't so much as peeped since I first came in.

She wasn't doing herself any favors by playing possum. The longer I stood there, the more vivid the images in my mind became. Pawing hands, masculine grunts and groans mingling with the sweet sound of quiet whimpers and pleas. My whimpers and pleas.

"God damnit!" I threw my fist into the wall. "Get the fuck out here, Freckles."

My heart thumped, shooting spurts of anger through my veins as I waited for movement to come from the other side of the room.

The door remained closed.

No shuffle, whimper, or squeak came my way. The only thing I could hear was a few soft ticks as drops of blood slid down my knuckles and landed on the floor.

The only thing that stopped me from storming over there and dragging her ass out was the rage burning through my system. When I was in this kind of mood, the only thing I wanted to do was destroy things. And while I did want to destroy Harper, I wasn't about to take my anger out on a defenceless little girl. Unlike the prick she was protecting.

Calm down, Mason. You need to get control of yourself.

I forced my fists to relax, and blew out a long breath while leaning my shoulder against the wall.

"You don't want me to come in there after you."

She and I had been here before. In fact, this was the very same bathroom I'd cornered her in on prom, but I wasn't picturing someone else stealing her tears that night. *If one single delicious drop of misery was taken...*

Nope, not going there. You're not even sure if anything happened.

But what if it did?

"Fuck," I grumbled, and gritted my teeth against the thoughts rolling around in my head. "You don't want to fuck with me right now, Freckles. Get the fuck out here!"

Still nothing. I did hear her moving around though.

Alright, have it your way.

I shrugged and pushed off the wall. Looked like I was going in. Which was exactly what I did. A fraction of a second later, I'd forced the door open and prepared to drag her out.

Then I froze.

Harper was seated on the closed toilet lid, gawking up at me with wide eyes, but my eyes were stuck on the thin line of red rolling down her thigh.

"What the fuck is that?"

She clamped her legs shut and shook her head. "Nothing."

Why wasn't I surprised?

That was clearly a lie.

There were a few things I could do in this situation. Like prying the truth out of her by forcing her legs open and seeing for myself why she was bleeding. But that would be too easy. Besides, I was much more interested in the hand she'd tucked behind her back.

"Whatcha got there, Freckles?"

Her face screwed up in a scowl. "Nothing."

Fuck me if that snarky little bite in her tone wasn't one of the hottest things I'd ever heard. Unfortunately for her, I wasn't in the mood to play games.

Intent on finding out for myself what she was hiding, I lunged forward and reached out. That's when her hand swung through the air, smacking me across the face. I'd never come full stop so fast in my life.

Did she just fucking slap me?

Did I like it?

I cocked a brow down at the surprise glimmering in her eyes. Yeah, I think I did. Little Harper Callaghan had some fight in her after all. A slow smirk spread across my face. This was going to be fun.

"Um... I-I....," she held her palms. "I didn't mean..."

"Oh, you didn't mean it." I cocked a brow down at her. "Was someone else controlling your arm, because I'm pretty sure you just fucking hit me."

Harper jarred back against the toilet and quickly muttered, "I'm sorry," as I stepped into the stall.

"You say that a lot." I flattened my palms on the wall behind her and leaned in to growl, "What are you sorry for this time, Freckles?"

The second she ducked to hide behind her hair, I reached out and snatched her arm. She tried to fight back. *Tried* being the operative word. I tore her hand out from her behind her back with minimal effort.

A nail file dropped from her grip and clacked down on the floor. If Harper thought I was mad before, she was wrong. The tiny specks of red dotting the edge of the metal file rekindled any of that fire I managed to tamp down.

"Did you fucking cut yourself?"

I could see the guilt in her eyes before she shook her head. "No."

Okay, now I was pissed.

"I'm getting real sick of your lies, Freckles."

"I'm not… I mean…" Her gaze fell down to the evidence laying on the ground. "I've never done it before."

Harper had some tells. A little twitch in her nose, a slight curl of the lips, and fluttering lashes were a few. For the most part she was a pretty good actress, but there was one thing she never could fake. Honesty. And the look on her face was too earnest for me not to believe her.

"You think that makes it any better?" I knew something about self-harm and the dark path of relief it pulled people down. If she wanted pain, I'd give her pain.

"Mason –"

My fingers speared in her hair, cutting her off before she could plead her case. I didn't give a shit about what she had to say, or why she did what she did. The end of my rope had officially been reached. It was time Harper Callaghan learned what would happen if she continued to spew bullshit my way.

Without a second thought I dragged her out of the stall and across the tiled floor. She fought to get away, flailing her legs while she clawed at my arm and begged me to let her go. But she wasn't doing herself any favors.

The only thing she was doing was turning me on. Every time her nails bit into my flesh my dick got harder. I actually had to pause and re-adjust before I slammed her face down on the counter.

"You want pain, Freckles? Fine." My hand landed firmly on her ass. "That one's for scratching me."

She took it pretty good, just pressed her face into the counter and whimpered. So I smacked her again.

"That one's for slapping me."

The second strike didn't elicit much more of a reaction. Apparently she had a higher pain tolerance than I thought. But I wasn't done yet.

"And this one," throwing my arm back, I cracked my palm down on her ass. "Is for lying to me."

This time Harper shrieked and threw her leg back, kicking her heel into my shin. A sharp stab traveled up my calf, pulling a deep groan from my chest.

Fuck yeah. That's what I'm talking about.

The way her face paled when I stepped in and pressed my cock up against her ass, now that really got me going. I tightened my fingers around the back of her neck, reveling in the way her pulse fluttered while I took my time to admire her folded-over form.

She had zero chance in this situation. Her feet weren't touching the floor, so she couldn't use that for leverage. My little toy was one hundred percent vulnerable. I could do whatever I wanted, and there was fuck all she could do to stop me.

It was so tempting to take her right then and there, and fuck me, I wanted to. But I couldn't. Not yet, and not in Ashworth's bathroom. There were too many nosey bitches around that would come to her rescue. When I did finally fuck Harper, it would be somewhere where she had no allies. So I could feed off her terror and tears.

That didn't mean I couldn't have some fun.

"I'm curious," I reached down to glide my hand up her thigh, "what panties are you wearing today?"

"Stop it." Harper jarred her hips, trying to wriggle away. A pathetic attempt if you asked me, but I did like the way her ass ground against me.

"Keep telling me to stop, Freckles," I leaned over to growl in her ear. "Find out what happens."

Standing back up, I glanced down to where we were pressed together. Her plaid skirt was annoying me. There was too much fabric between us. I wanted to feel her warmth and soak up the shivers trembling her body. That was easily remedied. One flick of my wrist and I had her skirt flipped over her back.

"Fuck me," I groaned.

White cotton panties. Couldn't get much more virginal than that. Then again, it could be another lie. As Silas pointed out, if someone was going to beat on her, what was stopping them from doing something else.

No time like the present to find out.

When I moved to tug on the waistband of her panties, Harper lurched forward.

"W-what are you doing?"

God, I loved the way she stuttered, all nervous and shit.

"What do you think I'm doing?"

"B-but you hate me," she argued.

"And?" Was she under some naive misguided delusion that I liked every chick I fucked?

"We're in the girls bathroom." Harper attempted to struggle against my hold by twisting her neck and throwing her arm back.

I glanced down at the fingertips feebly clawing at my chest. "Keep it up and you'll find yourself good and fucked in the girl's bathroom."

Harper stilled then. Went completely quiet, like a mouse playing dead for a cat.

"Aw, what's wrong, Freckles?" I purred, while dragging my finger down her spine. "You scared?"

She whined and buried her face in the counter. "Please leave me alone."

My gaze rolled over her shivering form, soaking up the way her chest shuddered with each breath. Digging my fingers into her neck, I slid my hand around the curve of her hip.

"Let's get one thing straight. This is my body. No one is allowed to touch it or mark it up. Including you." I folded back over her, pressing my weight down. "Try that shit again, and you'll really be sorry. Got it?"

She whimpered and nodded.

Good. Now I could do what I came in here for. One glance back at her panty-clad ass had me tempted to sink my teeth into those fleshy globes. And I might've, if it wasn't for the angry red cut staring at me from her inner thigh.

I wasn't sure if Harper could sense the change in mood. Maybe she knew what I was going to do. Either way, her fight picked back up.

My jaw twitched as her arms flew back and feet kicked. It was more of a nuisance than anything. I had that shit under control in a matter of seconds. Harper's wrists were grabbed and held against the back of her neck, while I forced my way between her legs. It wasn't her struggle that caused me to pause. It was what she said when I slid my palm around the front of her hip.

"Don't touch me down there. It's private."

Did she just call that shit 'down there'? Well, I guess that answered the virgin question. Still, it was better to be safe than sorry.

"How many times do I have to tell you? This is *my* body," I growled, and pulled her panties to the side, so I could slide my finger through her folds.

Fuck me, she was wet.

My intent was to shove a finger inside until I felt resistance – which I did – but the second her hot wet walls clamped around the tip of my finger, I snapped.

Before I knew what was happening, I had my cock out and was stroking my shaft. I wasn't even sure how I got my belt off, or my pants open. The only thing I did know was that I needed release more than I did my next breath or hit of heroin. The way she thrashed under my hold only amplified the primal need crawling across my skin.

This is what I craved.

I needed to feel her useless fight while I exploited her vulnerability and took what I wanted. I needed to dominate and mark her.

Teach the lying little bitch a lesson she wouldn't forget. I wanted to see her down on her knees with her eyes full of tears while she begged me to stop. I needed her to hurt.

Like I did.

"Mason," she cried out. "Stop it."

Not a fucking chance.

"Shut the fuck up," I ground out and pressed her face into the countertop. "When I want you to talk, I'll fucking tell you."

The tear that dripped from the side of her face threw me over the edge. I tore her panties off, roared and fought to keep my knees from buckling as I shot my load over her bare ass. For a split second I couldn't see or hear anything. I was completely lost in the erotic bliss bowing my back.

It took a bit for my senses to come back. When they did and I saw the mess I'd made, there was only one thing rolling through my mind. Disgust.

I hated Harper more in that moment than I ever did. It didn't matter how much I enjoyed the defeated sigh that shook her body, because she made me lose control. Control I promised myself I'd always hold onto around her.

Before I could do something else stupid, I stepped back and tucked my dick away.

"Stop crying," I growled and walked away. "It could've been worse."

Worse for who, I didn't know. One thing was for sure, I needed to put as much distance between her and me as I could.

Chapter 10
Harper

*I*t was a lot easier to avoid people at Mason's house than it was at school. But for the past eleven days, I'd managed to hide away in solitude. Other than having to sit beside someone in class, that is. Not even Star could find me in my secret spot behind the bleachers. I'd sit in that cubby where coaches used to store equipment and watch her scour the field for me.

A part of me felt bad for hiding from her. Especially when Lana joined in on the search. But I couldn't take any more questions or sideways looks. So solitude became my only friend, and it wasn't that bad. Actually, I kind of enjoyed being alone. I didn't have to lie to anyone if they weren't around.

And the best part... Mason Kessler hadn't said a word to me since that day in the bathroom. I'd see him making out with some girl in the hall, or laughing with his friends, but he didn't so much as look my way. He didn't even drive me to school. That job was left up to Marco. In fact, he was so absent that at one point I thought I might actually be able to go home.

That didn't happen. When I tried to walk out the door, Louis stopped me. And the time after that it was Marco. So while I was still a prisoner, I was a forgotten one. That suited me just fine. My weekend was spent in the Kessler's vast library getting lost in various fairy tales, and on the weekdays when I wasn't in school I hid in my room. No one bothered me or knocked on the door. Well, except for Shelby. She visited a few times, but Logan always pulled her away.

So, all in all the past two weeks weren't that bad. Actually, they were probably the best I'd ever had. My bruises were pretty much gone. I walked into school with a smile on my face for the first time in I don't know how long. I was happy. For the most part, anyways.

I peeked around my locker door to the spot down the hall where Mason had Tiffany pinned up against the wall. She leaned into his kiss, pressing her breasts up against him. I couldn't stop watching the way Mason's mouth moved, or how his arms flexed when he tightened his grip on her wrists. It had always hurt to see him with other girls. Since our last encounter, it was different.

The ache in my chest was still there, but something else mingled with it. Curiosity, maybe? I kept thinking about what he did. How I heard him grunting behind me but was too afraid to look in the mirror. Humiliation and Mason Kessler went hand in hand. He'd embarrassed me more times than I could count. In that bathroom, I felt my blush spread through my entire body, heating up my skin while making things clench that I didn't know could.

He'd violated me. Forced the tip of his finger inside me and I couldn't do anything to stop him. That achy stretch consumed my dreams. Sometimes it felt like Mason was still there. I'd clench my thighs and swear I could feel his hand. I didn't know how to handle it. So I watched him saunter around the halls, talking to

140

girls, and waited to see if any of them had the same confusion I did.

Tiffany sure didn't seem to mind it. Her legs were wrapped around his waist, flipping her skirt up so everyone could see her underwear. Didn't she care? And there wasn't much there to cover her up. There was a time and a place for G-Strings, and school wasn't one of them.

Was that what Mason liked? And why did I care what he liked?

Luckily, I didn't have to think about it for long, because my phone went off with a ringtone that I was more than happy to answer.

"Sean," I sang into the phone.

"Hey, Bug. Whatcha doing?"

Watching Mason make out with someone.

"Just putting my books away. Shouldn't you be in class?"

"I ditched." A disgruntled groan rang through the other end. "Physics is soooo boring."

Why wasn't I surprised? My brother never took anything seriously. Girls, school, his future, were all just passing whims for him. And why shouldn't they be? Unlike me, Sean had everything handed to him on a silver platter. That's what happened for star quarterbacks. Girls had cheerleading, and that was a hard pass for me.

"Sean," I sighed. "You shouldn't ditch."

"Listen here, small fry, I may be a million miles away but I have no problem coming home to nuggie your ass."

As much as I wanted to pay attention to my brother, I couldn't. My lip curled as Tiffany's tongue lunged into Mason's mouth. Was she trying to kiss him, or eat his face? That couldn't be pleasant.

"Who wants someone else's tongue in their mouth?"

Sean's tone instantly dropped. "What?"

Damnit.

"What?"

141

"You just said, 'who wants someone else's tongue in their mouth'?"

"No I didn't."

"Harper?" Sean sang.

Yeah, I didn't believe that either.

"Is someone trying to stick their tongue in your mouth?"

What? Eww. "No."

That would be gross. I cocked a brow over at Mason. *I think?*

Sean's voice took on that big brother tone I heard all too often.

"Alright Harper, you're going to tell me right now who's trying to fuck you."

Oh my God. "No one is."

"You better not be lying to me," he warned. "If I find out someone's been putting moves on my baby sister…"

Before he could finish the threat, I cut him off. "No one's been putting moves on me."

I stopped as my mind went back to that day in the bathroom, and how it felt when Mason's warm fluid landed on my skin. Did masturbation fall into the 'putting moves on' category?

"Harper," Sean yelled into the other end, snapping me back into the conversation. "What the fuck is going on?"

"Nothing. Everything is fine."

I'd never told my brother a bigger lie than that. Fine was pretty far off from where I was. I'm not sure why I thought he'd buy it.

"Bullshit. Now are you going to tell me what's going on, or do I have to come home and drag it out of you?"

The scary thing was that I knew he'd do it. To say my brother didn't like the Kessler's would be an understatement. Even when we were kids before everything went sour, Sean didn't like them. Though I think that was mostly because Mason broke his favorite truck. If he found out Mason took me to his house… One of them would end up dead.

I glanced back down the hall. Mason was whispering something in Tiffany's ear while she giggled and fluttered her eyelashes up at him. Maybe he did like what she was doing? He didn't have that same angry glint in his eyes that he always did with me.

Sean barked out one last warning. "Harper!"

"I don't want to talk about it," I sighed and fell back behind my locker door.

"You can talk to me about anything, Bug. You know that."

There were plenty of things I couldn't talk to him about, but was this one of them? My brother was experienced. He'd been with a lot of girls. Like a lot, a lot. His high school life might've been easier if he installed a revolving door on his bedroom. Would it really be so bad to ask him a few things? There wasn't anyone else in the world I trusted more.

Before I could lose my nerve, I blurted out, "Do guys like it when girl's stick their tongues in their mouths?"

"What?! No. We hate it. Don't fucking do it." I could practically see his hand waving through the air in a stern point. "Just a quick peck on the cheek, after you're married. That's all we like."

My brow arched. He didn't really expect me to believe that.

"You forget I lived in the same house as you." I couldn't count how many girls I'd seen shove their tongues down my brother's throat.

"That's because I'm a slut and a bad guy. You don't want to go out with someone like me. Date Robbie Peterson."

Robbie Peterson? "I weigh more than him."

"Exactly," Sean said. "You can kick his ass if he gets too handsy."

Maybe I liked handsy? I found myself once again peeking around my locker door. This time, though, Mason's eyes met mine. Two glittering green orbs that stole my breath and caused me to freeze. That is, until a smirk curled the corner of his mouth. Then I ducked back, slamming my back against the wall.

"What the hell was that?" Sean asked as some of my books fell on the floor.

"Nothing." I shook my head and told myself to snap out of it. "Look, I don't want to date anyone. I'm just trying to figure out why I got all hot and achy the other day."

Dead silence was the only thing that came across the other end.

"Sean?"

Still nothing.

"You there?"

I was about to look at my phone to see if I lost the signal when his voice came through.

"Sorry," he muttered. "I'm just trying to wrap my head around the fact that someone turned my baby sister on."

Was that what that was? I got turned on by Mason Kessler violating me? I suppose it made sense. Why would I dream about something some part of me didn't like? Then again, I had night-mares all the time, but those made me wake up in a cold sweat. Not a hot one. At least Sean understood what was happening. The only question now was...

"How do I make it stop?"

Sean's tone picked up an octave this time. "What?"

"How do I make it stop?" I repeated. I didn't like this tension I was feeling. It had me wound up and more jittery than normal. "There's got to be a way to release it."

The phone went quiet again.

I waited in silence as the minutes ticked by for what seemed like forever, before saying, "Sean, there is a way to stop this feeling, right?"

"Yes, there sure is."

Thank god. I was starting to worry.

"What is it?"

Sean let out a long, heavy sigh. "Sorry sis, I love you, but I'm tapping out on this one."

My brows knit. "What do you mean, you're tapping out?"

He was the one who said I could talk to him about anything.

"I mean, physics is better than this," he said, and hung up.

"Well that was super helpful," I muttered while shutting my locker.

The face that suddenly appeared caused my heart to lurch as I squealed and sprang back.

"Hey," Shelby raised her hand, giving me a small wave. "I came to see if you wanted a ride."

Although the smile on her face was creeping me out, I nodded. Anything was better than being stuck in a car alone with Marco. The huge beast that ran the Kessler's security was almost as terrifying as Mason. Almost.

She tipped her head, causing her blonde ponytail to sway behind her. "How's your brother?"

Oh my God, she heard.

"That was a great conversation by the way."

I could feel the mortification spread through me, heating my cheeks, chest and arms.

"Okay, first off." She waved her hand through the air, pointed a manicured finger at me. "Never ask your brother for sexual advice. Don't ask any man in your family. Their sole mission in life is to make sure you die a virgin."

Didn't really know what else to say to that other than, "Um... okay."

"Now, the kissing thing." Shelby threw her arm around me and led me down the hall towards the doors. "Boys love a little tongue action. There's this thing I do with mine that drives Logan wild. You gotta curl, swirl, and hook at the same time. I know it sounds tricky, but trust me it's doable. You take the tip..."

I trailed outside with her while secretly praying God would strike me down right then and there.

THERE ARE few things I never thought I'd be doing on a Friday night. Attending a party with the popular kids, watching the football game, or just hanging out with friends in general. Daddy had very strict rules that didn't allow me a lot of spare time or freedom.

When Star showed up and took me to Malum, he was not impressed. Just like he wouldn't be impressed if he knew I was currently sitting with Shelby in her room. He hadn't even met Shelby, which I'd tried my hardest to prevent. Sometimes when Daddy looked at Lana I'd get this icky feeling crawl up my spine.

In a way it was good that she had the babies and stopped coming around so much. Not that I thought he'd do anything. I'd seen the darkest parts of him and I'd never had any inkling that he would cross that line. But I was more comfortable without my friends around him.

"Here." Shelby held a piece of tissue paper up to my mouth. "Smack your lips together."

I internally shook my head. Just because I didn't wear make-up didn't mean I didn't know how to put it on. Then again, she wouldn't know that, would she? It's not like I talked to her very much. So I leaned forward and did what she said.

After that she sat back and eyed me for a second. Her whole face lit up as a proud glint filled her pretty cinnamon eyes. She was radiant, beautiful, and so happy I wanted to smile with her. Why hadn't I talked to her before? Why did she want to talk to me? Girls like Shelby usually ignored me, or picked on me. But she was always nice. Maybe Shelby had issues? Her best friend *was* Riley.

"That color looks gorgeous on you." Shelby clicked her tongue and swung her finger through the air. "Seriously, sleep in it, eat with it, never take it off."

I couldn't stop myself from turning in her dressing table chair to look in the mirror. When I saw the girl staring back at me, I was stunned. Her hair was cascading over her shoulders in the softest red curls I'd ever seen, and her brown eyes seemed bigger and brighter.

"Is that... me?"

"Yes, that's you."

I twisted my neck to argue, but was blinded by a flash of light. Did she just take a picture? I swear I heard a click. My heart all but stopped when my vision came back. Shelby was busy tapping on her phone. Was she sending it to people so they could laugh at me? Naomi did that once.

She pretended to be my friend just so she could get me in a compromising position, claiming I would look great in a dress. Once I'd stripped down to my underwear, she flicked on the light and everyone in the room laughed.

It was almost four years later and I still couldn't change in front of people. At school I hid in the bathroom stall and when Lana came home with me, I waited until she left to get out of my uniform.

"W-what are you doing?"

"I told Logan you were a hottie and now I have proof."

Her finger tapped down on the screen in her hands, sending a text that made my heart race.

"Why would you send that to Logan?" I was so stupid. How could I fall for the nice girl act again?

Inquisition furrowed Shelby's brow as she tipped her head and studied me. Attempting to get away from her scrutiny, I shifted and swung my eyes around her room. It was pretty in here, with splashes of pink and black on the bed and other furniture. This was what a teenage girl's room should look like. Even with the pile

of unicorns in the corner, Shelby's room was way more sophisti-
cated than mine.

"Harper," Shelby sighed. "You know I'd never hurt you, right?"

Wouldn't she? I was at the bottom of the food chain. It was
kind of my job to get kicked around.

She walked over and placed her hand on my arm. I tried not to
flinch away when she tipped her head to look in my eyes.

"I mean it. I really do think you look fantastic."

Silence filled the room as I stared back at her. I wished I could
believe what she said, but let's face it, I was anything but fantastic.

Still, I muttered, "Okay."

Whether she believed me or not, I didn't know. Before she
could say anything, we were interrupted by her phone. The ringtone alone was enough to tell me who was calling. Shelby rolled
her eyes as *'Pony'* by Genuine filled the room.

"That bastard changed my ringtone again."

I mean... was she surprised by this? She chose to date–sorry,
marry–Logan Hudson. Who I was pretty sure didn't have a sane
bone in his body. When we were kids he used to do stuff like walk
over hot coals and jump off cliffs, and his decision making skills
hadn't improved any over the years. My gaze narrowed on Shelby
as she answered the call. There was definitely something wrong
with her.

"What do you want?" she snarled while holding the phone out
like that could keep him away.

For a second I wondered what it would be like to have
someone that obsessed with you. Don't get me wrong, Logan
Hudson was not the kind of guy I'd want following me around.
But it had to feel a tiny bit good to know that you were someone's
whole world.

"What the fuck did you do to Harper?"

Logan's question made my eyes narrow further. I knew they
were going to make fun of me.

"Oh, calm down. I just put a little make-up on her." Shelby curled her lip at the phone. "It's not like I paraded her around in a sexy dress."

She paused, cocked a brow up at the ceiling, then looked over at me as if she was considering the dress part of her statement. I furiously shook my head back at her.

"Oh my god, Babe," Logan called out. "You need to stop and do that shit right now. And please, please send a picture to Mase."

What? No! Mason couldn't see me like that. The last time I let someone dress me up he was pissed. He didn't leave me alone for weeks.

Suddenly my lungs refused to work. All the air in the room had been sucked away. I couldn't take a breath to save my life. The only thing that saved me from collapsing in a shivering mess was Shelby's response.

"I'm not playing into your sick games."

Now I was really confused. Wasn't she on their side?

"Oh come on, Cherry Pie," Logan whined.

"No," she stated firmly. "And you know what else? I'm not fucking you tonight."

Then she ended the call.

I was stunned. She just hung up on Logan Hudson. Logan freaking Hudson. Who did that?

"You just hung up on him?" I whispered.

Shelby curled her lip at me. "Um, yeah. He's being an idiot."

"But... he's Logan?"

"Aaand?" she sang back.

Why wasn't she scared? "What if he gets mad?"

"Oh please." She waved her hand. "I have that boy wrapped around my finger."

I didn't get it. "Why would you stick up for me?"

Who was I to her? No one. I was nothing more than the quiet

girl who sat at the same table as her in the cafeteria. And not by choice. If I had it my way, I'd have been in the corner alone.

"Why wouldn't I stick up for you?" she asked while placing her hand on her cocked hip. "They're being assholes."

I hung my head and grumbled, "Maybe I deserve it?"

"No one deserves to be treated like that."

She said that now, but... "You don't know what I did."

"Yes I do," she said, making my eyes snap back to hers. "Logan told me."

That didn't make sense. If she knew what happened... what I did, then why would she ever talk to me? I didn't want to talk to me.

She let out a long puff of air. "Look Harper, I don't know what went down. If what you said was true or not. But we all make mistakes."

"What if it wasn't a mistake?"

As much as I regretted hurting the little boy I loved, if I had it to do over again I'd make the same choice. Mason may hate me, but he was still breathing.

Shelby thought about what I said for a second, then shrugged her shoulders.

"I'm sure you had your reasons. I'm the last person to judge." She swung her eyes my way and I swear I saw a hint of guilt on her face. "Trust me."

Her room suddenly seemed very small. I could feel the walls closing in on me as I sat there trying to figure out what to do or say. There was a big difference between making a bad decision, and destroying someone. Because that's what I did. That's what I was still doing by not saying anything. For the first time in my life, I wondered what it would be like to unburden myself. How relieving would it be to get this heavy weight off my shoulders?

Then again, it might just add more. Would Shelby, Riley, and everyone else look at me with disgust when they found out about the horrible things I'd done? The things my father had forced me to do. Would Lana hate me like Mason did? That was a thought that was too much to bare.

"I have to go."

I jumped up and scuttled out of the room before Shelby could stop me.

Tears sprang into my eyes as I flew down the stairs and around the corner. Lana was already mad at me. I should've said something when she asked me about Daddy. I should've convinced her that everything was okay, instead of hiding from her. What if she started asking questions? What if she asked him questions? Daddy was my burden. It was my job to protect people from him. If she got hurt, it would be my fault. I had to call her. I had to fix this.

At least that was my intent, until I turned down the hall for my room and ran into something hard. At first I thought it was a wall that knocked the wind out of me and sent me spiraling to the floor. Then I heard a familiar growl.

"Where the fuck are you rushing off to?"

My entire throat bobbed as I swallowed my fear and forced myself to look up at the huge form looming over me. Rolling my eyes up Mason's jean clad legs was agonizingly slow. I could not only feel the anger coming off him, I could see it flexing in the defined muscles under his dark t-shirt. Then my eyes met his bright green orbs, glittering with something dark. Whatever I was going to say was lost. I just stayed there, sprawled out on the floor, staring at him.

I couldn't quite put my finger on why, but Mason looked different. Bigger, and more masculine. I was very aware of how easily those hands could hold me down. Like they had in the bathroom. Though I didn't see what he was doing, I felt his arm moving. I felt the long strokes he was making. But were they long? It couldn't be that big, right? Curiosity drove my eyes to trickle down his solid form.

"Are you wearing make-up?"

My gaze instantly snapped back up to his. "Shelby did it."

Way to throw someone under the bus, Harper.

"I mean... I didn't tell her not to."

"Uh huh."

His eyes dropped down, making me realize my legs were open, displaying what I had on under my skirt. Mason smirked when I quickly clamped them shut.

I waited for him to say something and laugh at the make-over Shelby had given me, but he didn't.

He simply stepped over me and said, "I'm going out. Stay in your fucking room tonight."

"Where are you going?"

Not sure why I asked that. The answer I got was about what I expected.

"None of your damn business."

Well, at least some things never change.

"Oh, and we'll talk about what I found on this," the pit in my gut swirled when he held my phone up over his shoulder. "When I get home."

I watched him walk away, wracking my brain to think about anything I may have texted. Daddy checked my phone so I was usually pretty careful about what I said. That didn't mean I hadn't missed something. Like my chance to fix things with Lana.

Damnit.

Chapter 11
Mason

My fist tightened, pulling the ache in my knuckles across my hand and down my fingers. The tough bastard I was fighting got a few good hits in, but I took down. I took them all down. Maybe not as callously as I did him. There was a slight chance that I may have pounded on his skull a tad more than I needed to.

Okay, it was more than a chance. Probably should've stopped before Silas jumped in the ring and pulled me away. But hey, when someone stepped into that ring they weren't signing up for Care Bear camp.

A disgruntled sigh came from the back of the Hummer. "I hope you're happy with yourself."

"I didn't ask for your opinion, London," I snarled over my shoulder at the blonde in the back before turning my glare on Silas. "Why'd you have to bring her?"

He steered the Hummer down my driveway and shrugged. "She wanted to come."

"I thought Harper would be there," Star added.

'Why the fuck would I bring her?"

I already couldn't get those big brown eyes out of my head, the last thing I needed was another distraction.

"You can't keep her prisoner, Mason."

"Watch me," I growled, then added, "Besides, she can leave anytime she wants. All she's got to do is tell me who fucking hit her."

Star scoffed out a snicker. "Why would she tell the arsehole who torments her anything?"

My gaze snapped back to hers. "Has she told you?"

Her dark narrowed gaze and crossed arms were enough of an answer for me.

"That's what I thought."

"Says the arsehole who beat the bloody hell out of someone," she huffed while shimmying back against the seat.

"It's called a fight, London," I huffed back at her. "Don't like it, then don't come."

Besides, the shit that went down was all Shelby's fault.

What the fuck was she thinking, making up Harper like that? Her pouty pink lips were a distraction all night. I could smell the blood and sweat in the ring and hear the crowd cheering, but all I could see was her. All sprawled out on the floor and staring up at me like she was begging to suck my dick.

Fuck me.

I was doing such a good job ignoring her too. Only snuck into her room to watch her sleep four times this past week. Maybe five?

"Stop taking your shit out on her," Silas grumbled from behind the steering wheel. "I told you this would happen."

"Whatever." I rolled my eyes.

We were banned from Grey's and that's all he had to say? I told you so?

Asshole.

"Not my fault Ryan didn't put his big girl panties on today."

Old man Grey wouldn't have had an issue. Then again, he had no idea what his son had done with his beloved record shop.

"Look, Ryan might be a giant prick but this isn't his fault."

Someone was bitter. Let's just say my best friend wasn't too happy when his favorite sanctuary was transformed into mine.

"You have no control," Silas added, while sternly pointing at me.

"Says the guy who organizes his socks by color."

That comment made Star chuckle. At least we agreed on one thing.

His blue eyes swung my way. "That qualifying fight is in six weeks."

Terry Winters was a heavily sought after coach for MMA fighters. He stumbled across one of my matches this summer while he was vacationing and said he might be interested in taking me on. But I had to prove myself against one of his fighters.

"You can't lose control like that."

I waved my hand at Silas. "I'll be fine."

It wasn't like I walked around town fucking up faces for fun. Well, sometimes I did, but tonight was different. I was… unfocused, and maybe a touch enraged. Who could blame me though? I'd had the worst case of blue balls in the history of mankind, and the cause of that affliction was sleeping in the room next to mine. Don't get me wrong, I had options. There were plenty of chicks that'd happily jump on my dick, but that would be like eating a pb and j sandwich when you were craving a steak.

I scrubbed a hand down my face. "I shouldn't have touched her."

"What?" Silas and Star said in unison, which was creepy as fuck.

My eyes shifted from the girl in the back, to my best friend. "Do you two have individual thoughts anymore, or have you become a hive mind?"

"Asshole," Silas muttered and pulled to a stop in front of my house.

I eyed the door, wondering if I really wanted to go in there. That's where *she* was. Mind you, she was probably fast asleep. On the comfortable bed I *allowed* her to have. Every night I stood by the hidden door connecting her room to mine and considered making her sleep on my floor. Like a damn dog.

Maybe I should?

"Hey," Silas tipped his head to study me. "Do I need to worry about you?"

Probably.

"Yes," Star piped in.

I rolled my eyes. *Bitch.* "I'm fine."

"You sure about that? Cause you were sucking face with Tiffany today."

The grumble that came from the backseat made me chuckle.

"I loath that cunt."

Can't say I disagreed with Star. Tiffany was worse than Naomi. And I hadn't forgotten about that shit she pulled with Harper. Something I was more than happy to remind her about before I posted the videos of her making out with the school mascot costume. It was amazing what some girls would do to please a guy.

"If it makes you feel better," I looked over my shoulder at the dark eyes glaring at me, "she tastes like shit."

"Yeah, sure," Silas snorted. "You had your tongue shoved far enough down her throat, I'm not surprised you tasted her ass."

"Does Star know about your ass fetish? Cause I'm pretty sure if you shove that behemoth hanging between your legs up hers, she ain't never gonna shit right again."

Star's jaw dropped while Silas glared at me with his nostrils flaring.

"Get the fuck out of my car."

"Why so cold, buddy? I'm not judging."

He hung his head to pinch the bridge of his nose. "Why the fuck am I friends with you?"

That was an easy one.

"I am a very pleasant person."

"You're a pain in the ass." He sighed and looked up. "Get the fuck out of my car before I give you a bruise to match the one on your jaw."

"That's just mean." Didn't see me making fun of his obvious fetish, yet here he was pointing out the uppercut I failed to dodge.

"Oh, you want mean?" Prick looked me dead in the eyes and said, "Fucked Harper yet?"

This time it was my face that dropped as I smacked my lips together.

His comment also relit the fire under Star's ass. She sprang forward, getting right in my face. "You better leave Harper alone."

"We talked about this, Crumpet," Silas responded before I could.

Her anger was instantly redirected to him. "No, you talked about it. I chose not to listen."

A twinkle flashed through Silas's light eyes as a smirk tugged at the corner of his mouth. "Someone's angling for the belt again."

Well, that was my cue to leave.

"I'd hate to hold that up." I opened the door and stepped out, saying, "You two have a nice night. Don't get run over by any pirate ostriches."

Not sure what he was smoking that night, but the asshole should've shared.

"Eat a dick, Mase."

"As long as it's not yours." I waved over my shoulder and walked into the house.

There was a reason I typically went in through the garage, and that reason smacked me in the face the second I stepped through the doors. Moonlight streamed in through the skylight, high-lighting the large sundial set in between two staircases. It felt like the universe was mocking me. As if someone up there was saying, 'Hey check it out. Look what's still here.'

It wasn't the cold metal dial that got to me. It was the little girl I could still see pointing out the time we'd get married. Six o'clock, when the shadow of the dial had a slight pink tinge to it. She liked the way it looked against the black metal. It was one a.m. now. Seven hours too late to catch that tinge. But it wasn't too late to go through her phone.

I smirked and headed through the foyer for my wing of the house. That thing had been burning a hole in my pocket all night. Chicks lived their lives on their phones and now I could finally peek at Harper's.

Except she wasn't like other chicks.

There were a few texts from Star, Lana, and her brother, but not much else. Harper didn't even have Riley and Shelby saved in her phone. I recognized their numbers that showed up as unknown, and couldn't help but wonder if they knew how much she valued their friendship. They should have their own special ringtone and cutesy nickname. Even I did that shit. Silas was in my phone as Fuckwad.

Strange.

Oh well, maybe her pictures would have more information?

I scrolled through various images of Sean – *prick* – and Lana, then stopped when a familiar face filled the screen. The sparkling eyes staring back at me were the same ones that haunted my dreams. Every time I closed my eyes I'd see that innocent smile and hair, flowing like red waves. I could hear her laugh and call my name as clear as the little boy standing beside her did. Why the fuck was this picture on here? And it wasn't the only one.

I continued to flip through image after image of a time I tried so hard to forget. Each one pulled at my chest, tugged out a deep-seated ache I buried long ago with the words. Now that voice was filling my head until all I could see was the amusement in his green eyes.

Stopping in front of the parlor, I told myself to shut the phone down. My thumb hovered over the power button, but I couldn't do it. The only thing that chased away the feeling of rough hands greedily pawing at me was her face. An innocent smile filled with love that got me through the darkest parts of my childhood. Then destroyed it...

"MASON DID IT."

My jaw dropped. The video I was watching couldn't be real. Harper wouldn't say that. She knew I would never hurt her.

"No." I shook my head. "That's not right. You made that up."

Deputy Adams sat down on his desk and sighed. "I'm sorry Mason, but I didn't make it up."

"Yes you did."

"No I –"

"Stop lying!" This was all wrong. Harper was in the hospital and these people were trying to turn her against me. "You made her say that."

"Is that what you think?" The deputy's brow arched. "That someone made her say it? Who do you think would do that?"

"You did!"

He had the video, which meant he was the one that made her do it. Maybe he hurt her too? But would he do that? I'd never seen him hurt anyone. My dad didn't like him though. There must be a reason for that.

Maybe he was bad and no one knew it, like Ryker. My eyes narrowed in on him. If he hurt my wife...

"I just took her statement, Mason. I didn't make her say anything."

"Liar!" I sprang out of my chair and lunged at the deputy, clawing and slapping him.

He might be bigger than me, but I could still hurt him. Just like I did Micha. Sure, I might've had a paperweight at the time, but there was lots of stuff around here. I had to get him and make him pay. Harper was mine. I had to protect her.

I should've protected her.

I failed.

Snatching a stapler off the desk, I whacked it against the deputy's shoulder. I couldn't fail her again. They all needed to see that I wouldn't let them do this. Every strike I rained down told him that.

Thud.

You're a liar.

Whack.

Stop making her lie.

Smack.

You can't hurt her.

Clack.

You can't hurt me.

Next thing I knew, I was snatched away by a pair of strong arms.

"Mason, stop."

The spicy scent and suit jacket told me it was dad, but I didn't stop. I couldn't. Lunging forward, I tried to break free of my dad's hold. He tightened his grip and pulled me back against his chest.

"You need to calm him down, Louis."

"No," I screamed back at the deputy. I would not calm down. "You made Harper lie."

She wouldn't say that. Harper loved me.

My eyes swung over to the hospital room displayed on the TV.

Didn't she?

Why would she say that? She knew I would do anything for her. I had done anything. The boogeyman came for her, and I let him take me instead.

Would she show you the same loyalty?

I looked at the beautiful face on the video as a sharp stab tore through my chest. The pain was so strong that not even the tears burning a trail down my cheeks could chase it away. She didn't just say it, Harper looked right into the camera and lied. She looked right into my eyes and accused me of being a monster.

The boogeyman was right.

Looking up into comforting dark eyes, I sucked back a sob and pleaded, "Dad?"

"It's alright, son," he pulled me into him and smoothed his hand down my back. "We'll figure this out."

I buried my face in his chest and let the tears fall. He was wrong. Nothing would be alright ever again. The monster from my nightmares told the truth.

And the girl I loved lied...

MY EYES LANDED on a brown bottle sitting on the bar in the corner of the parlor. It was in my hand before I could blink and I was swallowing a welcome mouthful of scotch. This was my refuge. The only thing I had to feel when I was lost in a drunken haze was numb. That's usually how it went. Not this time. The smoky burn flowing down my throat was doing nothing to chase away the image I was staring at.

So, I drank more.

By the time I was on my second bottle it seemed to be working. I was stumbling around barely able to stand on my own two feet. Yet the faces displayed on the screen in my hand were just as vivid as the day the picture was taken.

I could feel the sun on my back and see Fin's chubby little

hands full of shimmering red hair. Every breath I took carried the scent of sand and water while her sweet voice thundered through my head. *'You better learn to like babies Mason Kessler, cause I want three.'*

My fingers tightened around Harper's phone. These children and their smiles were mocking me. I wanted to crush their happy faces and rid myself of what could've been. But no matter how many times I tried, I couldn't do it. Even if it was all a lie, memories were all I had. And I still loved the little girl in this picture.

I sighed and dumped the rest of the bottle down my throat. That girl was gone now. Maybe she was never here? Maybe she'd only ever lived in my head? She was fierce and loyal. The kind of person that had no problem pushing my brother when he was being a dick. She never would've betrayed me.

My eyes drifted through the moonlit room to the form on the bed.

I had a better idea of how I got in this room than I did of who the girl sleeping in it was. Was Harper ever the person I thought she was? Or just a trickster sent to crush my soul?

"Would she show you the same loyalty?"

That's what Ryker said when we first started our *sessions* as he called them. I told him he could do whatever he wanted to me if he didn't touch her. And what did he do? Questioned her loyalty and laughed like he'd just won a game. I could still hear that eerie chuckle. It followed me around, echoing in the background as I walked around Ashworth. It rang through my ears when I stepped in the ring and went to bed at night. I couldn't escape that laugh.

Just like I couldn't escape her.

That was the cruelest joke of all. After everything that sick fuck did to me, he was still right. And I was the dumb kid that he threw his innocence away.

I believed in our love so much that I managed to hold onto a piece of my soul. Ryker could put his hands on me. He could carve out as much pain from my young body as he wanted, but he'd never touch that part, because it was for her. And she took it. Harper tainted the last pure piece of me.

Stumbling through the fog hazing my vision, I moved closer to the bed. Back when all this first started, I thought someone made her say those things. Why didn't I remember that? Everything else was clear as a bell. Being taken down to the station and locked up. How afraid I was, sitting alone in that cell all night. And the way she ignored me for months afterwards. Every time I'd ask her about it, Harper would walk away. As if I meant nothing.

I dropped my gaze down to her slumbering face, all peaceful in the moon's soft glow. She almost looked like an angel. Too bad there was nothing divine about her. Even if someone told her to do what she did, it wouldn't matter. She made her bed and now she could lay in it.

When my palms pressed down into the soft mattress, I cocked a brow.

Or... I could lay in it.

Before I knew what was happening, I was crawling up on the bed beside her. Where my clothes went, I had no idea. Didn't even realize I was in nothing but my boxers until I felt her warmth hit my skin. Gotta say, this chick was one hell of a deep sleeper. I was so close that I could smell her minty breath, and Harper hadn't so much as flinched when I laid my head down next to hers.

Why the fuck was she in my bed anyways? I sure as hell didn't invite her. I didn't invite anyone into my room. Not even Silas. That was my domain, and now she was tainting that too.

A yawn widened my mouth as I settled back into the soft fabric under my head. I suppose there was no harm in letting her stay while I rested my eyes for a bit. I could kick her out in a few minutes.

I'd almost drifted off when a sweet breathy tone hit my ear.

"Don't do that."

What the fuck?

"This is my fucking…"

Wait…

My left eye creaked open to peek at the headboard. Was this my room? I guess technically it was, just not the one I slept in. Fuck it. I was too comfortable to move. And why the fuck should I? Harper was infringing on my territory. If she didn't like it, she could move and sleep on the floor for all I cared.

A soft giggle whispered across my cheek, making me once again pop my eyes open. I was about to open my mouth to tell her to shut up when I noticed that she wasn't awake. Quiet little Freckles was talking in her sleep.

A smirk curled my lips as I rolled over to watch her pretty pink lips part in a gasp. God she was beautiful. That much I'd give her. Harper Callaghan was perfect, with her full pouty lips and big doe eyes. She had no idea how many guys I beat down over the years because they'd noticed her.

Can't say I blamed them. Naomi and Shelby had the whole sex kitten thing going on. But Harper… When she walked in, it didn't matter how many people were around her, she was the only girl in the room.

"You're the queen of blue balls, Baby," I whispered, and slid a little closer to graze the tip of my nose off hers. "If you knew what you did to me…"

My fingers tightened around her hip, pulling her in so I could inhale the contented sigh she let out. Her sweet taste kissed the edge of my mouth, lingering on my lips. Suddenly all I could think about was devouring more. And why shouldn't I take her now? Lou was constantly preaching how alcohol clouds your judgment. I could blame it on that.

"Your tongue is hot."

And just like that I sobered up.

What the fuck?

166

Rage boiled through my veins, spreading in hot waves as a flush tinted her cheeks.

Oh fuck no. I banged enough chicks to know that look. Whoever this motherfucker was, he just signed his death warrant. That was my goddamn dream to invade.

Harper giggled again, making me ball my fist.

She better cut that shit out right fucking now. All breathing heavy as if she was enjoying what that asshole was doing.

"Stop it."

I gritted my teeth and hissed, "That's right, stop it."

When she huffed out a quiet moan, I had to stop myself from slapping her. If I did that, then she'd wake up and I'd never find out who this prick was.

One breathy word was all it took to stop my thought process dead. "Mason."

Did she just say my name?

The corner of my mouth lifted at the flush crawling down her neck.

Yeah she did.

Almost immediately my muscles relaxed, letting go of all my tension and allowing me to settle back in the mattress and enjoy Harper's shuddered breaths. Each little moan, gasp and groan filled my chest with satisfaction.

I yawned and rolled over. "That's right, Freckles."

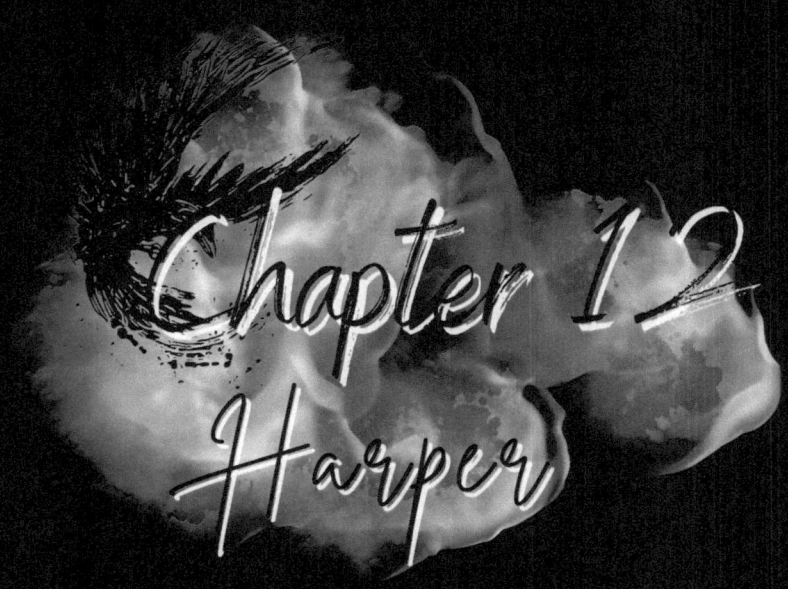

Chapter 12
Harper

Games were a part of childhood. We'd all gather together and play things like Red Rover, Tag and Hide-n-Seek, but my favorite was Red Light, Green Light. It wasn't the race across the room that I found addictive. It was having to instantly freeze when the person that was 'it' called out 'red light' and spun around.

Sometimes I'd get caught with my foot off the ground, or in another awkward position that was troublesome to hold. But I did it. I played statue better than the boys who were faster and stronger than me. That ability was one I never thought I'd use beyond the game. Yet here I was, laying in bed, perpetually stuck in red light mode.

Because Mason Kessler was laying beside me.

Having him around was normal. When he was in rehab I didn't know what to do with myself. It was weird not seeing him in school or around town. I missed those green eyes so much that I actually considered sneaking away to see him. But this…

This was too close.

Mason had his head thrown back on the pillow next to mine. I could feel the steady breaths that floated out of his open mouth. I didn't like it. I didn't like the faint hint of scotch tickling my nose. It made my heart stop every time he muttered or moved in the slightest.

At one point I even clamped my hand over my lips to quiet my own breathing. Scotch was Daddy's favorite. When I was little I'd sit on his lap and watch him sip on the amber liquid while wondering what it tasted like.

Back then that smell was comforting because it meant I was safe. Now that malted, smoky scent meant something else. Something that had me frozen in place beyond the fear of waking up the boy asleep beside me. Dealing with a monster was one thing. When he'd been ingesting the devil's nectar, bad things happened. The evidence of those bad things was what the sheriff asked to see.

I kept telling myself to get up and leave. Mason wasn't Daddy. He might be cruel, but he'd never hit me. Then he'd exhale and that scent would smack me back into stillness. There was a point when I thought Daddy wouldn't hit me either.

Accepting my fate, I let out a defeated huff and settled into the mattress. Maybe this wasn't so bad? At least I didn't have to worry about Mason waking up and accosting me. He might say something mean, but he certainly wouldn't touch me.

Like he didn't touch you in the bathroom?

My eyes slid along his right arm to the hand splayed out on his chest. Was that the one he used? Mason was left handed, not that anyone would be able to see that. The bulging muscle on his right bicep was just as hard and firm as the one on his dominant side. *He* was hard and firm.

The chiselled dips and grooves in his torso were testament to that. I always knew he was big, but I never imagined he was this big. It felt like I was laying next to a giant whose arms were thicker than my thighs.

I shouldn't be looking at him. It was wrong.

He's the one that climbed into your bed wearing next to nothing.

That was true. The only thing he had on was a pair of black boxer briefs. Not that I'd looked. He had... stuff in there. Stuff I didn't want to know about.

You sure about that?

Yes I was sure. *Wasn't I?*

Other than accidently walking in on Sean when he was changing, or seeing the swim team around school, I'd never really seen a guy's body. Would it really be so bad to take a peek? What kind of person laid down next to someone practically naked? Maybe he wanted me to look?

Next thing I knew, my gaze was drifting over the black rose inked into the side of his waist. His tanned skin was so smooth I couldn't help but wonder if it would feel soft. Would he feel warm pressed up against me? Would he wake up if I moved just a little...

No. Stop it!

I snapped my attention back to the flower on his side. That was much better to look at. There was nothing creepy about admiring the artistic beauty of a tattoo. And Mason had four that I could see.

A raven on the inside of his wrist, the rose, a white rabbit with broken ears and a gouged out eye socket, and under that, my name dripping blood. That didn't exactly bode well. Was the rabbit how Mason saw me? Or was that what he wanted to do to me?

Maybe that's what I did to him?

Apparently breaking him wasn't enough, I had to go and add gawking like a pervert to the list.

Say you're a bad person without saying you're a bad person.

Sighing, I tipped my chin to Mason's closed eyes. He looked so peaceful and serene that for a second I forgot about the monster I created and only saw the little boy I lost. I missed him. So much so that my chest ached when my hand lifted to reach out and sweep a lock of chestnut hair off his face.

I just wanted to touch him one last time. Feel the heat of his skin warm my hands like it used to when we were kids.

My hand stopped, so close that my fingers could almost graze his forehead.

We weren't kids anymore, and no amount of wishful thinking could fix what I did. The only fantasy I could hope for now was keeping the people I cared about safe. Meaning, no matter how desperately I wanted to reach out for that little boy, I couldn't. It was better if he stayed gone.

I quickly tucked my arm into my chest.

Mason didn't want me touching him anyways. He didn't want me near him. That much had been made perfectly clear over the years.

So, why was he here?

My brow cocked at the broad chest rhythmically rising and falling. Was this just another way to humiliate me? When Mason woke up he'd tell me how pathetic I was compared to the girl he was with last night.

It was probably Tiffany. Stupid Tiffany with her perfect smile and pretty face that boys always wanted to be around. It wasn't like I wanted the attention she got, but...

My eyes trickled over Mason's plump bottom lip.

"Would one kiss be so bad?"

My heart stopped dead in my chest when a green eye creaked open, pulling the room in around me as the lid slowly lifted.

Please tell me he didn't hear.

"Depends on where the kiss is."

I could feel the mortification pouring through me into my bones. Especially when Mason rolled his eyes my way.

"I wouldn't complain if you sucked my dick."

My jaw dropped. He did not just say that. I'm not sure why I was surprised. He was always saying stuff like that. Didn't mean anything. It was just another way to poke fun at me. When he reached down to slip his hand in his boxers, I thought I was going to die of embarrassment.

"What do you say, Freckles?" The way his bicep flexed as a soft groan escaped his lips was enough to make me shut my eyes tight. "Wanna help me get rid of this morning hard on?"

I whimpered and tried to press my body further into the mattress. Mason wouldn't really make me do anything, would he?

"Ugh," he grumbled. "You're fucking useless."

While I was a tad hurt, I was also thankful for the distinct slap of elastic hitting skin that told me he'd stopped doing what he was doing. At least I thought I was thankful? That day in the bathroom, I'd been too afraid to look, but a big part of me wondered what he would've looked like when he reached orgasm. Did it hurt in that moment? Did he like it? Did he like me?

"What the fuck are you doing in my room anyways?"

Guess not.

Confusion caused my eyes to flutter open as I whispered, "I-I'm not."

How much did he drink last night?

"Oh," Mason swung his eyes back to the headboard, then closed them and sighed. "Right."

A voice in the back of my head screamed at me to run away now, before he was fully alert. Unfortunately, my body refused to move. All I could do when he lifted his arms to fold his hands behind his head was lay there like a lump.

I just stayed there, staring at someone I shouldn't be, while praying that I'd be granted the use of my limbs. How sad was that? Couldn't even force myself to hide from danger.

I was useless.

I'm not sure if it was my internal fight that caused my body to shake, or the fear being pumped through me with every pounding heartbeat. But whatever it was, Mason noticed. This time when he opened his eyes there was a sparkle in them. A dark glint that grew as he slowly tugged the blanket off my quivering form.

"What's wrong, Freckles?" His deep voice vibrated through me. "You cold?"

I curled up in a ball and shook my head. Just when I didn't think things could get any worse, Mason rolled over and slapped his palm down on the mattress behind my back.

That scent of scotch hit me again when he leaned in and softly growled, "Are you scared?"

Yes. I was terrified. But it was the huskiness in his tone that allowed me to finally break free of my frozen hold and slip out from under him.

I sprang off the bed, declaring, "I need to brush my teeth."

His green eyes met mine for a fraction of a second before I spun around and rushed away.

The stupid thing was, the teeth thing wasn't an excuse. I was utterly mortified at the possibility of him smelling my morning breath. Just one more thing to prove how pathetic I was.

When I ran down the hall and closed the door behind me, I could've kissed the mosaic of skulls and roses tiled into the far right wall. I'd never been so happy to be in a bathroom in my life.

Sighing with relief, I clicked the lock in place and walked over to the closest of the two sinks.

It'd been two weeks since Mason brought me here and I was still surprised whenever I came into this room. Sean's was always a mess, with bottles strewn all over the counters, dirty clothes on the floor, and it smelled like socks. This one smelled clean and looked cleaner.

I could see my reflection in the white floors and black four claw tub. Even the glass walls on the shower were spotless. The roof–made up of one large showerhead–was clearly visible

RELAPSE

through them. That is, until someone clicked the door shut, then all the walls turned frosted.

I may have played with that for a bit when I discovered it. That would've looked great. I could just imagine what Mason would say if he walked in and saw me opening and closing the door.

A shiver ran up my spine as I reached out to turn the water on. The faucets in here were something I could do without. It seemed wrong to have a dark metal skull spew water on my hands.

Although, I suppose it was no more wrong than me being here in the first place. Or having the dream I did last night. I woke up all hot and sweaty and could still feel Mason's hands on me. Then looked over to find him actually there.

Everything about this was wrong.

The girl looking back at me in the mirror had her hair all up on end, as if she'd just been manhandled. And that tense feeling that I talked to Sean about was still there. Achingly taunting me whenever I walked.

I really wish he would've told me how to get rid of it. Shelby might've tried but she was talking so fast I only caught half of what she was saying. Maybe Lana would know?

Damnit, Lana!

I had to get my phone back. How, was the question? I highly doubted Mason would hand it over. That is, if he hadn't destroyed it already. I really hoped he didn't. Daddy was going to call in two days. If I didn't answer…

Suddenly I didn't feel so well.

"It'll be okay," I told myself.

Mason wouldn't destroy it because then he wouldn't be able to taunt me with it. It was odd how that one thought made me feel better. *Or sad.* Either way, I was able to relax enough to focus on my toothbrush, instead of what might or might not have happened.

Halfway through brushing my teeth the door flew open,

175

making me gag on the minty froth in my mouth as Mason strutted in.

Didn't I lock the door?

That thought fled faster than it came. Mason wasn't any more dressed than when I'd left him, and the part that I'd avoided looking at was very visible now. I couldn't look away from the large tent in his boxers.

Most people had some modesty and would cover up.

Not Mason Kessler. He walked in, proudly displaying his erection that bobbed with every step he took. It was kind of mesmerizing, the way that tent jostled up and down. Like a snake doing a dance. A very hard and large snake. How did anything that size fit inside of someone?

What if he wanted to put it inside of me?

I couldn't breathe. My lungs ceased all function, making me want to hunch over and cough. Somehow I managed to stay upright, but that one thought wouldn't leave my mind. I was small. I had to look up to see his shoulder. That thing would break me.

The sudden sound of Mason's voice caused me to squeak and jump back. "Is there a problem?"

"No," I quickly muttered around my toothbrush and snapped my attention back to the sink.

Of course there was a problem. Bathrooms were private spaces. He shouldn't be in here. What if I'd been doing something else? Oh my God, what if I'd been on the toilet?

I calmed down a bit when he walked past me and plucked a toothbrush out of a black cup next to the other sink. He was just here to brush his teeth, which as far as he knew, was what I was doing. There was nothing wrong with that.

I don't know what I was worried about. Of course Mason wouldn't try to do anything to me. The very notion was laughable. He hated me and guys didn't do that stuff with girls they hated. I really needed to stop overreacting.

My eyes shifted back over to Mason and that thing between his legs that was resting on the counter.

I was overreacting, right?

"Whatcha looking at, Freckles?"

Damnit.

"Nothing."

There was absolutely nothing to see in here. Except the sink. It was a nice sink. All shiny from water running down the black interior. Black? Just like his...

Nope... I'm not going to do it.

Shaking my head, I refocused on the ceramic bowl in front of me. Looking over there was not an option. Considering the mirror took up half the wall and covered both sinks, that was easier said than done.

Every time I looked up I could see that steel rod. It felt like it was staring at me through the fabric covering it. Why would he rest it on the counter? Maybe it got heavy? Sometimes my breasts did. I had a lot more than someone my size should, a fact that Lana was constantly reminding me about.

She claimed to be jealous of my cleavage, but she didn't know what she was asking for. My chest was always getting in the way and pulling on my bra, digging the straps into my shoulders. Maybe guys' members were the same? There were times when I'd like to rest my boobs, so...

My eyes wandered back over to Mason's side of the mirror.

Why shouldn't they?

"Keep eyeing my dick, Freckles, and you'll earn yourself an up close look."

And just like that, my curiosity melted away. The only thing I was concerned with now, was finishing up and getting out of there – which apparently I wasn't permitted to do.

Mason headed for the shower while stripping off what remained of his clothes, and I made a mad dash for the exit.

Almost made it, too. Had my hand on the knob and everything when his voice rang out.

"Where the fuck do you think you're going?"

Not wanting to risk looking over there, I hung my head. "Back to the room."

"Oh no you're not." His snicker hit my ears, mingling with the soft whirl of the shower door being pulled closed. "Take one step out that door and I'll drag your ass in here with me."

"But you're naked," I pointed out.

"I'm also hard as fuck." The warning in his tone was clear. "I wouldn't push my luck if I were you."

I don't know what came over me, but I couldn't stop myself from spinning around and snapping, "I'm not staying in here."

The frosted glass shield between us lasted about point two seconds. Next thing I knew, the door to the shower was pushed open and Mason's wet head appeared.

"What the fuck did you just say?"

Anger and hatred was something I was used to seeing in those bright green eyes. This was different. It was dark and threatening. An intense glare that told me one thing.

You just messed up.

Chapter 13
Harper

"I'm sorry," I muttered, while ducking my head and chewing on my lip.

The soft dig of my teeth helped ground me. It gave me something else to concentrate on other than the consequences of my stupidity. Don't talk back. Ever. It's not worth it.

Part of me hoped that Mason's grumbled 'uh huh' would be the end of it. It wasn't. If anything, things got worse. Because the next order he barked out caused my stomach to flip.

"Get the fuck in here."

No, no, no. I couldn't do that. I didn't want to be trapped in that tiny glass room. Alone. With him. A very, very naked him.

"I won't leave," I promised. "I'll stay right here."

There was a downside to staring at the floor. I wasn't able to judge his reaction and see if he believed me or not.

He didn't.

"You had your chance."

Even if I wanted to make my feet move, I wasn't sure I could. Nerves shook my entire body. So I tried another tactic.

"I'll get wet," I said, knowing it was a lame excuse.

"Like I give a shit," Mason barked back. "Now get the fuck over here before I lose my patience."

Out of options, I did as I was told and slowly made my way across the room. Forcing my feet to move was easier than I thought it would be. Perhaps that came from the years I spent trying to fly under Daddy's radar. Obedience wasn't an issue. Fear, however...

The louder the sound of trickling water got, the heaver my legs felt. Soon the thump, thump, thump, of anxiety ringing in my ears was all I could hear. It took a long time for me to learn how to avoid angering people, and I was good at it. Keep my head down, stay out of the way, and be quiet. Those three rules saved me more times than I could count.

But not this time.

The instant the white floor I had my eyes locked on met with the black tiles of the shower, my arm was grabbed and I was yanked into the confined space. Mason pulled me up against his solid form, making the glass walls seem much closer than they were. On instinct, my eyes shut.

Judging by the way he grabbed my chin, I assumed he didn't like that.

Mason gave my head a little shake. "Look at me."

I shook my head and squeezed my lids tighter closed. All I could feel beyond the dampness seeping into my clothes and heating up my skin, was his hardness digging into my diaphragm. A shiver ran down my spine when his hand wrapped around the back of my neck. It was terrifying how much bigger he was than me.

"Come on, Freckles," his voice purred down at me. "Let me see those pretty brown eyes."

Did he just call my eyes pretty?

Before I knew what was happening, my lashes fluttered open. That was a mistake. I couldn't look away from the way his dark wet hair stuck to his forehead. As if it was framing those bright green orbs I longed to save me from my torment.

When the darkness took over Daddy, I focused on those eyes and the things that might've been. Other people had the same color, but they weren't the same. Logan didn't have the twinkle Mason did, and Ryker...

I stopped and tipped my head, remembering the conversation Mason had with his father when he first brought me here. "Louis isn't your biological dad, is he?"

"Not that it's any business of yours..." I swallowed back a nervous lump when his gaze narrowed in on me. "But no, he's not."

Louis wasn't genetically Mason's father, and he cared more about him than mine did me. That hurt.

"At least you have a dad that loves you."

I wished I could take it back the second the words left my mouth. If Mason was eyeing me before, then he was completely zoned in on my face now.

"Why would you say something like that?" He tugged on the back of my neck, pulling me in closer when I tried to jar away. "Did Daddy do something to you?"

"No," I insisted, while silently cursing my stupidity. "My father loves me."

"Keep lying to me, Freckles, and I'll wash your mouth out with my cock."

To reiterate his point, Mason thrust his hip, grinding his hardness up against my ribs. My lips parted but nothing came out. All my mind could focus on was what something that size would do to my internal organs.

"You're small. It wouldn't take much." My pulse skyrocketed

when his fingers tightened, digging into my throat. "Just push your head down a bit…"

Freezing, I clamped my eyes and mouth shut. I waited for him to carry through with his threat. Water rained down, splashing off the floor and walls in echoing ticks that mingled with the fluttering in my chest. Each individual drop's slice through the air was so vivid, I could picture its path. Like time had slowed down around us.

Then it all stopped.

Mason pulled me away from him and sat me down in a dry corner on a bench.

Whether it was the click of the shower door or confusion that caused me to open my eyes, I didn't know. But there I sat, in the corner, staring at the back of a man I should be running away from. I didn't know what to do. Mason didn't seem mad or annoyed. If anything, he looked nonchalant. Casually lathering up his hair as if there wasn't someone in there watching him.

This wasn't the first time I was locked in a room. Daddy called it a time to reflect on my choices. Sometimes I did what he said and pondered over where I went wrong. Others, I imagined that my dad was a good man, and Mom was still alive. We'd go to picnics on the beach and music festivals at night.

The little boy and Lana would join us on occasion, and we'd all laugh into the wee hours of the morning. That was the place I wanted the white rabbit to take me. My wonderland. Where everyone was safe and happy endings never got torn away. A fairy tale where the prince and princess got to ride off into the sunset.

"Here," Mason thrust a soapy white loofa my way. "Make yourself useful and wash my back."

I'm not sure why I got up and walked over there, under the warm spray of the water. Nothing made sense anymore. I was avoiding my best friend. The sheriff was asking questions, and Mason took me from my house and brought me to his—for what?

To torment and humiliate me? Force answers out of me? I'd been here two weeks and he'd barely acknowledged me.

I slid the loofa across his skin and watched the muscles in his back twitch. He really was beautiful. Even his back called to me. A strange tingle surged through my belly when I reached up to wash his shoulder blades.

Our size difference was terrifying. But there was something else there. A spark settled deep inside. It was similar to the thrill one would get when they rode a rollercoaster, but a lot fainter. Did I like his body? Did he like mine? Did I want him too?

"Mason?"

"What?"

"Why did you put your finger inside me?" A better question was, why was I asking him this stuff in the first place?

"Why?" His shoulder jarred with a soft chuckle. "Scared I'm gonna fuck you?"

Yes.

"No."

Maybe?

He let out an annoyed sigh and shook his head. "There's that lying mouth again."

"I'm not–"

Mason cut me off before I could finish.

"Look, why don't you just save us all the trouble and tell me who the fuck hit you." He twisted his neck to look over his shoulder at me. "I'm gonna find out."

Scary thing was, I believed the determination on his face, which was what I should've been concerned with. Instead of trying to think of a way to steer him off that path, I stood there staring at the purple bruise on his jaw.

I didn't see it in the bed because I was facing the other side of his face. Now that angry mark glared back at me, making my ribs ache from the ghost of injuries that once were.

185

"What happened?" The question came out before I knew what was happening.

Mason's cold glare locked on mine. "I fell."

The physical hit from his statement knocked the air out of my lungs. My gut caved in as I stumbled back and collapsed on the bench. It hurt to have my excuse thrown back at me. Almost as much as it did to say it. I hated lying to Lana, but I took comfort in the fact that it was for her own good. Now all I could think about was if this was what she felt when I lied to her?

Was it what he felt?

"What's wrong, Freckles," the corner of Mason's mouth lifted in a smirk that was anything but playful. "Can't handle your own lie?"

The only thing that came out of my mouth was a stuttered, "I-I-I."

He was right. I couldn't handle my own lie. But I had to. I couldn't let anyone find out the truth. I'd been through so much to keep them safely away from Daddy. I couldn't give up now.

"You what?" Mason spun around and cocked a brow. "Were beat the fuck up by someone?"

My heart was pounding so hard that I had to clutch onto the bench to keep myself steady. "It was an accident."

After everything I'd done, it shouldn't be this hard to lie. Just say the words and move on. But the longer I stayed in this house, surrounded by judgemental glares, the harder it was to force the words out. Especially to him.

At school I could pretend that Mason was only angry with me, and went on with a happy life when I wasn't around. But he wasn't happy anywhere. He was snubbing his family, and arguing with Silas, while drinking himself into an early grave. I hadn't just destroyed the little boy, I crushed his soul.

"Oh, I see." He nodded and took a step closer. "So you accidently fell on someone's fist repeatedly?"

I was more worried about the determined glint on his face than

I was about his nakedness or what I might see. He wasn't going to back down, and I didn't know how to make him. He continued to advance. Taking long confident strides that I shimmied back on the bench to avoid.

When my back hit the wall, I whispered one word in panic. "Stairs."

"Are you talking about that big marble staircase in your house?" Slapping his palm down on the wall next to my head, Mason leaned in and added, "You know, the kind people die falling down."

What could I say? I tripped and only fell down a few steps? Somehow I didn't think he'd buy that. There was only one thing left to do.

Run.

A poor choice to make when one was trapped in a shower.

The wet man wasn't hard to slip past. I easily ducked under Mason's arm. The wet floor, however, posed a different challenge. My bare foot slapped down on the tile and immediately gave way to the slipperiness.

Mason's hand fisted in my hair as my legs flew out from under me. I barely had time to blink before he pulled me back and slammed my butt down, making me wince when the hard bench smacked against my tailbone.

"Trying to run from me, Freckles," he tsked. "I thought you knew better than that."

I thought I did too. But apparently my middle name for the day was stupid because I didn't sit still with my head down and keep quiet. I abandoned all three of my rules and lashed out. Throwing my arms wildly at him while kicking my feet when he tried to advance.

And God, did it feel good. The first slap I connected and the rake of my nails down his arm sent a surge of adrenaline coursing through me that I needed more of. It was freeing, empowering, and all consuming. I liked it far more than I should've.

Unfortunately, so did Mason.

"Yeah baby." He grabbed my chin and growled, "Fight me while I shove my cock down your throat."

My entire body instantly went stiff.

What?

His green eyes glittered at my shock. "That's right."

This couldn't be happening. It had to be a joke. Mason Kessler didn't want me that way. He was just messing with me because I was asking him questions. He was annoyed. That's all it was. I just had to apologize.

"I'm sorry."

Dread settled in when he cupped the bottom of my chin and lifted my head.

"I'm sick and tired of your fucking sorry's. Now open your goddamn mouth!"

Panic didn't fully hit me until his fingers dug into my cheeks, prying my jaw apart. I tried twisting my neck to pull my face out of his grasp while clawing at the arm holding me. That fight was more fruitless than the last.

Mason slammed my head back against the wall. "Keep it up and I'll take your ass instead."

Defeated, I tried to focus on something else. Like not hyper-ventilating when he stepped in and fisted his erection. It didn't matter. Whatever air I did manage to suck in was violently pushed out when Mason shoved his length through my held open mouth. It all happened so fast. One minute I was fighting him, the next his hardness was lodged in my throat.

"Fuck me." He let out a long, loud groan, then glared down into my watery eyes. "Your lying mouth is useful for something after all."

A few thoughts flew through my mind. Most of which were the usual fear filled feelings, except for one. A little voice in the back of my head commented on how silky his dick felt for being so hard. That one had me confused. Here I was, being forced to do something I didn't want, and some part of me liked the way he tasted on my tongue.

I really am pathetic.

That strange thought didn't matter the instant he thrust his hips, forcing more of this length down my throat. I couldn't breathe. Couldn't suck in the tiniest bit of oxygen. My chest tightened as I gagged around his girth and slapped his thighs. Mason didn't care. He just growled out another groan while holding me firmly where I was.

Blackness started to seep into my vision and I couldn't help but wonder if this was how I was going to die.

What would my tombstone say?

Here lies Harper.
So useless she couldn't even handle a dick.

Just when I thought all hope was lost, suddenly I could breathe again.

Mason pulled away and let go of my mouth, allowing me to hunch over and cough oxygen back into my body. My lungs burned with each staggered breath while my mind kept preparing me for when he did it again. But that's not what happened. What came next was completely unexpected.

He didn't force my mouth open, or say something vile about my pathetic nature. No. Mason reached down, threaded his fingers through my hair, and started stroking the back of my head in a mockingly tender gesture.

"Because I'm not a complete asshole, I'm going to give you a choice."

I begged to differ on the asshole part. Not that I'd ever tell him that. But I would say he was good with his hands. The tingling that his strong fingers were eliciting from my scalp was oddly relaxing. I almost leaned into his touch. It felt… nice.

"I can keep fucking your face…" He tugged on my hair, pulling my eyes up to his.

So much for nice.

"Or you can wrap those pouty pink lips around my cock yourself."

Should've known something like this was coming. Mason never made things easy. Why would he start now? How was I supposed to pick between those choices? One option I might suffocate from, and the other…

I was too afraid to look at his member. How was I supposed to touch it?

Come on Harper, you can do this.

Letting out a breath, I wiped the tears off my face and slowly pushed myself up. I wished I hadn't. Seeing it through a reflection in the mirror while being covered up by a pair of boxers was much different than being eye to eye with the thing. I wanted to duck away from the vein running down the side of his shaft.

It was big. Really big and angry looking, with a wet drop sliding down the tip. Much more intimidating than I thought.

"Well," Mason tapped his foot on the floor. "What's it going to be?"

I lifted my chin and sucked back a breath at the heat burning in his gaze. How many times had I wished he'd look at me like that? He really *did* want me to do this. I wasn't sure how to take that.

I eyed the smooth head staring at me. Maybe it wouldn't be that bad? I was probably over exaggerating the size. He did get it down my throat, after all.

Yeah, and almost suffocated you in the process.

That was true. But if I did it myself then that wouldn't happen again. Besides, it couldn't be that hard, right?

Curious, I gingerly reached out and touched the tip with my

finger, then immediately sprang back against the wall when it twitched like it was going to attack me.

Mason's brow arched. "Did you just boop my dick?"

"Um... maybe?" *That thing was scary.*

He rolled his eyes and scrubbed a hand down his face. "Alright Freckles, I'm getting impatient. So I'm gonna give you five minutes to make me come or I'll take over."

My eyes widened. "That's not fair!"

"Who said anything about fair?"

Not a surprising statement coming from him. My gaze dropped back down to his cock. Say I did what he asked, what would stop him from taking over regardless?

"If I do it, will you sit down?" At least then he couldn't thrust down my throat.

"No," he grumbled and lifted his hand to look at his watch. "Four minutes and forty-five seconds."

Well there goes that idea.

"But I don't know how to do this," I tried to argue.

He responded with, "You have four minutes and thirty seconds to figure it out."

It seemed like I didn't have a choice. So I slowly inched forward and forced myself to reach out and wrap my hand around his shaft. The throb under my fingers scared me away. It took a couple times for me to actually keep my hand there, which wasted another thirty seconds.

"Four minutes," Mason barked, reminding me of the timer ticking down.

I took a second to study my hand – which looked tiny in comparison. I couldn't even get the whole thing around it. There was a gap between my finger and thumb. And I was holding on tight, otherwise I might let go. My thumb was literally moving with the pulse in his shaft.

"Is it supposed to be this hard?"

"Do I look like I want to play twenty questions?"

No, he looked pissed off.

Alright.

I took a deep breath and mustered all the courage I had to suck the tip into my mouth. It wasn't that bad. I kind of liked the salty taste flittering across my tongue. The only question was, what did I do now?

While sliding my mouth further down Mason's shaft, I tried to remember conversations I'd heard Sean have with his friends. Benefits of having a whore for a brother. He liked to talk about his conquests in description.

'She sucked my cock so hard', led me to suck as I bobbed my head. *'That bitch had a tongue that could lap up a lake'* made me swirl mine, and his comment about some girl playing with his balls pulled my hand to gently cup Mason's.

All of which he seemed to like. Mason closed his eyes and threw his head back while letting out a soft groan of satisfaction. "Suck me harder."

Mason's hand threaded through my damp locks, guiding my head as I did what he asked. When he told me to stroke him with my hand, I did that too.

"Fuck." A deep growl emanated from his chest, vibrating through the moist air. "Good girl."

After that it didn't take long for me to fall into a rhythm. Every grunt and groan that I pulled from him sent a warm feeling through my chest. It took a second for me to realize what it was. Pride.

How long had it been since I'd done something right? It felt like forever. The feeling was addictive. I wanted more of it. I needed it more than I needed my next breath. Maybe that's why I rose up on my knees and tried to swallow him down my throat.

That didn't work.

I gagged the second his dick hit the back of my mouth. But the way Mason's hand tightened on the back of my head drove me to do it again. The more his face twisted in pleasure, the more proud I felt. I may fail at everything else in life—I was too afraid to stand up for myself, and I'd destroyed the people I loved. But this...

This I was good at.

I wanted to do it all the time.

"Jesus fuck," he growled and pushed me further down his cock. "Keep going Freckles, I'm gonna come."

Tears streamed down my face as I bobbed faster, taking him in deeper. Mason released a long guttural growl and slammed my head down. At first I thought he was going to suffocate me again, until I felt him twitch in my mouth. Then something salty covered my tongue. I choked and coughed, trying to spit it out. He didn't like that.

Mason pulled himself out of my mouth and clamped his hand firmly over my lips.

"Swallow it." There was more anger in his eyes than I'd ever seen before. "Right fucking now."

I obeyed and swallowed until there wasn't a drop left. The taste was still there, though.

He eyed me for a second before dropping his hand, which was when I smacked my lips together. While I enjoyed seeing the pleasure on his face, I could definitely do without the flavor of said pleasure.

"Open up."

The order was unnecessary, considering he stuck his hand in my mouth and pried my lips apart. I sat there trying to squirm away from his inspecting fingers swirling around my tongue and dipping in the corners of my mouth. Once he was done, he let me go and grabbed the towel hanging on the wall behind me.

I watched him dry off, wondering what I was supposed to do now? Did people just go about their day after? Or did they talk? Because I had questions.

Deciding to test the waters, I said, "That was really salty."

"You better get used to it," was the only response I got.

Not sure I'd never get used to that taste. Or the shame rushing through me. Did I really enjoy that, and with him of all people? I let Mason Kessler in my mouth. What was wrong with me? I hadn't even kissed anyone yet, and I let him do that.

"You have hair on your pussy."

Okay, that one caught me off guard.

"Umm… yeah?" Didn't everyone my age?

Mason wrapped the towel around his waist, then looked over at me. "Shave it off."

"Why?"

"Because I fucking said so!"

I jarred back from his barked out response. "Okay."

"Good." He lifted a hand and pointed his finger at me. "I'll be checking on that later."

Checking? What did he mean by that?

"Oh and Freckles," Mason opened the shower door, then paused to look back at me. "If you lie to me again, you'll get another mouthful of my salty come."

A heavy swallow bobbed down my throat. I knew I'd lie to him again, just like he did. I didn't have a choice.

Chapter 14
Mason

So far this day was off to a good start. Got my dick sucked, had steak and eggs for breakfast, and now I was lounging in one of the patio chairs out back while watching said dick sucker have a tea party with Maggie. Not that I necessarily wanted her that close to my little sister, but Maggie was excited to have a girl to play with. So I let it go.

That didn't mean I'd leave them alone. I didn't trust Harper. Even if she did suck the soul out of me a few hours ago. I never came so hard in my life. My knees damn near gave out from under me. For years I promised myself all I'd ever do was fantasize. Kind of ironic when I thought about it. I was pissed at Lou, my brother, and everyone else for hiding shit, and here I was, lying to myself.

I sat here with my eyes fixed on the table on the other side of the patio under the guise of protecting Maggie from deceitfulness. When all I could think about was how it'd take me five seconds to tear the royal blue jumper Harper was wearing to shreds.

Even the sun seemed to be against me. The way it beamed down, glittering off the water in the pool Lou recently had put in, seemed to highlight every inch of her exposed flash. My entire being was focused on her ample cleavage and smooth creamy thighs. That, and the voice in the back of my head reminding me of what she'd said in the shower.

At least you have a dad that loves you.

Harper may as well have pointed the finger at her old man with that statement. As much as I would love to kill Ned Callaghan, I wouldn't just yet. Assumptions were the mother of all fuck ups. For all I knew, he simply didn't like his daughter – which didn't exactly coincide with his doting daddy act. Then again, his daughter was a liar, so… Besides, I wanted to hear Harper say it. She owed me that.

"Mason," Maggie's sweet voice wafted across the pool. "Come play with us."

My eyes followed Harper as she bent over to scoop a stuffed animal off the ground. Her jumper rode up, giving me the smallest peek of the frilly edge of a pair of white panties.

Fucking white!

There was something insanely hot about a girl that pure wearing that color. And fuck me was she pure. I'd popped a few cherries in my time, but I'd never seen a virgin jump away like my dick was gonna bite them. Though in this case, there was a high probability of Harper getting bit. My dick didn't have teeth, but I did, and I'd have no problem marking up that perfect complexion of hers. I wanted to do it.

Would she fight me? Fuck I hoped so. I damn near bust a nut when Harper scratched me in the shower. I bet she'd cry when I sunk my teeth in her flesh. How hot would it be to lick the tears off her face while her blood stained my tongue?

"Mason?" Maggie called out, killing my hard on. "Are you ignoring me?"

I gave the little cockblock a smile and called back, "Would I do that?"

My gaze floated back over to Harper as she piled her hair on the top of her head and fanned the back of her neck.

Don't worry about that sweat, Freckles, I'll happily lick that shit off.

"You're doing it right now!"

Shit. I snapped my gaze back to Maggie, who was tapping her foot impatiently.

"No I'm not."

Her face screwed up in annoyance. "Then come play with us."

Should've seen that coming.

"Do you really want me to interrupt girl time?"

When her mouth tightened I thought she might argue with me, but instead she nodded and said, "You're right. Boys ruin everything."

Damn kid.

Ah, whatever. It was better if I stayed over here, away from temptation. Otherwise Maggie might see some shit she was way too young to see. I might have 'the talk' with her when she was thirty-five. Until then, I'd kill any motherfucker that tried to defile her innocence.

"Ugh, is she having another tea party?"

Speaking of defiling motherfuckers...

My glare zeroed in on Junior as he walked out the glass French doors to stand beside me. "Yes, she is. Now fuck off."

Don't get me wrong, I liked the little shit. But he spent way too much time with Maggie. Mind you, most of those times were against his will – the girl was a force to be reckoned with. But still.

"What's wrong, Mase," Junior returned my glare with one of his own. "Afraid I'm gonna steal your girlfriend?"

I couldn't stop the chuckle from bellowing out. Both from the confidence in his statement, and the fact that he called Harper my girlfriend. That'd be the day.

"First off, I don't do girlfriends, and secondly." My hand dismissively waved at him. "Get the fuck out of here with that shit."

He huffed and crossed his arms. "Bet I'd treat her better than you."

Who the fuck did he think he was? Don Juan? Uptight angry little prick's face might actually crack if he smiled.

"The scum on the bottom of my shoe treats her better than I do."

That statement should probably bother me, but it didn't.

"So what you're saying..." My eyes narrowed at the smirk curling the corner of his mouth. "Is she'd be easy to steal from you."

Was he serious with this shit?

"Have your balls even dropped yet?"

"Maybe Harper can find out," he shot back.

"Yeah," I snickered. "Good luck with that."

She was too afraid to touch me. There was a reason I told her to wash my back, yet the only thing I felt was the damn loofa. I should've put the soap in her hand.

Junior's dark eyes slid my way. "You don't think I can do it?"

"Fuck no," I snorted.

He was a twelve-year-old kid. I wasn't worried. Though part of me did respect the determination displayed on his face. Junior had more balls than most of the men I knew. The other part wanted to kill the little prick when he shot me a smile and skipped around the pool to join the tea party.

Maggie was happy to see him, of course. That wasn't what had me clutching onto the sides of my chair. Harper's mouth curled in the same bright smile I used to get. There was a time I'd have done anything to see her face light up like that. Was she trying to fuck with me, making me think about shit that was dead?

I watched her hand reach out to playfully tousle Junior's hair and I heard the chair creak as my fingers dug into the metal frame. And she didn't stop there. Harper let out a little chuckle and dropped her hand on his shoulder. Oh sure, she had no problem touching *him*.

To add insult to injury, the smug little prick wrapped his arms around her, laid his head on her shoulder, then looked right at me and smiled. I damn near jumped out of my chair. Luckily for him, Logan showed up.

"Damn," he clicked his tongue while strutting out to drop down on the lounger beside me. "Someone's angling for a beat down."

"It's fine." My eyes narrowed at the hand on my woman's back. "He's just a kid."

"I don't know, man." Logan tipped his blond head towards Harper, who was now giggling like a fucking school girl. "He's bigger than her."

Why did he have to point that out? Now all I could see when I looked over there was some suave dipshit with dark hair and a charming smile hitting on my girl. I get that Logan wasn't the kid's biggest fan, but did he want me to kill him?

Harper said something that looked an awful lot like *'you're so sweet'*, before kissing Junior's cheek.

No, she wanted me to kill him.

Logan chuckled. "Look at that player making the moves on your girl."

This mother...

"Is there a reason you're here?" I snarled.

"The girls went to the spa. So we decided to come hang with you."

Figures Shelby would be behind this. I was starting to think that girl liked pushing my buttons. Wait...

I cocked a brow at Logan. "We?"

My eyes rolled when he nodded at the person stepping out to join us.

Micha.

I should've known my brother was home when Junior showed up. Technically he was the kid's guardian, and a better parent than his mother had ever been. Who no one had seen since she signed over her parental rights. Couldn't help but wonder if Micha got rid of her. Junior should consider himself lucky. Most kids in his position barely made it through childhood. Who knows where he would be if he'd never stumbled across my brother.

Kind of like how you lucked out with Lou.

And just like that, I was pissed for an entirely different reason.

Micha tipped his head down at me.

"Mase."

I tipped my head up at him.

"Micha."

I could taste the tension in the air. We hadn't talked since the day I sucker punched him, or seen each other, for that matter. Micha was hiding out at Logan's place. At least that's what I assumed. I heard him say something to Lou about Riley not liking it here. That was a lame excuse, if you asked me.

My brother didn't let anyone tell him what to do, least of all his girl. If he wanted Riley here, then here is where she'd be. Whether she wanted to come or not. But hey, who was I to judge. There was nothing stopping me from going to Micha. Besides the pain that shot through my chest whenever I saw him, that is. That was easily remedied with a couple of shots though.

Micha hung his jacket off the top of the chair on the other side of me and sat down. I watched his arms flex under the red shirt he was wearing and wondered if Lou had any scotch left. I'd kill for a drink right now.

If Silas was here he'd say some shit about being the better man, but fuck that. That's what Micha was supposed to be for me. The better man who always had my back. Not another liar who hid the truth from me.

"What took you so long?" Logan asked Micha.

Micha rolled his dark eyes Logan's way. "Had to check in with the old man."

I couldn't help but snort at that.

"You got a problem, little brother?" His brow arched, darkening his glare. "Because I wasn't asking for your approval."

"Do you ever?" I shot back.

Micha's chest lifted with a heavy sigh. "And what, exactly, am I leaving you out of now?"

"I wouldn't know now, would I?"

Big brother didn't include me in his decisions. No one did. I was a Kessler by name and a Hudson by blood. The second born in both family lines – which inducted me into The Order, but didn't make me important enough to be consulted on anything. They could wrap their reasoning up under the guise of protection all they wanted, but I knew the truth.

"Is this about that shit I said to Harper?"

That got my attention. "When the fuck did you talk to Harper?"

"The first morning she was here," he explained, making me roll my eyes.

Of course he did.

"I can handle my own shit, Micha."

"I know you can."

Did he? Because everything in our past said the opposite. My brother didn't even trust me with my own genetic background.

"Look Mase," Micha scrubbed a hand down his face and sighed, "I was just trying to…"

Not wanting to talk about it, I cut him off. "It's fine."

My entire life I'd been dealing with shit on my own. I didn't need his help now.

"I'm sorry. I shouldn't have–"

"Seriously Micha." I slid my gaze his way. "It's fine."

I was tired of sorries. Tired of telling people it was fine. It wasn't fine. Micha knew that, but he let it go anyways. Letting out one last sigh, he laid back and turned his attention to the other side of the patio. Where Harper appeared to be instructing Maggie on the proper placement for a tea party.

Her tiny arm swung through the air, delicately repositioning things. My dick jumped at the way her fingers curled around the tiny flowered piece of China. All I could see was how those pink nails looked wrapped around my shaft. She was holding on so tight that it bordered on painful.

Micha cocked a confused brow. "What is she doing?"

"Having a tea party." *Duh.*

"Willingly?" Logan piped in.

To say he and Maggie didn't get along would be an understatement. That stemmed mostly from her uncanny ability to miraculously appear behind him with her swear jar every time he spewed out a cuss. I, however, thought her tactic was smart. Why wouldn't she follow the money? Every second word that left Logan's mouth was fuck.

"Fuck me."

And here we have exhibit A.

Logan sat up and rested his forearms on his thighs. "She's actually having fun?"

"She has a thing for Alice in Wonderland," I explained.

Micha grumbled, "That explains the rabbit tattoo."

Guess big brother didn't know everything after all. I had more than one rabbit tattoo.

"What is she? Five?" Logan snickered.

He had no idea. There was naive, and then there was whatever the fuck Harper was. I kind of liked it though. The way she looked up at me with her lips wrapped around my cock all full of fear and uncertainty was continuously playing in the back of my mind. I was getting hard just thinking about the way she meekly reached out with one finger.

"Good luck with that." Micha scoffed. "It's hard to break someone that naive."

"You're telling me." What kind of chick Harper's age hadn't at least peeked at porn. I wouldn't be surprised if she hadn't looked at her own pussy. She better not have done a shoddy job shaving that shit. "You ever have anyone boop your dick?"

Both Logan and Micha slowly turned their heads my way.

"What?" Micha asked.

"Okay, hold up," Logan lifted a finger in the air and made a motion like he was tapping a nose. "Are you talking like boop, booping?"

"Yeah."

"What the fuck?" He paused and looked up, pondering something, before adding, "Was it hot?"

So fucking hot.

I shrugged.

Logan grunted out a, "huh," then laid back down.

If I were a betting man, I'd say Shelby would be booping a dick before the day was done.

No sooner had the thought left my head than Logan jumped up and declared, "We should go get the girls."

Should've made that bet.

Micha cocked a brow. "They're not done yet."

"They will be when we get there."

Meaning Logan was going to drag Shelby out of whatever chair or mud bath she was in.

Despite not wanting to leave, Micha grumbled and pushed himself up. When Logan got something in his head, it was useless to argue with him. Not that I was complaining. I was more than happy to get away from my brother. And Junior, who flipped me off as he walked past.

Little shit.

Not too long after that, Cheyenne came and grabbed Maggie

for dance lessons. Leaving me alone with nothing to focus on. Except the redhead packing up the table. Harper now had her hair piled on the top of her head in a messy bun, allowing me to roll my eyes down the side of her throat.

My fingers tapped along with the hurried beat pulsing in the column of her neck. I could practically feel the fluttering of her fear under my palm. She knew I was watching her.

Every time her gaze shifted my way, a faint pink flush rushed across her cheeks. A nice tint that turned bright red when she realized that the teapot box was under the table. Down nice and low, in a place where she'd have to get on her hands and knees to reach.

Her eyes met mine.

Go on, Freckles.

Poor little thing was hesitant. She carefully peeked under the table before looking back at me.

That's right. Better get your ass down there.

I wasn't making it any easier on her. When Harper moved to duck down, I reached in my jeans and blatantly readjusted myself.

For a second I thought she was going to abandon her quest and walk away. But the sneaky little liar thought she could outsmart me. Harper tiptoed around to a side of the table where I couldn't see her disappear under the lacy pink cloth. Well, that wouldn't do.

I was up and over there before she could back out.

Let me just say, seeing some chick on porn crawling around wasn't anywhere near the turn on that this was. My dick hardened as Harper's legs slowly scuttled out, followed by a pert ass that I couldn't help but bend down and smack.

I'm not sure if it was the force of my hit that pushed Harper back under the table, causing the China to clatter, or if she jumped away on her own. But the squeal of shock that rang out shot right through my chest and into my dick. A few seconds later, a small hand gingerly lifted up the tablecloth.

Harper's lashes fluttered as she peeked out to roll her eyes. "I-I didn't see you there."

The only thing I wanted to do to that innocent look on her face, was defile it.

"Do you need something?"

Yeah I need something. You, naked and riding my dick.

My silence was obviously making her uncomfortable, so instead of answering I just cocked a brow.

"I have to finish cleaning up."

The only answer I gave was a further arching of my brow.

That's when she muttered, "umm..." and shifted her eyes around.

Was she looking for something to save her? Isn't that cute. What was I going to do to her? I had no clue, but I had a few ideas.

"Are you mad that I was ignoring you?"

What the fuck?

Half our lives were spent avoiding each other. There were so many other things that pissed me off. My brother. Lou. Her existence. The way she looked down there, all vulnerable and helpless. Out of all of those things, she decided to go with ignoring?

I shook my head. "Get out from under there."

'It's hard to break someone that naïve.'

While Micha had a point, Harper wasn't as innocent as he thought. She'd been taking beatings and keeping them secret for god knows how long. Not exactly the actions of someone innocent.

Neither was the way she slowly shuffled forward and shifted her body so I couldn't see her ass while she pulled herself up. Using the table for leverage, I might add. Harper was very careful about not touching me. Didn't have a problem touching Junior though.

Huh?

The first time in seven years that Harper slipped up was when I pulled her in the shower. My sweet little liar may be well versed at hiding her pain, but when it came to a naked man... she crumbled like a wet paper bag on a windy day. And that was something I'd happily use to my advantage.

"Put that shit down." I waved for Harper to follow me. "You're coming with me."

When she opened her mouth to argue, I bent over and scooped her up on my shoulder.

"Mason," she squealed. "I have to put the teapot down."

"Fuck the teapot." The damn thing could come with us for all I cared.

Chapter 15
Harper

*E*veryone had comfort items. Lana had her Troll dolls, Riley her art. I'd even seen Preston playing with little tin foil flowers. Books, stuffed rabbits and a picture of a little boy were a few of my items.

A teapot was something I never thought would end up on that list. Yet here I was, once again slung over Mason Kessler's shoulder while tightly gripping onto the handle. As if that tiny bit of porcelain could whisk me away from this nightmare.

While I didn't know where Mason was taking me or what was going to happen, I did know there were three blue flowers and four pink on the teapot. The blue ones had the smallest touch of yellow in them, and the pink had darker shades of the same color.

Both types were beautiful, but I preferred the one closest to the top. The chip missing from one of the petals told me how much this little dish was used.

"Maggie really loves this tea set."

"I think you have other things to worry about, Freckles," Mason growled while rounding a corner. "Why the fuck are you talking about a tea set?"

His logic was sound. The corridor Mason was walking down led to a set of stairs. And up there... my room. Was it weird that I thought about it as mine? I didn't have to think about that right then. Just like I didn't have to think about what he was going to do to me in that room. Not as long as I focused on the dish in my hand.

It was a pretty little thing, with a gold tip on the lid that glinted when we passed a light. Did her mother get it for her? Maybe her father did? I'd only seen Shelby's parents a couple of times, but they seemed like nice people. Shelby was crushed when her father died. When I saw her moping around school, I wanted to hug her. I didn't.

That would only encourage her to do something like show up at my house, and Daddy would have someone else to put on his radar. Star, I couldn't stop him from finding out about, but Shelby and Riley I kept safely tucked away. He didn't even know their names. Every time they'd text I'd tell him it was someone from school that needed help with an assignment.

If this tea-pot did come from Maggie's dad, it might be the last thing she had of him. Something so precious needed to be taken care of.

"Mason, please let me put this down."

He grumbled something inaudible then stomped up a step, making me slap my free hand down his back to clutch his shirt as I was jarred on his shoulder. On the upside, my bruises were healed so this ride didn't hurt as much as the last. But it was still uncomfortable.

"Please," I tried again.

"Drop it. Who gives a shit about a tea-pot."

"Maggie does." I quieted my tone when his shoulder twitched, tightening the muscle under me. *Don't poke the beast.* "She'd be disappointed if it broke."

"Oh for fuck sakes," he muttered.

Next thing I knew, my feet were placed back on the ground. It was seriously scary how easily he did that. Mason lifted me like I weighed nothing. I couldn't even see any labored breathing as I stared up at him, confused.

"What the fuck are you waiting for?" He swung his hand at a small table next to us. "Put it over there."

It took me a second to absorb the fact that he'd listened to my pleas. Was this real? Was Mason Kessler actually letting me do something I asked? Last week, when I wanted to go for a walk in the garden, he locked me in my room. *What world did I land in?*

"I don't have all day."

Mason clapped his hands in front of my face, spurring me to jerk back and rush over to the table. I ever so carefully placed the precious pot next to a vase of flowers. The instant my fingers were free, my wrist was seized and my arm yanked back as I was pulled away. Not sure why I was surprised. Patience was never Mason's strong suit. Still, I thought he might have given me a few seconds at least.

Even though I knew where he was dragging me, I asked, "Where are we going?"

"Shut up."

Geez, I thought guys were supposed to be in a better mood after having stuff done to them?

My eyes locked on Mason's back. Is that where we were going? Did he want me to put my mouth on him again? Because I couldn't do that. I shouldn't have done it in the first place. Not that I had much of a choice. That didn't make my reaction right.

"Can we go back outside? It's so nice out–"

He cut me off with a loudly snarled, "No."

I thought about tearing my arm out of his vice-like grip and running the other way. Even tried giving a tug once. That action ended the second Mason arched a brow over his shoulder. I needed to get away. I couldn't be alone with him. That's when I started to think about things I shouldn't. Like the way his butt looked in those jeans, or how his forearms flexed below the charcoal shirt rolled up past his elbows.

A spark of annoyance played across Mason's face when he glanced back at me. It was time for me to keep my head down and be quiet. Whatever was coming would be over soon. He was probably just going to push me in my room and leave. That I could deal with. In this house, I preferred the solitude.

That's not what happened.

Mason didn't stop to open the door to the room I'd grown comfortable being in. He tugged me down the hall towards another. One I hadn't seen the inside of.

My footsteps slowed down, stretching my held arm out as I stared back the way we came.

One rough yank had me tripping over my own feet to keep up with the man leading me. Even that couldn't make me look away from that brass doorknob. I longed to feel the metal cool my palm. I wanted to escape into that room and wrap myself in its familiarity. I knew what to expect in those walls.

That fantasy was ripped away when I was yanked in front of Mason to stare at a skull etched into a doorhandle. A shiver raced up my spine as he plucked a key out of his pocket. As far as I knew, this was the den of death, where I'd be trapped inside and forgotten in the dark.

The soft click of a lock opening thundered through my ears like a stampede. I could feel my heart sink as the door swung. It felt like the whoosh of air toying with my hair was going to blow me over, but that could've been the fear weakening my knees.

"Go on," was the only warning I got.

One quick shove of my shoulder jarred me across the precipice of no return. The first thing I noticed was the smell. Crisp and fresh with a hint of oak. A lot like the air outside, which is what I assumed it was when a breeze cooled my skin. That's when I realized that my eyes were closed.

I told myself to open them so I could look around and see my fate. But the sound of the lock being slid back into place weighed my already heavy lids down. Mason moved around and I stayed where I was. Listening to his footsteps echo while my body trembled with fear. The bunny was out in the open, locked in the den with the lion.

If I open my eyes then I might find someplace to hide.

That thought sounded so comforting that my left eye creaked open. As soon as I saw where I was standing, the left followed suit. The black marble flooring beneath my feet spanned across the entire room, then flowed up the bottom part of cream colored walls. I looked over to the left where sheer white curtains were billowing from the breeze blowing in through two large open glass doors. Beyond those was what appeared to be a balcony with two cast iron chairs and a table.

On the other side was a fireplace encased in the same marble as the floor, with a large TV hung above. My eyes swung from the soft cream rug in front of the fireplace to a black leather bound chair in the corner, next to a cherrywood shelf. I couldn't help but notice the book on the top. *Alice In Wonderland.*

Mason sauntered over to the raised part of the floor in the middle of the room. My pulse picked up as he stepped up to a large circular bed and sat down. The bed itself looked soft, with lots of pillows, black sheets, and a cream blanket. It was a stark contrast to the punching bag hung beside it. Just like the man sitting on the edge of the mattress.

I couldn't help but ask, "Is this your room?"

The hardened glare he shot my way caused me to take a step back. I was going to assume that this was indeed his room, which broke my heart. The little boy I knew would never sleep in a place like this. Sure, there were personal touches in here. A little blue pillow on the chair and an antique candelabra that had been repurposed as a chandelier – but they were all sharp and cold.

Like how I made him.

Mason dropped his elbows on his thighs and gave a small wave, "Come here."

"Why?" Being around Mason on a normal day wasn't a good idea, but adding a bed in the mix meant something else entirely.

His green eyes locked on mine and I could practically hear him say, 'because I fucking said so.' I couldn't escape out the door – that was locked. That didn't mean I couldn't hide. The wardrobe looked big enough for me to shimmy into. Or I could go for the door on the other side of the room, which I assumed led to the bathroom.

"You want to play a little hunter-prey, I'm game." The smirk that curled his lip was anything but playful. "But I might get a little too excited."

I'd seen Mason angry, pissed off, and pissed off while lustful. My aching jaw was a stark reminder of that. Wasn't sure I wanted to add excited to that.

"Now, Freckles!"

My feet were moving before he could finish speaking my nickname. Unfortunately they weren't taking me away from danger, but closer to it. I stopped at the bottom of the two steps leading to the bed and stared at the floor.

"What are you going to do?"

"I'm not going to do anything. You are."

My wide eyes snapped back to the man leering down at me. What did that mean, *I was*?

"Now come here," he growled, while pointing at the spot between his open legs.

If I went along with what he said, then maybe I could trick

myself into believing that this was just another day. Another time Mason Kessler would get his kicks by humiliating me. The unfamiliar and I weren't friends. Survival depended on knowing what was coming next. But as much as I tried to fool myself, this wasn't normal behavior. I had no idea what was going to happen, and that was utterly horrifying.

Panic had me spinning on my heels to run away, but Mason caught me before I could take a step. He grabbed my arm and roughly yanked me in between his legs, bringing me face to face with the beast. And I meant beast. The darkness twinkling in his bright jade eyes stole my breath. I stood there staring back at a man who was so much bigger and stronger than me that we were the same height when he was sitting.

"There." Mason's expression softened a touch. "That wasn't so hard, now was it."

"I guess not." My trembling body would disagree.

"Alright," he leaned back, placing his palms flat on the bed behind him. "Now we can get down to business."

I wasn't sure I liked the sound of that.

"Take off my shirt."

Yep, definitely didn't like it.

I stared at the black buttons on his shirt that seemed to get bigger every time his chest expanded. The voice in my head mingled with the fresh citrus scent filling my nostrils. Every breath Mason took brought a new taunt.

Inhale.

Come on.

Exhale.

Just pop one open.

Inhale.

You know you want to.

"I can't."

Mason Kessler was a sculpted god with dark hair, and I was

just a sad little girl who wanted to hide from the world. It hurt to look at him. How was I supposed to touch him?

"Is there a problem?" Mason tipped his head and narrowed his glare. "You don't seem to have an issue putting your hands on someone else."

My nose scrunched up.

What was he talking about? I'd never put my hands on anyone, which I would've pointed out if he didn't look so angry. His scowl was so embedded that the lines on his forehead darkened his entire face, and I couldn't help but notice the way his fingers pressed down, digging into the mattress.

"Are you fucking deaf!" Mason barked. "Take my goddamn shirt off!"

My hands shot out, going for his shirt. It was a lot harder than it should've been to pop a button through a hole. My shaky fingers kept jerking away. Mason's impatient huffs weren't helping any. But after a few attempts, I finally managed to pop the first one open. I worked my way down to the second and third. By the time I got to the last one, pushing that small round button open was as easy as pie. I clicked it through the fabric with confidence and pride.

Then his shirt fell open and once again I was trapped in red light mode.

Nothing in my life was more intimidating than those solid planes of tanned skin. I wanted to bypass the chiselled lines in Mason's torso and curl up with the broken bunny over his heart. Even the six pack in his abdomen was clearly visible, despite the fact that he was sitting down.

Would he notice if I slowly backed away?

"My shirt's still on, Freckles."

Guess so.

"Um…" My eyes swung from one broad shoulder to the other, trying to figure out how to carefully remove the fabric from his frame. I wanted to touch him – my hands were twitching at the thought of gliding over his smooth skin – but I couldn't make my arms move.

"Fuck this," Mason growled while snatching a handful of my hair. "If you won't touch me, then I'll touch you."

I slapped my hands down on his chest and cried out, "No…"

One word was as far as I got. My mind checked out the second my palms made contact. *Oh my.* He really was as firm as he looked. And warm, and smooth. Did he always smell this good? Because I couldn't get enough of it. I wanted to soak up every inch of him.

Leaning in, I slid my hands down to the firm ridges of Mason's six pack. I didn't care about the fist tugging on my scalp, or the nose running up the side of my neck. I kind of liked the tingle it caused to shoot up my thighs. That was nothing compared to the primal grunt Mason breathed across the shell of my ear.

A shiver wracked through my body when his tongue laved a hot wet trail up the column of my throat. "I should fuck you right now."

The very thought of him trying to put that thing inside me made me whimper. Yet I couldn't pull my hands away. It felt nice to be this close to someone. Was I so starved for affection that I'd take it from anyone? Including him.

This was wrong.

The man that I had my hands on was the same boy I'd destroyed. I needed to get away from him before I destroyed what was left of his soul, so I did the only thing I could think of. I shoved Mason back, then swung my hand through the air.

The second I saw the corner of his mouth curl, I knew I'd made a mistake.

Chapter 16

Mason

Most of my life I'd been dreaming about this girl. How it would feel to have her struggle underneath me. The bite of her claws as I held her down, and the sweet taste of her tears got me through more nights than any drink or drug out there. None of those fantasies came close to the real thing. When Harper pressed her tiny palms against my chest, I felt her touch sink into my soul.

I wanted more. I needed to feel her curious fingers roam over every inch of my body while I soaked up her pure scent. The only thing I could think about in that moment was killing any mother-fucker she'd laid her hands on. Including that little prick, Junior.

Then she slapped me.

The sweet sting searing across my cheek snapped the darkness inside me to the forefront of my mind. Her tender little pokes and prods weren't enough to feed that beast. He wanted fear and blood, and I was more than happy to give it to him.

The corner of my mouth lifted when Harper's big doe eyes rounded with fear.

"I thought we were having a moment, Freckles," I tsked, then leaned in to growl, "but if you want to play rough, I'm game."

A single tear slipped from the corner of her eye.

"Mason –"

My fist twisted in her hair, cutting her off by pulling tightly on the soft locks until she released an anguished cry that had my dick jumping. Was I a sick fuck for getting off on her misery? Probably. But I was spawned by one, so why not go with it.

"Please," she cried out while clutching onto my arm in an attempt to relieve some of the tension I was putting on her scalp. "I'm sorry."

The dark chuckle that vibrated from my chest echoed around the room.

"You have no idea what sorry is." I yanked her forward, pressing her nose against mine. "But you're about to find out."

I felt some of her strands tear free as I lifted Harper up and slammed her down on the bed. Two seconds later I'd ripped open the front of her jumper, sending buttons flying around the room. The quiet little tinks rang through my ears, mingling with her squeal. My eyes were locked on the firm creamy mounds covered in white lace. I couldn't stop myself from bending down and sinking my teeth into one.

Harper screamed and lashed out. Slapping my head and tugging my hair. But I was too far gone to give a shit about her useless struggle. Nothing on God's green earth could pull me away from the delicious taste of her blood. I greedily laved at the mark and groaned as nirvana flowed across my tongue, lighting up every nerve in my body.

I'm not sure how or when my mouth slammed down on hers. All I remember was wondering how she would taste in other places, next thing I knew my lips were moving against hers. Well, my lips were moving. Harper had gone stiff, which pissed me off.

"Open your fucking mouth," I growled, while reaching up to pry her jaw apart.

She whimpered, but gave in when my tongue wrapped around hers. Harper was tentative at first, carefully trying to mimic the movements I was making, which was hot as fuck. It was obvious that she'd never kissed anyone before and knowing that I was the only man to have his mouth on her did something to me. Something primal took over, making me grab her wrists and slam them down on the bed while I pressed in to deepen the kiss.

Fuck she tasted good. The warm buzz lingering in the back of my throat with every tiny little sound she made was more addictive than alcohol. My cock ached at the heat of her breath on my mouth. I'd happily stay there inhaling every fiber until there was nothing left. But I hated her at the same time. I wanted to watch Harper cry out in pain while I crushed her heart in my hands.

I needed to destroy her. But I couldn't pull my mouth away from hers. Couldn't stop tingles from traveling down my spine every time her tongue swept over mine. I tried to tell myself that it was just a kiss and wouldn't go any further. Then I wedged my knee between her thighs.

The heat from her pussy burning through my jeans. She was turned on! I wasn't the only twisted fuck here. Innocent little timid Harper got off on this shit. Suddenly it felt like I was wearing too many clothes.

I pulled back and tore my open shirt off, which I wouldn't have had to do if she'd fucking listened to me.

The second I let her go, Harper scuttled back.

I tsked and grabbed her ankle.

"Where the fuck do you think you're going, Freckles?" She was wearing too many clothes too. "We're not even close to done."

She flipped over and kicked out when I reached for her jumper. "Get away from me."

"Not a fucking chance," I growled and pulled her back down the mattress.

Harper flopped her body this way and that. It was kind of annoying. Squirmy little thing was hard to hold onto. Her ankle kept slipping out of my grasp. Her clothes, however... I had that shit pulled down her hips and off her legs in thirty seconds flat.

That's when her struggle really picked up. She clambered across the bed while kicking her feet back at me, and I'd never had more fun in my life. I sprang forward, pouncing on Harper before she could get too far away. We could play a little hide 'n' seek another day. Right now, I had other things in mind. Like how loud she's scream when I bit down on her clit.

"No!" Harper cried out when I clamped down on the back of her neck and pressed her face into the bed. "Stop Mason, I don't want to do this."

Stop. There was something about that word that got me hard. Especially when it came from her.

"I could give a fuck what you want."

The crack from my hand landing on her ass was so enticing that I did it again. This time pausing to give that firm globe a squeeze. Harper winced and stilled, but not completely. Thank fuck. Now that'd I'd seen this side of her, I was over the possum bullshit.

Though I did appreciate the fact that she'd calmed enough for me to enjoy the white fabric covering her ass. They were pretty standard, with just a touch of frill on the seams. But to me those panties were the hottest thing I'd ever seen.

I smoothed my hand over her left cheek and groaned, "Did you do what I asked?"

The flush crawling down across her cheek was all the answer I needed. Still, it was better to be safe than sorry.

Keeping my grip on her neck, I flipped Harper over and shoved my other hand down her panties. She tried to keep me out by clamping her legs together and tugging on my arm, but I was a determined motherfucker.

I forced my way between her thighs and slid a finger through her silky folds. Her wetness coated my skin, making me groan. She was fucking soaked, and so wound up that her entire body twitched when I flicked her clit.

"You like that, Freckles?" I asked while doing it again.

Harper answered me by slapping her hands over her face and shaking her head. I felt the smirk spread across my face. That was the response I was waiting for.

"Did you just lie to me again?" Spearing my fingers in her hair, I lifted her upper body off the bed, bringing her face to my groin. "You know what to do."

When I told her that she'd get another mouthful of come the next time she lied to me, I wasn't kidding. That didn't mean she'd listen. Harper jerked back, trying to twist out of my grasp. One firm pinch of her clit stopped that shit cold.

She flew forward and pressed her face against my groin while crying out, "Please stop."

I watched tears drip down her cheeks as her legs kicked from the pain and considered telling her to go fuck herself. But that would accomplish nothing. Besides, why would I want her to fuck herself when I'd do a much better job.

"I'll stop when you start." I tipped a brow down at her pleading gaze. "Make me wait too long and I might decide to use my teeth instead."

That got her going. Harper's fingers shot up and began unbuckling my belt. I eased up on my pinch just a bit. Not enough to stop the pain, but enough that she could concentrate on what she was doing. It seemed to take forever for her to open my jeans. I felt every tick, tick, tick of the zipper sliding open in my dick.

When it finally sprang free, I didn't waste any time. I tugged on Harper's hair, sliding her hot mouth down my shaft. Fuck that felt good. If struck down right now, I'd die a happy man. But not before I was done.

I tightened my grip, controlling the mouth swallowing my cock while I slid my finger through Harper's tempting pussy. It didn't take much to pull a moan out of her. A few flicks and swirls had her ecstasy vibrating through my shaft.

"Fuck me," I grunted when the tip of my dick hit the back of her throat and she gagged. "You're such a good little cock slut."

Harper whimpered and I couldn't help but notice the gush of moisture washing over my hand. Did Freckles have a praise kink? This was gonna be fun.

I stroked the back of her head and purred down at her. "You like that, good girl?"

She wriggled her hips and tried to shy away from my touch. She wasn't going anywhere. I pressed the tip of my finger in her opening and shoved her head down, forcing her to take more of my length. Harper choked and sputtered, but I held her there, enjoying the way her throat pulsed around me while her pussy fluttered.

Her orgasm was almost there. A few more flicks, then I could watch her fly over the edge. At least that was my plan, but when I pressed down on her clit, Harper jumped back.

"Stop," she shook her head. "Something's wrong."

Aw, isn't that cute. Poor little thing was afraid of her own orgasm.

"Did I tell you to stop sucking my dick?" I grabbed the top of her head and growled, "Get your fucking mouth back on there."

She did it, reluctantly mind you, but Harper obeyed and sucked me back into her mouth. Not like I'd have given her a choice. If I had to hold her mouth open again I would. Right now though, I was more interested in holding another part of her still.

Folding over Harper's small body, I clamped my hand down on

her hip and continued working her clit. Let me just say, seeing her cry didn't have shit on watching her come. Her body seized, bowing her back as she called out my name.

"Fuck," I growled and flipped her onto her back to bury my face between her thighs.

No taste in the world compared to that first swipe of my tongue. Unfortunately her panties were in my way. I made quick work of those, despite her feeble attempts to fight me off. After that I was lost. Harper fought. Smacked her hands on my head while trying to wriggle away. But I just dug my fingers into her ass and continued feasting on her sweet nectar. She was going fucking to come for me again. Even if I had to drag it out kicking and screaming.

Which is exactly what I did.

Harper threw her head back and screamed, "Oh my god."

Fuck that.

I rose to my knees and watched her body twitch with after-shocks while I stroked my shaft. God could fuck right off. This shit was mine, and I was going to prove it right fucking now. A heavy groan escaped my lips as I slid my cock through her folds.

Harper instantly stilled. "What are you doing?"

"Shut the fuck up." I slapped my hand over her mouth and lined up with her entrance. "If you move, I'll fuck you."

The fear sparking through her wide eyes was all I needed. Every muscle in my body tensed as I shot my load inside her. Each wave of come pulsing through my cock darkened my vision, until I couldn't see anything but the white spots of bliss fogging my mind.

When I finally came back down, I stared at my seed leaking out of the prettiest pussy on the planet and realized my mistake. While I didn't fuck her, I did cross yet another line I'd given myself. And I didn't think I could go back.

I'm fucked now.

Chapter 17
Harper

"Stop squirming." Mason tightened his arm around me and growled, "It's fucking annoying."

It wasn't my fault he was insatiable. Not only did he make me put my mouth on him twice more, but he kept touching me. No matter which way I wriggled, I couldn't find relief from the achy soreness tearing through my body. Talk about annoying.

"It's uncomfortable," I whined while shifting my butt down the bed.

Apparently Mason didn't like that.

"Too bad." He slapped my butt and pulled me back into him. "I thought chicks liked cuddling."

Maybe, but with him it was just weird. Usually when Mason Kessler was this close, it was to taunt me. Not for... Comfort? My natural reaction was to try and get away, which, considering his forearm was almost as thick as my chest, seemed like an impossibility.

I huffed out a sigh and shifted my head on the pillow to look up at Mason's closed lids. He seemed pretty content. Maybe I should give in and go with it? I did feel oddly safe wrapped in his arms. Kinda of like I was wrapped up in a hard, protective cocoon of warmth.

What, no! Mason Kessler is not a white knight who's going to save you!

What was I thinking? I wasn't safe here. I wasn't safe anywhere, especially with him. The only question was how did I get away? Mason was pretty determined to keep me here. The sun set hours ago and yet we were still in his bed. He wouldn't even take a break to go down for dinner…

My brow rose.

Could it be that easy? Only one way to find out.

"Mason, I'm hungry."

Hope sparked when he lifted his lids, then soared when he sighed. "Alright. I guess we did skip dinner."

He unfurled his arms from around me and pushed off the bed. I did a silent fist pump and watched him strut over to the dresser, where I assumed he was going to get some clothes. He couldn't exactly go downstairs in front of everyone wearing nothing but grey sweats.

I was so excited I almost tore his charcoal shirt off my body to hand to him. But seeing as it was the only thing he let me put on, I'd be naked if I handed it over. That proved to be a good choice, because Mason wasn't rummaging around for clothes.

Confusion furrowed my brows when he spun around. There was no cloth in his hands, just two foil wrapped bars. One of which he tossed on the bed for me.

"Here."

I stared down at the words on the brown and tan wrapping. *Aunt Mae's Caramel Protein Bar made with all natural ingredients.* This was what he wanted me to eat?

Mason flopped back down on the bed and clicked on the TV while kicking his feet up. He appeared to be enjoying this. There was a second one sitting on his lap. I guess I couldn't complain. At least he didn't pull me back into 'cuddle'.

Ah well, when in Rome.

The scent was the first thing to hit me when I tore open the foil. Caramel should not smell like this. Maybe ass, but not caramel. I officially knew what ass smelled like. Did I really want to know what it tasted like?

"Is something wrong?"

Yes there was something wrong. My head cocked at the tiny piece Mason had left of his. Did he eat this stuff all the time? How did his breath smell so fresh?

He tipped his chin at me. "You gonna eat that?"

If I didn't, how long would I be able to keep this shirt on?

"Of course I am." I gave him a smile, then chomped down on the bar.

Or at least I tried to. The thing was made of rubber. I had to pull it back and forth while grinding my teeth just to tear the smallest chunk off. And let me just say, the reward was not worth the effort. It took everything in me to hold back my gag. Clearly Aunt Mae had never had caramel in her life.

And now I know what ass tastes like.

The second Mason turned his attention to the TV, I spat it back into the foil and pushed the piece down. I didn't want to hurt his feelings, but maybe in this case honesty was the best policy.

"This is kinda hard to chew," I said, while gingerly setting the bar down.

"Really?" This time it was his nose that scrunched up. "I don't find them hard to chew."

That's because your teeth are made of metal.

I had the mark on my left breast to prove it.

"Here." Without even looking, Mason pulled open the drawer on the bedside table and plucked another bar out. "Try this one."

This bar had black and white wrapping and said cookies and cream. I was terrified to find out what Aunt Mae thought that would taste like.

"That one's too sweet for me, so if you don't like it I think I got some peanut butter ones left."

How many of these things did he have? Were they just randomly stashed around his room? Why on earth, out of all the things he could hide away, would he choose this? And what was wrong with real food? Pizza, salad, heck I'd take a cheese sandwich over this and I was lactose intolerant.

Sighing, I scooped up the new bar. May as well get it over with. Besides, Mason did say it was sweet, and sweet was good, right? Wrong. While this one was easier to chew, it had the consistency and flavor of chalk. Where was the sweet?

Mason cocked a brow. "Well?"

I didn't want to disappoint him. So I smiled, said, "Mmm, so good," then forced it down my throat.

The thing hit my belly with the weight of a lead balloon. I could feel it in there, swirling around. But Mason seemed pleased so I took another bite, then another after that. His smile somehow made it taste better. Before I knew it, I'd eaten the whole thing, and I instantly regretted it. I'd never been so full in my life.

Mason chuckled when I groaned and laid back down. "A little full there, Freckles?"

A little was an understatement. It felt like my stomach was going to explode.

"How did you eat two of those?"

He shrugged. "I burn a lot of calories."

His statement drew my attention to the punching bag. It was obviously used a lot. In some places I could see his knuckle marks on the canvas. I understood why he had one. Everyone in

Ashworth knew about Mason's proclivity to fight. But there was one thing I didn't get...

"Why do you have that next to your bed?"

"It's easier than trying to find something to hit in the dark."

That was a strange response. "Why would you want to hit anything?"

"Because it's fun, Freckles." Mason released an annoyed huff and turned his attention back to the TV. "You should try it sometime."

Was that why Daddy hit me? Did he get some sort of enjoyment out of it? Because it didn't seem like he did. He was just angry, or frustrated, or disappointed. Daddy was always disappointed. If he knew what I had done with Mason...

Proper girls don't look at boys, Harper. They keep themselves pure until marriage and obey their husbands.

I shouldn't have done that. I shouldn't have let Mason touch me. I was stupid, naive, foolish and everything else Daddy said I was. A useless little girl that couldn't even listen to one rule. Stay out of his office...

I GIGGLED *and skipped across the wooden floor. The shadows dancing on the walls kept trying to reach out and grab me, but I was quicker. I swirled around one black tendril, then hopped over another. Then, when one tried to sneak up to the roof, I did what Mason taught me and flicked on my flashlight sending it back to the dark underworld where it came from.*

"I'm the greatest shadow vanquisher," I called out and rushed down the hall.

I'd never been up this late and was a little scared to come out of my room – monsters liked to eat things when it was dark – but I forgot to tell Momma about the beach tomorrow. Mason had a surprise for me and said I had to get there at twelve pm sharp or it would be ruined. So I had to tell Momma before she went to bed, otherwise we'd be late.

And wives were never late for appointments with their husbands.

Her room was the first place I checked, but she wasn't there. Now I'd come down here because Sean said that sometimes Daddy and Momma had 'special time' in his office. It couldn't be that special if we weren't there. Parents never did anything fun without their kids.

"Please Ned..."

Oo there's Momma.

"I won't say a thing. I swear."

My nose scrunched at Daddy's office door. Why would Momma say that? She's the one that told me secrets were bad. Maybe this one wasn't? Mason and I had secrets and none of those were bad, but I still told her about them. That way Mason and I could still keep them quiet, but they weren't a secret.

"Why were you talking to Dean Whitley today?"

Daddy sounded mad.

"I just ran into him downtown –" Momma tried to explain, but Daddy cut her off.

"Enough!"

I jumped back a little. He was really mad.

"I've worked too long for this to let you fuck it up, Ivy!"

That was a bad word. I wish I had my swear jar.

I heard something smash on the floor, then what sounded like a slap.

"Please Ned," Momma pleaded, "I love you."

It went quiet, but if I listened really hard I could hear someone crying. Was it Momma? Daddy shouldn't make her cry. Even if she did break something. I had to help her. That's what Mason would do. He'd barge right in there and save the person crying.

I puffed my chest out, rolled my shoulders back and pushed the door open. "Leave Momma alone!"

My feet instantly froze. Momma was laying on the floor next to a broken lamp, and sitting on top of her was Daddy. His hands were *around her neck, squeezing so hard her eyes were bulging out of her head.*

I couldn't move. Not even when Momma turned her strangled face my way and croaked out, "Harper, run."

"HARPER, CALM DOWN."

No, I couldn't. I had to listen to her this time and run. I threw my hands out, lashing out at the man who was going to hurt me. Who hurt her. Angry brown eyes glared down at me. The same eyes that used to hold warmth and lovingly tuck me into bed. Why was he hurting me? What did I do?

"I'm sorry," I cried while kicking him in the shin. "I didn't mean to go into your office."

"God damnit!"

It wasn't until I was slammed back on something soft that I realized the eyes staring down at me weren't brown. They were green. I wasn't seven-years-old, and this wasn't Daddy's office. It was Mason's room.

My heart broke when he smiled down at me and whispered, "Hey, it's okay."

There he was. The green-eyed little boy. I missed him so much that I couldn't stop myself from throwing my arms around him. Mason didn't say a thing. He just held me and let me cry into his chest. I silently let go of everything. All the misery and anguish. The solitude, lies and heartbreak all came out in those tears.

Once those were gone, I stayed there clinging to the memory of the one person I needed most in the world. For half a second I allowed myself to think that everything was okay. No one knew anything, so Daddy wouldn't hurt them. I could steal this moment for myself.

Then Mason spoke.

"Your father's a dead man."

Chapter 18
Mason

"**S**on of a bitch!" I roared while punching the dashboard.
Fucking Harper.

Little liar was gone when I woke up. I spent an hour looking around the house for her and found nothing. Except the key to my room and a note laying on my dresser saying, *I'm sorry.* Are you fucking kidding me? I was so tired of her bullshit.

When was she going to get it? There were no options for her in this situation. No out, or secret escape. The only place she had to go was where I fucking told her to. There was only one place I could think of where I'd find my little escapee. Harper didn't feel safe in many places – thanks in large part to me.

I yanked on the steering wheel, kicking up dirt as I rounded the corner to a familiar Antebellum house. Why she'd feel safe at home I had no fucking clue. Didn't really care. If she wanted to be stupid that was her problem. Besides, I could have fun with a girl that liked a little pain. Because masochism is the only reason I could see for *this* being her refuge.

Sunlight sparkled off a red BMW parked at the end of the driveway. At least my back-up was already here. Though I could've done without the way Preston was casually leaning against his car smoking a cigarette. Out in the open where everyone could see. A couple of the gardeners working at the side of the house were giving him the side eye.

Weren't hitmen supposed to be inconspicuous?

Should've called Silas. But then I'd run the risk of Star tagging along and bitching in my ear about my improper treatment. Micha would ask too many questions, and dealing with Parker meant I'd have to deal with Lana – which would result in more bitching – and Logan was, well... Logan. So that left one person.

Preston showed up to the last job we did with a bucket of fried chicken. Who the fuck brought food to a body dump? There was something wrong with that prick.

Asshole didn't even bat an eye when I revved my engine. He just stood there, sucking on his cigarette. I did get a brow arch though when I parked right behind him. So close that my hood was kissing his bumper.

"Who the fuck taught you to park?"

He had weird attachments to objects. Like the jean jacket around his shoulders. That thing looked like something left over from a nineties teen movie. The kind where some hot-ass girl wasn't hot because she wore baggy clothes and a ponytail. There must've been some blind motherfuckers going to school back then. I'd never miss that shit.

I flashed Preston a smile, then stepped out onto the gravel driveway. "Aw, is Mr. Hitman worried about his flashy car?"

He leaned over and cocked a brow at my Corvette.

I rolled my eyes. Yeah, okay so it might be a tad decked out, with gold rims and a streak of fire down the side. But... "I don't kill people for a living."

"Neither do I." He breathed out a cloud of smoke and flicked his butt on the ground. "I don't need the money."

I don't know if I'd ever heard a more fucked up statement in my life. Did I want to know why Preston killed people? Fuck no. I still wasn't sure why I called him. Seemed like a good idea at the time. I might need a distraction. Harper had staff in her house, some of whom wouldn't be too keen on letting me drag her out by her hair.

"Gotta say, I was a little surprised you called me."

There was the understatement of the year.

"Yeah, well," I sighed. "Some people can't keep their noses out of my shit."

Lou, Micha and Logan were so far up my ass I wouldn't be surprised if they could taste my farts. Even Silas was starting to give me a hard time.

"Can't imagine why they'd do that." Preston slid his cold grey eyes my way. "Someone fresh out of rehab is definitely reliable."

Ha, ha motherfucker.

"I'm clean now." Kind of.

"Addicts are never clean." He cocked a brow at me. "They just find new things to get addicted to."

Harper's face flashed across my mind. All twisted in a mix of agony and pleasure while I forced an orgasm out of her. The image was so vivid I had to shake my head to get rid of it. "Can we just get this over with?"

Preston pushed off his car and swung his hand towards the door. Silently saying 'lead the way.' Which was exactly what I was going to do, until I heard a muffled cry and knock.

"What the fuck was that?"

"What?" Preston asked back.

Knock, knock.

"You don't hear that?" *Was he deaf?*

"Nope." He shook his head. "I don't hear shit."

Whatever. We weren't here to seek out strange noises anyways. I took a step, then stopped. Could've sworn I saw Preston's trunk vibrate.

Knock, bang.

There it was again. It was almost like…

"Do you have someone in your trunk?"

Preston rolled his grey eyes my way. "Don't worry about it."

I opened my mouth but nothing came out. How the fuck was I supposed to respond to that? Call him a dumbass for bringing a hostage to a meet? Somehow I didn't think that would fly very well and I wasn't in a hurry to have his knife pressed up against my balls again. I couldn't help but wonder if it was Marnie Dupire trapped in there.

He was pretty pissed when I hit on her and her sister. I believe his exact words were, *"Touch the one with glasses and I'll cut your dick off and shove it down your throat."* Nothing killed a hard on faster than the threat of castration, especially when you knew said threat would be followed through with.

Fuck it. His business was his business. I didn't want to know what he was doing with his toy.

Or did I?

I crossed my arms and eyed the psycho up. Preston was one cold, calculating bastard, but he got shit done. "What would you do?"

"What do you mean?"

"What if it was Marnie in there?" I tipped my chin at Harper's house.

His brow arched. "Are you asking for my advice?"

Yes.

No.

"Maybe?"

I didn't think he was going to say anything at first. He just stood there looking at the house, then shifted his gaze over to me.

"First off, my Bird won't be able to run anywhere." He lifted his hand and pointed a finger. "Trust me."

Bird? Interesting nickname considering Marnie's wings were clipped the second Preston decided that he wanted to... play with her? Fuck her? Kill her? Who the fuck knew what he wanted to do with her. Whatever he was after, there was no doubt in my mind that Marnie was well and truly fucked. This methodical bastard probably had every last detail planned. And back-ups just in case plan A got bumpy.

"But say she could..." Preston sighed, sat down on the hood of his car and studied the house. "I'm guessing this isn't just about her taking off?"

My response to that was a derisive snort. Harper running away was only the most recent in a long list of infractions.

His gaze slid my way. "You sure you're ready for the answers you want?"

"You're fucking kidding, right?"

He shrugged. "Everyone thinks they're ready for the truth, until they get it."

"Are you gonna give me some speech on the proper way to handle shit too?" Lou and Micha had that conversation covered. Ten times over.

"I don't give a shit what you do, Mason. Snort all the coke and smoke all the crack you want." The creepiest grin I'd ever seen washed across his face. "Just know that I will kill the guy who sold it to you."

Couldn't help but wonder if that's what happened to Keith. I hadn't seen him since I got out of rehab, and I was pretty sure that's where Ryker gotten the shit I almost overdosed on. I recognized the pink label on the bag.

I brushed the thought away. "We're not here for this."

"Okay," Preston let out a huff. "There's only one way to drag the truth out of someone."

"Care to share that secret with the rest of the class?"

He turned his head, locked eyes with mine, and said, "Break them."

My face dropped. Really? Break them? That was his grand advice. "What the fuck do you think I've been trying to do?"

"Nothing. That's my point." Preston tipped a brow and crossed his arms. "You're the same asshole who's been terrifying her for years. Why the fuck would she tell you shit? That little boy she fell in love with however…"

Huh?

As much as I'd like to argue the love part of his analogy – you didn't throw someone you loved under the bus – Preston did have a point.

"You're saying I have to be nice?" Just saying that made me want to gag.

"Not all the time," he explained. "But a kind word here and a tender moment there will really fuck with her head. Can't keep a secret when you're trying to figure out why you're seeking comfort from the guy that makes your life hell."

"So… I need to be her enemy, and her friend?"

He clicked his tongue and waved a finger. "Exactly."

Yeah, I could see how that would fuck someone up. I kind of felt bad for Marnie. Poor girl had no chance.

"Okay." I rolled my shoulders, filling them with determination. "Let's do this."

I had to give props to Preston. The asshole was efficient. He walked right up, kicked the door open, and strutted into the house like he owned the place. I'd barely followed him before the first scream echoed out the door. By the time I stepped inside, he was pushing two of Harper's staff into a closet.

My brow rose as he picked up a broom and slid it through the door handle, locking them in the tiny room. "Is that necessary?"

He stopped and glanced over his shoulder at me. "I could shoot them?"

It was disturbing how casually he said that. He wouldn't have an issue putting a bullet in everyone we came across. Hell, he'd probably skip through the house while doing it.

I waved at his makeshift lock. "Carry on."

We were here to get Harper, not turn this place into the house of death and blood. If Ned was in town, however...

The first place I checked was Harper's room. I thought I'd find her huddled in the corner hugging one of her stuffed rabbits, but no. She wasn't there. The interrogation began after that. There was an upside to bringing a known psycho to a shake down. The third maid we came across happily gave up that information when Preston threatened her. Freckles was apparently holed up in the library.

When we rounded the corner, I was ready to kick the door in until a familiar face stepped through.

"Fuck me," I grumbled as Mrs. Benson crossed her arms.

I was hoping to avoid this drill sergeant bitch.

"Mason Kessler. Why are you causing a ruckus in my house?"

I wanted to point out that technically this wasn't her house, but she did run shit around here. Uptight prude probably knew we were here before we stepped inside.

"I'm just here to collect my property."

There wasn't so much as a twitch in her expression when she argued, "Harper is not your property."

"I beg to differ." The corner of my mouth curled. "Or did her Daddy not tell you about the contract?"

She could stand there with that look on her face as much as she wanted. There was fuck all she could do to stop me.

"I don't care about your contract," she shot back. "If you think

I'm going to let you take that girl out of this house and terrify her more, you're sorely mistaken."

Well shit. I didn't see that coming.

Preston leaned over and whispered, "Can I shoot that one?"

I was thinking about it.

"Try it, boy." Mrs. Benson's glare narrowed on Preston. "And I'll beat you to death with that bust."

Preston and I both looked over at a marble bust of Einstein sitting on a small table next to us. That thing could do some serious damage.

"She'll never make it," Preston scoffed.

I wasn't as confident in that statement as he was.

Sighing, I scrubbed a hand down my face. "Don't you have a floor to clean or something?"

Why I thought that would help I had no idea. If Silas had a 'stick up the ass' twin, it would be Mrs. Benson. Though her stick was thicker and shoved up there further.

Her shoulders rolled back, firming her stance. "I will not stand for disrespect. Not from you, or the rag-a-muffin boy you sent here."

Rag-a-muffin? Who the fuck talked like that? Not to mention... "What boy?"

"I don't know," she waved her hand dismissively. "Tito, or Taco."

Preston and I arched a brow at each other. "Tico?"

"Yes. Yes, him."

Tico was Star and Riley's friend who was killed. I didn't personally know him, but I knew of him. Mostly because of the raven carved into his chest. The Order took an interest in that. What the fuck was he doing here? How many secrets did Harper have? I could deal with that after I got her home. First things first...

My eyes locked on the drill sergeant in a pencil skirt. I was over there wrapping my arms around the uptight bitch before she could utter another word. Gotta say, carrying someone over my shoulder was a lot easier than trying to frog walk them in a bear hug.

I thought about switching her up, but all that would get me was a shredded back. Despite the movement restriction, Mrs. Benson was a fighter. Jabbing me in the side and kicking my shin while I inched us towards the next door. It was her incessant yelling that was annoying. I barely heard Preston over her death threats.

"You want me to go get your girl?"

"Yeah," I glanced back at him. "Take her ass home."

Mrs. Benson dug her claws into my side and demanded, "Let me go!"

"Ah fuck." I grunted and tightened my hold on the wriggling woman. "I'm gonna deal with this."

If I didn't, she was likely to follow us back and I had enough problems at home. Didn't need to add Harper's governess to my list of lecturers.

Preston gave me a ten-four sign and sauntered into the library.

"Try not to shoot her," I called out after him while dragging the wriggling woman in my arms into the next room.

My plan was to get Harper's self-appointed protector alone and have a little chat. But the second I closed the door, I froze. My eyes swung from the bookshelf in the corner to a large desk on the other side of the room.

'I didn't mean to go in your office.' That's what Harper said when she was freaking out yesterday. What were the odds that this would be the room I'd wind up in? Seemed like divine influence if you asked me. Someone up there must want me to have a look around. It would be wrong to deny them.

The smile curling my mouth was wiped away when a stapler cracked off my cheek. I completely forgot about my captive until I locked eyes with her angry glare.

"I warned you, Mason Kessler," Mrs. Benson growled and came at me again.

This time I ducked under her swing, which was a pretty impressive feat considering I had a good foot on her. Might've even patted myself on the back if she hadn't dug her elbow into my gut.

"God damnit," I snarled.

A feral cat was more controllable. Luckily there was a small closet with just enough room to push her in. I only took two more hits doing that, and with a chair propped up under the handle she wasn't going anywhere. I stood back to admire my handiwork. Even smiled a little when the door vibrated with her fists. Maybe Preston was onto something with his boom handle lock?

"Let me out of here!"

"Pipe down," I snickered and sauntered over to the desk.

It was time to see what old Ned has been up to.

Turned out, he wasn't up to much. Most of what I found was pretty standard stuff. Business letters, accounting crap, shit like that. What did catch my eye were the two letters sitting on the top of the desk. Both were opened and one was signed. The interesting part... they were dated two days ago. It was kind of hard for someone out of town to sign a document. So the real question was, where the fuck was Ned Callaghan?

My thought was interrupted by a buzzing in my jacket pocket. It was probably Lou again. He'd called three times since I ducked out this morning. Guess I should answer, even if it was just to tell him to fuck off. He'd keep calling if I didn't. But it wasn't Lou's name I saw on the phone. It wasn't even my phone.

I cocked a brow down at the white jewelled case then smirked at the name lighting up the screen.

Setting the phone down on the desk, I clicked on the speaker phone and said, "Hey Ned. Long time no see."

"Mason?"

That's right, motherfucker.

"Where's my daughter?"

"Harper's a little tied up at the moment." It wasn't necessarily a lie. For all I knew, Preston had her bound in the trunk with his current victim. Why did that bother me?

A light sigh wafted through the speaker. "I want to talk to my daughter."

I just bet he did.

"I'm afraid you're stuck with me." I braced my palms on the desk and bent over, bringing my lips close to the phone. "Or do you only like hitting little girls?"

Ned wasn't the only one that went quiet. The closet door had stopped thudding. Interesting. Did the almighty Mrs. Benson not know what was going on under this roof, or was she afraid that I knew?

If Ned didn't want to talk, that was fine. I could handle the conversation. I'd even spur him on a bit while I did it. I pulled open one of the desk drawers and loudly rifled around with the stuff inside.

"You have a nice office, Ned. Very... clean."

A grin spread across my face when his voice came from the other line.

"I like to keep things in order."

"Like your daughter?" I shot back.

"Indeed." He hummed. "You should be thanking me for that."

Did this motherfucker just say I should be thanking him? "What exactly should I be thanking you for?"

"Has Harper given you any problems?"

She *was* my problem. I wanted to kill her and wrap her up in a bubble at the same time. For the first time in seven years, I started to wonder if Harper had a choice in what she did. Was she an innocent victim with big daddy Callaghan pulling the shots?

"Why don't you tell me where you are Ned." I turned my glare back on the phone. "And I'll come thank you personally."

His response caused my fists to ball.

"Ask my daughter."

I looked down at the letters I'd found and gritted my teeth. "Harper knows where you are."

"Why wouldn't she?" Ned stated flatly.

Don't know why I was surprised. She lied about everything. Star and Riley grieved over their friend while Harper conveniently forgot to mention that Tico paid her a visit.

"She is my daughter."

I scooped the phone up, growled, "Not anymore," and hung up.

Harper's time of playing daddy's little girl was done. She was mine now.

And after tonight, she'd never forget it.

Chapter 19
Harper

When I heard Mrs. Benson yell, I knew I'd been found. I'm not sure why I came here, of all places. Before I'd even realized I'd left Mason's house, I was standing in my yard next to the patch of black-eyed Susan's marking my mother's grave. All night long the only thing I could think about was how she used to smile at Daddy.

One minute I was laying in bed next to a snoring Mason, staring up at her bright sparkling eyes, and the next I was here. In the place where she died. It'd been a long time since I thought about that night – maybe it was too painful? Or maybe I didn't want to remember the last expression I saw on her pretty face. Momma wasn't worried about herself.

She was terrified for me.

Was history repeating itself? Had I turned Mason into the same monster Daddy became? Despite everything that happened, I still loved my father. Yes, he had a darkness inside him, but he was still the same man who checked under my bed before I went to sleep. The glimpses I got of that man were enough for me.

The problem was, I'd seen the same glimpses in Mason. That green eyed little boy was still there, fighting to be seen. Was my sweet prince buried so far under the beast I'd created that he couldn't be pulled back? And if I did pull him back, would I lose the man who raised me?

That's why I was hiding in here, because I knew eventually I'd have to pick a side. I even tried to convince myself that everything would be fine. I could tuck myself back into my shell of invisibility. But Mason would come for me. I knew that long before the door to the library was kicked open.

Except it wasn't Mason that strutted in.

My heart dropped down into a dark abyss of dread as I sprang out of my chair. Instead of a pair of sparkling green eyes, I was met with cold, grey, soul-sucking ones. I could literally feel the heat drain from my body.

I guess Preston could see my change in temperature because he tipped his head and arched a brow. "Are you gonna faint?"

Maybe. Considering who I was staring at, it might be a good idea. I grew up with Preston. I'd seen some of the things he did. And trust me when I say, none of the rumors came close to what this man was capable of.

"Can you speak?" he said, taking two steps closer.

My answer was to jump away, smacking my back against one of the bookshelves. That didn't accomplish anything, other than apparently amusing him. A cold chill coursed through my bones as a smirk spread across his face.

"I could have fun with someone like you."

Oh god no.

"It's too bad Mase claimed you."

Yes, Mason! "Where is he?"

"He's busy. So I'm going to take you home." Preston's glare

narrowed, making me wish I could meld into the wood at my back. "Are you gonna give me any problems?"

I shook my head. He'd never met anyone more compliant than me. Daddy and Mason had different things that would set them off. Preston Whitley was a whole other breed of monster.

I'd follow him out, get in his car – backseat, of course – and not utter a single word. Which was exactly what I did. When I heard some banging and muffled cries echoing through the backseat, I kept my mouth shut. Nor did I say anything when he pulled over and popped open the trunk.

I didn't even peep as he swung a tire iron and filled the air with the sickening sound of wet crunches. No, I sat where I was, staring out the windshield, while playing the best game of red light, green light that I ever had.

A part of me wanted to speak when he took a turn next to Cherry Lake – Mason's house was the other way – but who was I to argue with Death? It was comfortable back here. The seat was kind of soft, and I liked the checkered pattern on the headrest in front of me.

There were twelve black squares and eleven grey ones. The fifth grey one had a slight deformation that led me to believe the stitching was off. I wonder who made them? They seemed out of character for someone with his social standing. Then again, so did that jean jacket. But that was something I could think about another time. Right now, I was going to stay where I was and study the headrest.

My game of red light green light came to an end when we pulled over next to an ice cream stand. He opened his door and I retained my silence, but when Preston looked in the rearview mirror and jarred back a touch, I damn near jumped out of my skin.

"Oh shit. I forgot you were there." His brow arched. "Want some ice cream?"

"Sure," I whispered while trying not to cry.

When he pranced over to the stand I was tempted to run, but my feet wouldn't move. Aside from the wild fluttering in my chest, I had become one with the backseat. I could barely get my arm to lift and accept the cone he held out for me. My tears, however, were flowing freely.

"You seem like a vanilla kind of girl."

I preferred strawberry, but I did what any rational person would and ate my treat. It was weird driving down the road to hell with the devil at the helm, while I cried like a baby and ate quite possibly the best vanilla ice cream I'd ever had. Thank god Mrs. Benson made me take my pills this morning, otherwise I'd be in pain for the rest of the day. Not that my lactose intolerance would've mattered either way.

My heart didn't calm down until I saw the Oakleigh Manor sign, and when Mason's house came into view I practically leapt out and scurried inside. I wasn't even sure if the car had come to a complete stop. I did hear Preston yell a 'you're welcome' before I closed the door though.

The raven sprawled across the Kessler's floor used to creep me out. I hated being under the scrutiny of that big amber eye. It felt like that thing followed me everywhere. Today, however, that eerie orb was so much better than the dead glare I'd escaped. An object made out of tiles had more life in its face than Preston did.

The question I had now was, where did I go? Did I go to my room, or wait here? I sure as heck wasn't going to Mason's room. The one and only time I was there stuff happened. Don't get me wrong, it felt good. At least it did at first. I spent the last seven years in the aching embrace of pain, but none of the injuries I'd endured came close to the fiery slice of pleasure overload.

Not to mention that I didn't like being that close to Mason. It reminded me of a time when I believed in fairy tale endings. When I was happy. And that was dangerous. Twice now I'd let something

slip. How much would he find out if I did it again? Would everything I'd worked so hard to protect come crashing down?

"Harper?"

"Riley?" My brows furrowed.

What was she doing here? Then again, why was I surprised?
She was dating Micha, so it wasn't entirely out of the realm of
possibility that she'd be here.

She rushed forward and grabbed my arm. "Thank god."

"Um… okay?"

"I'm so happy you're here." She tugged on my arm, pulling me
off to the right.

Okay, this was weird.

Other than Lana, no one was ever happy to see me. Yet the
relief on her face was very evident. So much so that I began to
wonder if this was some kind of trick. It was a crazy thought to
have – Riley wasn't that kind of person. Once upon a time she was
in my shoes, except her bully was Mason's brother, which in my
opinion was worse.

Micha literally sought Riley out, whereas Mason only picked
on me when I was around. Sure, some of those run-ins were
strange. Like why would Mason be at the private beach behind my
house. But that didn't mean he looked for me. Right?

I twisted my neck and looked over at her dark blue eyes. Riley
and Micha weren't the gooshy couple that Logan and Shelby were,
but I could see how much they loved each other. Even when they
fought – which was a lot. How did they go from hate to that?

Mason didn't look at me like he used to. There was something
else behind the anger sparkling in his eyes. Was it pain, sorrow, or
something else, like love? Could there be a part of him that still
cared about me? Would I sense it if there was? Did Riley? Would
she tell me if she did?

Should I ask? No, I shouldn't be prying. It felt wrong. Riley's
personal life was her business. But what if she could help? What if

Riley Adams held the key to saving that green eyed little boy? Micha Kessler was a monster and she softened him. Did that mean I could do the same with Mason? Did I want to?

"Is Micha ever nice to you?"

"Oh yeah, he's a regular paragon of sweetness." She snorted.

"But... he has to be... sometimes. Right?"

She stopped and eyed me, making nervousness dig my teeth into my lip. On a normal day, Riley Adams scared me. She was a tiny ball of force that knocked everyone out of her way.

"Alright," she sighed and propped her hands on her hips. "What did he do?"

That was a weird thing to ask. "Who?"

"Micha."

Now I was really confused. How did my question get her to that conclusion? Did I give something away about her boyfriend's visit to me? No, I didn't think so. Then again, I did inadvertently give information to Mason, so...

"Micha didn't do anything."

Riley's eyes narrowed. "Uh huh?"

"Really." I hoped my voice didn't sound as high pitched and squeaky as I thought it did. "I haven't even seen him."

Thankfully, we were interrupted by a new voice.

"There you are."

We both turned as an older woman with dark hair walked out of the kitchen.

Riley grumbled, "Fuck, she found me."

I tipped a brow and studied her flowery black dress and tightly pinned up bun. I didn't know who she was, but she seemed familiar. Especially around the eyes. It felt like I'd see that spark in those deep chocolate depths before.

When she spotted me, a smile so bright that it lit up her whole face spread across her mouth. "Oh, you brought a friend."

"This is Mason's girlfriend, Harper." Riley thrust me in front of her. "Look at how small she is."

What? Since when did Riley refer to me as Mason's girlfriend? The last time Mason talked to me at school she threatened to cut his balls off.

The woman tsked and shook her head. "That won't do. Come with me, Harper." She spun around and walked back in the kitchen, while waving for me to follow. "I'll have you fattened up in no time."

I glanced over my shoulder at Riley. "What's going on?"

"Apparently we need meat on our bones to feed her great-grandbabies," she growled while pushing me to follow the older woman.

Great-grandbabies? Wait...

"That's Mason's grandma?"

She rolled her eyes and muttered, "Welcome to my hell."

I'd heard talk about the mysterious resurrection of the older generation of the Order. Riley was constantly complaining about Logan's grandparents – who were, according to her, so sweet it made her sick – but I hadn't heard a thing about a Grandma Kessler. Maybe I just wasn't paying attention. It's not like Mason and I ran in the same circles. I didn't have a circle.

My eyes widened when we walked in the kitchen. There was so much food. It was everywhere. Lasagna, a couple casseroles, some cupcakes, and what looked like a roast. Who cooked this much? I'd seen buffets and catered events smaller.

"Come, come," Grandma Kessler sang while pulling out a chair next to a table piled with food. "Sit."

She seemed very nice and I didn't want to be impolite, so I walked over and sat down.

Riley spun around to leave, but Grandma Kessler quickly added, "You too."

I don't think I'd ever seen a more disgruntled march than the one Riley gave as she made her way across the room to flop down on the chair next to mine. Not sure what she was so upset about. There was nothing wrong with someone wanting to feed you. It was kind of nice, right?

Wrong.

Mrs. Kessler started scooping food on our plates, and every time I thought she was done, she'd add more. By the time she stopped, my stomach was churning. I had to look around the pile on my plate to see the table.

I leaned over to Riley and whispered, "Are we supposed to eat all this?"

"When I stab her with this," Riley picked up a fork and glared over at Mrs. Kessler, who was pulling something else out of the oven, "I'm claiming insanity."

She was just trying to be nice. That didn't warrant a stabbing. Then again, everything warranted a stabbing in Riley's mind. Just last week she threatened to stick a fork in Silas's leg because he got the last cupcake in the cafeteria. Fortunately for me, I had an excuse to get out of this.

"Does this have cheese in it?" I asked while looking over at the older woman.

"Of course," she nodded. "What kind of lasagna doesn't have cheese?"

"I'm lactose intolerant." I faked a smile and pushed the plate away. "I'm sorry."

For half a second I thought Riley was going to stab *me* with the fork.

"That's fine, dear." Mrs. Kessler waved her hand through the air. "We have plenty of food without dairy."

Damnit.

Riley straightened up and shot me one of the smuggest smirks I'd ever seen. Maybe the fork idea wasn't so bad after all. That thought didn't last long, because I heard footsteps coming our way.

Determined and angry footsteps that could only belong to one person. My pulse picked up before Mason's deep tone echoed through the room.

"Harper can eat later."

I didn't have to look at him to see Mason was mad. I just like I could feel his stare boring into me.

"We have some business to take care of."

Riley was quicker to respond than I was. "What kind of business?"

"Let's go, Freckles," he barked out, blatantly ignoring his brother's girlfriend.

As much as Riley wanted to stick up for me, she couldn't. Besides, defying Mason would just make things worse. But that didn't stop her. When I moved to get up, Riley reached out and pushed me back into the chair.

"She's not going anywhere."

Why was she antagonizing him? His grandma wasn't poking her nose into things. She was singing quietly while stirring something in a bowl. Was that her way of coping? Paisley hid everything behind a smile. Maybe Mrs. Kessler cooked her feelings away?

Mason's green eyes darkened, making me drop my head. "Now, Freckles!"

Once again I moved to jump up and Riley intervened.

"You listen to me, Mason Kessler, I'm pissed off, full of food I didn't want to eat and armed…"

His next statement caused my eyes to snap to his.

"I talked to your father, Freckles."

What did Daddy say to him? What did he say to Daddy? Did Mason know? Did he threaten him? This was bad. He had no idea what Daddy was capable of.

"I should go," I whispered, and slipped away before Riley could stop me.

Every move I made was weighed down and tense. My muscles

seized while my mind screamed to run away and hide. By the time I stepped up to Mason, my heart was ready to burst out of my chest. I flinched when he reached out and pulled me in close to him.

"You've been a bad girl, Freckles." I couldn't tear my gaze away from the darkness in Mason's eyes. Not even when he shoved me out of the room. "Get your ass moving."

"You're on my shit list, Mason Kessler," Riley called out after us.

But it didn't matter what she said. It didn't matter what anyone said. The time I dreaded had come. There'd be no more secrets or lies. This was it. One of us was going to break.

And I had a feeling it wouldn't be him.

Chapter 20
Harper

Apparently I wasn't walking fast enough for him and his long strides because he growled, "Hurry the fuck up," and gave my shoulder a shove.

I was trying, but my legs couldn't move any quicker. And his pushiness wasn't helping. It was kind of hard to speed walk when I was tripping over my feet half the time. I wanted to get away from him and the oppressive weight of his glare. Every corner we turned, I prayed to find a secret door or hole to drop into.

The only thing I found was a staircase filled with an impending sense of dread. Every step brought me closer to a door at the end of a familiar hallway. A door that taunted me with the dark desires that had happened the night before. I didn't like how Mason made me feel in there, or the how my knees trembled at the possibility that he would do it again.

But this wasn't some erotic tryst. The scowl on Mason's face told me that. He wasn't going to take me in there and make me feel so good it hurt. Judgment was the only thing I'd find on the other side of that door. This was my day of reckoning, and Mason was my executioner.

I peeked back over my shoulder, looking for something familiar in the glare watching me. A spark that I'd seen the night before. The green eyed little boy was in there somewhere. The flash I'd seen was brief, but it was there. *He* was there.

Maybe it wasn't too late? I just had to figure out a way to take a step back and steer Mason in another direction. One that didn't lead to Daddy's wrath. Which would be a lot easier if I knew what was said. Did Daddy call him, or did he call Daddy?

"Do you still have my phone?" It was a redundant question. I knew he did, and I should've grabbed it before I snuck out this morning.

When I looked back at him, Mason shoved my shoulder again. "Why?"

I lurched forward, barely stopping myself from falling face first on the floor.

"Well if Daddy called on my phone," I looked over at the door taunting me. It was getting closer. "Then he was probably mad that I didn't answer."

"What's your point?"

At least he was responding. That was more than what I had a few minutes ago. I never realized how deafening silence could be. Yelling and anger meant bad things were coming, but silence was calm and peaceful. At least that's what I thought, until Mason dragged me through his house without uttering a word. It was disturbing how terrifying quiet rage was.

I preferred the sound of his voice over the fear pulsing in my ears. But I didn't know what to say. What was my point? That Daddy got mad? He got mad a lot, not that I could ever admit that to Mason.

I did the only thing I could think of and said something my

mother used to tell me. "Sometimes when people are mad, they say things they don't mean."

Her words of wisdom helped me more times than I could count. This wasn't one of those times.

Before I knew what was happening, I was slammed back against the wall and staring up at the very pissed off face of a green eyed demon.

"Is that what you tell yourself when you're licking your wounds at night? That Daddy didn't mean it because he was mad?" His hand shot out and wrapped around my neck. "News flash, little girl, your old man doesn't give a shit about you."

The truth behind his words stung so much that all I could say was a stuttered, "I... Uh... He..."

That wasn't a suitable answer. Not in Mason's opinion, anyways.

"He what?" Mason snarled, "Beat you? Pushed you down the stairs? Locked you in a closet maybe?"

Unable to risk looking him in the eyes, I ducked my head. Just because he was right didn't mean he needed to see my pain. I would keep that to myself and stare at the swirls in the marble floor.

A determination I managed to keep until Mason bent over and added, "Or is it that he's hiding somewhere in town?"

My brows furrowed as my head snapped up. What? Why would he think that? Daddy didn't hide. Well, not physically anyway. It was only the darkness inside him that he kept secret.

"He's out of town," I said. "For business."

"Your lies and betrayal are one thing, but this..." Mason shook his head and grabbed my wrist to drag me down the hall. "Just shut up."

It felt like I was on a death march. Each step we took vibrated up my body to thunder through my head. Our feet clacking off the floor was all I could hear. It was all I could feel. The walls were closing in around me. They moved with my breaths. Sucking in when I did, then pushing out a little less each time, constricting the heavy weight of panic pumping through my veins. There was only one thing I could do.

Try and reach a softer side of the man dragging me to my doom.

"Mason…" If Riley could do it, why couldn't I? "I don't know what Daddy said, but…"

He cut me off. "Oh, stop protecting him."

"I-I'm not." Daddy wasn't the one who needed protection.

"That's right." Mason's hand tightened on my wrist as he stopped and glared back at me. "Not anymore."

My heart dropped as the darkness in his eyes deepened the scowl on his face. Mason was beyond pissed. Beyond the enragement that the dark abyss of hatred brought. He was the beast.

Like Daddy…

"I'm sorry Daddy." Why was he hurting me? I didn't mean to go in his office. I didn't mean to interfere with him and Momma.

Momma...

She was right there but I couldn't look at her. Her eyes were dull and empty... wrong. Like she wasn't there anymore.

Daddy walked around me and kicked a lamp on the floor. "I love you, Harper, but you need to learn."

I hid under my arms and waited for the next blow. Was he going to take me away like he did Momma? Everything was in pain. My arms were on fire, my legs were aching and my chest hurt when I breathed.

"You need to do what I say."

"I will, Daddy." I choked back a sob, "I promise."

I'd do anything he said. I'd be the bestest daughter so he would love me again. Then maybe he'd bring Momma back...

. . .

I DON'T KNOW when we got to the end of the hall, or how I wound up in Mason's bedroom. But the second his grip loosened, I did what I should've seven years ago.

I ran.

Where was I going? I didn't know. I just knew that I needed to listen to Momma this time and get away. I needed to find a place to hide. Somewhere where Daddy couldn't find me. Except it wasn't my father I was running from, it was the green eyed little boy. Because if I let him catch me, Mason might find out everything. And that was so much worse.

"What the fuck?" Mason bellowed. "Get back here!"

Every fiber of my being twitched to obey his command, but I couldn't. I couldn't let him get close to me. I had to save what was left of the boy I loved. Even if it was just a spark.

I dove for the first place I could think of. Under the bed in the middle of the room. It was the one place he couldn't follow. Squeezing in that small space was a tight fit for me. There was no way Mason would fit. No sooner had I escaped into those safe shadows than the most disturbing laugh I'd ever heard echoed through the room.

"You want to play hide 'n' seek, Freckles. Alright."

I could barely twist my head enough to watch his feet. Those black boots mocked me as they moved, vibrating light thuds through the floor as they got closer. Why couldn't he just leave me alone and go back to the semi-happy life he had before?

When the toes of those boots stopped at the edge of the bed, I wanted to reach out and touch them. I needed to feel him just one more time and see that spark I missed so much.

"Come out, come out, wherever you are."

"Please leave me alone," I whispered, while tucking my face in the crook of my arm.

If I was quiet or pathetic enough, maybe he'd leave me alone. That hope was quashed when the bed was suddenly gone. A gush of air swept across me as my security was torn away. That was followed by a deafening crash and deep chuckle.

"Found you."

I looked up at Mason.

He glared down at me.

This was not like the games we used to play as kids. There was no glimmer of innocence in his victorious expression, or excited crack in his voice as he ran off to find his own place to hide. And why should there be? Mason wasn't that boy anymore. He was a man with broad shoulders and bulging muscles. So why couldn't I look away from the playful smirk on his face?

Even when he was angry, he was the most beautiful thing I'd ever seen. A monster in pretty wrapping. I rolled my eyes up his jean clad legs to the black t-shirt with a fist on it. The wrapped up fingers and tight knuckles sent a shiver down my spine. Mason humiliated me every chance he got, but he'd never hurt me. Right?

Are you crazy? Of course he would. Now stop gawking and run away!

All it took to snap me back into reality was a single twitch of his jaw. I was up on my feet in a flash, ready to run again. This time, though, I wasn't fast enough.

Mason grabbed my hair, causing my body to twist and slam back into him. I toppled to the floor. My legs went one way and my arms another. The worst part was, I brought him down with me.

Kissing the hard marble didn't hurt as much as I thought it would. Part of me wondered if the grunt I heard Mason give meant that he took part of the force for me. But I didn't have time to think about that. Bracing my palms on the ground, I attempted to wriggle my left leg out from under his weight. Thought I might make it, too. Until a large form crawled over me.

When the solid planes of Mason's chest pressed down on my back, I tried to tell myself to stop. The fight was over, I couldn't win. But panic had too much of a hold on me. It coursed through my veins making me flail and cry, while taking over my mind. My desperation caused me to say the stupidest thing I could've in that moment.

"Daddy didn't do anything."

That's when everything went quiet. It lasted for a fraction of a second, but it felt like forever. I heard everything. Every beat of our hearts resonated through my ears. The grinding of Mason's teeth, and the way his muscles tensed, stole the breath right out of my lungs. Judgement was here and she wasn't just carrying the scales, she was banging them on the floor next to me.

"Daddy didn't do anything." Mason's hot breath trickled across the back of my neck. "Daddy didn't do anything!" he repeated while slamming his fist down next to my face. "No, fuck that. This shit ends now. You are not his, you're mine."

I whimpered as his hand flattened on the back of my head, pressing my face into the marble beneath us. Nothing good ever came from being the brave one.

"When are you going to get that through your thick fucking skull?"

I played possum while his weight lifted off my back. Didn't even twitch when I felt his eyes pour over me. I stayed as still as a statue and repeated my mantra. *Stay quiet, don't talk back, keep your head down.*

"If you want to continue to lie for him, that's fine." The growl in Mason's tone sent alarm bells ringing in my head. "I'll show you whose little girl you really are."

By the time I sensed the change in the air, it was too late. He was already yanking my shorts over my hips. Fighting him was useless. I knew that, but rational thought fled along with my shorts that were tossed away. Despite my struggling to get away, the next to go were my panties.

Which, by the way, wasn't anywhere as easy as Shelby made it seem. Fabric dug into my hip, biting my flesh as Mason tore through one leg, leaving the other to hang haphazardly off my thigh.

I thought he might do what he did last night. That wasn't so bad. I kind of liked how his fingers felt, and I didn't get many pleasures in life so why not enjoy it? I even managed to calm down a bit when Mason wedged his knee between my thighs, forcing my legs open.

Then I heard the jingle of a belt.

My pulse instantly skyrocketed as tension poured back through me. "W-what are you d-doing?"

"Shut up." He clamped his hand over my mouth and snarled, "I hope you're wet, Freckles. Otherwise this is really gonna fucking hurt."

I whimpered as his weight settled down on my ass and something much bigger than his finger slid through my folds.

"Cry for me, Freckles," was the only warning I got before he pressed the tip of his dick to my opening and pushed in.

God it hurt. Hot white dots of pain blurred my vision as all my air was violently pushed out of my lungs. My lips parted to scream but I couldn't even do that. The tears he wanted however... those flowed freely. The pressure was too much. Mason had barely entered me and I was ready to do anything to make him stop.

"Fuck," Mason hissed and tried to force more of himself inside me, but my body fought against it. Squeezing around his tip in the most painful muscle clench I'd ever experienced. "You're too goddamn tight."

What was he complaining about? He was the one that was too big.

"Please stop," I blubbered. "It hurts."

When I tried to wriggle away he laid down on me, keeping my body in place with his weight. Then, when I thought I couldn't take anymore, the pressure on my core eased up. Next thing I knew I was being lifted in the air and flipped around. My brain didn't have time to register what was happening before Mason grabbed my hips and buried his head between my legs.

Any pain I had was washed away with one swipe of his hot tongue. I let it all go in one long moan. A moan that apparently spurred him on. Mason's fingers dug into my flesh as he lifted my ass off the ground and feasted like a starved man.

The hard marble dug into my shoulder-blades, but I didn't care. My entire being was focused on the tiny bundle of nerves his lips latched onto, and the tension his tongue brought. I held onto his hair and rode the waves of pleasure, until my tightly wound coil snapped, letting me free fall into the blissful land of ecstasy.

This I could handle. I was more than happy to get lost in the haze clouding my mind. I could spend an eternity here where pain didn't exist and I could let go. Unfortunately, that didn't happen. Not this time. I was slammed back down to earth by the hand around my neck. My vision didn't come back because the satisfied haze dissipated. Terror and fear cleared my head when I felt the same pressure on my entrance.

"No, don't..." I was cut off by a single thrust.

Mason grunted, "Fuck me," and forced in more of his thickness, tearing through something inside me.

This time I could scream.

I screamed loud. I screamed long. I screamed until I couldn't scream anymore. And he still wasn't all the way in. My pain didn't matter to Mason. He kept inching his way into my body. I tried to stop him. I swung my arms, slapping his chest and clawing at his face, but he pushed those away.

Mason pinned my arms down on the ground without a modicum of effort. I was completely vulnerable and trapped. Unable to do anything when he gave his hips one hard thrust, driving the rest of his length inside me.

He released a feral groan and all I could do was suck back a sob and whimper.

Something weird happened then. Mason didn't move or twitch his hips in the slightest. He stayed seated inside me and swept his hand over my sweat soaked forehead.

"Shhh, it's okay." Despite my discomfort I couldn't help but sigh when his lips pressed down on the top of my head. "The hard part's over."

I buried my face in his chest and whispered, "Are we done?"

"Not even close," he snickered. "But don't worry, you'll like the next part."

I highly doubted that. I didn't like anything about sex. It hurt. Well… I wriggled my hips. It didn't really hurt so much anymore, but there was something impossibly large wedged inside me. It felt wrong. Like I was full in a way that I shouldn't be. I wanted to squirm away from it. And I tried, but that was apparently the wrong thing to do.

Mason clamped his hand down on my hip and growled, "Hang on, Freckles."

Then he fucked me.

The first couple strokes brought back the ache in my core, but then something else took over. Something wild and feral. A beast that had me clawing at his back and begging for more. And Mason gave it. He fisted my hair and pounded into me with so much force we slid across the floor. All I could do was what he told me to. Hang on.

"Jesus fucking Christ, Freckles, I should've fucked you years ago."

When his fingers wrapped around my throat, I thought it was just another 'stay where you are' move. Until he tightened his grip, choking the air out of my lungs.

"Lying little bitch."

The anger sparking in his green eyes was more terrifying than the fact that I couldn't breathe. He wanted to kill me. I could see it all over his face.

"You ruined everything," he growled, while driving into me, over and over again.

Every thrust he gave was filled with more and more rage. He was pumping his anger into me. Forcing me to taste the bitter betrayal I fed him, and all I could do was cry.

My lungs were on fire and blackness started to seep into my vision.

"I fucking hate you," Mason hissed as he gave one final thrust and emptied himself inside me.

The beautiful boy I loved wasn't just broken. He was destroyed.

And it was all my fault.

Chapter 21
Mason

I fucked her.
    Son of a bitch!

That was one line I should've never crossed. Now not only did I damn near kill her, but I wanted to fuck her again, and again, and again, and again. I couldn't stop thinking about the way she felt wrapped around me and how her walls squeezed my cock.

Even her taste lingered on my tongue – which was something I wouldn't have had to do if Harper wasn't so tight. Ever try to force your way in a dry hole? That shit wasn't fun. And even when she was wet, I still had to inch my way in. It was fucking annoying. Not that my dick cared. He was hard and ready to go again.

God damnit.

Maybe I should've killed her and put us both out of our misery? That would've been the smart thing to do. Just keep on choking her and call it a day. Disposing of a body was always a pain in the ass. That would've been better than sitting in a bathtub with the object of my desire between my legs.

Harper shifted her ass, causing water to slosh against the cast iron sides. I couldn't help but sneer at some of the bubbles sliding down her back. What kind of man puts bubbles in a bath? A pussy ass bitch whose first thought is 'girls like bubbles', that's who.

Who the fuck cared what girls liked? I should've left Harper on the floor looking like a mess with half her clothes on, crying. But no. I had to scoop her up for a nice soak in the tub. And all because I'd seen something that I couldn't unsee.

There I was, lost in the way her warm walls wrapped around me, then I looked down. At her. It wasn't the fear twisting Harper's face that set me off. It was the way she was reaching out to me. That pull on her lip and glimmer in her big brown eyes that told me she needed me. She needed my comfort and protection, and fuck me I wanted to give it to her. I wanted to wrap her up in my arms and kiss the top of her head like I used to.

It'd been a long time since I'd seen that look, or that girl. I couldn't handle it, so I decided to destroy it. Smash that expression to bits until it was pushed away like the memories in the back of my head. Then when it was gone, I wanted to bring it back. Bring back the girl who'd never side with a piece of shit over me. Except that girl did side with him. Harper chose Ned seven years ago and threw me under the bus.

That wouldn't happen again. I'd kill her before I let him have her.

I tipped my head and pulled my eyes down Harper's back, to the wave of her red hair floating in the water. She was so sad and pathetic. Huddled up as far away from me as she could get, hugging her knees. I should just kill her.

My hand lifted out of the water and flattened on the top of her head. It wouldn't take much to hold her under until she stopped struggling. Just a couple minutes and it'd all be over. Quick and easy. But I couldn't do it. As much as I wanted to end it all, I couldn't let her go.

Fuck!

Letting out a breath, I slid down closer and rested the back of my head on the wall of the tub. How did things get so fucked up? Micha and I were barely talking, Silas was pissed at me, and Lou... well, that was a whole clusterfuck all on its own. All that shit going on and the only thing I could think of, was bending Harper over the bathroom counter. My skin was literally itching for me to do it.

"Mason?"

Why the fuck did she have to talk?

I blew out a sigh and closed my eyes. "What?"

"Can I get out now?"

Did she just ask me permission? If my dick wasn't hard before, it sure as hell was now.

Fuck my life.

"No."

"Why not?"

Then she had to go and question my authority. If Freckles wasn't careful, she would end up bent over the counter.

"Because I fucking said no," I barked back at her.

She squeaked and shuffled away.

Well that won't do.

While I didn't have an issue, per say, with the space between us – it might give me some time to get myself in check – it was the point of the matter that made me grab her hair and pull her back. "Don't move."

My tone dared her to move. Just a little twitch or small shuffle. That would be all I needed. I liked punishing her. It would give me a reason to fuck her again without worrying about how sore she was. Because for some fucked up reason I gave a shit about that.

But Harper didn't move. She stayed perfectly still like some

277

obedient little pet that she was. Which wasn't helping my situation any. I don't think anything would help, except for feeling her sink down on my shaft. The wet skin of her waist was brushing against my thighs, shooting sparks of electricity up my legs.

My balls were aching for release while my dick bobbed in the water trying to get closer to her. Couldn't be anymore than twenty minutes since I shot my load and I was half tempted to jerk off just to relieve some tension.

Or I could fuck her? Pull her on top of me and let that sweet silky cunt milk my cock. I could already feel her hands on me. Fingers wrapping tightly around my shaft while she stroked up and down. Wait…

I cracked an eye open and glanced down at the hand jerking me in the water. My hand. Fuck sakes. Pulling my arm away, I let out a frustrated breath and gripped the edge of the tub. Alcohol was an easier addiction than this shit. Maybe I should have a drink? Smoke a joint, or do a line, anything to take the edge off.

"Are you going to do that to me again?"

Ugh, her again. "Do what?"

"Um," I felt her shuffle between my legs. "You know."

That made my eyes pop open. "No, I don't."

"You know," she whispered while peeking shyly over her shoulder at me. "What we just did."

Aw, poor innocent little Freckles couldn't even say it. Why was that so fucking hot?

I sat up, grabbed her hips, and pulled her back into me so I could whisper in her ear. "What did we do?"

Nothing was as beautiful as the flush that crawled down her neck.

Harper quickly turned away from me and dropped her head. "It's not important. Nevermind."

Nevermind? What kind of crap was that? Suppose I shouldn't expect anything else. She'd been feeding me bullshit for years. But no more. The time for lies and silence was over. If Harper had a question, then she was going to damn well ask it. Besides, I was dying to hear the word 'fuck' slip through those plump pink lips.

"Say what's on your mind, Freckles." I swept her hair over her shoulder and watched the pulse in her neck flutter.

"I don't want–"

Cutting her off, I grabbed her neck and tipped her chin back. "I don't care what you want."

Harper whimpered and I damn near groaned. If I could bottle that sound I'd never need porn again. When she tried to wriggle away, I clamped legs around her. Her softness pressed up against me felt too good. I couldn't stop myself from sliding my palm down her side.

I liked how tiny and fragile she felt in my arms. What I didn't like was the way she was hugging her knees to her chest. It stopped me from sliding my hand around her hip.

"Put your legs down."

Her plump bottom lip popped out in a pout that I wanted to sink my teeth into. "But..."

"What did I just say?" I dug my fingers into her throat, applying just enough pressure for her to know I meant business. "Do it."

Her meek little whimper of defeat shot straight into my dick. By the time she started lowering her legs, I was practically salivating. Especially when she tried to pull a fast one and keep her legs together.

I half snorted and half tsked. Did she really think I'd let her get away with that shit? "Don't play with me, Freckles. You better spread those legs. I want to see my pussy."

There was that pout again, but she did as she was told and ever so slowly parted her thighs. Too slow, in my opinion. That was remedied with a firm pinch of her nipple. Then I got to see my glory land. A perfect, pink, glistening cunt. Harper did a good job shaving. It was clean, smooth, and soft.

"Good girl," I breathed in her ear, partly because I knew that shit got her off and partly because I got to watch that perfect pink cunt clench at my words. Even her pussy obeyed me.

"Now, I want you to touch yourself."

Her wide brown eyes snapped to mine. "What?"

"You heard me. Touch your pussy." I didn't like the hesitation that flashed across her expression so I added, "Right fucking now."

Her hand slapped down, cupping her mound. I waited for her to do something and give me a show, but it didn't happen. There was no sliding of her fingers over her clit, or shy little swipes. Harper just sat there covering her cunt. Was Harper trying to piss me off?

"What the fuck are you doing?"

"What you told me to," she whispered back.

"That is not what I told you to do."

I cocked a brow down at her hand. She didn't seem to be playing me. If anything, the girl looked confused. That's when realization hit me.

"Have you never fingered yourself?"

The flush flooding her face was all the answer I needed.

Damn. Don't get me wrong, I loved that no one else had touched her – there were no other cocks tainting my pussy – but everyone should know how to get themselves off. Luckily for her, I was more than happy to play teacher.

I had to hold back a snicker when I reached down and placed my hand over hers. "Loosen up your grip there, Hercules. It's a pussy, not the edge of a cliff."

"I'm scared." That same glimmer of needing protection flashed through her eyes when she looked up at me.

This time I didn't quash the ache in my chest. I went with it.

"It won't hurt, I promise." I ran my nose up the side of her neck and grazed my lips off the shell of her ear. "You need to trust me."

But it was more than that. I needed her to trust me. I needed her to give me some sign that the girl I once loved was still alive. That I hadn't lost her, and there might be a way to come back. I knew it would be a lie, but I didn't care. For just one second, I wanted to be that little boy again. To remember what it felt like before the betrayals and secrets tainted my soul. I wanted to have one pure moment in this craphole called life.

It felt like forever as I waited for Harper to ease up her grip. I was just about to give up when I felt her hand relax. Not completely, but enough for me to take control. Satisfaction filled my chest as I curled her hand in mine and slid our fingers over her clit.

Her lips parted in a gasp that had me mesmerized. I continued to guide her hand and watched the way her face twisted – tiny little nose all scrunched up while her tongue darted out to moisten her bottom lip. God she was beautiful. I wanted to sink my teeth into the pink hue tinting her cheeks. I wanted to feel the pleasure making her pert nipples hard. I wanted to watch her come apart.

Harper dropped her head back on my chest and moaned, "That feels good."

"Oh yeah?" I grazed my lips off hers and inhaled her shuddered gasp. "You want more, baby?"

She nodded her head and breathed out, "Yes please."

Please? Fuck me. I wanted to hear her say please while I drove my cock into her over and over again. But this wasn't the time for that. Fighting to contain my urges, I gripped onto the side of the tub with my free hand, then pushed her finger and mine inside her entrance. Her walls clamped down as Harper's eyes rolled into the back of her head and she let out the sexiest sound I'd ever heard.

That's when I snapped.

Before I knew what I was doing, I'd lifted her up and twisted her around to sit on my lap. The instant her heat met my cock, I knew I was addicted. No alcohol or drug in the world felt better than this. Groaning, I grabbed Harper's hips and rocked her forward, sliding her pussy over my shaft. She liked it too. I could tell by the way her fingers were digging into my chest. But that wasn't enough.

I needed to be inside her, so deep that my name would be branded on her soul, like my mark was on her neck. When I threw my arm under her ass and lifted her to line up my fist thrust, Harper shot up on her knees.

"No... wait..."

It was too late for waits. One quick readjustment and it didn't matter how stiff she went, I was still able to sink into nirvana. My brain barely registered the bite of her nails in my shoulders, but I did pick up on the quiet little wince she let out. Her inner walls were fighting back, trying to push me out. One hard thrust while I slammed her down solved that problem.

Harper tried to wriggle away but I just dug my fingers into her hips and held her where I wanted her. Despite what she thought, I wasn't deep enough.

"I can't," she whined while shaking her head.

Yes she fucking could.

"You're going to take every..." *grind...* "last..." *thrust...* "inch."

I couldn't help but smirk at the way Harper buried her face in the crook of my neck. "I'm sore."

"But it feels good, doesn't it?"

"Mason—"

"That's it baby, say my name." I slapped her ass, spurring her to jerk forward.

Now that felt really fucking good. I wanted more of that.

"I'll tell you what, Freckles. If you don't want it to hurt..." I pinched her chin and pulled her in so I could suck that plump bottom lip in my mouth. "Then you better fuck me."

The shock on her face got me hard, but the curiosity shining in her eyes... that shit was euphoric. "B-but... I don't..." My breath hitched when she peeked up at me through her lashes. "I don't know how."

This girl was going to be the death of me.

"It's not that hard," I said while clinging onto the edges of the tub to stop myself from taking over. "Bob up and down on my dick until something feels good."

Her face screwed up in the cutest confused scowl. "How will I know if you like it?"

"Trust me, I'll like it." She could sit on top of me and sneeze for ten minutes and I'd like it. "I want to watch you make yourself come."

My forearms flexed, pressing my fingers into the cast iron. If she kept wriggling her ass like that, I was gonna blow my load before she did shit.

"Hurry the fuck up, Freckles." I arched a brow at her. "Unless you want me to take over?"

That worked. Harper gave one little tiny jump that shot a lightning bolt up my spine. Then she gave another and another. Until finally she was moaning and riding me like the wanton little slut I wanted her to be.

It took everything in me to hold back. I imagined Micha in lingerie, Logan getting his dick booped, and even tried picturing Grams in her underwear. None of that could overshadow the way Harper felt wrapped around me while she clawed at my chest. When her pussy clamped down on my shaft, I couldn't contain myself anymore. I slammed her down as hard as I could while biting into her neck and emptying my load in her warm, wet walls.

We sat there for a bit, Harper slumped against me while I fought to catch my breath. But when the haze of our erotic moment passed, reality came back. As much as I wished the girl in my arms was the same one I picked all those years ago, she wasn't.

This Harper Callaghan was the one that killed mine. Even if I wanted to go back, I couldn't. My soul was tainted long before her betrayal. She was supposed to be the thing that kept me going, not the final nail in my coffin.

I looked down at the satisfied smile on Harper's pretty face, then at my arms tightly wrapped around her. As long as she was around, I wouldn't be able to move on.

So why couldn't I let her go?

Chapter 22

Harper

I never wanted anyone to go to sleep more than I did Mason last night. He'd had sex with me twice and still kept pawing at me. After we got out of the bath he insisted on brushing my hair, then held me for what felt like forever.

It was kind of nice to feel wanted, but his touch kept creeping down to parts that needed a break. Even when he finally fell asleep, it was with his hand on my breast.

Was this what all men were like? I couldn't recall a single girl that Sean let spend the night. According to him, they were done and therefore had no reason to stick around. So I'd seen plenty of pissed off marches when he kicked them out, but not a single frustrated 'leave me alone' huff.

Mind you, Mason was back to normal in the morning. He pretty much pushed me out of his room the second he woke up. His exact words were, 'get the fuck out of my face'. Maybe he liked spending a little more time with girls than my brother did?

At least that's what I thought until I saw him at breakfast. It couldn't have been more than five minutes before he slid his hand under my skirt. Thankfully Mason didn't argue when I jumped up and said I was going for a walk. He did give me a dirty look though, so I was probably going to pay for that later.

His dad was right there, not to mention his soon to be step-mom and brother. What was he thinking? That was the million dollar question. What was Mason Kessler thinking? One minute he glared at me with hatred, then the next it was like he couldn't get close enough. I didn't know what to do. Should I keep hiding? Run away? Or should I give him what he wanted?

The truth.

I huffed out a sigh and ran my hand along the soft green leaves of the hedge. There was a time when all I wanted to do was confide in Mason. Daddy would be in one of his moods and my mind would go to that green eyed little boy. I'd imagine that I was a princess locked in a dragon's tower, and he would swoop in to save me. But little boys couldn't defeat dragons. They got eaten by them.

So I did my best to forget about my hero and faced the monster myself. That way I'd be the only person who got hurt. But that wasn't the case, was it? I didn't realize until Mason brought me here.

Sighing, I turned the corner to the tower in the middle of the hedges. I looked up at the vines of ivy climbing the stone exterior. The sign saying 'Fort Kessler, no girls allowed except Harper,' was still hanging next to the door. It was faded and covered in dust, but it was still there, just like the carving in my tree. Why did I come here?

This place was nothing more than faded memories. A reminder of a time best forgotten. And yet here I stood, staring at it in wonderment like I used to. The first time Mason brought me here he was so excited. I'd never forget the sparkle in his bright eyes. It felt like he was letting me in on some grand secret fairy tale. Now this place just looked sad and lonely. A crypt entombing all of our happiness.

My eyes fell to the shadow filled archway. I could hear the innocent giggles of our childhood wafting down the stairs. It called to me, pulling me through the ivy hanging over the door and up the stairs where I could smell the grass stains on Mason's jeans.

"Come on, Harper," the ghostly figure of a little boy waved for me to follow. "Wait till you see this."

He skipped away with a smile on his face and disappeared around the corner.

"Wait," I called out and rushed up the stairs.

He laughed when I caught up and ran away. His joy was so contagious I couldn't help but join in. My giggles got louder the faster we raced each other up the tower. The ghostly little boy would duck behind one corner where I'd jump out and say "boo," before he took off again. Our little game was so freeing that I forgot about everything and enjoyed the wind in my hair and the smile on my face.

Then we got to the room at the top of the tower and I stopped cold.

The little boy was gone but the items he'd put in this room years before weren't. My gaze swung from the red velvet pillow covered in dust, to the wooden sword in the corner. Everything was here. The stuffed rabbit I brought to keep guard out the window, and Mason's monster hunting plans – which were hanging on the wall next to it. Even the pink water bottle I drank from the last time I was here still sat in the place I left it.

The longer I looked around, the more my chest ached. It wasn't the cherished memories that caused the tears to drip from my eyes. It was because nothing had moved. Every single item was exactly where I'd last seen it. Meaning Mason hadn't come back in here. Not since that day. I didn't just break him, I took his innocence. And now he'd taken mine.

I walked over to the far wall and ran my hand along the crayon drawings. A prince and princess, a dragon, and a little boy holding his mother's hand next to a lake. My brows furrowed at that one. I didn't remember seeing it before. But it had to be here. If Mason hadn't been back here, then it...

My breath hitched as I stumbled back. Mason didn't draw it. I did. Two days after I got out of the hospital, I snuck out and came here, hoping I'd find Mason waiting for me. I sat here all night, but he never came. So I left him this because I wanted him to know I loved him. How did I not remember that?

This picture was my secret message to him. I chose his mother and the lake because they were like Daddy. Julia Kessler did a bad thing, but Mason still loved her...

"Do you think if someone hurts you, they can still love you?"

I brushed the dirt off Mr. Bunny's head and shrugged. "I don't know? Maybe?"

"Yeah." Mason's chest puffed out with a heavy sigh.

He'd been sad lately. Moping around with a frown on his face. I just wanted him to be happy again. That's why I was here. To make him smile. But he hadn't smiled all day. Maybe he needed a hug? So that's what I did. I walked over, sat down on the floor beside him, and threw my arms around his neck.

"It'll be okay," I promised and gave him a kiss on the cheek.

When Mason lifted his green eyes to mine, I wished I could wipe away the sorrow in them.

"Can I tell you a secret?"

"Of course." I was his wife, and wives always kept their husband's secrets.

"I think my dad is lying to me. Micha too."

My nose crinkled. "About what?"

"Member when my mom died and I was in the hospital?"

I nodded. "Yeah."

That was last year. My dad said Mason's mom did it to herself 'cause she was crazy. All I knew was that Mason missed her and he cried lots. If I could've brought her back for him, I would've.

"I remember things." He dropped his head back on the wall and stared out the tower window. "Things like Micha yelling for me to wake up, and Mom singing while water rushed in. I think we were in the car with her?"

"You mean when she..." I didn't want to say it, so I looked to the side and swung my hand out.

Mason nodded.

That didn't make sense. If Mason and his brother were in the car, then how come they got out and their mom didn't? Then again, they were in the hospital for a couple days and no one would tell me why. Even Mason didn't know why he was there. Maybe he was in the car?

Mason sniffed back a sob, but I could see the tears in his eyes. "Do you think if my mom tried to hurt me, that she still loves me?"

"Yeah." Mother's always loved their kids. "Sometimes grown ups do dumb things."

Trying to hurt your son was a really dumb thing.

"Your parents don't hurt you," he argued.

Daddy spanked me sometimes when I was bad, but that was punishment. He didn't hurt me.

"No," I said, "but they fight lots." I always heard them yelling. "And they still love each other."

Sean didn't think so. He said Momma and Daddy were going to get a divorce, but they still slept in the same bed. And you didn't sleep next to someone you didn't love. That's why when we had campouts I slept beside Mason.

"But they don't hurt each other," Mason argued.

He had a point. I looked up at the roof and said, "Maybe she just didn't want to leave you here without her?"

"You won't leave me, right?"

I puffed my chest out and shook my head. "Nope. Never."

His eyes narrowed. "What if your dad tells you to? Or your brother?"

"Then I'll run away," I stated confidently. "I don't need them, 'cause I have you and you'll protect me from anything..."

I STUMBLED back and fell down to my knees. That drawing taunted me with the words of the little girl who made it.

'You'll protect me from anything.'

Mason trusted me with his secret. He had no problem confiding in me. And when it came time for me to be put to the test, I failed. He was the one person I needed, the one person I tried to say something to. Even if it was in a cryptic drawing, I came here. To him. And when he came to me with questions, I blew him off.

All because I believed I was protecting him. At the time it made sense. Mason was a little boy. But did it make sense anymore? Or was I just scared that if he found out the truth, he'd hate me more.

They'd all hate me.

Chapter 23
Mason

I was that annoying kid that woke up at the crack of dawn ready to take on the world. I'd come flying out of my room and jump on my parents' bed. The sooner they woke up, the quicker I'd get to see her. Harper was the reason I started my day, and the person I dreamt about when I closed my eyes at night.

Now, I slept in for as long as I could, hoping that that part of the day would pass before I opened my eyes. There was no reason to open my eyes, because my entire world died with three words. The only place that girl lived was in the dark, hidden below the nightmares that woke me up.

This time when I opened my eyes, Harper wasn't behind the tears and screams of a little boy. She was lying beside him. Wrapped up tightly in my arms with her head nestled in the crook of my neck. It was the first morning in seven years that I woke up feeling whole.

Then I remembered, and kicked her out.

When people called me cold and cruel they were right. Not caring was the only way I could survive. That's what I told myself, anyway. The truth was a much harder pill to swallow.

I flattened my palms down on the bar and blew out a breath. I'd been standing in here for god knows how long, staring at the bottle of scotch in front of me. One drink, that's all I wanted. Yet every time I put that open bottle to my lips all I could see was Harper's face.

If anyone deserved my hatred, it was her. But if I took a drink and lost control, was I any better than the man who turned her against me?

"Found him!" I looked up as Logan waved at someone down the hall and then sauntered in.

Great, just what I needed.

"Hey Mase, we've…" He stopped and cocked a brow at the open bottle. "Whatcha doing?"

That cautious look of worry that everybody gave me was really starting to get on my nerves.

"Staring at a bottle of scotch."

"Just staring?" another voice asked, making me roll my eyes as my brother rounded the corner to join us. "That bottle's open, Mase."

Well, if it isn't Captain Obvious.

I pushed off the bar and folded my arms over my chest. "What do you want?"

"That depends," Micha's chocolate eyes shifted from me to the bottle and back. "You been drinking?"

"You wouldn't know if I was."

Harper wasn't the only one good at hiding shit. Half of my last year was buried in a drunken haze and my brother had no idea.

"Yes I would," Micha insisted.

That made me snort. "Why? You got a breathalyser in your back pocket?"

It wouldn't surprise me if he did.

Did I back down when Micha locked his hard ass glare on mine? Nope. I glared right back at him. If he wanted to try and intimidate me, he could go right ahead. I grew up with this shit. It didn't work on me when I was little, and it sure as hell wouldn't work now.

Logan, however, had had enough of our silent stand offs. He sighed and shook his head.

"You've gotta stop holding this shit against Micha, Mase." Logan tipped his head and looked right at me. "I didn't tell you either."

I huffed out a snicker. "Who says I don't hold anything against you?"

There was plenty I held against Logan. But Micha... He was my brother. The other half of my soul. The one guy I should've been able to count on no matter what. I never would've kept something like this from him.

"So get mad at me then." Logan tapped his chest. "I'm the one that wanted to keep it from you."

"Right," I snorted. "Because Micha always listens to other people."

No one told Micha what to do. Even when we were kids and the rules of a game were clearly lined out, he changed them. And everyone else went along like little lap dogs.

How did my brother respond to my comment? He huffed out a heavy breath and shook his head. "Stop acting like a child, Mase. Let it go."

"Huh? Let it go?" I snatched the bottle off the bar and moved to shoulder past them. "Why didn't I think of that?"

Great advice there, big brother.

"Mase, stop." Logan gripped my shoulders, stopping me before I could leave. "There's a reason we never told you." He dropped his forehead on mine. "Ryker Hudson is my cross to bear. You don't want any part of his legacy."

Genetics didn't give a shit about want. Monster's bred monsters. Harper was just the match that lit the fire.

"Oh fuck you, Logan." I shoved him off and took a step back. "You think you're the only one that was subjected to Daddy's special games?"

Both their faces dropped.

"What?" Micha grumbled.

I'd never heard him sound so shocked. It was kind of funny when I thought about it. Big bad Micha Kessler. Thought he had everything figured out, but he didn't know shit about his little brother.

"No." He shook his head. "You were never left alone with him. I made sure every time he was around that someone was with you."

"Not at Harper's house." And Ryker was there a lot.

I watched the denial in their faces morph into the realization that all their careful planning had failed. Their excuse was protection. I got it. I fell for the same line of bullshit. Take the pain for her and she'll be okay. Look how that turned out. A secret was a lie that no one heard. And lie was a fantasy that people wanted someone to believe because it made them feel better.

We stood there for a few minutes in silence before Logan whispered, "Why didn't you say anything?"

"Why didn't you?" I shot back.

"We were trying to protect you," Micha argued.

That made me laugh. "Protect me? You know what your protection did. It left me alone. You all had each other to talk to. I had no one."

For years I thought I was the only one. Why did Ryker hate me so much? Was I a bad kid? And all that time it was happening to them. They all knew about it, of course, but no one told me shit. While they comforted each other and whispered about the horrific things they experienced, I was in the background wondering what was wrong with me.

Logan furrowed his brows. "What about Harper?"

"What about her?"

"Did my old man get her too?"

"No." I shook my head and pushed down the urge to bring the bottle to my lips. "She got out clean."

Micha stepped forward and gave my shoulder a squeeze. "You can't know that."

Yes I could.

"Ryker was a sly motherfucker. He could've gotten her alone..."

"I took it for her," I growled.

They both stood with their mouths open while I sighed and looked out the door to the hall.

"The first time he took me in that room, I knew something was wrong. I could just feel it. Like the air around me had changed. After awhile I became numb, and eventually I wasn't even scared anymore. It all just kind of blurred into one big nightmare. Like I was there, but wasn't. But you know what I remember the most?"

Micha and Logan remained quiet and let me continue.

"It was what he said when I told him to leave Harper alone. That son of a bitch leaned in and whispered, 'are you sure she'd show you the same loyalty'?"

I'd heard those words everyday for seven years.

Micha let out a breath. "Mase..."

"Guess he was right. The first chance she got, she threw me to the wolves."

My tears weren't pulled from my eyes by the hollowness in my chest. They came in the form of scotch, when I chucked the bottle across the room and watched it twist through the air. Shards of glass fell to the ground as amber liquid flowed across the wall in a beautiful puddle of rage and sorrow.

Micha opened his mouth a couple times, but nothing came out.

I didn't know what to say either. We just kind of stood there staring like it was the first time we were seeing each other, and maybe it was. All our cards were on the table now, laid bare for the other to see.

I looked from the brother I grew up with, to the one I shared a father with. Neither one tried to comfort me or say some bullshit about it not being my fault, because they were just as confused as I was. But they were still here. Standing next to me. And that said a lot.

Logan was the first to break our silence.

He flipped over a table in the corner, sending the contents clattering around the room. "Motherfucker! You were supposed to make it out clean."

The single tear rolling down his cheek hit me harder than anything Ryker had ever done to me. Logan Hudson didn't cry. He didn't feel sorry for himself or anyone else, and yet here he was, giving me some of his pain. But he wasn't the brother I used to admire. It wasn't Logan's bed I snuck into when I had a nightmare. It wasn't his smile or approval I sought out.

Micha was the brother I needed.

I looked over at his furrowed brows. He was pissed. Not at me or Ryker, but at himself.

"When Riley was in the hospital, Chase said something to me. He said that if I loved her, I'd let her go. That she didn't belong in our world." Micha sighed and walked over to a painting of a sailboat on the wall. "Maybe he was right?"

"Riley can handle it," I said. "She'll be fine."

He rolled his dark eyes over his shoulder and looked back at me. "She's not the one I'm worried about."

"Oh, so now I can't handle shit?"

Fuck him.

Logan argued, "That's not what he's saying, Mase."

But Micha retaliated with, "That's exactly what I'm saying."

"Fuck you, Micha."

"No Mase, fuck you. Look at Logan." Micha tipped his chin in Logan's direction. "How many scars does he have? Don't hear him complaining."

Gritting my teeth, I puffed my chest out and grumbled, "I'm not complaining either."

Until a few minutes ago they had no idea what happened to me.

"That's my point. We thought Ryker was dead for years and you didn't say shit."

I sighed and crossed my arms. "So?"

"So, don't hold us to a higher standard than you hold yourself."

"This isn't the same thing." I wasn't holding back Micha's DNA.

What happened to me as a kid was my business. Still, I couldn't help but wonder why I didn't say anything? If the threat was gone, why didn't I tell someone? Lou, Micha, Silas, even Harper. I used to tell her everything, but I didn't tell her about this. Why? Was I ashamed? Was I scared that the boogeyman would come back?

Is she scared?

"Sure," Micha snorted. "Tell Harper it's not the same thing."

"Harper betrayed me!"

"I don't know, Mase," Logan interrupted. "I hate to say it, but Micha's got a point. We all assumed she was skittish because, well, you're an asshole." He slapped his hand on his chest. "While I admire your tactics, if you think about it, she changed before you started tormenting her."

"So?"

"So," he continued, "what changed? What happened the day she fingered you?"

That's when realization dawned on me.

"Her mother," I whispered.

Ivy Callaghan disappeared right around the time her daughter was in the hospital. I remember people talking about how horrible of a mother she was for not visiting her sick child, but that wasn't the woman I remembered. Hell, half the band-aids I wore were put on by her.

Micha's brow rose. "Have you ever looked into where she went?"

"No." I was too busy hating her daughter to give a shit.

"Maybe you should?" Logan suggested.

A new voice interrupted us. "That can wait."

The annoyed grunt Micha let out told me who it was before I turned around.

Gramps stood in the doorway with sternness glimmering in his dark eyes and his arms crossed over his suit jacket.

He looked right at me and said, "I have a job for you."

Chapter 24
Harper

My brows knit at the white house Mason pulled up to. "We're going to Lana's?"

"No," he ground out while pulling the car to a stop. "You're going to Lana's. I have shit to do."

When he first found me, I thought that he knew I was eavesdropping and was in trouble. It wasn't like I was trying to listen in. I was just too afraid to walk past. Micha, Logan and Mason were in that room.

Getting by them without being seen would be like trying to sneak past the Devil's office while he was talking to Death and War. And the outcome if I got caught would be better in that situation than it would with Mason and his friends.

So my first instinct when Mason came in to my room was to hide. Until he told me to get my sweater cause we were going out. It wasn't even cool enough for that, but I took it anyway. I wasn't about to argue. Not after what I heard.

Ryker Hudson was a bad man. The entire time we were driving all I could think about was how terrified he must've been. That sweet little innocent boy, cornered by a monster. I couldn't imagine the things he went through. For me.

I looked over at the scowl on Mason's beautiful face. This man had literally walked through hell for me. And what did I do in return? I threw him right back into those fiery pits.

I should tell him. He deserved at least that.

"Mason," I reached out and placed my hand on his arm. "I..."

"Look Freckles, I don't want you to mistake this shit for kindness. I'd rather lock your ass up in a closet at my house than bring you here. But," he let out a huff and cocked a brow my way, "I can't trust you not to take off."

That didn't make sense. "But this is Lana's house?"

If there was anyone in this town that would tell Mason to go to hell and help me hide, it was Lana. And her Nan, of course.

"I'm well aware that this is your friend's house. But her father's men know how to listen to instructions." He got out of the car and grumbled, "Unlike Lou's."

Oh yeah, I forgot about that.

Being surrounded by a bunch of armed men wasn't exactly a comforting thought. I looked out the window at a man walking around the side of the house. Lana didn't like them either, though she said they were necessary – which I understood. Her son was heir to the Russian mob and had enemies from the day he was born. I couldn't imagine how terrifying that must be for her.

Mason stopped outside my door and cocked an impatient brow, spurring me to quickly hop out of the car and join him.

I was excited to see my best friend, but dreaded it at the same time. For weeks I'd been avoiding her, because it hurt to lie to her. That look she gave me when I refused to answer her questions was permanently burned in my brain. Through all this stuff, she was the one person I had. The only one who never turned their back on me, and she paid for it. It wasn't just me that Mason picked on. Lana got the brunt of his wrath too, and therefore everyone else's. She just didn't know why.

My stomach flipped when we walked through the door. But it wasn't Lana that greeted us.

"Hey." Parker tipped his chin at Mason.

Mason tipped his chin back. "Hey."

Parker shifted a bit and cleared his throat, while Mason swung his gaze around.

"Nice place you have here."

That made Parker's brow rise. "You've been here before."

"Right," Mason nodded.

After that they just kind of stood there for a second, staring at each other.

Well, this is awkward.

"Umm…" I looked from one to the other. "Are you guys okay?"

"I guess that depends on him," Parker said while waving at Mason.

Mason snorted in response. "Of course we're okay. Why wouldn't we be?"

"Um, maybe because you showed up here last month looking for a repeat performance?"

Confusion crinkled my nose. "Repeat performance of what?"

"Nothing." Mason gave Parker a dirty look. "Don't listen to him, he's crazy."

"Says the guy who asked me to suck his dick."

My jaw dropped as my eyes flew to Mason's. "You sucked his penis?"

"Okay, first off," he pointed at me, "we really need to work on your anatomy words. It's a dick, or cock, period. And secondly no, I didn't suck his dick." He raised his fist to his mouth and coughed. "He sucked mine."

My jaw was officially on the floor. I could taste the carpet.

"Close your mouth, Freckles, you're gonna start catching flies."

I quickly clamped my lips shut. That didn't stop the shock from widening my eyes. Did that mean Mason liked boys too, or was this an experimental thing? Lana told me about some of the things her and her husband did. Would Mason want me to do those things?

"I don't want to have sex with anyone else."

Parker burst out laughing while a murderous look washed over Mason's face. "That's fucking right you don't!"

"I don't know," Parker snickered. "I could probably talk Lana into swapping."

What? No. I could not do anything with him. He was my best friend's husband. I spun around and wrapped my arms around Mason's waist and clung to him.

"I want to go home."

Mason sighed. "You see what you did? Go play with your wife and keep your dick away from mine."

I couldn't stop the smile from curling my lips.

He called me his wife.

He hadn't done that since we were kids. I nuzzled in closer, enjoying the way he smelled. All fresh and masculine. I didn't even mind the hardness pressing up against me. It was still scary, but I kind of liked it too. Mason was still the guy that made my life hell, but he was also the guy that took on a monster for me. It felt warm tucked up against him, almost like I was safe. That feeling didn't last long.

"Alright, that's enough of that." Mason pried my arms off him and pushed me back. "Now go find your friend."

I didn't want to find my friend. I wanted to curl up with him again. To feel safe for once in my life.

"Keep looking at me like that, Freckles, and I'll fuck you right here in front of Parker."

That snapped me out of it. The smile dropped off my face and I took a step back. Would he really do it? That was the dumbest question ever. Of course he would. Mason wasn't exactly the subtle type. Then again, he told Parker to stay away from me so he might not.

It wasn't Mason's cocked brow that made me spin around and run away, it was the obvious bulge in his jeans.

He'd definitely do it.

Parker chuckled and called out, "She's out back."

And that's exactly where I went, as fast as I could. Even when I heard them leave I didn't slow down. I'd been tricked before and wasn't about to fall for any games. Especially when they involved possible nakedness.

When I turned the corner towards the backdoor, I practically ran into Lana.

"Whoa," she held up her hands. "What are you–"

My arms were around her before I could blink. I was too happy to see her sparkling hazel eyes to care what she was going to say.

"I'm sorry," I cried, while hugging her as tightly as I could.

If I let go she might disappear and I couldn't risk that. It had killed me to avoid her. I needed Lana. Her smile was the bright spot in my day.

I guess she felt the same way, because next thing I knew her arms were around me and she was crying too.

"I'm sorry too."

"I missed you," I sobbed back.

Could I really get mad at her for asking questions? If the roles were reversed, I'd have done the same thing. Besides, what good was all this secrecy if it drove away the one person I needed most? Every time I spoke a lie, or made up an excuse, I was just delaying the inevitable. I couldn't hide it forever. Lana was every-thing I wasn't. Strong, confident, and smart. How did I think she'd react?

"No, I shouldn't have pushed you."

"It's okay," I sniffed while clinging to her like she was my only life line – which in a way, she was. "You were worried about me."

Minutes ticked by as we stood there holding onto each other. By the time we let go of each other, neither of us had anymore tears to let fall.

I gazed up at the smile on my beautiful friend's face and let the dam break. Lana always stood by my side. When Naomi and her minions cornered us in the hall, she never left me alone. She stood up to Mason, Logan, and anyone else that bothered me. When the world was beating me down, Lana carried me on her shoulders. She deserved to know why. She deserved to know everything.

"Lana..."

My words were cut off by the finger pressed to my lips.

"It's okay, Harper."

Lana had this infectious smile that made everyone in the room feel her joy. But the one she was giving me now lacked that warmth. She was happy to see me, but the curl in her lips was filled with sadness.

"You're not the only one who's been keeping a secret." She cupped my cheeks to brush the tears off my face with her thumbs. "We should talk."

I nodded. Lana had no idea how true that statement was.

Lana led me out back where we sat down on some of the patio furniture, and almost immediately she started talking. I sat back and listened to her tell me all about her first night with Parker. How he threw money at her afterwards, and then how scared she was when she found out she was pregnant.

I knew what it was like to suffer in silence. To walk around with a smile on your face while you were dying inside. It killed me that she went through that. And when she told me how Parker tricked her into marriage and the things his mother did, I wanted to hurt him so much that my fists balled. Not that I would've been able to do much to a man his size, but I would've tried.

Yes, he'd taken care of everything, but the fact that he'd put her in that situation at all was infuriating. Then again, was I any better? While I did my best to protect her from the darkness of my world, I also didn't give her any information about what she was walking into. Was it too late to give her an out?

But every time I opened my mouth to say something, my stomach flipped. Would she hate me when she found out? Would the girl who sat with me night after night while I cried about my mother leave when she found out that I'd helped bury her ashes?

"Harper," Lana blew out a long heavy breath. "There's one more thing."

Now my stomach was flipping for an entirely different reason. The look on my best friend's face didn't show relief or happiness. Her expression was shadowed with the weight of something she'd been carrying around. I knew something about secrets, and this was one Lana was terrified to tell. But it was more than that. She wasn't scared to speak it.

"I hate myself for telling you this." My heart picked up its pace as she sat back and stared at the sky. "But I have a feeling you already know your father's not a good man."

Did Daddy do something to her? I'd never forgive myself if he did.

A chill ran down my spine, making my shoulders straighten. "Why would you say that?"

"Stop lying, Harper." Her hazel eyes swung my way. "I know who gave you those bruises."

The words, "I fell," just slipped out.

Jesus, Harper, just tell her.

"No you didn't. You wanna know how I know that?"

I was pretty sure I didn't.

Lana sat up and looked me directly in the eyes. "I know it was your father, because he…"

311

Before she could finish speaking, she was cut off by another voice singing, "Babies, babies, babies. I got me some babies."

My brows knit at the opening patio door. "Who's that?"

"Ugh, that's just Ava," Lana said and flopped back on her chair as if Ava Whitley was an annoyance, and not the crazy psycho daughter of the devil.

My pulse skyrocketed as the door swung open and a blonde sauntered out with a baby on each hip. My eyes flew around frantically searching for a place to hide before she saw me. Unfortunately it was too late for that. The blonde's grey eyes landed on me as I squeaked and jumped back.

"Oh hello. Who are you?"

All I saw in Ava Whitley's smile was pain and misery.

"Ava," Lana waved at me, "this is Harper."

I never wanted to disappear into a chair more than I did when Ava tipped her head and searched my face.

"Harper?" Ava looked up and crinkled her nose while bouncing the babies sitting on her hips. "Why does that sound familiar?"

Dear God, please don't let her know who I am.

I damn near jumped into the pool when Ava's eyes dropped back down to mine and narrowed.

"Do you know Mathers?"

Okay, I wasn't expecting that.

"Umm…" I looked over at Lana, who just shrugged. "No?"

"Oh, okay." Ava seemed disappointed for about half a second, then she turned her attention to the babies. "Who wants to see the pool?"

Weston just stared up at his aunt, while Winslow giggled and grabbed a handful of Ava's hair to shove in her mouth. Brave kid.

Ava walked past us and I leaned over to whisper to Lana, "Who's Mathers?"

The only person I knew with that name was some guy named

Chase that Riley talked about. Though I didn't see how Ava would know him.

"Don't ask," Lana grumbled. "There's something about fires and a dragon."

A dragon? Ava really was off her rocker.

"Are you sure she should be around the babies?" I got that she was their aunt, but was she stable enough? I mean, the girl was talking about dragons.

"Actually, she's great with them."

Huh?

"Sometimes I think she's a better mother than I am."

"I doubt that," I argued.

Lana was a great mom. She loved those babies and would do anything for them.

I looked over at Ava, who had the brightest smile on her face. She always had this spark of sadness when we were kids. It was nice to see her happy. Even if she was crazy.

The song *Cover Me In Sunshine* rang through the air, making Lana let out a disgruntled groan.

"It's Parker," she grumbled while picking up her phone. "I better get it or he'll keep calling."

I gave her a nod. Lana didn't like being interrupted, she thought was rude. Funny, considering half the time she was so busy talking that she didn't notice the people around her.

All hell broke loose when she answered the call. At first I thought a rock or something had flown into the glass jug of juice sitting on the table beside me. My brows knit as glass shattered and juice splashed on my leg. Then another quiet slice cut through the air as a light bulb burst apart.

After that, all I could hear was pops, rings, and dings, as a shower of plaster and glass rained down on us. Men came from everywhere, bursting out of the house and running around the yard with their guns drawn. The world slowed down as gunshots echoed through my ears.

Oh my god, I was in the middle of a firefight!

I couldn't breathe past the pounding in my chest. I could barely scream as someone grabbed me and threw me in the house. What the hell was happening? Who would shoot at us?

All I could do when Ava dropped a baby on my lap was gawk open mouthed at Lana, who looked just as terrified as me. She was clinging to Winslow so hard her knuckles were white.

"Don't worry," Ava plopped a pot on her head, grabbed a cast iron frying pan, and ran out the door. "I got this."

I looked down at Weston's calm face and prayed that I'd live long enough to see that bright sparkle in a set of green eyes again.

Chapter 25
Mason

*P*arker swung his hands back and forth, continuing to negotiate with the shop owner. I just rolled my eyes. Not only was I sent to 'Sam's Bait 'N' Tackle' to collect video footage of the night Tico was found, but I was sent with Parker. Mr. There's Always A Diplomatic Solution.

This shit could've been done in less than five minutes. All it would've taken were a few punches and threats. But noooo, Parker wanted to try and talk to him first.

I'm pretty sure we wouldn't have been sent here at all if talking worked. Gramps said that they were having issues getting the owner to cooperate. But hey, who was I to argue with Ashen Springs' golden boy?

"You'd be really helping us out." Parker braced his elbows on the counter and leaned in closer to the old man, eyeing him. "It couldn't hurt to be owed a favor, right?"

Grumbling under my breath, I ran my hand over a nearby shelf filled with feathered tackles. Favor my ass. Why the fuck should we do shit for him? Without counting in the fact that we owned this town, this grumpy ass fucker was neglecting the fact that a kid was killed. I should just beat it out of him.

I was about to spin around and show Parker my version of diplomacy when something caught my eye. My head tilted as I walked over to the window. Across the street was a small café with red checkered tables sitting out on a patio. Most were occupied with people happily eating, but it was the couple at the end that made my lips curl in a smile.

"No fucking way."

I could barely contain my laughter as Silas's grandpa reached over to sweep some hair off Gretta Crawford's forehead. Mr. Governor was on a date with Lana's nan. This was the best day ever. I stood back to snap a couple pictures, then texted my best friend.

Me: Hey man, what's up?

Silas: Not much just hanging out with Star.

I rolled my eyes. Nothing new there.

Me: Oh yeah, that's cool.

Silas: Hanging out with Star is cool?

Me: Yeah, she's your girl. You should hang out with her.

Silas: Alright, what's wrong?

Me: Nothing's wrong.

Silas: Then why are you acting weird?

Me: I'm not acting weird, you're acting weird.

Silas: You're the one that messaged me!

"Suspicious bastard," I snorted.

Me: All I did was ask how you were, asshole.

Silas:...

Me: You've known me long enough, you'd think you'd trust me by now.

Silas: That's exactly why I don't trust you.

Me: Fine then. Go back to your girlfriend.

Silas: I will.

Me: Wait, before you go...

Silas: What?

Me: Have you seen your gramps lately?

Silas: Yeah I saw him this morning. Why?

Me: No reason.

I sent him the pictures I took then pocketed my phone, ignoring the series of dings that followed. That should sufficiently ruin his relaxing afternoon. Maybe I'd send him a bouquet of flowers later, brought by a barber-shop quartet, of course. It'd been awhile since I sent him a strip-o-gram. Star would love that. If she wasn't such a pain in my ass, I might send her one too.

Huh? That wasn't a bad idea. I'd love to see the look on my best friend's face when some ripped, naked guy ground up against his girl. Now that would make my day.

"Hey," Parker waved me over to him. "Trent is going to let us have a look at his footage. Isn't that nice of him?"

I scowled right back at the old man behind the counter. "Yeah, that's real generous."

There was a reason we were interested in this store in particular. One of the exterior cameras was pointing at the only road leading to Cherry Lake. I tried to argue that someone could've walked Tico in. From what I heard, he wasn't a very big guy. But then Micha pointed out that that would be a long way to carry a body without being seen.

Sometimes I really hated logic. Especially when it had me stuck in a back room with Parker Whitley scrolling through hours of footage. This whole thing would've been a lot easier if Trent dated his tapes. I was about to walk out when Parker tapped the screen.

"Here we go."

There was Star's car, driving right past the camera. About a half hour before that a black town car rolled down the street. I couldn't tell who was driving, and the car itself didn't have any defining features. But I did pick up on one thing. Silas's Hummer drove by before we saw it leave. Meaning the fucker stayed to watch.

Judging by the look Parker gave me, he picked up on the same thing.

"You think he was after Star?"

Yes, but not for the same reason's Parker did. "I think it's a message."

There was only one thing Star and Tico had in common. Harper. Riley and Shelby had never been to Harper's house. I knew this, because I overheard them asking Lana where she lived.

Why hadn't my little liar invited her friends over? I didn't think she had anything to do with Tico's death, but I think she knew who did. It was all making sense now.

Harper's mother disappearing, her constant excuses, and now Tico. A great way to scare a little girl into compliance was by taking away the things she loved. And I contributed to her downfall. If I'd paid a little more attention...

Fuck.

I pulled out my phone and texted a number I recently added. I couldn't go back and change the past, but I could damn well make sure she was safe now.

> Me: Carving the raven in his chest was a nice touch.

> Ned: I don't know what you're talking about?

> Me: Don't play games with me, asshole.

> Ned: The games have just begun. Besides, I think you should be a little more concerned with the living than the dead.

A shiver ran down my spine as my eyes shot up to Parker. "Call Lana."

"What..."

"Right fucking now!"

"Alright," he muttered and made the call.

Relief washed over me when Lana answered and said they were having a drink on the patio.

Then Parker shot out of his chair. "What the fuck was that?"

The horror on his face chilled me to the bone.

"Angel, answer me!"

When no response came, Parker snatched his jacket. "We gotta go."

"What's going on?" I asked, following him out the door.

The entire world stopped with four words.

"Someone's shooting at them."

I SLAPPED the dashboard of Parker's station wagon. "Hurry the fuck up."

Why the fuck did we take the mommy mobile? My Corvette would've been there by now. Instead we were trudging along, as fast as this thing could go, and I was ready to jump out and race it down the driveway. What if Harper was hurt? What if she was shot, or worse?

Everywhere I went I'd see that red hair that pissed me off. She was always there. In school, around town, fuck, I'd even run into her at the doctor's office. I'd spent so much time consumed with making Harper's life hell, I never thought about what I'd do if she wasn't there. How empty would the halls in Ashworth feel if I didn't see her?

No, stop thinking like that. She's fine.

There was another time I thought those exact words. *She's fine.* But she wasn't fine. Not at all. Harper was drowning, and I took away her life preserver. I just couldn't see it.

Please God let there still be time to make this right.

Would I suddenly become a pussy ass bitch that rolled over and took shit from his woman? No. I'd still be the same asshole I always was. But I'd make damn sure that Harper was safe and no one ever hurt her again.

Harper was mine. She'd always been mine. And despite how much I hated her, I'd always been hers. That's what it all boiled down to in the end. Her and I. All the bullshit with Micha, the crap with Lou, even my addiction issues, were all because I couldn't admit one thing to myself.

I still loved her.

I never stopped.

And now I might never get to tell her.

I was out of the car before Parker pulled to a stop.

One of the men outside tried to stop me, but my fist met his face before he could do more than raise his hand. Nicolai Ivanov could kiss my ass, because the only thing I could see were the holes riddling the siding of Parker's house. Why did I bring Harper here? She was safer at my house.

'Dad, I need to get to Harper. She's hurt.'

'I know Mason, and we'll go just as soon as you get your sweater.'

I tore through the interior, knocking shit over as I went by. Images filled my mind as I searched. Images of a perfect freckled nose dotted with blood and big doe eyes that no longer sparkled. Ned Callaghan was a dead man. I was going to rip his heart out of his fucking chest. I'd make him pay, even if it was too late.

No, I couldn't think that.

But what if you're right? What if Harper's already gone?

I stopped and hunched over to catch my breath. Where was she? I couldn't find anyone other than Nicolai's men.

'I'm sorry Mason, but I didn't make it up.'

'Yes you did.'

The second I saw that tape I should've known something was wrong. I should've seen it. I should've saved her.

"Where the fuck is she?" I bellowed while flipping over the couch.

"They're over here." My gaze snapped up to the suited man coming down the stairs. "We put them in the safe room."

"She's okay?"

'Harper's fine, but you're going to have to come with us.'

The man nodded and waved for me to follow him down the hall. The voices of the past continued to speak as I walked with him. I could feel the handcuffs being clipped around my wrists. The click of a tape being played followed us around the corner. When we stopped in front of a door, I heard the clang of my cell being locked shut. Then when the door swung open and I saw the sparkle of fear in Harper's big doe eyes, three words rang through my head.

'Mason did it.'

She was right. I did do it. I abandoned her, because my monster wouldn't let me see hers. All these years Ryker Hudson's taunt sat in the back of my head when it should've been the broken look in her eyes on that video tape. Never again.

I rushed forward and scooped her up in my arms. "I'm sorry, baby. I'm so fucking sorry."

And what did my sweet girl do? She wrapped her arms around me and kissed the tear sliding down my cheek.

"Don't worry. We're all okay."

God damnit.

I cupped her cheeks and peppered her with kisses, making sure I didn't miss a single one of those thirty-seven dots. I couldn't get close enough to her. And when I pulled away to memorize every inch of her face, she smiled back at me. I snapped. Slammed my lips down on hers and pushed her back on the ground. I needed to be inside her.

Right.

Fucking.

Now.

I didn't give a shit who was there. Didn't care when Lana muttered something and ran out of the room. Not even Harper could stop me, and she was trying. When I unclasped my belt she pushed on my shoulders and argued that people could see.

Good. I wanted them to see. I wanted everyone in this house, including Harper, to know who she belonged to. Besides, the babies left with Lana, so who the fuck cared who else was watching? Not even God himself could stop me from reaching up under her skirt and tearing her panties off.

"Mason, stop." Harper wriggled to the side, trying to buck her hips away, but I was already there, pushing into her tight walls.

I groaned as the heat of her pussy enveloped my cock. Then slammed into her when she moaned in response. She could tell me to stop and shake her head all she wanted, but she liked this shit just as much as I did. Proof of that came three pumps later when her back bowed and she screamed out my name. Did I get off on forcing girls? No, I got off on forcing her.

I fucked her hard all over that room. Knocking stuff off the counters and breaking shit as I enjoyed the way her face twisted in pleasure. But I needed to feel something else. I wrapped my hand around Harper's neck and slammed her down on the floor.

"Hit me."

Her flushed face screwed up in confusion. "What?"

"You heard me." I gave her just the slightest swivel of my hips. "I said hit me."

"No." She shook her head. "I don't want to."

I didn't ask if she wanted to.

"What's wrong, Freckles? Too pathetic to fight back?" I pushed my cock in as far as it would go and leaned down to growl, "Too beaten down by Daddy to grow a backbone?"

That did it. Her tiny hand swung through the air, slapping off my cheek. The bite from her strike shot straight to my dick.

"Again," I growled while thrusting into her.

This time she didn't hesitate and I groaned as her nails raked across my flesh.

"That's it, baby." I drove up into her so hard she slid across the floor. "I want all your anger."

Oh and she gave it to me. Harper lashed out and screamed.

Beating me with her fists while I fucked the shit out of her. Nothing could compare to how hot it was to see her lose control. Her hot little cunt squeezed around my shaft, sending sparks of electricity up my spine that mingled with the burn in my scalp and the sting of her teeth.

I'd never come so hard in my life. My heart literally stopped when I shot my load inside her. It took a few minutes for me to catch my breath to a point where I could roll off her and collapse on the floor.

Harper panted from beside me and stared up at the ceiling. "Mason, I'm sorry…"

"Don't." I rolled my head to swing my gaze her way. "Don't ever apologize again."

"B-but, I hit you?"

I tipped my eyes down to the red mark of her teeth on my arm and smiled. *Yeah she fucking did.*

"I didn't mean to hurt you."

"Trust me, Freckles." I reached over and rolled her on top of me. "You didn't hurt me."

It was so fucking cute how she dug her teeth into her lip, unsure if she should believe me. Well, she better get used to it, because the only person she'd be taking orders from was me.

"Stop that," I growled while popping her lip out of her mouth with my thumb. "Or I'll fuck you again."

The color drained from her face as she shook her head. That small timid act was getting me hard again. Unfortunately, we were interrupted.

Parker walked up to the open doorway and threw his hand up in front of his face. "Oh god, put that shit away."

"Why?" I cocked a brow at him. "You've seen my dick before."

"It's not your dick I'm worried about."

Oh shit.

I reached down and flipped Harper's skirt back in place. "Stop staring at my girlfriend's ass!"

"I'm your girlfriend?" Harper smiled down at me.

"Until I put a ring on your finger, you are."

Parker waved his hand at us. "Can we do this later? We have a problem."

Damn cockblock.

"Ugh, fine." I rolled my eyes and pushed Harper and I up to sit. "You're acting like someone died."

"Someone did. My nanny."

Damn. I was so happy to find Harper okay that it hadn't occurred to me that there might be other casualties.

Parker's light eyes locked on mine. "And she had a raven carved in her chest."

Chapter 26
Harper

The drive back to Oakleigh Manor was a quiet one. I sat quietly in my seat while Mason fisted the steering wheel and stared out the windshield. He was obviously angry, I just didn't know if it was because of me, or Lana's nanny.

I could understand it being the later. Bernice was such a sweet lady, who loved those babies. Poor Lana was broken up about it. I spent the last hour we were there trying to comfort her.

What kind of person would do something like that? How callous did someone have to be to open fire on innocent children? Daddy had his faults, but I'd like to think he'd never do something like that. Then again, there was a time I thought he'd never hurt me. Maybe I was a bad judge of character? I mean, I did sleep with Mason Kessler. And I liked it.

There was something wrong with me.

Mason pulled up to the house where Mr. Kessler was waiting, and grumbled, "Great. Just what I fucking need."

My gaze swung from one to the other. I didn't understand Mason's animosity. Louis might not be his biological father, but he was more of a dad to Mason then mine was to me. Didn't he realize how much something like that was worth? I'd sacrifice anything to have someone care about me the Louis did Mason.

Maybe I did have someone?

I couldn't get what happened at Lana's house out of my head. Mason clung to me so tightly, it was like he thought I'd vanish. No, he was scared I'd disappear. My gaze trickled over his dark hair and down to those bright green eyes sparkling with annoyance. Could that be true? Was Mason Kessler afraid he'd lost me?

"Come on." He swung open his door and huffed back at me. "Don't answer any of his questions."

"Um… okay?" How exactly was I supposed to ignore Louis Kessler? Mason did understand who his father was, right?

He ducked down to glare in the car where I was still seated. "I mean it, Harper. Don't say shit."

"But–"

"Not buts. You're mine, not his. Got it?"

I wasn't sure if I could do what he said, but nodded anyway and stepped out into the fading evening sun. The events of the day caused one thought to roll through my head. It was warrior's hours. How ironic was that? The pink hue in the sky was extra bright, as if the world itself knew I had to find the courage to go back in the past and unravel the tangle of lies I'd created.

Mason barged into Lana's house, panicked that something had happened to me. The least I could do was give him the answers he wanted. Funny thing was, I wasn't scared. I was relieved.

"Son." Louis gave Mason a small nod.

He rolled his eyes in response. "Louis."

"We need to talk."

Mason clasped his hand in mine and shouldered past him. "We really don't."

"Yes," Louis reached out and grabbed his shoulder, stopping him, "we do."

When I felt Mason's fingers tighten around mine, I thought he might hit his father. I kept waiting for his fist to swing through the air. But it didn't.

Instead, Mason looked at the hand on his shoulder and said, "Not right now."

And to my surprise, Louis sighed and let him go. I couldn't help but stare back at the look on his face as Mason pulled me away. Louis Kessler was quite possibly the most self assured person I knew. Yet right now he looked defeated. It broke my heart to see such a strong man broken.

"You should be nicer to him."

"Oh yeah?" Mason snorted. "And why's that?"

"Because he's your father. He loves you." Why couldn't he see that?

When he dropped his eyes down to me, I could feel the anger burning in Mason's glare. "He's not my father."

It killed me to see him like this. I couldn't fix the damage I did, but maybe I could help him see the light in this situation.

"I don't hear you saying the same things to Maggie," I pointed out. "She's not your biological sister, and you still love her."

Anyone who spent half a second with that little girl would know that. She spent most of our tea party talking up her big brother.

"I never said I didn't love him. I'm just..." Mason huffed out a heavy breath. "Mad at him."

My brow rose. "Does he know that?"

He stopped and narrowed his eyes. "Why do you care?"

Because I care about you.

As much as I wanted to tell him that, I couldn't. So I hung my head instead. "Not all kids have good parents."

"Yeah, well." Mason pulled me up the stairs that led to his room. "Maybe if they told someone about it, their life would get better."

My mind screamed to tell him, but my mouth wouldn't work. The only thing I could do was chew on my lips as we walked down the hall. I'd never been more nervous than I was when he unlocked his bedroom door. My pulse was beating so fast, I thought he could hear it.

"Don't look so scared, Freckles," Mason smirked and pushed me in the room. "I'm not going to do anything to you that I haven't done before."

The bright red scratch marks on his cheek caused my hands to wring. I did that to him. I marked his beautiful skin with my anger, just like I marked his soul with my lie.

Mason locked the door then turned around and demanded, "Strip."

Neither of us expected what came out of my mouth.

"He killed my mother."

God it felt good to say that.

Part of me expected Mason to push me for more. But all he did was cross his arms and arch a brow.

"Okay."

I was officially confused. "You're not going to ask for more?"

"Would you give it to me?"

Yes.

No.

"Maybe?"

Mason rolled his eyes and sauntered across the room. "I'm tired of trying to pry information out of you, Harper."

Wasn't this what he wanted? Was I too late? Had he already written me off completely? I watched him sit down on the bed and take his shoes off. No. He wouldn't have looked at me the way he did if he'd given up, right? I had to try.

Taking a step forward, I swallowed down my nerves and asked,

"Do you remember the day I was supposed to meet you at the beach?"

"Kinda hard to forget the day the love of your life stood you up because she was in the hospital." Mason reached back and pulled his shirt off. "Especially when she said you put her there."

Ouch. If someone could be sucker punched by a statement, I just was. Was this a good idea? When I told him, would he hate me more?

Come on Harper, you can't stop now.

"I forgot to tell my mom about it before I went to bed, so I looked for her that night."

Mason didn't say anything. He sat there quietly, watching me inch slowly closer to him.

Tears dripped down my face with my next words. "I found her. In my father's office, and he was..."

It hurt too much to say it. I wanted to tell him. The truth was right there, but I couldn't spit it out. All I could see was the cold empty look in her once vibrant eyes.

"He, um..."

"He killed her." Mason finished for me. "Then he beat you to keep you quiet."

I nodded and waited for him to tell me how pathetic I was. Seconds ticked on, thickening the silence in the air. I could feel his judgment weighing me down. It was so heavy and suffocating that I could barely breathe.

Mason's chest rose with a huff that thundered through my ears like a drum. This was the moment that he cut ties. The time when my tiny spark of hope was squashed forever and I was sent back to my father for the treatment I deserved.

His hand lifted to give a small wave. "Come here."

Of all the times I walked across this room, this one was the hardest. My mind was a whirlwind of emotions. The heaviness of my choices weighed my steps down, while my heart pattered with hope that made it flip anxiously. The thoughts running through my head only added to my internal storm.

Does he hate me? Does he care? Should he care?

By the time my foot flattened on the floor in my last step, I was ready to collapse. My knees were trembling so bad that the motion vibrated up my body, tensing every muscle I had.

"I'm going to be real with you, Freckles." Mason pulled me in between his legs then smoothed his palms down my arms. "Whatever you tell me won't erase the past."

My heart dropped along with my hope.

"But," he tipped my chin up, forcing me to look into his eyes. "You weren't the only one at fault."

What did that mean? How was he at fault? The only thing Mason did wrong was trust me.

As if he could read my thoughts, he said, "I could've asked more questions instead of abandoning you."

"You didn't—"

"Yes, I did." He exhaled, causing his shoulders to rise and fall. "You need to understand something. I'm not that little boy anymore. He died a long time ago."

"He's still in there." I could see him sparkling in the glint in Mason's eyes.

He leaned forward and placed a tender kiss on my forehead. "Only the part that loved you."

What? "You still love me?"

"I never stopped." The corner of his mouth curled in a crooked smile. "Why do you think I was so mean to you?"

I didn't know how to feel about that. People weren't cruel to the ones they loved. But they also didn't break their hearts either, and that's exactly what I did to him. There was no stopping my tears. They burst forth like waterfalls as I flung my arms around his neck.

"I'm sorry. I didn't want to hurt you."

"Shh," he soothed while stroking my back. "It doesn't matter anymore."

But it did matter. Mason took on the boogeyman for me and I folded under my monster's threat. He deserved better. He deserved someone who would stand up for him like he did for me. He deserved someone strong. Could I be that person for him?

"You need to understand something." His grip around my waist tightened, pressing me up against him. "Your father's going to die."

Panic soared through my heart, thumping it loudly against my ribs. "No! You can't. You have to leave him alone."

"That's not gonna happen."

Yes it was. I struggled to get away. He couldn't do this. All my suffering and silence would be for nothing if he confronted my father.

"You don't know him." Daddy was capable of horrible things.

"He's gonna die, Freckles." He fisted my hair and yanked my head back. "You need to make your peace with that."

My entire body shook as I stared up into Mason's hard stare. "But... he's my dad."

The same man who kissed my forehead when I was sick and tucked me in at night. When I fell and hurt myself it was him I ran to. I called out his name when I had a nightmare, and held his hand when I was scared. The first hint of warmth I ever felt came from him. He was my father. My first love.

"No, he isn't," Mason growled. "He stopped being your dad the second he beat you."

"You hurt me," I snarled back. "You hurt me all the time."

"That's right I fucking do, and I'm not gonna stop. You like it when I hurt you." He leaned in, bringing his lips a breath away from mine. "I bet your pussy's soaked right now."

So what if he was right? It didn't mean anything. It was his fault I reacted this way. He's the one that turned my body against me.

"Admit it, you like it when I tell you what to do."

No. Screw him. The only thing I would admit to was how much I wanted to slap that smug grin off his face.

"Fuck you, Mason."

"Careful Freckles," he tsked. "You're in danger of becoming a potty mouth."

I lost it. I lunged forward, forgetting that my hair was in his grip, and tried to claw his face. The chuckle Mason let out when he yanked me back only spurred me on.

"I hate you," I yelled while kicking at him.

Not even the ache traveling up my foot from the solidness of his shin could stop me. Somewhere in the back of my mind flashed the brief thought that I shouldn't be doing this, but I couldn't stop lashing out. It was like all the anger I'd been suppressing all those years broke through the dam I tucked them behind. Rage poured out of me like a fountain. I smacked him in the face, bit his arm, and stomped on his feet. None of which phased him.

Mason didn't so much as flinch when I struck him. He continued yanking on my hair and glaring down at me as if I was nothing more than a nuisance. He didn't even cock a brow when my arms finally fell down, exhausted.

"You done?"

And just like that, I found my second wind.

Fat drops burned in my eyes as I screamed my hatred and swung my hand.

"I hate you." *Smack.* "And your stupid smile." *Slap.* "You ruined everything."

Except it wasn't Mason that ruined things.

I collapsed down on the ground, out of breath.

It was me.

The way Mason petted the back of my head was a stark contrast to the tone in his growl. "Throw another tantrum like that and I'll show you just how much I can stretch all of your holes."

My glare locked on his and the words slipped out before I could stop them. "You're no better than him."

Instead of punishing me – like I thought he would – Mason picked me up, gently placed me on the bed, and strolled over to the door.

"When you're ready to stop acting like a child and have an adult conversation, I'll be back." He paused with the door open and glanced over his shoulder. "Oh, and Freckles, don't ever compare me to that piece of shit again."

After that, Mason left, locking the door behind him.

And I'd never felt more alone.

Chapter 27
Mason

*M*oonlight glowed around me as I sat in the kitchen staring at a cup of juice. Fucking. Juice. And why had I chosen this to drink instead of something with a bit more bite? Because Harper said I was no better than her father.

I knew it was only said out of anger. Trust me, I got it. I'd babbled off more stupid shit than anyone I knew because I was pissed. But in this case, I couldn't help but wonder if she was right?

I'd never be the nice guy who sugar coated shit. Hell, I wasn't even sure if I'd be able to calm down when I fucked her. Not that she seemed to mind. But I could make sure that I maintained as much control over myself as possible. And that meant no more alcohol – which was a lot fucking harder than it should be.

I swallowed down the rest of my G rated apple nectar and cursed the bottle of wine locked in the cabinet above the fridge. How good would that shit taste right now? Every time my hand twitched with need, I reminded myself that what was in that bottle wouldn't have half the sweet flavor as what was waiting for me upstairs.

"You're still up?"

The internal groan rolling through my chest threatened to burst out full force when Lou clicked on the light and waltzed in.

"Why are you sitting in the dark?"

"A bright shining light kinda puts a damper on the 'wallow in one's misery' ambiance I was going for."

Lou braced his forearms on the opposite side of the island and cocked a brow. "Are you okay?"

Was I ever okay?

"I'm fine."

"You know what they say about the word fine?"

Please enlighten me.

"It's seldom associated with its true meaning."

If that wasn't a statement to make someone shake their head, I didn't know what was. "As always, you're a true paragon of information."

He sighed and pushed off the marble counter to open the fridge. I ran my gaze over the black silk pajamas he was wearing – button up, of course. This was as casual as Louis Kessler got. I suppose it was better than the suit he was always wearing, and the slight mess on the top of his head made me have to suppress a smile. There was only one way a man would get a knot like that in his hair.

"I don't hate you."

Lou paused with a bottle of water pressed to his lips. "I know."

"I'm just…"

"Angry," he finished.

"Hurt," I corrected.

"I can see that." He set his bottle down on the counter and nodded. "But I want you to know something, Mason. You were never not my son. Never. I don't care how you came into this world, you were always my boy."

That was a nice idea, and he may say that now, but, "How old was I when you found out?"

"I knew before you were born."

What? If he knew I wasn't his, why did he let my mother have me?

"As I said," his dark eyes met mine. "You were always my boy."

I wasn't really sure how to respond to that. Honestly, I thought my DNA was something he figured out when I was like five and he was attached already. It had never occurred to me that he knew before I took my first breath. I guess I shouldn't be surprised. The information that man knew astounded even Micha.

"So no more of this 'I'm not your son' bullshit."

"Alright," I rolled my eyes and mockingly sang, "Dad."

He let out a small snicker. "I'll take it."

I sat there in the kitchen while he made us a midnight snack. Peanut butter and jam with the crusts cut off. Just like we used to have when I was a kid.

He picked half the sandwich up and slid the other half over to me. "We should talk about what happened at Parker's house."

"There's not a lot to talk about," I said while taking a bite. "His nanny was found with a raven carved in her chest. Not much more I can tell you."

"I'm more interested in how you knew something was going to happen?"

I forced the bite down my throat and looked up at him. "I don't know what you're talking about?"

"Parker said you two might not have made it in time if you hadn't insisted he call home."

Fucking Parker.

"So?"

Lou crossed his arms and leaned back. I could see him studying me, searching my face for signs of deception. "Does this have anything to do with what's going on with Harper?"

"If it does, then it's my business." I could lie, but the man was a human lie detector.

"And you," he pointed at me, "are my business."

He had a valid point. There was no reason for me not to tell him about Ned, other than the fact that I wanted the pleasure of ending his life. Someone had to make him suffer.

"When that guy was stalking Cheyenne, did she ask for any of our help?"

"That's different."

"No it's not," I argued.

She was his woman, and Harper was mine. If he could protect Cheyenne all on his own, then I could make sure my girl was safe.

Lou's nostrils flared, telling me he didn't like the idea. "Do you have things in order?"

By order he meant, stacked to my side.

"Yes."

There was a reason Mrs. Benson didn't come back here with me. Let's just say Harper's staff was less than impressed when they found out what their employer was doing to his daughter. The second he set foot in that house, I'd know. I'd also reached out to an old contact. A dealer named Blake who had his fingers in the New Haven police department.

That's how I found out Ned Callaghan didn't exist until he moved to Ashen Springs. That little tidbit of information I was given about an hour ago. Couldn't help but wonder how much Harper really knew about the man she called father.

"Alright," Lou sighed. "I'll leave it be for now. But if you run into any trouble, come to me."

I gave him a salute. "Ten-four."

"Your grandfather is not going to be happy about this."

That made me smile. "And I bet you'll be real upset about delivering the update."

Pissing Gramps off had become my old man's favorite pastime.

Speaking of pissing people off...

I still had a brat upstairs to deal with. She'd probably calmed down by now. It'd been a couple of hours. Still...

I eyed a bottle of olive oil on the counter next to my arm.

Lou was always saying that actions had consequences, and I was a firm believer in learning one's lessons. Harper still had yet to learn the most important one.

She belonged to me.

HARPER LOOKED SO beautiful sprawled out across my bed with her red hair fanned out over my pillows. I'd been staring at her for a while now. Listening to her quiet little snores, then snickering when she woke herself up for a split second.

She'd even taken the time to change into one of my shirts. There was nothing sexier than the sight of my girl wrapped up in my clothes. She swam in it, but every time she moved the blue fabric would ride up a little more.

Best strip tease ever.

I crawled up on the mattress, over her sleeping form, then reached down to graze my fingers up her leg. "You're so fucking cute."

Harper grumbled something and squirmed, while popping her bottom lip out in a grumpy little pout. Guess she tired herself out with that tantrum. The nice thing to do would be to let her sleep, but then I ran the risk of her clamming up again, and we weren't done talking.

Folding over her, I brought my lips to her ear and whispered, "Wake up, Freckles."

There was that pout again. If she wasn't careful she'd wake up to me biting her lip.

"Come on, baby," I coaxed while caressing her cheek with my thumb. "Open those pretty eyes."

Finally her eyelashes fluttered as her lids rolled open. "Mason?"

"Hi." I couldn't stop my mouth from curling as the moonlight sparkled off her big doe orbs.

"Are you still mad at me?"

That made me chuckle. "I wasn't the mad one."

She was the one who lost her shit. I had a couple bruises to prove it. Not that I minded. I kinda liked seeing her like that.

Harper, however, didn't see it as a good thing. Her eyes dropped guiltily away from mine as she whispered, "I'm sorry."

"Hey." I pressed my finger under her chin, forcing her to look back up at me. "What did I say about sorry's?"

"No more."

"That's right."

"But I hit you?"

"Yeah," I said, "and I told you I was gonna kill your old man."

Her mouth clamped shut and I could see a spark of anger flash through her eyes.

"It's okay, Freckles. I get it." Regardless of how much of a piece of shit I thought Ned Callaghan was, he was still her dad. "I don't accept it, but I get it."

I was the one who felt like a piece of shit when her face brightened up.

"So you're going to leave him alone?"

"No," I shook my head. "I'm still gonna kill him."

It wasn't that I wanted to squash her hope. It was that I didn't want her living under any false delusions. We'd both put up with enough falsehoods. Reality was a bitch sometimes. That, I couldn't change. But I could make sure that hers didn't include bruises and broken bones.

When she rolled her head away I sighed and rolled it back. No more avoiding each other.

"Let me ask you something, Freckles. Do you want me?"

Her big brown eyes gazed up at me. "Yes."

"Do you love me?"

There was no hesitation in her answer. "Yes. But you scare me."

"I know." I raised my hand and swept a lock of hair off her forehead. "And there's only one way that will change. I need you to give me your complete and utter surrender."

Her eyes widened and I could feel her heart hammering against her chest. She was scared – which was turning me on – but if she didn't give me what I asked for, things would continue the exact same way. I needed to know that she trusted me enough to not question the things I told her to do. I needed her to be my perfect obedient pet. Not all the time – I liked forcing her – but tonight. Because if she could hand her life over to me, then I'd know she was truly mine.

"Can you do that for me, Freckles?" I slid my hand under her shirt while laving my tongue on the side of her neck. "Can you be my good girl?"

"I can't do it again." She wiggled her hips, trying to shift away. "I'm sore."

That was fair. I hadn't exactly given her a break since I stole her virginity. But that wasn't what I had in mind.

"I promise I won't fuck your pussy." I couldn't stop the smirk from washing across my face.

Harper chewed on her lips for a second before shyly saying, "Okay."

Half a second later I had her shirt pulled over her head. To her credit, she didn't argue. Though she did look hesitant.

"Put your arms over your head."

I had to arch my brow to get her to do that one, but when her shaky arms slowly lifted, something swelled deep inside me. A warm glow in my chest that I hadn't felt in seven years. It shook me up for a moment. I had to blink my eyes and make sure the beauty under me was real. That perfect button nose with the thirty-seven freckles didn't disappear.

She stayed right where she was, staring up at me with big wide eyes, while her bottom lip quivered. All I wanted to do in that moment was kiss the fear off Harper's face and reassure her that despite everything, she would be okay.

We would be okay.

And that's exactly what I did. I folded over her, brushing my lips over every inch of her skin. Cheeks to mouth, then across her chin and up to the tip of her nose, and then over her soft fluttering eyelids, until she let out a contented sigh. That's when I clipped the handcuffs on her wrists.

This bed was a lot more than it seemed. I had all kinds of things tucked into it. Each and every item hidden within I'd handpicked. For her.

"Mason?" Harper tugged on the chains binding her arms down. "What are you–"

"Shhh." I grazed my lips over hers and whispered, "You need to trust me."

She didn't want to. I could feel that in the way her muscles tensed. At this point, trust was a foreign feeling for both of us. That's why this was so important. It was the first step to rebuilding that bond that we used to have. A bond that had never completely broken.

I moved down her torso, taking my time to worship her flat stomach, tiny hips, and full breasts. Sucking a pert nipple into my mouth, I let out a growl when she moaned. I could spend the rest of eternity right where I was, listening to the way her breath quickened. My dick, however, wasn't satisfied with a taste.

When I began shimmying her shorts down her legs, Harper scooted up the bed and sat up.

"You said you wouldn't…"

"And you said you'd give me your surrender," I said, while grabbing her ankles to yank her back down where I wanted her. "You gonna change your mind? Because I can too."

She shook her head and closed her eyes.

When I striped her panties off I had every intention of sticking to my word–which was that I wouldn't fuck her pussy. That didn't mean I couldn't steal a few licks. Especially considering it was right there, all pretty and pink. Oh, and I gave it the attention it was begging for.

I laved my tongue through her folds and nipped on her clit until Harper was moaning and bucking her hips. Just when she was about to come, I flipped her over. Nothing in this world sounded better than the disgruntled little huff of frustration she let out.

"Sorry, Freckles." I said while snatching the olive oil I'd brought up with me off the bedside table. "You don't get to come yet."

First I needed her to relax. so I poured the oil over her back and began kneading her muscles. When I felt her body loosen under my touch I moved to another spot. I took my time working her shoulders all the way down to her legs, but my one hand never left her ass. That one I rubbed over her firm globes and down to the sweet spot between her thighs, then back up again, mixing her own lubrication with the one I'd brought.

Harper was so wound up she was pressing back into my hand every time my finger flicked her clit. But that wasn't the hole I was going for. I swept my thumb over her tight back hole and while she was lost in her lust filled haze, pushed it in.

"What are you doing?" she squealed, while attempting to lift her head off the bed.

I pushed her head back down and continued to fuck her ass

with my thumb. If I wasn't so enthralled with what I was doing then I might've been able to make out what she was saying. I tried to listen. Heard something along the lines of no, it won't fit, but once I'd added a finger to my thumb's movements, I was lost.

Before I knew what was happening, I had my jeans pushed over my hips and was lining up my cock.

"It's okay, Freckles," I grunted and forced my way in. "You just need to relax."

I think she screamed. Could've been a cry. I wasn't sure. My entire focus was on watching her tight little ass stretch around my shaft. It was so fucking hot that I pulled her cheeks apart so I could watch myself sink into her. And when my pelvis finally smacked against her backside, I saw stars.

Shit. This wasn't going to take long.

My balls were already starting to pull up.

Gritting my teeth, I reached down to finger her clit while I fucked her. Not hard, like before. I slowly pulled my cock out of her, then gently thrust back in. So she'd enjoy it as much as I was. I wanted to revel in this moment. Take my time to admire the little twitches and soft moans my girl was letting out. Harper's body looked so small against mine. Like I was shoving a telephone pole up her ass. Yet she took every last inch like a champ.

"I wish you could see this," I groaned and pinched her clit. "You're taking my cock like a good girl."

Those last two words caused Harper's back to bow. She shoved the blanket in her mouth to muffle her scream, and I drove in. Clamping my teeth on her shoulder as I shot my load inside her. I'd taken every hole she had now. I growled as the tinge of her blood ran over my tongue and thrust into her a few more times.

The beast wanted to come out and play, but this time I was able to push him back. Harper Callaghan was mine. I would love her. I would fuck her, and I would take care of her. Even if that meant protecting her from myself.

Chapter 28
Harper

*A*ll day long I wandered around not knowing how to act. Mason was being weird. When we woke up, he was smiling and said good morning. At breakfast he made sure I got the last blueberry muffin – which he argued with Logan over – then he took me up to his room to watch a movie and cuddle. And the movie was what boys would call a chick flick.

"Hey baby, you look great." Mason kissed my forehead and smiled. "You ready?"

I don't know if I was ready. Mason had a fight tonight, and for some reason he wanted me to come. I wasn't sure how I felt about that.

"Why do you want me to come?"

Watching someone get beat up wasn't exactly my idea of fun. I got enough of that all on my own.

"I need my good luck charm."

Good luck charm?

My eyes narrowed.

Why was he being nice? Was this a trick? Whatever it was, I didn't like it.

"Come on."

He grabbed my sweater off the dresser, where he placed it after he folded it. Yes, folded. What the hell? Earlier I tried to make him mad by slapping his hand away when he pawed at me. And know what Mason did? He placed his hand on my leg and left it there.

Mason opened his bedroom door and gave me a smile that lit up his eyes.

Was he mad at me? Did I do something wrong? Was this his way of punishing me? Because I couldn't take it any more.

Even the tone in his voice was playful. "Well don't just stand there, Freckles. You don't want to be late, do you?"

Alright, that's it.

"Stop being so nice," I yelled while stamping my foot.

His brow arched and for a second I thought maybe he would spank me or something. Heck, I'd take another rough sex act over this nice guy stuff. My girl parts might complain, but I'd feel better. I was half ready to whip down my jeans and bend over for him.

Until he laughed. And not just a small chuckle, but a full on clutching his belly laugh.

My face dropped. "Can you stop already?"

"Is there something wrong with me being in a good mood?"

"Yes," I said. "You're supposed to be mean and grumpy while you choke me, or pull on my hair and shove things in places where they shouldn't fit." I even gave my hair a little tug to show him what I meant. "Not… this."

I waved my hands over the pod person that had taken over Mason Kessler.

"Don't worry, Freckles, I'm still all those things." He flashed his perfect teeth at me and I wanted to slap the smile off his face. "This is just my pre-fight mood."

This time it was my brow that arched. "So, you're happy before you get beat up?"

That was messed up on so many levels.

"Okay, first things first, I'm the one that does the beating. And yes. I'm in a good mood before." He grabbed my hand and shot me a wink before pulling me out the door. "Gotta keep my anger for when I step in the ring."

Oh. I guess that made sense.

"So you'll go back to being a jerk when you're done?"

"Yes, Freckles," he chuckled. "I'll go back to being a jerk when I'm done. I might even punish you for calling me one."

That shouldn't be comforting, but it was. I kind of liked regular Mason. This guy put me on edge. When someone had seen the darkest parts of another's soul, it was hard to accept the light. At least in my experience, anyway. The sun may come out to shine, but the clouds were always waiting near-by. And the longer it took for them to loom over the horizon, the worse the storm would be.

Mason Kessler himself was a force. I didn't want to find out what would happen if he let those clouds build. There were plenty of people on his list. Including my father – who I still had yet to figure out how to save. There was a good man somewhere inside him, and that man deserved a chance to thrive.

We walked down the hall to the raven that spanned across the entryway, where another monster was leaning back against the wall. Logan Hudson had his ankles crossed while he stared down at the phone in his hands. A part of me hoped we could sneak past without being seen. That didn't happen.

As soon as we turned the corner, Logan's eyes rolled up. "Hey."

"Hey." Mason nodded at him. "You waiting for Shelby?"

"You could say that."

Why else would he be here? Please don't let him be coming with us.

A female voice I recognized to be Shelby echoed out from the kitchen. "It's not that big a deal, Mom."

"Not that big a deal?" said another voice I'd only heard a couple of times. "You are seventeen years old!"

"Lot's of seventeen-year-olds get married."

Wait... what? Logan and Shelby were married? When? How? I was pretty sure I didn't miss a wedding. Then again, would they have invited me?

"This is exactly what I'm talking about." Shelby's mom sounded mad. "You are not old enough to make these kinds of decisions."

Something crashed on the floor, urging me to tuck myself into Mason's side. There were a lot of things in a kitchen that you could hurt someone with. I could almost hear the crack of a rolling pin smacking off my leg.

"It's okay," Mason whispered, while smoothing his hand down my back.

I jumped to wrap my arms around him when Shelby yelled, "I'll be eighteen in two months!"

Why couldn't they stop yelling?

"Oh, is that so?" her mom sang. "Well if you're so grown up then maybe you should live with your new husband."

Almost instantly Logan pushed off the wall. "And that's my cue."

I watched him walk away, then looked up at Mason. "Can we go?"

Shelby and her mom were still yelling, although now it was at Logan. I didn't really care. I just wanted to get out of there. The haunted memories of painful strikes and hateful words were creeping up on me.

'Too stupid to do anything right.'

'Why can't you do anything right?'

'You're such a disappointment.'

'Useless.'

'I wish your mother never had you.'

It wasn't until we stepped outside that I realized none of the taunting phrases running through my head were Mason's.

Mason cupped my face and gazed down at me. "You okay, beautiful?"

"Yes," I smiled back at him.

All I saw of Star before she tackled me was a streak of blonde hair.

"I was so worried about you." One second she was hugging me and the next she was slapping Mason's chest. "You arsehole! What did you do to her?"

The wicked smirk that spread across his face was answer enough, but of course he had to go a step further. "Oh, I did plenty."

My jaw dropped. He did not just say that.

"I knew it." Star's eyes narrowed into tiny angry points as she swung her glare to Silas – who was standing next to his Hummer. "I told you he'd take advantage of her. But nooo, you said he wasn't that kind of guy…"

At least I wasn't the only liar in this group.

"Calm down, London. She liked it."

Star was small, but I was pretty sure Mason shouldn't be antagonizing her. Judging by the look on her face when she turned back around, I was right.

"What did you just say?" She looked like she was going to pounce on him.

As much as I wanted to run and hide, I couldn't abandon Mason to her wrath. So I summoned all my strength and stepped in between them.

"It's okay, Star," I reassured her. "Everything's good. I promise."

Can't say I was surprised when she didn't automatically believe me.

"Are you sure?"

I tipped my chin back and looked at Mason. The way he was staring down at me with a twinkle in his green eyes caused a tingling sensation to fill my chest.

Mason Kessler wasn't adding to the voices in my head anymore.

He was battling them.

I DIDN'T LIKE it in here. There were so many people, I barely had space to breathe. And they were loud, yelling stuff at the ring someone had set up in the middle of the bar. I clung onto Star's shirt and stared up at the bearded man behind us. He was big, tattooed, and mean looking. Just the kind of man I'd expect to see in New Haven.

Why were we here anyway? This was the place where bad things happened to good people. Mason and Silas could probably take care of themselves, but Star and I were little. Neither of us came up to a single person's shoulders. She didn't seem worried though.

Star stood beside me quietly humming while she sipped on a mug of beer. As if there was nothing wrong with this situation. Maybe she hadn't heard the stories about New Haven?

I tucked myself up against her and said, "We shouldn't be here."

"Why not?"

"This is a bad place," I explained.

Star flipped her ponytail over her shoulder and shot me a wink. "Don't worry, we're fine."

How could she say that? It was kind of hard to miss the mob of hopped up men around us. One of whom was creeping up really close to her. I was about to open my mouth to tell her about it when Silas suddenly appeared and yanked the guy away by his shirt.

"Hands off, asshole."

Star slid her dark eyes my way and smiled. "See."

That didn't make me feel any better. I still wanted to escape out the doors. Unfortunately, the streets in this town weren't any safer than this bar. So I stayed tucked into my friend and kept my eyes dutifully on the crowd. I knew better than to let myself get caught off guard. That was a lesson I learned a long time ago, and one I promptly forgot when a voice boomed overhead.

"Last call to place your bets, boys." A dark haired man stood in the middle of the ring with a microphone in his hand. "Will it be our very own Tony Gratta?"

He waved to the left where a bald man covered in tattoos emerged from a room. My stomach flipped when he raised his arms in the air and his muscles bulged. That's who Mason was fighting? Jesus. He looked like a juggernaut made of stone.

"Or will it be the pretty boy from Ashen Springs, Mason Kessler?"

Someone needed to stop this. That guy was huge. Mason couldn't...

Oh.

My.

God.

I couldn't look away as Mason strutted out from a room on the right side. He was wearing nothing but a pair of dark jade shorts and some tape on his knuckles. The light shining down enhanced every hard edge on his sculpted body. Confidence rolled off his shoulders and sparkled in his eyes.

People cheered as he threw his arms up in the air. I barely heard them. My eyes were stuck on a lock of chestnut hair that flopped over his forehead. I wanted to crawl all over him while running my fingers through those soft locks.

"You're drooling."

I straightened up and shot Star a dirty look. "No I'm not."

I was simply admiring the male form. And oh what a form it was. All those times Mason did stuff to me, I must've missed something. He always looked good, but right now he was so mouth watering that all I wanted to do was run my tongue up his torso.

My brows knit.

Was I going crazy? Did I really just think that about Mason Kessler?

Mason marched forward and shot me a playful wink before ducking under the rope to get in the ring.

Yes, yes I did.

I was too busy gawking at the graceful way his feet bounced around to notice that the bell had rung until the first punch was thrown. My nerves skyrocketed as Mason ducked under. That morphed into adrenaline when he returned the strike with an upper-cut of his own. His fist connected with the juggernaut's bottom jaw, twisting his head to the side.

I'm not sure what it was that had me entranced. This wasn't a sport I ever thought I'd like, but it was kind of like a dance. A primal, feral dance that between two nearly naked, sweaty men. Every time Mason was hit, I'd grimace. Then he'd deliver a blow of his own and a strange tingly feeling would spread through my core. He seemed so powerful up there. Like a god among men.

And this god was mine.

"Yeah," a man behind me yelled and rushed forward, slamming into my back and nearly knocking me over. "Kick his ass."

"Hey!" I spun around and wagged my finger at him. "Do you mind? I'm trying to watch."

Whoa, where did that come from?

His lips curled, revealing his yellow teeth. "Well aren't you a sweet little thing? Wanna come back to my house and play?"

"No thank you." I did not want to go anywhere with him.

"You're polite." He stepped in, crowding me with the stench of rum on his breath. "I like that."

This was getting out of hand. Where was Silas? I put up my hands to keep him back and scanned the crowd. Silas and Star weren't anywhere to be seen. I thought I saw him in the back, but it turned out to be someone else with black hair.

Yellow teeth wasn't backing down. He snatched my wrist and hissed down at me. "You ever been with a real man, doll face?"

A familiar panicked flutter pounded in my chest. Then, just like that, the grip on my wrist was gone and yellow teeth was on the ground. I blinked down at the trail of blood trickling out of his mouth and wondered what happened. My silent question was answered when a pair of strong arms wrapped around my waist.

"You okay, baby?"

Mason.

Any concern I had vanished the instant I looked back at his face. Sweat was trickling down his brow, glistening on his tanned skin like a beacon of temptation.

"Can I touch you?"

A wicked smirk tugged at the corner of his mouth. "You want me to fuck you right here in front of everyone?"

Kinda.

Boos echoed through the room, and that's when I realized the fight wasn't over. The juggernaut was standing in the ring giving Mason a 'what the hell' eye, because he'd stepped out to protect me. Which just made me want to crawl all over him more.

"You should probably finish the fight."

He kissed my forehead, whispered, "Meet me in the back room," then climbed back into the ring.

For the first time in years, I didn't feel alone.

Chapter 29
Mason

My fists clenched, pulling at the tape around my knuckles. It'd been awhile since I had a challenge like that. Tony didn't go down easy. I could still feel the fucker's skull in the ache spreading across the back of my hand.

Sybil's fingers twirled over my palm, unwinding the wrapping on my left fist. "That was a good fight."

What she meant by that was, 'did I want her to suck me off?' Sports bunnies were a real thing, and it just so happened that Sybil had a degree in sport medicine. So it was handy to have her around. In more than one way.

"I'm good."

"You sure?" Her eyes dropped down to my shorts. "I know how pent up you get after a fight."

She wasn't wrong. Sometimes I could ride the high for hours afterwards. Getting off helped tame some of the adrenaline surging through my system. But my dick only wanted one person.

My eyes rolled up to the red-head timidly slipping into the room.

Sybil kept her focus on what she was doing and sighed when the door clicked closed. "You shouldn't be in here."

This wouldn't be the first time some chick tried to sneak into find me, so I couldn't fault her for trying to protect me. Plus, I liked the look Harper shot her in response. The snarky way her mouth curled was hot as fuck. If I didn't know any better, I'd say Freckles was jealous. I was tempted to tell Sybil to get on her knees just to see what Harper would do.

The snarl in her lip deepened when Sybil shifted over in between my legs so she could grab my other hand.

"I can come back later if you're busy."

She was definitely jealous.

Did I comfort Harper, or tell she didn't have anything to worry about? Fuck no. Why would I do some dumb shit like that?

I simply looked at her and said, "You're fine."

My dick twitched at the pissed off glare in Freckle's eyes, which made this entire situation better. Sybil noticed the movement and licked her lips.

"I knew you needed some relief."

Harper's mouth fell open as Sybil smoothed her palms up my thighs.

"Hey," Harper yelled. "You can't do that."

The chick between my legs rolled her gaze over to the one staring her down. "And who are you?"

"I'm the one that's supposed to be doing that."

Yeah you are.

"I think you should leave," Harper huffed and crossed her arms.

Look at timid little Harper Callaghan staking her claim. *Good girl.*

Annoyance toyed with Sybil's features as she spun around. "Look, I don't know who…"

"Get out," I snarled, cutting her off.

That caught both of them off guard. Harper jumped, while Sybil cocked a brow my way.

"What?"

"I said," my eyes snapping up to hers, "Get out."

It wasn't like we were a couple or anything. Sybil didn't even like me that much. It was the blood and sweat that got her going. That didn't mean she took rejection well.

She shot me a dirty look, snarled, "fine," and snatched her purse off the table. "You're not as great as you think you are, Mason Kessler."

Harper stepped back and watched the other girl storm out, slamming the door behind her.

"I don't like her," she muttered after Sybil was gone.

I snickered. "I could tell."

"It's not funny, Mason."

Isn't that cute? She's mad at me now.

"No, it's not." I reached down and moved my shorts out of the way to fist my cock. "It's fucking hot."

Even though her gaze followed my hand's movements, she asked, "What are you doing?"

Fuck, I loved that nervous little twitch in her tone. My grip tightened around my shaft as I trickled my gaze over the jeans hugging her hips. Why the fuck did I let her wear those? Her ass looked fucking delicious, but there was way too much fabric covering her.

"Take your pants off." I could sense the argument coming when she parted her lips. So I added a, "Now, Freckles."

That was officially my new favorite phrase. Every time I barked out those two words, she jumped to action. And this time wasn't any different. Harper had her pants unbuttoned and off in record time. There was only one problem...

My brow arched. "Panties too."

She blushed, but did as she was told.

"Good girl," I groaned and continued to stroke my shaft. "Now I want you to climb on the table and get down on all fours."

Unsure, Harper looked over at the table, then back to me.

"Go on," I coaxed, urging her to slowly take a few steps.

There was nothing quite like the sight of her gracefully climbing up on the wooden table-top. My mouth watered at the way she shakily pressed her palms down. I could practically taste her on the tip of my tongue. This girl was made for me. Her submission was beautiful, while the fear in her trembling body was intoxicating.

I took a minute to admire her glistening pink slit before I rose from my seated position and made my way over to her. My balls were ready to burst even before I slid my shaft through her folds. But the instant her sweet nectar coated the tip of my cock, I was done. I grabbed her hips and slammed into her hard.

"Oh my god." Harper cried out while clawing at the wood under her.

The pain in her tone was evident, but I didn't give a shit. And neither did she, because the harder I hammered into her the harder her walls clenched around me. I'd barely started and she was already screaming my name. Now that I didn't like.

"Shut the fuck up," I growled while pushing her face down against the table. "Your screams are mine."

I didn't want any of those jackasses out there to hear her. Harper's pleasure was mine and mine alone. Unfortunately wood wasn't a very good sound dampener. She was trying to swallow back her moans, but every time I'd drive into her, one would slip out. The third time she called out my name I'd had enough. I pulled out of her heat long enough to flip Harper around so I could slam her back against the wall and clamp my hand over her mouth.

That's better.

"Fuck I love your tight little cunt."

I thrust in and grunted as her walls fluttered around me. This was how I wanted to die. Hard as fuck and buried deep inside the most perfect pussy on the planet. The beast came out full force. Barrelling through any logical thought I had to drag me into a feral cloud of lust and desire. There was no gentleness or tender touches as I pounded into Harper, and she loved every second of it.

She ground her hips and begged for more of what only I could give her. Oh, and I gave it to her. I fucked her against the wall, on the table, chair, the bar in the corner, and any other surface I could find. Then I stood up and palmed her ass, bouncing her up and down on my cock. until my knees buckled as I shot my load and we collapsed on the ground.

That's when I knew how truly fucked I was.

This girl wasn't just made for me, she was my kryptonite. The thing I'd rip my own heart out to taste. Yes, I was an addict, and Harper Callaghan was my drug of choice. No rehab in the world could help me with that.

"HUH?" Silas glanced back at me. "You have a visitor."

I peeked over Silas's shoulder and grumbled under my breath at the guy leaning against a navy blue Audi parked in my driveway. Fucking great. This was the last thing I needed.

"Fucking Callaghan." Sighing, I looked down at Harper – who was asleep with her head on my lap, and swept my hand over her forehead. "Wake up, Freckles."

Guess I shouldn't be surprised. The asshole was bound to show up sooner or later. At the very least, this shit should be interesting.

"Are we home?" Harper yawned and rubbed her eyes.

"Yeah." My glare met Callaghan's through the windshield as Silas pulled to a stop. "And your brother's here."

"What?" Harper shot up.

The smile that washed over her face before she jumped out of the Hummer wasn't dulling my hatred for her brother any. Then she had to go and throw her arms around him, like he was the greatest person in the world. Fuck him. Why did he get a hug like that? Prick.

Silas tipped his chin at me. "You want me to stick around?"

"Nah." My gaze shifted to Star dozing in the passenger seat. "I got this."

He arched a brow while I fought to stop my hands from fisting. "You sure?"

"Yeah," I said and stepped out. "Take your girl home."

I have to go pry mine off her brother, and maybe kick his ass a bit.

Silas nodded and drove off, leaving me alone to watch Harper fawn over her brother.

"I missed you so much."

Oh please.

I rolled my eyes. It wasn't like Sean just got home from war. He just went to college. The only thing that stopped me from charging over there and ripping them apart was the look on Callaghan's face. Harper was happy to see her brother, but I don't think he felt the same.

"What the fuck, Harper?" He pulled his sister back by her shoulders and scowled down at her. "I don't hear from you for days, so I drive home thinking something happened, and I find you here. With him."

He shot me a dirty look which I returned with a smirk.

"It's not what you think," Harper exclaimed.

I snorted. "It's exactly what you think."

If Little Miss People Pleaser thought I was going to let that one fly, she was wrong.

Sean threw an angry finger up at me. "What did you do to her?"

"A better question would be, what haven't I done to her."

Oh, he didn't like that answer. "Fuck you, Kessler."

"Sorry," I crossed my arms and sat down on the hood of my Corvette. "You're not the Callaghan I'm interested in fucking. Isn't that right, Freckles?"

Harper's jaw dropped while Sean's nostrils flared. I was wrong. This wasn't interesting. It was fucking fun.

"Don't listen to him, Sean."

Freckles was starting to piss me off though.

"Yeah Sean," I snidely sang back. "Don't listen to me. Instead have a look under your sister's jeans. I'm pretty sure my cum is still running down her leg."

"Motherfucker!"

Here we go.

Callaghan charged past his sister while I pushed back onto my feet and got ready for the first punch.

"I warned you, Kessler." His fist sailed through the air, narrowly missing my jaw as I ducked back. "Stay the fuck away from my sister."

"She's mine, asshole." I twirled around, threw my forearm up on his shoulder blades, and smashed his face down on the hood of my car before leaning over and whispering, "Or did you forget Daddy already signed the contract?"

I may not like Sean Callaghan. In fact, I fucking hated the guy, but there was a reason he was a damn good football player. He knew how to take a hit and didn't go down easy. The second I folded over him, he threw his elbow back into my gut. Then snapped his head up, cracking the back of his skull off my chin. That was enough to make me stumble back.

"Fuck your contract," he growled while slamming his fist against my jaw. "I'll be damned if I let my sister ever end up with the likes of you."

We used to get in tussles all the time, but I had to hand it to the guy, he picked up some skills in college. Unfortunately, he still wasn't as good as me. I bent down and charged forward, scooping him up with my shoulder, then knocking him back against his car.

If Logan was here he'd be crying right now at the sound of metal denting. That would've been better than Harper screaming at us to stop it. At least I wouldn't feel bad then. But one look at the tears on her face caused my fist to freeze in the air.

Sean, however, either didn't care or didn't notice his sister's state. He jumped back up and shoved me hard.

"What's wrong, Kessler?" Another shove. "Can you only beat up little girls?"

My fist was flying before my eyes had time to snap back to his. "You're a little too late to play the protector."

My knuckles connected and Sean's head twisted to the side as he stumbled back. Harper chose that moment to step between us and hold up her hands. "Stop it."

"Get out of my way, Harper," Sean demanded.

Gotta say, I'd never felt more satisfaction then I did when Harper shook her head.

"Please just stop."

She'd listen to me, but she wouldn't listen to him.

Sean wiped the blood from the corner of his mouth with the back of his hand and hissed, "I am not going to let him put you in the hospital again."

"Before you start pointing the finger," I snorted, "you should take a look in your own backyard."

"What's that supposed to mean?" he growled back.

"I'M NOT THE ONE YOU NEED TO PROTECT HER FROM, ASSHOLE!" I screamed over Harper's head.

The fact that she had her back to me and not him proved who she trusted in this situation.

When her brother jerked to the side to lunge at me again, Harper called out, "Mason didn't hurt me, Daddy did."

If there was an invisible wall for Sean to hit, he just ran into it. I'd never seen anyone stopped so fast in my life.

His face screwed up in confusion as his gaze rolled back to Harper. "What?"

"Mason didn't do it," she repeated. "Daddy did."

Everything went quiet. I could see Sean mulling over his sister's confession. I almost felt sorry for the guy. If anyone could understand what a slap in the face this was, it was me. Parents were supposed to be godly icons that children aspired to be. Finding out the truth about someone who was once your hero was a hard pill to swallow. One that apparently Sean couldn't force down his throat.

"No." He shook his head. "I don't know how he did it, but this asshole," the finger aimed in my direction made me snort, "has twisted your head. Dad would never hurt you."

I wanted nothing more than to kiss the tears off Harper's face when she whispered, "But he did."

"No," he insisted. "You're wrong."

"I'm not wrong. He killed Mom, Sean."

"Mom left, Harper. She'll be back."

"She won't be back!" Harper yelled. "She's buried under the black-eyed Susans in our yard. Daddy made me help him put her there."

What? I didn't know that. Was that what she was seeing when she was freaking out and apologizing for going in his office? Fuck Ned Callaghan. I was going to bury his ass under those fucking flowers.

"No," Sean stated with a firm head shake.

Stubborn asshole still couldn't accept it. I could see the heartbreak on Harper's face. What the fuck was wrong with him?

"Dad wouldn't do that."

"Yes he would."

We all turned to see Lana standing in the beams of light coming from her car. I had no idea when she arrived or how long she'd been standing there, but there were more tears streaming down her face than Harper's.

Lana's eyes were focused entirely on Harper as she took a step closer. "That's what I was trying to tell you. Last year, when I was at your house, your dad… he raped me, Harper."

I could see the color drain from Harper's face. I wanted to grab her and wrap her up safely in my arms. But I was too shocked to move. If this happened last year, why didn't Lana tell her before? And did Parker know? If he did, I was pretty sure Ned Callaghan wouldn't still be breathing.

Lana held her hand out and moved towards Harper, but she took off with Lana hot on her heels.

"Wait, please don't hate me…"

I looked at Sean, who looked back at me as realization set in his brown eyes.

Welcome to the party, asshole.

Chapter 30
Mason

S ean paced around the driveway muttering under his breath, while I leaned back on his car and waited for Lana to leave. As much as I wanted to go after Harper, she needed time to work things out with her friend. Never thought the day would come when I'd want Lana Crawford in her life. The chick was a major pain in my ass – not as much as Star, but still...

"This can't be happening."

I watched Sean kick a rock, sending it skipping across the ground.

"Well, it is." He better make his peace with that. No amount of denial could wash away the bitter taste of betrayal.

His jaw clenched, darkening his glare. "Why the fuck are you still here?"

That was a good question. A few times I considered walking away, but for some reason I couldn't leave him alone.

"Just enjoying your misery," I said, while folding my arms over my chest.

"I don't need your sympathy, Kessler."

I snorted out a chuckle. "No worries there."

Wrapping Sean Callaghan up in a warm, fuzzy hug was right up there with arming my brother's girlfriend with a bunch of forks.

"I need to talk to my sister."

When he walked towards the house I called out, "I wouldn't do that if I were you."

He stopped next to the hood of his car and gave me an 'are you kidding me' eye.

"Fine. If you want to make your sister relive all that bullshit, be my guest." I waved him off. "I personally think she's been through enough, but hey, go ahead and retraumatize her."

There was a reason I stopped asking Harper for specifics. For years Logan suffered through flashbacks, and every time he'd get this dull look in his eyes. The same dullness I'd seen in Harper's the other day. I was just too pissed off to put the pieces together.

"God damnit." Sean slammed his fists down on the top of his car. "I lived in the same fucking house."

The guy had a point. He should've fucking known. Then again, the same could be said about myself, or Lana, or Star. Anyone in her life, really. We'd all failed. Including Harper. She could've said something, but fear was a powerful motivator.

"Why didn't I see it?"

I shrugged. "She was good at hiding it."

Sean's head cocked my way. "Why the fuck did she tell you?"

She didn't. I figured that shit out on my own. Though I guess one could argue that she did tell me at least some of it.

"I saw the bruises," I explained.

"Fuck me, she had bruises?"

I nodded. "Probably a couple broken ribs too."

My goal wasn't to hurt Sean. Actually, I sympathized with the bastard. I knew what it was like to find out the people you grew up with lied. While I had time to work through some of it, Sean was just starting to traverse the dark web he was tangled in. Couldn't help but hope he didn't head down the same drug and alcohol fueled road I did. Harper didn't need to suffer through that shit show.

Neither did Micha, and yet I put him through it. Was what he did really so bad? Yes, my brother was overbearing and a giant prick, but he'd never gone out of his way to hurt me. Sean was beating himself up over what happened to his sister, like it was his fault their old man was a piece of shit. So could I really blame Micha for wanting to protect me?

"She should've told me," Sean muttered.

My brotherly issue could be dealt with another time.

"Okay, say she did tell you." I rolled my neck, swinging my stare his way. "What would you have done?"

Why did I ask him that? Maybe I was testing him? Maybe some small part of me thought he deserved revenge as much as I did? But would he have the stones to carry through? There was a difference between being pissed off about being kept in the dark, and actually doing something.

When Sean answered me there wasn't a single tremor or crack in his tone. "I'd have killed him."

But would you?

"There's still time," I pointed out.

His eyes locked on mine and I didn't just see the rage burning in that gaze, I felt it. If his old man was here right now, there was no doubt in my mind that he wouldn't hesitate to slit his throat. But that privilege was mine. I'd let him get a few good shots in, though.

"But would you say the same thing tomorrow?" I challenged.

"Why wait until tomorrow?" He glanced down at his watch. "He's supposed to meet me at the house in an hour."

That was all I needed to hear.

"Alright then," I walked over to open the passenger door of his car. "Let's go Mr. Borden and give your father forty whacks."

WHEN WE PULLED up to the house, wrath surged through my veins, turning my blood into lava. It poured through me, twitching my muscles and clenching my jaw. By the time we stepped out into the evening breeze, my fists were ready to pound all Harper's pain and misery into her old man's face.

I wanted to feel his skull crack while his eyes bulged out of his head. Ned Callaghan's blood would still be coating my hands when I went back home and fucked his daughter. I'd strengthen her will while feeding her his pain. And when my sweet little liar sucked my fingers clean and moaned my name, she'd know she was safe. No one would ever hurt Harper again.

Except me, of course, but she'd like that.

Rolling my neck, I headed for the door. Sean didn't come with me.

I cocked a brow as he veered to the left. "Where the fuck are you going?"

He did live here. We should be able to walk through the front door unquestioned.

"Mr. Borden is going to get an axe," he called back.

Well shit. Callaghan didn't play around.

Pure morbid curiosity drove me to follow him to a shed around back. That, and I kind of wanted to see what other fun little toys were stashed in there. Fists were fun, but there was something to be said about a man wielding hedge cutters or a chainsaw. Scariest thing I ever saw was when Preston decided to rake a guy to death. I didn't know human vocal cords were capable of making sounds like that.

My pulse thrummed as Sean pulled out a key and clicked open the padlock.

Wonder if Ned has a rake?

When he swung the wooden door open I was reminded of all those dark garages and sheds of death in movies. My gaze swung from the hooks hanging off the roof to a wall filled with sharp instruments. This was definitely the kind of place someone in a horror movie would come to die.

"Well," Sean tipped his gaze back to me. "See anything you like?"

All I could do was purse my lips and nod. Every possible instrument I could think of to end someone's life was in here. Including a shotgun hanging on the wall. But that weapon was a little too easy for my liking. Why would I give Ned a quick death when I could draw it out?

I reached over Sean's shoulder and plucked something off the wall. His brows rose in response.

"A cultivator? That's what you're going with?"

A slow smirk spread across my lips. "Looks like a hand rake to me."

With three hard sharp points. Yeah, this would do nicely.

"Whatever," Sean shrugged and headed over to the far wall where an axe hung as the light above flickered.

Tink, tink, tink.

What the fuck? "Did you hear that?"

"Hear what?" Sean asked back.

Tink... Tink...

There it was again. "That."

This time when I pointed it out, his forehead furrowed. "What the fuck is that?"

That's what I was saying.

We both stood there listening as the sound quietly echoed again.

Tink, tink, tink.

It was weird. Like a clanging, tapping sound, with a rhythm to it. Three quick taps followed by three long, then…

Tick, tick, tick.

Was that morse code? I really should've paid more attention in Boy Scouts. The sound was quiet, like it was coming from far away. No, not far away.

My eyes fell to the wooden floor. "Do you have a basement in here?"

"No." Sean looked around as the taps came again. "At least, I don't think so?"

We stared at each other for a second, then went about searching the shed. It didn't take too long for us to pick up on the fact that every time the sound came, the light flickered. So we followed the cord to a hole in the floor under one of the shelves. And that hole turned out to be a trapdoor that led to a set of wooden stairs.

Sean and I exchanged a look before we headed down.

There were a lot of things I thought I might find in a secret hole in the ground at the Callaghan estate. Blood, a piece of Tico's clothing, or a furnace – Ned had to clean up after himself somewhere. Hell, I wouldn't have been surprised to find this place as nothing more than a wine cellar. Dean Whitley's Mike Brady smile was the last thing I expected to see at the bottom of those stairs.

"Hello Mase. What are you doing here?"

My eyes roamed over the large cage he was in, to the twisted and malformed way his left arm hung. "What are you doing here?"

"Not sure where here is?" Dean lifted his good arm and tapped his chin – which was covered in blood that I assumed came from the cut under his eye. "Are we still in Ashen Springs?"

"Yeah?"

Sean climbed down the last step, then promptly hunched over and threw up. Can't say I blamed him. Dean was beyond fucked up. There was a deep cut across the left side of his head, bruises covered his face, while dried blood caked his tattered clothes.

"Are you okay?" Given the circumstances, it seemed kinda stupid to ask that question, but the fucker was smiling like he was going for a walk in the park.

"Now that you mention it, I could use a glass of water."

Water? Really? That's what he was going to ask for?

"How about we get you out of here first?"

Dean clicked his tongue while wagging his finger. "I always knew you were a smart one."

"Thanks?" I said, not knowing how else to respond.

The smile on Dean's face widened. "You're welcome."

Right?

"Well," I shook my head and blew out a breath. "If you'll tell me where the keys are…"

"Oh," Dean grimaced. "You didn't take care of Nate."

Who the fuck was Nate?

The door being slammed shut vibrated through the room. My brain barely had time to register that before a soft hiss wafted in, along with a smoky cloud.

Fuck.

We had to get out of here. A thought that Dean apparently didn't share. He calmly walked over to the corner of his cell and sat down.

"You boys might want to do the same. That fall can really hurt your noggin."

He could do what he wanted, but I wasn't giving up. Neither was Sean. He'd already run up the stairs and was trying to bash the door open. Since he had that covered, I moved around down here, looking for another way out.

The cloud filled the room, making every step I took feel heavier as a haze floated through my mind. Coughing on the chemical taste filling my lungs, I stumbled over to a table in the corner where some tools were laid out. If I couldn't get out, then at least I could be armed. I didn't know where my hand rake went.

The last thing I saw was Sean's limp body tumbling down the stairs.

Chapter 31
Harper

*L*ana and I spent over an hour crying into each other's arms. She thought I hated her, but that could never happen. I hated myself. All this time I thought I was protecting people from Daddy. I did everything he asked, and never said a thing about what was really going on. And that was okay, because the people I loved were safe.

But they weren't.

He hurt Lana. Not only that, but he broke a part of her soul. He took something she could never get back, and she'd lived with it in silence because she didn't want to hurt me. Lana cared about me so much that she kept his secret so I wouldn't lose my only parent. How did I repay that kind of love? I couldn't. But I could make sure that Daddy didn't hurt anyone else.

Even if that meant helping Mason.

I didn't want my father to die. There was still a piece of the man I loved inside there. The darkness that ruled him though...

The weight of a man was measured by his actions and Daddy's scales were tipped so far in one direction that it didn't matter how much good he was capable of. So if he had to go, I could live with that. But death wasn't the only option. If he was locked up then he couldn't hurt anyone else, and maybe he'd take the time to think about the kind of man he wanted to be.

Daddy may have given up on his soul, but I still believed in him. I just had to convince Mason to do the same. Which would be a lot easier if I could find him. I'd been looking all over, searching every room I came in, and found no sign of him.

The only places I didn't go were the east wing – that was Micha's – and any place I thought might be Mr. Kessler's space. While I was somewhat comfortable with Mason, his family was another story. A stronger person might've risked going in their spaces, but that person wasn't me.

Sighing, I headed across the entryway for the only room I hadn't been in. If I didn't find Mason in the kitchen then I might have to swallow my nerves and infringe on territory I didn't want to. My heart stopped when I walked through the archway.

Micha was standing behind the island.

He looked at me.

I looked at him.

My brain screamed at me to ask him, but my throat couldn't choke the words out. I just stood there opening and closing my mouth while my heart thundered in my chest. I could feel his dark eyes boring into me, yet I couldn't move. All I could hear was his voice saying, *'I'll remove the problem.'*

Maybe I should leave?

Micha's eyes narrowed as he dropped a water bottle on the counter.

It took everything in me to gulp back my yip and stay where I was. His annoyance was heavy in the air. I wanted to speak. I told myself over and over to say something. But the only word that came out was, "Mason."

His brow rose. "What about him?"

"Um… He's… Not…"

"Speak up." His voice thundered through my ears, making me jump back.

Once again I choked on my words. "He's not… I can't… where…"

"Where what?" Micha asked. "Where's Riley? Where's Mason? Where's your cold heart, or the truth that will set my brother free?"

Ouch, that hurt.

"Mason," I whispered.

"Not that it's any of your business," he rolled his eyes, "but he went somewhere with your brother."

What? "Why?"

That didn't make any sense. Mason and Sean did not get along – which was a nice way of saying they hated each other.

Micha waved his hand through the air. "I don't know. Maybe Mase is going to kill him or something."

That's when panic struck my heart. No, they wouldn't. Would they? The look in my brother's eyes flashed through my mind.

Oh my God, they would.

"You have to stop them!" I cried out desperately. "They don't know what he's capable of."

Micha's brow knit. "What who's capable of?"

"My father."

Chapter 32
Mason

$\mathcal{T}$he distinct grinding shriek of metal on metal burned through my subconscious. At first I thought the slight throb in the back of my head was a sign of a hangover – wouldn't be the first time I woke up having no idea where I was or how I got there – but the musty scent of earth seemed familiar. Where the hell was I? I didn't hear Harper.

Like a slap in the face, everything hit me. Sean showing up, Lana's confession, the secret dungeon under the shed, Dean Whitley, and the cloud of gas.

My eyes flew open and I was instantly met with the source of my anger. Ned Callaghan stood over by the table, sharpening a knife. The asshole couldn't be too smart, because he had his back turned to me.

I lunged. Or at least tried to. Something snapped me back, drawing my eyes down to the rope binding my wrists to a metal chair. Which, considering it didn't move with me, I assumed it was bolted to the ground.

God damnit.

"You really should take better care of yourself. That gas should've kept you out for at least another twenty-minutes." Ned tipped his chin and looked back at me. "Just how many drugs have you poisoned your body with? I'm not sure I want my daughter around that kind of influence."

This motherfucker.

"Too bad you didn't have that much concern for your daughter when you were beating her."

"What you call beating, I call lessons." He sighed and returned his attention to the blade he was sharpening. "If she'd have listened in the first place, then none of this would've happened. It was a simple rule. Don't go in my office."

The fact that he was trying to justify his actions only strengthened my resolve to end him.

"Is that what you're going to tell your son?" I asked while looking around for Sean, who I didn't see anywhere.

I remembered seeing him fall down the stairs, so I knew the gas knocked him out.

"My son was never supposed to be a part of this." Ned placed the sharpener back on the table, then spun around and pointed the tip of the blade at me. "I blame you for that."

"Right, cause it couldn't possibly have anything to do with what you did to his sister." I tipped my head to the side and looked right at him. "Or Lana."

That surprised him. Ned's eyes widened just a bit.

That's right, asshole. I know about that, and soon Parker will too.

"Lana's a beautiful girl who I would've left alone had she never gained the interest of a Whitley."

The way he said Whitley, full of disgust and hatred, made my gaze shift over to Dean, who was still asleep. If his beef was with the Whitley's then why Tico, or Harper? Why any of it?

"That's a big cell for one person." I didn't really care why Ned did what he did, but the longer I could keep him talking, the more time I had to loosen the rope on my wrists.

"It was originally built for four." Ned twirled the knife in his hand and walked across the room. "But I had to escalate my plans and settle for one."

If Dean was one of the four he was talking about, then I could only assume he was talking about the other kings. Which again, didn't make sense. If someone was going to go for one king, then why not cut the head off the snake? Taking out the king of kings would pack a much bigger punch. Then again, my dad wasn't an easy man to target.

"Why Dean?" I asked while twisting my left wrist, stretching my bindings.

Light glistened off the blade's metal edge as Ned tossed it from one hand to the other. For half a second I thought he wasn't going to answer me. Then he clicked his tongue and looked up.

"Children are like sponges. They take in the world around them and absorb it into their very being. A parent can turn their child into pretty much anything they want. If they go to church, their children will learn the glory of their religion. Do good unto others and all that. However, if they hate something," he stopped and rolled his eyes over to Dean's sleeping form. "Their children will learn to hate that thing too."

My wrist was starting to burn, so I had to control my tone when I spoke. "So your parents hated the Whitley's?"

"No." Ned's eyes snapped back to mine. "My parents hated The Order."

What? I knew we had our enemies, but the name Callaghan had never popped up.

"I grew up hearing stories about how the Order Of Ravens and

Wolves scorned our family," he explained. "I didn't really pay any attention to it until one night, twenty-five years ago."

What the fuck happened twenty-five years ago?

"Ten is such a fragile age," he paused to wave at me. "As you know."

Fucker.

"It's kind of ironic, when you think about it. Though I wasn't arrested..."

I couldn't wait to kill this asshole.

"I was the same age when my world fell apart."

The smile on his face made me grit my teeth.

"You have no idea what it means to have your world destroyed." But he was about to find out.

"Oh, but I do." Ned's hands slammed down on the chair over my wrists as he brought his face right up to mine. "I had to watch my brother's murder."

What? "You don't have any brothers."

"Ned Callaghan doesn't have any brothers." He pushed off the chair and shot me a wink. "But Nate Fenton had one."

Fenton? Why did I know that name?

My eyes widened as I remembered the poster Silas found Star clutching. The same one on Tico's body that caused all the grandparents to come back from the dead. Niles Fenton. That was the name of the guy who went missing.

"Is that why you killed Tico? Because he found out about your secret identity?"

When I felt the rope tear under my wrist, I concentrated on working the other.

Ned shrugged. "The boy started asking too many questions, and I couldn't have Harper growing a backbone. Do you have any idea how exhausting it is to groom someone? A father should never have to beat their child. Harper has you to thank for that."

"Why me?" Dean groaned from in the cell. He was fucked up already, and I didn't want Ned's attention detoured back to him.

"When I put my daughter in that book, it was so Parker or Preston would choose her. That would've been so much simpler. A quick 'I'm sorry Dean, your son fell off the bluffs playing with my girl.' But you picked her." I could see his jaw twitching. "Not a Whitley, but a fucking Kessler."

I knew what he meant by that statement. All the families in the Order were powerful, but the Kessler's were at the top of the food chain. No one messed with my old man. Except for...

"Is that why you teamed up with Ryker?" That was the only thing I could assume. Otherwise, why would Ryker be at his house so often? And it *was* often.

"Oh no, I befriended him long before that. The first trick to taking down an organization is to cause dissension in the ranks. Your father helped with that. All I had to do was make a few comments to Ryker about how he was better fit to lead and he did the rest. You were the only crimp in my plan."

A few more twists of my wrist and I'd give him a crimp in his fucking plan.

"Oh well," he sighed. "I suppose it worked out for the best. Actually, it worked out better than I ever could've imagined. I made my daughter tell one lie, and I got to sit back and watch you destroy yourself."

That got me. I felt the punch of his implication deep in my gut. Not because he'd orchestrated everything that led to my downfall, but because I let myself fall. I relied on alcohol and drugs to numb my pain instead of talking to my brother, who I should've trusted.

"Why?" I shook my head. "Did you get some sick thrill out of watching me crash and burn?"

"Why. WHY?" Ned yelled. "The Order took my brother." His eyes locked on mine. "So I took theirs."

I was wrong. *That* punched me in the gut. All this time I'd been blaming everyone, and all I had to do was open my eyes. Finn wasn't the connecting link in the chain that could tear everyone apart. I was, and I broke. But the others didn't fall like he thought they would. They held me up. And now...

I yanked on my wrist, snapping the last rope in half, and lunged at Ned.

Now I would hold *them* up.

Red filled my vision as my fists flew down in a fury. I beat him for my brother. I beat him for the shit he put my father through. For how he tainted Ryker, and ruined Logan's childhood. But mostly, I beat him for Harper. I threw my fists against his ribs and skull until I felt bone crack. Then I hit him some more, so he would, with his last dying breath, know that the only good thing he ever brought into this world was mine now and he would never touch her again.

With every hit I landed and grunt he made, I wiped away the fear on her face and bruises covering her body. I mended her bones by breaking his. I did what I should've done seven years ago. I fought for the girl I loved.

When I finally came out of it, there was nothing left of his face but a caved-in mess. That's when I noticed the knife in my side.

"Fuck," I grumbled, and fell over, giving into darkness.

Chapter 33
Harper

The beeping of the machines along with the green line moving with Mason's pulse reminded me of another time in a different hospital room. I did lose him that day, but I got him back. If Micha hadn't found him when he did, I might've lost Mason again. The thought terrified me so much that I couldn't stop clinging to him in the hospital bed.

Sean was in the room down the hall in a medically induced coma. He had a bad reaction to whatever drugs our father gave him. He would be okay though. The doctors said it was easier on his body if he slept until the drugs were out of his system.

Mason would be okay too. Or at least I hoped he would. His addict status caused him to refuse pain meds, so I stayed here with him every night to help him sleep. I would fight for him just as hard as he fought for me. Though I doubted Mason needed anyone to fight for him.

Was I sad that Daddy was gone? Yes. It broke my heart that I would never see him smile again, but he didn't do that much anymore. I still loved the man I grew up with – him I would mourn – but the other guy? That one hurt the people I loved? Including my father. The beast of wrath that consumed Daddy and tainted everything good about him? That man, I wouldn't miss.

After Mason and Dean were found – who was in amazingly good spirits considering – the Order combed through my house. The things they found terrified me. My father had been planning this for twenty-five years. His family used to be part of the Order but were cast out over fifty years ago. Apparently my grandparents – who were still alive in another city – didn't take this well.

My uncle rapped Dean Whitley's high school sweetheart and paid the ultimate price. Daddy only saw what happened to his brother and not that poor girl, Cora. But that's what happens when you're raised around anger. It festers and breeds until that hollow emptiness is the only thing a person knows.

Hate begets hate.

I never hated Mason, and I don't think he ever hated me. We just needed to find each other again.

"Hey Freckles, you're hanging on a little tight there."

"Oh no." I instantly loosened my grip. "I'm sorry."

His green eyes glowed as he gazed down at me. "What did I say about sorry's?"

"No more." I rolled my eyes. "But sometimes an apology is needed."

"Only if you have a reason to be guilty." He wrapped his arm around me and kissed the top of my head. "And you don't."

I smiled and snuggled up into his embrace. Mason wasn't talking about me squeezing him too hard or accidently breaking something. That was his way of letting me know that he'd forgiven me. I just hoped he could forgive himself.

"There is something you could do for me."

He was going to ask for sex again, wasn't he? Mason was

injured, he needed time to heal, but that didn't stop him. Last night I had to sleep in the chair because he wouldn't stop touching me. The man was insatiable.

"I would love some of that peach pie in the cafeteria."

Okay, that I would do.

I sat up and gave him a smile. "I'll get you the biggest piece they have."

My reward was the happy glimmer in his bright eyes.

I gave him a kiss and hopped off the bed to get my man his pie. Sean's room was on the way, so I stopped in there to check on him. I knew he was in a coma, but I wanted him to know that I was there with him. Every hour I stopped by and told him a story – which Mason didn't like – but he would have to get used to it. My brother was a part of my life and always would be.

After that, I headed down the hall for the cafeteria, where I was sure Margret would be working. She was usually on the late shift and very sweet. Last night I stayed up for hours talking to her about her grandbabies.

Before I could walk into the room filled with tables and chairs, I was cut off. A man in a suit stepped in front of me.

"Harper Callaghan?"

I stared up at the wrinkles around his chocolate eyes. He kind of looked like an older version of Louis Kessler. Was this Mason's grandpa? "Yes?"

"You need to come with me."

My brows knit. "Why?"

I couldn't leave Mason.

He grabbed my arm and pulled me down the hall. "It's time to pay for your father's sins."

Chapter 34
Mason

What was taking Harper so long? I was starting to worry. She should've been back by now. This didn't feel right.

I climbed out of bed and grunted as the stitches pulled at my flesh. This shit fucking sucked. I really wished I could take something for the pain, but I didn't want to risk falling back down the hole. There were other people I had to think about. Like the girl of my dreams, and the children we would have.

She could be pregnant right now. Harper wasn't on birth control and I had yet to pull out. That didn't mean I would point it out to her. I kind of liked the idea of putting a kid in her belly and watching her swell with my seed. How fucking hot would that be?

I palmed my dick and made my way across the room. I was so fucking hard it hurt. If I didn't get some pussy soon then I was going to beat her ass.

Speaking of beating her ass...

I peeked out into the hall. Harper was nowhere to be seen. But I did see someone else.

My brow arched at Preston, who was leaning against the wall next to my door. "Hanging out in hospitals now?"

"The morgue is a good place to dump a body. No one's ever really sure how many they have."

I didn't want to know.

"Whatever floats your boat." I rolled my eyes down the other side of the hall.

"You looking for Harper?" Preston asked.

My eyes narrowed. "Yeah?"

"Your gramps took her."

That wasn't what I was expecting. "My gramps took her?"

He nodded.

Riley I would get, but Harper? Gramps barely talked to me. Now Micha, however, was constantly catching his attention – which I thought was hilarious. The old man wasn't doing himself any favors. My brother knew how to hold a grudge.

"Why the hell would he take Harper?"

"I don't know." Preston shrugged. "He said something about father and sins."

Father and sins? Wasn't there an Order doctrine about that? What the fuck was it? I really should've paid more attention when I read that damn book. Probably would've helped if I wasn't high when I did it.

Okay, I just needed to think. The Order's fathers never sin? No that was fucking stupid. Everyone in the Order sinned. We were raised in a den of lust and blood. Wait... Blood?

> King blood that is spilled by the father,
> shall not be forgotten by the child.
> Should the father fail to pay the price,

Then the sin shall pass down to the next in line.

THAT COULDN'T BE IT. The next in line in this case was Sean...

Who was currently in a coma.

My eyes widened.

Oh shit.

I TORE up the road to Manning Keep. Preston would probably kick my ass later for taking his keys. He really didn't see that sucker punch coming. At least he took it like a champ. That'll make me feel better when he beats my ass for stealing his car – which, by the way, was absurdly clean. I half expected to sit in a puddle of blood.

Micha's Jeep, however, might need a little work. I may have bumped into it, but that would've never happened if they hadn't decided to take Harper. What the fuck were they thinking? The girl wasn't even five foot.

I sprang out of the car, barrelled through the door and down the stairs. It didn't occur to me that the door shouldn't have been open until I was already halfway around the corner to the meeting room where I could hear people talking.

"Are you insane?" Silas yelled out. "We can't fucking do this."

My friend didn't need to worry. There was no way those fuckers were doing shit.

"Does Mason know about this?" my old man asked.

"No," Micha snorted. "There's no way he would've let this shit happen."

Look at my brother standing up for me.

Parker's voice was the next to bark out. "I'm not doing this."

I knew I always liked that guy, and not in that way. Yes, I'd done some shit with Parker, but it wasn't like that. The first time was after I'd had a nightmare about Ryker. I flipped out when Parker touched me, which was when he fell to his knees. It wasn't attraction that led me to do the things I did. Parker helped me get something back. Something I lost as a child.

"I say we whip them," Logan growled as I stepped up to the large wooden door with a raven carved on it.

"Enough," Gramps boomed, reminding me of when our old man would yell at Micha and I. "Like it or not, this is how things are."

"Maybe in your generation," Micha argued.

Gramps wasn't going to let that go. "My generation and yours follow the same rules. Something your father seems to have forgotten."

I threw open the door just as Logan jumped out of his large wooden throne. "If your generation's dead, then we can make up our own rules."

"It doesn't work that way," Gramps stated, as his eyes swung my way. "Hello Mason. Welcome to the meeting."

Meeting my ass.

All the kings were here. My old man, and Silas's, even Dean was sitting all fucked up in his seat. Logan, Silas, Parker, and Micha were at the right side of the grand oak table. Preston's spot was empty though, and I didn't think he was going to show up any time soon. *Oops.* And in the middle, sitting like regal kings on their thrones, were the grandparents. All of whom were staring directly at me. But my focus was on the girl huddled up in the middle of the room.

Harper was shaking like a leaf. All I wanted to do was wrap her up in a bubble of safety. So that was exactly what I did. I rushed over and threw my arms around her.

"You okay, baby?"

Her big brown eyes filled with worry. "You shouldn't be out of the hospital."

"I'm fine." I wasn't. My side hurt like a bitch and was bleeding a bit. But I'd be damned if I was going to let them do this to her.

My glare locked on my grandfather's firm expression. "What the fuck is wrong with you?"

"Order doctrine dictates..."

"I don't give a fuck what Order doctrine dictates!" Fuck him, and fuck the others too. "You are not doing this."

"This is why we took power back," Gramps explained. "None of you understand the rules of this game. This town is ours, yet you let the docks get overrun with gangs and crime. These people follow us because we protect them. We make sure they are safe to walk their children at night, and we don't allow strangers like Ned Callaghan to move in and disrupt that peace. Regardless of how much money he could bring in."

"You can't keep everyone out of this town," my old man spat back.

"Yes we can. Ashen Springs stands on its own because of the Order." Gramps sighed and scrubbed a hand down his face. "You were given this power too young, Louis, and I'm sorry for that. But we all have to make sacrifices. This is Mason's."

Silas's grandpa tipped his head and stared at me with sympathy in his bright eyes. "I'm sorry, son, but we have to do this."

I looked down at the beautiful girl in my arms. She was so brave, stroking my face while whispering that it was okay. It wasn't okay. The punishment for a father's sins was twelve lashes. Harper had been hurt enough. I couldn't let her take anymore pain.

"If this is my sacrifice," I looked back at the grandfathers, "then let me do it."

Gramps shook his head. "It doesn't work that way, son."

"Why not? Ned Callaghan spilt king blood, right? Well I spent fours years in his house and didn't pick up on shit. So one could argue that I spilt king's blood."

The older generation looked at each other as if they were considering it, which Micha did not like.

He slammed his fist down on the table. "No. This is not an option." He threw his hand up in my direction. "Look at him. He is still in a goddamn hospital gown."

Hey now, I think I rocked this shit.

"You're right. We're not doing this." Gramp's eyes locked on my brother. "You are."

"What?" Micha sprang out of his chair. "No fucking way."

But Gramps wasn't looking at him anymore, he was staring at me. "If you want to do this Mason, then your brother has to be the one to punish you."

Everyone else joined in Micha's objection. Logan started tipping shit over, Silas was yelling at his old man, who in turn was yelling at his. Parker was shaking his head, while Harper was crying in my arms begging me not to do this. Hell, even Dean had gotten up and objected.

The only one who wasn't losing their shit was my old man. His eyes met mine and with one single glance I knew, he understood that I had to do this. I couldn't fail at protecting her again. One single phrase caused the room to go quiet.

"Parker, will you kindly escort Harper from the room." My old man tipped his head at the girl in my arms. "She doesn't need to see this."

I mouthed a thank you to him and handed Harper over to Parker. She screamed and lashed out as he dragged her away. It broke my heart to see her so scared, but my dad was right. She didn't need to see this.

Micha shook his head when my old man went to hand him the whip.

"No." He crossed his arms. "I won't do it."

"What if it was Riley?" I shot back at him.

I could see the pain in his eyes when he sighed. "Mase…"

"She's my Riley, Micha, and if this is what I have to do to keep her safe…" I walked across the room and took my position with my hands on the wall. "Then I'll do it."

This was hard for Micha. He spent his entire life trying to keep me safe. But this was how he could protect me now.

"Mase, you're my brother…"

"Then be my brother," I cut him off, "and do this for me."

Silence hung heavy in the air. I could feel him staring at me, but I knew if I looked at him it would only make this more difficult. So I focused on the wall and waited until I heard his voice whisper, "I love you, Mase," followed by a crack across my back.

Epilogue
Harper

THREE MONTHS LATER:

"*O*uch." I squeezed Mason's hand and tucked my head in the crook of his arm while he smoothed his hand over my head.

"It's almost over," he shushed.

I hated needles, but birth control was important. The fact that I wasn't already pregnant was a miracle. But I hadn't even thought about it. Not until last week, when Riley came storming into the house and smacked Micha across the head with a positive pregnancy test. And she wasn't the only one. Shelby had jumped up all excited because she was also expecting.

That's when Riley accused Micha of arranging this whole thing. But I didn't think he would do that. Logan, however, openly admitted to messing with Shelby's birth control. Hence why I decided to go with the shot. There was no way Mason could switch that out. Not that I thought he would... but if there was anything I learned from past experiences, it was that it was better to be safe than sorry.

"All done," Dr. Creswell said, then stood up and dropped the needle in a bio container.

"How long before I can fuck her?" Mason asked.

I dropped my face in my palm. Was that all he thought about?

The doctor looked back at me and shrugged while saying, "You can fuck her now if you like." Then walked out the door.

Now why would he tell him that? I could already see that sparkle in his eye. One would think Mason had been deprived of my touch for years. It'd only been a week. And I still did other stuff during that time.

Mason walked over and locked the door so fast that I barely had time to pull myself up on the bed.

He tsked and grabbed my ankles to yank me back down. "Not so fast, Freckles."

"We can't do this here," I argued while my feet were placed in the metal stirrups.

"The fuck we can't."

"Mason," I huffed despite the dampness seeping into my panties. I missed his touch too. "You said..."

"I said I wouldn't fuck you until you were on birth control." His hand swept over my panties, with his finger pressing down on my clit, sending a spark of lighting up my spine that pushed a moan past my lips. "And you're on birth control now."

He had a point. And it wasn't like we were being watched. Not that he needed my consent. My panties were ripped down my legs and tossed across the room before I could blink. Half a second of cool air grazing over my wet folds was all I got before he was pushing inside me.

I groaned as I stretched around his thickness. Dear God I

missed this. I expected him to use me hard. Mason Kessler didn't do sweet and slow, but that was okay. I didn't want sweet and slow. I wanted to feel his hands digging into my flesh while he used me. I wanted him to get mad and tell me what to do, then punish me when I didn't listen. But my favorite part...

"No," I snarled and swung my hand to slap him. "Stop, Mason."

"Not a fucking chance, Freckles," he growled and wrapped his hand around my neck to slam me back on the bed.

"No," I cried out again and fought to squirm away.

Mason grunted and thrust hard inside me.

"Shut the fuck up," he hissed, while cramming his hand in my mouth. "You'll take my cock like a good fucking girl."

That was all it took to send me over the edge. I screamed around the fingers gagging me and fell into that cloud of bliss where I could ride the waves of pleasure coursing through me.

This was the game we played. I was the prey and he was the predator that took what he wanted, when he wanted. And I loved every second of it. The way he manhandled me and the pain he inflicted like he knew I needed it, were an intoxicating blend. What I didn't expect was for him to stop and cock his head to the side.

My eyes flew open and when I followed his gaze my pulse picked up. He was staring at an ultrasound machine sitting next to the bed.

"No."

A wicked smirk spread across his face. "Yes."

He wouldn't.

Yes, yes he would.

All I could do as Mason clicked on the machine and flipped up my dress was watch. His grip around my neck had tightened to a point where I couldn't move. Other than grinding my hips to beg for more of the girth inside me, that is. And he gave it to me.

Mason pumped slowly inside me while he squirted gel on my

belly. I was too lost in the way he felt to pay much attention beyond that, until he said, "Fuck me, would you look at that."

When I looked at the screen, my jaw dropped. I could see my walls clenching down on his shaft. It was oddly erotic watching his dick shove my flesh out of the way. It went so deep. Apparently not deep enough for him, though. Mason spread the stirrups wide and slammed in as far as he could go.

My back lifted off the bed as I screamed. It felt like he was fucking his way into my soul. I could feel him everywhere. In my bones, in the slight stab in my gut, and in the way he was staring at me, like he could feel the very fiber of my being with each thrust of his hips. We were one in that moment. One being, moving in sync.

Then when he roared and drove into me one last time, I didn't just feel his dick twitch, I could see it. I could see his essence spurting out of him and into me. I orgasmed so hard, I blacked out.

"YOUR GRADUATING CLASS, EVERYONE."

The crowd stood up and cheered. I never imagined this day would be so full of happiness, but when I looked down at the people watching and saw all the smiles, I felt overwhelmed with love. Sean was there, of course, and so were so many others. Louis Kessler looked so proud. Martin Creswell also had his chest puffed. Even Dean Whitley had come, despite his kids having already graduated.

The person that made me scoff out a snicker was Riley's dad. He was in the back with some big tattooed scary looking guy, and both were hooting and hollering like they were at a rock concert.

"Oh my god," Riley smacked her face against her palm. "Can you believe that shit?"

I smiled. "They're proud of you."

"They're idiots," she grumbled back.

If she was going to complain about anyone, I'd say it should be the row of bikers in the back. Half the parents were terrified out of their minds. Especially when the one with blonde hair jumped up on some woman's chair and yelled, "Fuck yeah, my girl kicked all your asses!"

I wasn't sure whose ass he was talking about. Riley did well, but Silas was valedictorian. I wasn't about to argue though. When one woman looked back at him and told him to quiet down, he stared back at her like he was going to kill her.

Mental note, when that guy talked to me I was going to act like Riley Adams was the greatest person in the world.

After we'd all gotten our diplomas, we gathered in the gym for a celebration. I stayed away from Riley's table though. All the bikers were there, and when that blonde guy found out she was pregnant, he threatened to shoot Micha right then and there. Mason thought it was funny, but I wasn't so sure the guy was kidding.

Lana threw her arms around me. "I told you we'd survive high school."

"Yes, you did," I said and hugged her back.

My friend was the one who always insisted that high school was nothing but a stepping stone, and that nothing that happened there mattered. But she was wrong.

I gazed up at Mason, who was stuffing his face with a cupcake. One thing mattered.

He cocked a brow at me. "You want some?"

"No," I shook my head. "I'm just admiring the view."

"Oh yeah." A smirk spread across his face. "Well, if you come with me to the storage closet, I can give you a better view."

I was half tempted to go with him, but Louis walked up and stopped any idea of that happening. It would be rude to leave before talking to his father.

"Congratulations everyone." He nodded at the people around the table, then stopped when he looked at Silas and Mason. "Don't forget we have a meeting tonight."

By 'meeting' he meant Order business. Unless I asked, Mason didn't tell me what they were doing, which was fine with me. That part of his life I didn't need to know about. Nor did I want to. If something was important, he'd let me know.

Preston walked up behind Mr. Kessler and said, "I thought we were done with all the Nate stuff."

It was weird to hear people refer to my father by that name. Even if it was the one he was given at birth. I preferred to think of them as two people. Ned was the man who raised me and tucked me in at night. Nate was the other guy.

"We are," Louis nodded. "The only thing we haven't been able to figure out is the card left on your nanny's body." When he said the last part, he looked at Lana.

I tried to tell them that my father wouldn't have done that, but they wouldn't listen. He had many dark parts, but to openly shoot at a house with babies in it... I just couldn't see him doing it.

Preston cocked a brow at Mason's dad. "A card?"

"Yes," Louis said. "An ace of spades."

Preston's eyes widened for just a second before he announced, "I gotta go," and walked away.

Maybe someone did believe me after all?

Spitfire

I found something in Ned's office, Don;t
tell Micha I gave it to you.

Sincerely,

Mason

Riley

I don't know how much time I have, or if you'll even get this, but I'm writting it anyway. I've been down here in this dungeon for two days now and I want you to know i've accepted my fate. You can't blame yourself for what's about to happen. There's nothing you could've done to stop it. I'm at peace.

You need to let me go. I had more love from my friends then most people get in a lifetime. But there is something you can do for me. Take care of Harper. She is not safe. Look out for her like you did me, and don't trust her father. He makes mine look like a teddy bear. He's coming back, I have to go. Tell Star i'm sorry I tried to help, but someone had too. Good bye my friend. Even if you don't believe in that stuff, I'll be watching over you.

Love always
Tico

Note from Preston

Before we begin I'd like to clear a few things up. This isn't going to be another tale where the villain finds his heart. I'm not some damaged soul that does things because someone hurt me. I do them because I want to. So, get rid of any romanticized ideas you have of a dark prince falling in love.

This isn't that story.

This is my story.

There will be no moment of tenderness where I pet your head and call you good girl. SO get rid of that hopeful spark in your eye. The only thing you have to be hopeful for is a quick end.

I will fuck you.

I will break you.

Then when I'm bored, I will kill you.

Now take a few moments and reflect on the decisions you made that brought you to this place. Once we begin there is no going back. I will not relent, I will not back down, and I will not feel sorry for anything I do.

There is no heart beating in my chest, or soul to be damned. The only thing you'll find here in this dark abyss is the pain and suffering I feed off of.

For I am the Devil of Death.

And you are my next victim.

Thank you for reading Relapse.

This book has been bittersweet for me. Even though it's not the last in the series it feels like and end of something else. Mason and Harper tested my emotional limits, and I will miss them terribly.

I would like to thank my beta readers, you guys are great and I'd totally forget stuff if it wasn't for you. You keep me going when writing gets exhausting.

And to my work wives, who are always inspiring me to keep going, I love you guys.

And a special thanks to Vee who spent hours helping me work through the mess that was Mason's head. I dedicate Mason and all of his beautiful brokenness to you. And Harper loves you reguardless.

Curious about the grandpa's? If we reach 100 reviews I'll write a short about how the Kessler brothers deal with older generation.

Preorder for book six Panic-Button

ABOUT THE AUTHOR

T.L. Hodel is a Canadian author, poet and artist. Through coming up from a difficult childhood she excelled at writing, having her first poem published in junior high. When not writing she occupies herself with numerous crafts, hobbies and is an avid gamer and horror movie fan. She lives in Calgary with her kids and cat, (who is a complete asshat), and may have a slight weakness for true crime shows.

Connect with T.L. Hodel online:
www.facebook.com/groups/272402970612789/?ref=share
www.instagram.com/tarahodel
www.facebook.com/Author-TL-Hodel-102923044775313/

Also by T.L. Hodel

The Order Of Ravens And Wolves:
Aftereffect
Scartissue
Happenstance
Accident-Prone
Relapse
Panic-Button (coming soon)

Deviant House:
Innocence
Innocence corrupted (coming soon)

The Lost Souls:
Adversaries
Frenemies

Brothers Of Shadow And Death:
Backfire
Backstab (coming soon)

The Seven Sins Series:
Pride

The Buchanan Brothers
Twisted Abel
Twisting Tallon (Coming soon)

Embrace the Darkness

T.L.Hodel